DELUSIONAL

ANDREY LONDRA

DELUSIONAL

A Novel

bent meow
books

First published in Great Britain in 2019 by
Bent Meow Books

Copyright © Andrey Londra 2019

Paperback ISBN 978-1-9160993-0-2
eBook ISBN 978-1-9160993-1-9

A CIP record for this book is
available from the British Library

In memory of uncle Chris

"We should indeed keep calm in the face of difference, and live our lives in a state of inclusion and wonder at the diversity of humanity."

— George Takei

FOREWORD

Apartheid (South African English pronunciation: əˈpɑːrteɪd/; Afrikaans: [aˈpartɦəit]) was a system of institutionalised racial segregation and discrimination in South Africa introduced by the governing National Party in 1948.

Under this system of segregation, South Africans were divided into groups of whites and non-whites, of which the latter was made up of Blacks, Indians and Coloureds. Non-whites had no say in the politics of South Africa.

Under the apartheid system, non-whites were forced to live in separate areas from whites in both rural and urban areas and were required to have documents or passes, known as passbooks, in order to move from one area to another as well as to take up employment.

During this period, the declaration of a state of emergency gave police the right to detain any person for renewable periods and imposed severe restrictions on media coverage of Black political violence.

The majority of white South Africans were opposed to these apartheid rules.

Apartheid came to an end a year after the release of Nelson Mandela, who went on to become president of South Africa in 1994.

PROLOGUE

Jason woke from whimpering coming from somewhere in his bedroom. The boy took a peek from underneath his bedcover and glimpsed at his electronic clock on the bedside table, flickering twelve o'clock. He then glanced towards the door, where the tall dark shadowy figure stood in silence. The moonlight dripped through the curtains but fell short of illuminating the faceless thing. A light draft coming from the open window carried *its* distinctive odour of burning timber and ash.

Jason pulled his head back under his bed sheet and could hear himself swallowing hard with his mouth gone completely dry. His heart beat in his ears. Seconds felt like minutes. He could feel *its* presence as it moved toward the bed faintly whimpering.

Jason dug his fingernails into his own forearm, pressing his nails as deep as he could into his skin and biting into his fist in an attempt to make the figure go away.

PART 1

CHAPTER 1

Saturday, 14 April 1984.

Johannesburg, South Africa.

Eleven year old Jason Rothshen and Pedro Catara raced each other over the green manicured front lawn in the lush exotic garden and over the cobbled driveway towards the enormous wooden front door of the ten-thousand-square foot Rothshen mansion.

"In here," Jason instructed and grabbed Pedro by the back of his shirt and pulled him behind a pruned bush.

"Remember our mission," he whispered. "We're spies and need to blend in. We only have one chance to find the human transformation venom which is locked inside the secret room. And remember, everyone is our enemy. They only pretend to be normal. Trust no one."

"Trust no one." Pedro giggled and tried to pull a serious face.

"Ready?"

"Yes man," Pedro said as he held an invisible weapon in his hand and pointed it into the air before he stuck an invisible gun into the front of his trousers.

"Go," Jason said and dashed into the grand foyer filled with dozens of smartly dressed people laughing and chattering over live piano music playing in the background.

"This way," Jason said and pulled his olive-skinned friend by the arm and zigzagged through the countless guests towards the west wing of the mansion. "Keep to the wall."

Both boys froze in position against the wall and smiled when a tall waiter in a black suit walked past with a golden tray floating over their heads.

"Let's go," Jason said and gave a few quick steps in the opposite direction and stopped by two large double wooden doors. The entrance to the secret room.

"We have to make sure no one sees us going in. Pretend we're looking at the paintings on the wall."

"This is so exciting," geeky Pedro said. "I need to pee."

"You always want to pee when we're on a mission."

"Can't help it," Pedro said, looking slightly uncomfortable while holding his pretend weapon. "My mom says I have a weak bladder."

"Weak bladder?" Jason rolled his eyes. "You have to keep it in. Okay, no one's looking, quick get inside." Jason opened the door and pushed Pedro through the gap and quickly closed it behind them.

"Wow, this is awesome man," Pedro gasped. "This is massive." He spun around, taking in the luxuriously decorated study with dark wooden bookshelves filled with thick books spanning all four walls, with a huge dark-wood office desk, grand paintings and one enormous self-portrait of Jason's father hanging above the fireplace.

"Told you, your dad's study ain't this big," Jason said proudly.

"Maybe, maybe not," Pedro said and as he turned around he spotted something extraordinary looking. "Wow," he said and ran towards two pistols encased in a protective glass box that sat on the side of Jason's father's large wooden office desk. "This is so super cool. Do you shoot with them?"

"Don't open it," Jason cautioned at the same moment Pedro opened the glass encasing designed to protect the multi-million dollar flintlock pistols that used to belong to Jérôme Bonaparte.

"I just want to hold it."

"No," Jason gasped and grabbed Pedro's hand and pushed him away from the antique weapons. "You almost triggered the fucking alarm, you stupid."

"Stop swearing and don't call me stupid." Pedro reached out to the weapon a second time.

"I said no," Jason yelled. "I'm not joking. It will activate the alarm and my dad will be super angry. So don't touch it."

"I thought we're best friends."

"We are, but you can never touch them. My dad said those pistols are worth more than a life, that's why they're in this protected case."

"What does that mean?"

"I don't know. Remember, we're still on a mission. Don't touch anything. No fingerprints."

"I don't want to play this stupid game anymore," Pedro said and sat down on the floor. Jason walked to the floor-to-ceiling bookshelf behind one of the sofas and climbed onto the armrest.

"Don't be like that. Watch this." Jason pulled one of the thick books outwards, and as if out of a movie, part of the bookshelf silently opened a gigantic metal door stuck to the bookshelf, almost thirty centimetres thick, that glided effortlessly towards the two boys.

"Bloody hell," Pedro said in awe and jumped up and gawked at the appearance of the hidden room.

"Wait until you see inside. Come on, we have one minute before the alarm is triggered."

"What is this place?" Pedro said as he slowly walked inside the dimly lit room.

"The panic room."

Part of the wall to the right was filled with rows of red wine bottles lying flat.

In the centre of the room stood a luxurious grey L-shaped sofa on a thick grey carpet.

To the left, behind the sofa, four bunk beds were built into the wall and made up, ready to sleep in, and in the right far corner was a small kitchen unit. To the side of that was a shower and toilet hidden behind a frosted glass screen.

On the wall straight in front of them hung a large gold framed oil painting of a man dressed in some type of old style military outfit, holding a shotgun with three dogs standing by his feet, all looking in one direction.

"Doesn't look like a room. It's more like a house inside a house. Why do you have a house inside a house?"

"It's where we'll hide if we get attacked, silly."

"Attacked by whom?" Pedro laughed.

"Terrorists," Jason said with big eyes.

CHAPTER 2

On the other side of the mansion, a man in his late forties, dressed in a white slim fit tailor-made suit, stood inside an elegant bathroom and gazed at himself in a Broadway theatre-style mirror and stroked his manicured beard.

On the marble bathroom counter lay a small vanity mirror with four lines of white powder scraped together.

Sir Patrick Rothshen, the managing director of Rothshen Diamonds International and Jason's father, took a bank note, rolled it up between his fingers, and in a swift move, sniffed two of the lines of powder.

"Jesus fuck," he muttered and sniffed a couple of times before he snorted the remaining lines of cocaine and smeared some powder particles onto his gums with his finger.

He glanced at himself for one last time in the mirror and said, "Showtime," and pulled his suit jacket in place, opened the bathroom door, and walked along the carpeted hallway on the upper floor of his double-storey residence.

He sniffed constantly as the powder, now turned liquid, dripped down the back of his throat.

The sound of live piano music echoed through the Rothshen mansion and got louder as Patrick reached the stately white marble staircase.

He stopped at the golden railing that overlooked the grand reception hall, illuminated by an opulent chandelier hanging like an upside-down hot-air balloon, with thousands of glittering pieces of crystal.

Below him, the floor filled with dozens of smartly dressed men and women, all showing off their very best and most precious jewellery.

Suited waiters glided between the guests with golden platters filled with glasses of imported champagne and caviar on blini topped with a dollop of crème fraîche.

Patrick lit a thick Cuban cigar and floated down the stairs, trying his best to look as elegant and calm as possible as the psychotropic drug lifted his body into the air with every step.

"Congrats on the acquisition, Patrick," a partly balding man with a neck as thick as a tree trunk said as Patrick reached the bottom of the stairs.

"We're going to make fucking millions, mate," Patrick said in a toff British accent. "No, fucking billions." He laughed out loud and double puffed his cigar.

"You can buy me a new car now, mate," a tall, pale, skinny man with spiky blond hair said while he also clutched a fat cigar between his nicotine stained teeth.

"Jimmy, old pal," Patrick said, "good to see you made it all the way from London. How's the Queen doing? We should have a talk about that documentary you're planning to make. It sounds like good fun."

Right about the same time, a tall woman with long blond hair and dressed in a tight figure-hugging black dress firmly took

Patrick by the arm and half whispered, "Darling, wipe that bloody white stuff from your nostrils," and dug her perfectly manicured nails deep into his skin as she led him through the crowd of people to the opposite side of the reception hall. Patrick gracefully wiped his nose and smiled at the guests who all wanted to share their congrats.

"Patrick Rothshen," a man said and walked directly into the path of Patrick and extended his hand to Patrick's wife. "Sarah-Jane."

"Inspector Deventer," Patrick said with a sense of disappointment, "I wasn't aware you were on the guest list. I'm afraid I'll have to ask you to leave immediately, this jamboree is by invitation only. One of the staff will show you out." Patrick indicated with his hand for someone to come over.

"I don't need an invitation," Deventer chuckled. "Somewhere private we can have a quick chat? I won't take much of your time. And you have some white stuff on your nose." The inspector pointed at the side of his own peculiarly flat nose.

Patrick moved slightly closer to the inspector and wiped his nose with one hand before he half whispered into the inspector's ear, "It's Sir Patrick to you, you arrogant fuck," and sniffed loudly. "Take yourself and your cheap smelly suit and get out of my fucking house before I get you arrested for trespassing on private property."

"Patrick, sorry Sir Patrick, that's no way to speak to an officer of the law," Deventer said calmly. "Right here in my hand, I have evidence that connects you to a known eastern European syndicate. I can arrest you right now, right in front of all these smartly dressed ass lickers with their fake smiles and overdrawn bank accounts. Imagine how well that will go down with that free bubbly and fish eggs they're stuffing their faces with."

"Stop wasting my time," Patrick hissed and grabbed the police inspector by the arm and pulled him toward the front door. "You got fuck-all on me. Now get the fuck off my property."

"Salisbury," the inspector said. "Ring any bells?"

Patrick stopped, and Deventer pulled his creased jacket in place.

"And how about Ling-ling?" the inspector said and grabbed a caviar nibble from one of the passing waiters and gulped it down in one go.

Patrick looked back at his wife, who flicked her long blond hair to the side and gave him her perfect fake smile and made big eyes at him, as if trying to tell him to hurry up.

"What do you want?" Patrick said and took a long drag from his cigar and blew the smoke in the inspector's face, who in turn gave a few deliberate coughs.

"Just a few minutes of your precious time, Patrick, sorry Sir Patrick. In private if you don't mind."

Patrick nodded towards the left. "You have one minute, then we're done. I have guests to attend to."

"Bloody hell, I don't think I will ever get used to the taste of these damn fish eggs."

"Maybe it's because you lack any taste, inspector."

Meanwhile, back inside the panic room, Pedro noticed part of a photo visible from underneath the sofa. He picked it up and looked at it for a split second before Jason snatched the photo from Pedro's hand and held it behind his back.

"Where did you get this?" Jason said.

"Who's that?"

Jason stuck the photo into the back of his underwear. "We have to go," he said and pushed Pedro towards the panic room door.

"Let me see." Pedro grabbed the back of Jason's trousers and tried to reach for the photo.

Jason pushed Pedro backwards, causing him to fall over the side of the sofa.

Pedro got up and chased after Jason out of the panic room and into Patrick's study and jumped on Jason's back.

They both fell to the carpet and began to wrestle.

"Give me the photo," Pedro shouted and tried to turn Jason around.

Jason pinched Pedro on his belly, rolled over and managed to get on top of him.

"Get off me," Pedro yelled as Jason pinned him down with both his knees on Pedro's arms. "Please, you're hurting me."

Jason playfully hopped on Pedro's stomach.

"Stop it, I'm going to pee."

"Say pretty please," Jason laughed and placed his hand on top of Pedro's front part of his trousers.

"Stop it. Get off me."

Jason laughed and said, "Something is getting hard."

"No," Pedro yelled as he tried his very best to get out of Jason's grip.

"You like it, don't you?" Jason kept rubbing on the same spot.

Pedro stopped resisting and looked at Jason, confused.

"Shhh," Jason said and pushed his fingers underneath the waistband of Pedro's trousers. "It's our little secret." He submerged his hand fully inside Pedro's trousers.

The double wooden doors burst open and the dreaded deep voice of Patrick said, "What the fuck are you two doing in my office?"

Both boys looked up.

Patrick's face went blood red from anger, and the vein on his forehead bulged like a purple worm while inspector Deventer stood behind him, looking a little dumbstruck.

"We're just playing," Jason said with a quivering voice.

"With your hand inside his trousers? And how many times have I told you to stay out of my bloody office? And why the hell is the panic room open? Who gave you permission to open it?"

Jason kept quiet and looked down at Pedro.

"Look at me when I talk to you. Answer me."

Jason looked up at his father as the tears flooded down his white freckly face and said, "I'm sorry, dad."

"Pedro, go home," Patrick said and pointed his finger towards the door. "And as for you, I'll deal with you later. Go up to your room and you stay there. Do you understand? Move."

Pedro ran out the door crying, followed closely by Jason.

CHAPTER 3

Later that evening.

The lavish party at the Rothshen mansion had come to an end and the last few tipsy guests had just left.

Jason laid in his bed in darkness, hoping his father would forget about what happened earlier in his study.

He could feel the warm tears rolling down the side of his face, leaving cold trails on his skin while he gazed out of the window at a summer thunderstorm brewing over the city. He held onto Juju, his beloved monkey doll with its missing eye, given to him in secret as a gift by their maid, Emma.

"God," Jason whispered to himself, "if you really exist, please strike our house with one of your thunderbolts and burn it to the ground."

Almost on cue, a lightning strike lit up the sky near the mansion, followed a second later by a deep roaring sound that rattled the bedroom windows for a few seconds.

"Almost," Jason whispered and squeezed Juju's head flat, "one more."

But instead, Jason's bedroom door swung open and the light switched on.

"Jason," his father growled and sniffed a couple of times.

Jason closed his eyes and pretended to sleep.

"Jason. Get over here this instant. I'm not calling you again."

Jason kept his eyes squeezed tightly as he heard his father stomping closer. Suddenly, he was pulled out of his bed by his arm.

"How many times have I told you to stay out of my study? Look at me."

Jason looked up towards the big-eyed man who stood in front of him with his angry red face and the bulging vein on his forehead while wagging his long finger that smelled like cigar in his face.

"I'm sorry," Jason sobbed and looked towards Juju where he had fallen on the floor.

Patrick removed his leather belt. "You will be bloody sorry, boy."

"Please, dad," Jason begged. "I'm sorry, not the belt. I won't do it again, promise, please-please-please, don't hit me, I'm really sorry."

The brown leather belt clapped with a muffled sound over Jason's white pyjamas as it struck his bum.

"Please," Jason cried out.

Patrick lifted Jason into the air by the arm and gave him another whip with the belt over his backside.

"What the hell are you doing to him?" Jason's mother yelled from the door before she pushed Patrick to the side and covered Jason with her body.

"Get out of my way," Jason's father growled and grabbed Sarah-Jane by the back of her nightgown and pulled her away.

"If you touch me again I swear—," Jason's mother said as she stood up to her raging intoxicated husband who towered almost two heads taller than her.

"Or you will do what, woman?" Patrick said calmly with his hand clutching the belt raised in the air while sweat ran down his flushed face. Then almost immediately, as if coming out of some type of trance, Patrick blinked a couple of times, lowered his arm and walked towards the door before he turned back to her. "Remember who's the boss in this fucking house. I am. You remember that before you give me orders again." Patrick disappeared down the hallway.

Jason's mother put her arms around him. "Are you okay, my baby?"

"Yes," Jason sniffed. He rested his head against her chest and rubbed his burning bum.

"I don't know what has gotten into him. Did you do something to upset him?"

"I went into the study."

"Oh, my son, you know how he gets when we go into his office."

"I said I'm sorry, but he just got so angry at me. He hates me." Jason began to cry again.

"It's over now. Stop crying. He doesn't hate you. He's just under a lot of pressure from work. Let's get you back into bed.

Tomorrow will be a fresh new day and all will be forgotten and we can go to the cinema and have those massive chocolate swirly cones you love so much."

"Promise?"

"I promise, my baby boy."

"I'm not a baby anymore."

"You're still my baby. You'll always be my baby boy."

Jason's mother tucked him into bed and sat beside him and gave him a kiss on the forehead.

"Mommy will always be here for you. You know that. I love you very much. Now close your eyes and I'll see you in the morning before breakfast."

Just as Sarah-Jane stood up, Jason grabbed hold of her soft hand and whispered, "Mommy, can I show you something?"

"Yes, my love, of course you can." Sarah-Jane sat back down and gently brushed his curly blond hair with her warm hand that smelled of sweet fudge. "What do you want to show me?"

"Please don't tell dad I showed you this. Promise me."

"I give you my word." She looked at him with her big powder blue eyes. She had removed her makeup and her face looked flawless, almost glowing.

Jason got out of bed, lifted the side of his mattress and pulled out a wrinkled photograph and handed it to his mother.

Sarah-Jane gave a light gasp and stood up. "Oh my god, where did you find this?"

"In the panic room."

She gaped at the photograph for a moment while a lone tear escaped her left eye and rolled down her cheekbone.

She took a deep breath and composed herself, then slipped the photograph into her white silk nightgown's pocket.

"Please don't tell dad."

"I promise you, my baby. You go to so sleep and I'll see you in the morning."

CHAPTER 4

0:10 a.m.

Jason woke to a loud noise and sat up in his bed. The bedroom lit up from a lightning strike with heavy rain pounding against the large windows.

Muffled voices could be heard coming from somewhere in the house. It sounded like his parents were having another argument, then a sudden "no" was followed by a deep dull thump.

Jason's heart pounded in his throat, and he scuttled to his bedroom door and listened before he carefully opened the door and tiptoed along the upper floor towards his parents' bedroom, four rooms further down.

Jason kneeled down on the thick carpet and waited in the same spot for what felt like minutes while he intensely listened for any other noise.

But the torrential rain clobbered against the windows and the thunder made it difficult to hear anything.

Then, all of a sudden, his parents' bedroom door swung open and his father's monstrously large silhouette stood in the doorway.

"What are you doing up?" Patrick said with one hand behind his back. "Go back to bed." He ushered Jason back into his bedroom and closed the door.

Jason stood by the door until he began to feel sleepy again and decided to climb back into his bed, grabbed Juju and drifted off to sleep.

CHAPTER 5

"Jason?" Patrick called from outside his bedroom door the following morning. "Jason? Are you up?"

Jason kept silent and hid underneath the bed while he clung onto dirty Juju.

"I can hear you under the bed," Patrick said as he walked into the room.

Jason crawled out from underneath the bed and looked up at his father, who was dressed in a light grey three-piece suit and wearing black round-framed sunglasses.

"Why are you still in your pyjamas?"

Jason shrugged his shoulders. "I don't know," he muttered and looked down, too afraid to look at Patrick wearing his sunglasses that made him look even scarier as they hid his big eyes.

"What do we do on Sundays?"

"Church?" Jason said with some hesitation.

"Take a bath and get dressed. I'm leaving in thirty minutes."

"Where's mommy?" Jason said, as she usually woke him up in the mornings.

Patrick sat down on the bed beside Jason and looked towards him without taking off the glasses. "Your mother left last night and went back to London. She wasn't happy anymore, so she packed her bags and left."

"I don't understand. How can she just leave me?" Jason began to cry. "I want mommy."

"Jason, your mother is not coming back. She made the decision to abandon you and me, so we are now on our own. You have to be strong. You are a man now, okay?"

"She left because of me," Jason sobbed and threw Juju against the wall.

Patrick kept quiet and patted Jason on his head and sighed. "No, son, she didn't leave because of you, she left because she was not happy. Go take a bath and get dressed. And brush your teeth."

"But how can she just leave like that without even saying goodbye to me?" Jason burst into a crying fit and pushed his face into his pillow.

"We'll talk about it when we get back from church. Go get ready. God doesn't wait. Thirty minutes," his father said and walked out of the room.

Forty-five minutes later, Jason and Patrick arrived at the church.

The familiar faces of snobby Sunday people stood outside on the perfectly manicured church lawn, dressed in their best suits and dresses, and held onto their luxury Bibles with their golden edged pages and leather covers, and looked on as the other worshippers arrived. The church bells chimed in the background and echoed throughout the neighbourhood.

Jason followed his father into the angelic reception of the newly built Catholic church where Father Michael, a balding, cleanly shaven elderly man with very small, round, wireframe glasses stood and greeted the worshippers as they entered.

"Good morning, Jason, and good morning, Sir Patrick," Father Michael said enthusiastically in his distinctive Irish accent. Without giving any room for a reply, he continued, "So glad you could make it on this glorious sunny Sunday morning. And where's the lovely Mrs. Rothshen? Still on her way? You must have had a really good celebration last night."

Father Michael tapped Patrick on his shoulder and glanced down at Jason. "Just a pity about that wild thunderstorm from last night. We even had a power outage on the east side of the city. Electricity only came back on about an hour ago. I had to have a shower in cold water this morning, not that I mind. God wanted to tell us that we're using too much electricity and tested my devotion to the Lord's cause and my resilience with that cold shower."

Father Michael gave a hearty laugh. "And why the sad face, young man? You should be happy to be alive."

"Mommy left us," Jason blurted out.

"Oh dear, did I hear correctly, she left? Patrick?" Father Michael gaped at Patrick with raised eyebrows.

"Jason, go and sit," Patrick instructed with clenched teeth and pushed him forward.

Jason slowly walked towards long pews and glanced back to see if he could make out what his father said before he sat down on the hard wooden bench. He turned his whole body sideways and watched as Patrick gestured with his hands, looking slightly sheepish as he spoke to father Michael.

A few minutes later, Patrick sat down beside him and whispered in an agitated tone, "Don't you ever chip in on an adult conversation again. Do I make myself clear?"

"Yes."

"Yes who?"

"Yes, dad."

"I think now that we're here in the house of the Lord Jesus, this would be the right opportunity to set a few *rules* you must abide by from here on, as you will not only make a promise to me, but also to God. Two rules. One, you will not make any contact with *mother* again, and secondly, you will not *try* and make contact with her ever again. Do you understand, Jason? She has abandoned you. She has abandoned me. She abandoned all of us. She most probably abandoned God, too. She is a bad mother, a bad wife, and a bad person."

Jason shook his head. "How can you say mommy is bad? She has never been bad to me. You are the bad one."

"Look at me," Patrick said with gritted teeth. "You will do as I say, do you understand."

"But—," Jason said and could feel the tears building up in his eyes and looked away.

"No *buts,* if you disobey my rules and the rules of God, then you will be punished by God as well as me, and I'll send you off to a boarding school on an island in Asia where you will stay until you finish your last day of school when you turn eighteen. And you will not get anything from me, not a single cent. Do you understand? I will disown you completely if you attempt to make contact with her ever again."

"But I miss mommy." Jason burst into tears and began to scratch his arm.

"Stop crying for God's sake," Patrick whispered and pushed his white handkerchief with PR embroidered on it into Jason's hand.

Jason wiped his tears then scratched his arm more vigorously.

"Why are you scratching?"

"Nothing."

"Did you play with the neighbour's cat again?"

"No."

Patrick took hold of Jason's arm and pulled up the sleeve which exposed large raw cuts on his upper arm.

"What is this?" his father hissed and inspected the marks.

"It's nothing." Jason pulled his arm away and turned his body away from Patrick.

"Don't lie to me, Jason. How did you get these marks?"

"Leave me alone."

"Jason, you tell me now how you got those cuts or I'll ground you for a month."

"You did this to me," Jason sobbed and shifted his bum one space away from Patrick.

"Excuse me?" Patrick said and looked around while a couple of people turned their attention towards Jason's undesirable behaviour. "You're starting to make up stories again."

"No, I'm not. You did this to me when you hit me before mommy left because of the photo. I should have never shown it to her."

Patrick went quiet and looked at Jason with a surprised expression which turned into an angry frown and then a second later morphed into *the look*. He said, "What photo?"

Jason realised what he had just said and felt the world was about to suck him in. "Leave me alone."

"Keep your voice down, for God's sake."

"I hate you," Jason screamed, jumped up and threw his black hardcover Bible at Patrick, which ricocheted off Patrick's shoulder and flapped through the air like an injured bird before it landed face down in the centre of the aisle.

The entire church fell silent, followed by gasps and everyone's attention directed at father and son.

Patrick gave a half smile at the gazing eyes and whispered to no one in particular, "Typical tantrum."

Patrick stood up and in a calm tone of voice said to Jason, "We're leaving," then elegantly took Jason by the arm and partly lifted him as they walked towards the rear of the church.

"You're hurting me," Jason muttered as he tried to keep up with Patrick's large steps.

With every step they took, heads followed Patrick and Jason until they marched past father Michael, who gazed down at Jason with angry eyes and shook his head in disappointment. He clutched onto his own burgundy leather Bible and made the sign of the cross on his chest.

CHAPTER 6

Jason and Patrick arrived home.

"Go to your room," Patrick said and walked to the study.

"Please, dad, I'm sorry."

"I said go to your damn room, and I don't want to hear another word out of your mouth."

For fuck's sake this cannot be happening, Patrick thought to himself, opened his desk drawer and took out the tiny 14 karat gold plated bottle with an attached snuff spoon. He took the top off, then dipped the small little spoon inside the bottle and snorted a heap of cocaine in each nostril.

"Jesus," he sighed and pushed back in his chair and glanced at the dark wooden framed photograph standing on his desk of him and Sarah-Jane, side by side on a ski slope in the French Alps a couple of years earlier.

Her flawless face looked radiant against the glimmering white slope with her ski mask on top of her head.

Patrick sniffed a couple of times and placed the photograph face down.

"You leave me no choice." Patrick walked up to the bookshelf and pulled one of the Encyclopaedia Britannicas outwards.

The bookshelf silently slid open to reveal the panic room.

Patrick walked to the large painting of the Hunting Man and the Dogs that dominated the wall, pulled the artwork out like a door to reveal the build-in safe and used a long specially designed key to unlocking the heavy reinforced steel door.

Inside the safe stood a number of weapons ranging from high calibre hunting rifles to a double barrel shotgun for duck hunting, and above that a couple of shelves stacked with small bullion gold bars, packets of bullets, and two silver metal boxes, each roughly the size of a shoebox, fitted with locks.

Patrick pulled out a notebook and walked back to his desk.

His hands shook uncontrollably as he flicked through the pages that were labelled in alphabetical order. *This is the only solution, Patrick. You have to do this. There is no other option.*

He stopped at 'D', took a deep breath and ploddingly dialled the number on his desktop telephone.

The phone rang a couple of times before a woman answered, "Good morning, Sandy Hill Hospital, how can I help?"

Patrick paused and slightly hesitated to speak as he didn't expect a woman to answer.

"Hello, anyone there?" the woman said.

"Yes, well, I thought I dialled the office number of Doctor Swanepoel. I must have dialled the wrong number."

"You've come through to the switchboard. All the numbers are now coming directly to me."

Patrick cleared his throat and said, "How can I get hold of Doctor Swanepoel?"

"Please hold, I'll transfer you to his ward."

"Hello, psychiatric unit," another woman answered.

"May I speak to Doctor Swanepoel?"

"He's busy with a patient. Could you perhaps call back later?"

"Tell him it's Patrick Rothshen. It's urgent."

"Are you a patient of his?"

For a moment Patrick wanted to tell the woman off, but then took a deep breath and said, "Can you please locate him and tell him I need to speak to him? He's expecting my call, I'll hold."

"I'll see if I can find him."

A muffled conversation followed on the other side of the telephone. "Patrick, my friend, how can I help?"

"It's Jason. I'm concerned."

A slight pause came from doctor Swanepoel's side, then he said, "I see, are you sure?"

Patrick sighed and said, "I'm positive. I think it's better you take him in, things are getting out of control."

"Shall I come over now?"

"As soon as you can."

"Not a problem. I'll get my team to prepare a bed before I make my way over."

"Can you keep this under wraps please. No marked vehicles or anything that can attract attention. You know how the fucking paps are. I already had an incident in the church this morning which attracted undesirable attention."

"I'll come in my car and we'll check him in under a pseudonym. Leave it to me. I'll see you in an hour."

Jason stood by the door and eavesdropped on the conversation.

Patrick looked in his direction and said, "Didn't I tell you to stay in your room?"

"I'm not going," Jason cried. "I hate you. Why are you doing this to me?"

Jason ran back to the kitchen and towards the rear of the house.

"Jason, come back here this very instant," Patrick yelled, his deep voice echoing through the enormous ground floor. Jason could hear his father running after him as he ran out onto the patio, but he didn't dare look back as he went around the gigantic swimming pool, over the manicured lawn, past the tennis court and headed straight for the huge lush bush on the far edge of the rear garden, straight towards the exotic plants.

"Jason, don't go in there," Patrick shouted from afar.

Jason deviated from the narrow little footpath going through the lush bushes and fought his way past the ferns and imported plants before he stepped on a saturated patch of ground that gave way under his foot.

Jason fell flat onto the dirt with his foot stuck in muddy gravel. He turned on his back and pulled his leg from the mud, which sucked off his shoe.

The next moment, Patrick burst through the ferns and grabbed Jason by the arm. "I told you not to come here, haven't I? Do you want to get bitten by the snakes? Open those bloody ears when I speak to you."

"Leave me alone," Jason cried and tried to get out of his father's grip.

Patrick picked up Jason and carried him back towards the house.

"Enough is enough. I had it up to here with your tantrums and misbehaviour. You *will* go for treatment this time."

"There's nothing wrong with me," Jason screamed and kicked while his father pinned his arms against his body and locked muddy Jason in the downstairs guest bathroom.

An hour later, a white luxury car drove towards the entrance of the Rothshen home.

Out climbed a Caucasian man with mammoth sideburns and large thick-framed black spectacles. He carried a fat black doctor-style briefcase, flanked by a man dressed in an all-white uniform, even the shoes.

"Doctor Swanepoel," Patrick said as he showed the man into the grand foyer.

"Stay here," Swanepoel instructed the man in white.

"Do I call you sir or mister now?" Swanepoel joked.

"It will be *lord* soon, but stick with *sir* for now," Patrick said smiling.

"You're getting greyer every time I see you, my friend," Swanepoel said and eyed Patrick up and down.

"And you're getting chubbier," Patrick said.

"That's what married life does." Swanepoel laughed. "But honestly, you look stressed, Patrick."

Patrick took a long, deep breath and said, "I've had a bit of an eventful twenty-four hours to say the least, but nothing I can't handle."

"Looking at the mud stains on your suit, it certainly looks like it. Do you want me to give you something to relax before I attend to Jason?"

"I'm alright for now, thanks. I took a *relaxer* a couple of minutes ago. Can you refresh my memory about the new treatment you had in mind?"

"The electroconvulsive therapy?"

"Yes, do you think it will be a suitable treatment?"

"We perform the procedure on a range of patients suffering from severe depression to schizophrenia. So the answer is yes, in most cases. I think Jason would be a suitable candidate for the treatment, however he is still very young and the brain is still in development. We should know for certain after a couple of weeks post-treatment. With these things you never really know as it's not an exact science. But we've had positive and lasting results so far. So the chances are it will work. Fingers crossed."

"Short to long term effects?"

"Well, there are several possible outcomes which will have their own short to long term effects. The one we'll be aiming for is retrograde amnesia, where the memories of the last twenty-four hours prior to treatment are usually lost. In some cases, even up to a couple of weeks. But there is also a risk of anterograde amnesia. As the name suggest, forwards in time. The ability to store and retain new memories might be lost, permanently. In cases like that, the person would still be able to recall data and events that happened previously. And then there's a slight possibility of global amnesia. Now this is not what we want, and these cases are very rare, but they do happen, where the patient experiences both retrograde and anterograde combined. No memories can be recalled, nor can new information be stored, similar to a severe case of dementia."

"The retrograde, are the effects permanent?"

"From experience, in most cases, yes. However, certain events might trigger part of the memories to come back. But because of the missing memories, the brain will attempt to fill in the missing parts by confabulation, like fake memories. So the patient might think they remembered, but part of those memories were created by themselves and can be so powerful that the patients actually believe they really happened."

Patrick pondered the doctor's explanation for a moment and stroked his grey beard.

"Do you want to take some time to think about this? I know this is a big decision," Doctor Swanepoel said.

"I think you should continue. His behaviour has been erratic, especially this morning when he attacked me with a Bible in church."

"Jesus," Swanepoel said and took out a notepad. "Has he been speaking to himself again?"

"He has had a few conversations."

"When was the last time?"

"In the car on our way back from church."

"What did he say?"

"It wasn't a conversation. He just kept saying 'leave me alone.'"

"How about seeing things?"

"He must have. He kept trying to fend off someone coming closer to him. Like when you slap someone's hand away when they try to touch you."

"Interesting," Swanepoel said and scribbled on his notepad. "Everything has been arranged and he'll be checked in under the name John Smith. Not very original, but it does the job. We'll conduct a few tests before we proceed with the actual treatment, just to be one hundred percent certain. Will you or your wife accompany Jason to the hospital?"

"Unfortunately, Sarah-Jane left for London yesterday."

"I will need both parents' consent before the procedure can go ahead."

"She went back to London permanently, so we'll just have to work around that technicality."

"I'm sorry to hear that. Well, I think we can make an exception then. For you. May I see Jason now?"

"Follow me. I've locked him in the bathroom."

Jason sat bundled up in the corner of the shower, still in his church clothes, covered in mud and shivering.

The door unlocked and opened.

"Hello, Jason, I'm Doctor Swanepoel. Wow, what happened to you, young man? You're all muddy."

"He fell facedown in mud. The heavy rain from last night made everything muddy in the back."

"So that's why your father has mud all over himself?" Swanepoel crouched beside Jason and held out a chocolate bar. "This is for you. I'll have one too."

Swanepoel took out another chocolate bar, unwrapped it and took a bite from it. "I love these chocolate bars. They're the best ever chocolates. Go on, have yours."

Jason looked at his father and then at the doctor and said, "What is wrong with me?"

"There is a tiny part in your brain that's not functioning properly, and it's my job to make it better. Would you like me to help you get better?"

Jason looked away. "There's nothing wrong with me. You just want me to forget, don't you?"

"Go on, eat your chocolate bar," Swanepoel said and pushed it into Jason's hand.

"No," Jason said as he grabbed the chocolate bar and threw it against Swanepoel's head. "Leave me alone!"

"Where's your bloody manners, boy," Patrick said and grabbed Jason by the arm, "apologise to the doctor."

Swanepoel took out a syringe from his jacket. "Could you hold out his arm? This is something to calm him down."

Patrick clamped a crying Jason halfway between his legs while Swanepoel stuck the needle into Jason's arm and emptied the contents.

Within seconds, Jason went limp and unconscious.

CHAPTER 7

Jason lay strapped to a bed inside a room with a humming ceiling light right above him.

"How are you feeling?" the nurse said as she brought a rubber mouth guard closer to his mouth.

"Sleepy."

"Good, now open your mouth for me." The nurse placed the mouth guard between Jason's teeth and wiped his temples with some kind of cold ointment.

"Set to one hundred," Doctor Swanepoel said and placed an instrument against Jason's temples.

"Ready," the nurse said and held Jason down with both hands.

Jason looked at Swanepoel, then a flash of white blinding light surged inside Jason's eyes as an electrical current zapped through his brain.

His muscles contracted for a second before they went into spasms then slowly calmed down until they stopped completely.

PART 2

CHAPTER 8

Six years later.

Friday, 5 October 1990.

Jason's hand shot up from underneath a crisp white satin bed sheet to silence the beeping sound of an alarm clock.

Holding the clock in one hand, now dangling from the side of the bed, he lay with his head slightly on his other arm and looked in the direction of the drawn curtains.

A slight gap between the dark grey blackout curtains allowed orange-red pencil-like rays of the African sun to trickle through and land across his face and over the king-size four-poster bed.

"Jason, are you up? It's 6:30," the deep mature voice of his father called from outside Jason's bedroom door, followed by three loud abrupt knocks. "Jason? Are you up?"

"I'm awake," Jason said and pulled a pillow over his head.

"You don't want to be late for your last day of school. Hurry up. Emma already made breakfast."

The seventeen year old, soon to turn eighteen in a couple of weeks, rolled towards the edge of the bed and sat up. His short milky-blond hair stood in all directions like a porcupine, with one side flat against his head.

Still half asleep, Jason walked to the curtains and jerked them open, as if trying to surprise himself with the bright morning rays as they flooded into the room.

He opened the door to his balcony and walked naked to the edge overlooking the one acre rear garden and urinated from the balcony down into the plants below. He took a deep breath of crisp morning air, with the distinctive sweet scent of spring filling his nose.

"Jason, I'm waiting," Jason's father called from somewhere on the ground floor.

"Yes, I'm coming! Wish you can leave me alone." Jason shuffled off to his en-suite bathroom.

He splashed his face with cold water and briefly inspected his green eyes in the mirror before he ran his fingers through his hair to flatten any pieces sticking up. He then checked out his fit, athletic body sideways for a couple of seconds, looked at a single lost hair that had appeared on his chest about a month ago, smiled at himself and put on a t-shirt and shorts. He walked down the cold, elegant marble staircase leading to the grand foyer, with the invigorating aromas of freshly brewed Kenyan coffee and a mixture of bacon and toasted bread drifting toward him. The all too familiar smell of breakfast each morning in the Rothshen family home. And Emma's perfectly fried eggs on homemade wholewheat bread was the only thing Jason enjoyed waking up for.

"Morning," Jason said as he took a seat on the opposite side of the dining table from his father.

"Finally decided to get up?" Patrick said and glanced at Jason over the newspaper with his round black reading glasses sitting on the tip of his nose.

"Why do you always have to be so bloody annoying in the morning?"

"Watch your language, young man. You're treading on thin ice. If no one checks, you'd probably sleep all day."

Jason looked at his father with a surprised expression and a forced smile as he poured orange juice into a glass without replying.

"How does it feel to know it's your last day of school for the rest of your life and you're about to enter the real working world?"

"Just another day, I guess," Jason said, uninterested in further conversation.

Patrick sighed loudly and dropped his newspaper on the table and took a sip of coffee. "I've arranged for you to start working at one of the mines in the beginning of the new year."

"As what? I thought you said I can go on a gap year and travel to South America before I start university."

"You'll start as an apprentice and work alongside one of my senior production resource geologists who will show you everything you need to know about the sector. Once you've completed your training with him, you will work with me in the head office and then we will decide what you will study to further your career in the company. That's a great way of getting to know yourself and to see what direction you want to go in."

"I don't want to work for you."

"You don't have to work for me. I'd like for you to study business and one day take over the company, but you have to start somewhere and work your way towards a certain goal."

"If you say so," Jason said and gulped down the glass of orange juice and turned his attention towards the window.

"You're such an ungrateful child. I give you everything in life, hand you a job on a golden platter in a tough but lucrative industry, and that's your reply. There are people out there who can't find work and with the direction this country is heading into with Mandela being released, things will change for the worse, and you will have to one day stand at the back of the queue as the minority white man. And you'll be the last to be offered a job. You've been spoilt too much. Perhaps you should go on a gap year to Asia. Go and work in the rice fields in Thailand or Vietnam, and you will come to your senses."

"Thank you, dad," Jason said with a hint of sarcasm.

Patrick shook his head unconvinced and said, "We'll talk about this later. I have a meeting at the mines at eight. You'll need to make your own way to school."

"What's new. And when am I getting a car?" Jason said impatiently and knocked his fork on the table.

Patrick elegantly lowered the newspaper once again and said, "Usually, what normal people do is pass their driving test *before* they get a car. But with your fucking erratic behaviour in the last few months, I highly doubt you'll get anything other than a bloody good hiding against that thick head of yours. Finish your breakfast and go get ready for school. You're really starting to wind me up now. And how many times have I told you to sit upright, you're slouching over like a street bum."

Jason pulled his shoulders back and pressed his chest and sarcastically said, "Like this?"

Patrick just looked at Jason and shook his head slightly in disappointment.

"Edward got a car three months before he could even apply for his driving test."

"And?" Patrick said.

"And what?"

"What's your bloody point?"

"Nothing," Jason said and rolled his eyes at his father right at the moment he lifted the newspaper.

"I saw that."

Jason looked at Patrick with surprise and said, "How could you even see that?"

"I see everything."

"Yeah, like the devil."

The newspaper flapped down and an uncomfortable few seconds of silence followed as Jason and his father eyeballed each other. Not even a blink from either side of the table before Patrick's face slowly disappeared behind the elevating newspaper once more.

"What's our net worth?" Jason said.

The newspaper lowered yet again, and Patrick looked at Jason, this time rolling his eyes. "And what made you ask such a specific financial question? All of a sudden decided to show an interest in business?"

"Pedro said they are richer than us."

Patrick gave a dry laugh and said, "I highly doubt that," then continued reading.

"Pedro said his parents don't have to work anymore and will soon retire."

Patrick sighed loudly, closed his newspaper and threw it to the side. "Who on earth wants to retire? His parents are just commercial lawyers. The chances of them retiring early is highly unlikely at their age, unless there's something else he's not telling you."

"So they are richer than us?"

"The correct term is *wealthier* or more *affluent*. Poor people say rich."

"So are we *wealthier* than them?"

"Let's just say that if you combine the total net worth of Pedro's parents and add all three of them to my personal payroll for the next forty years, it will equal about one percent of our personal income in the last year."

Jason gazed at his father, frowned and pondered for a few seconds before asking, "So what is our total net worth then?"

"My god, looks like I wasted my money on a private school. Do the calculations, Jason, it's simple maths."

"I'm not asking for the last financial year. I've said for our total net worth."

Patrick took a quick sip from a cup of coffee. "I have to go," he said and inserted his diamond cufflinks into his shirt cuffs. "You know what to do in an emergency?"

Here we go again. "Yes, dad. Panic room, press alarm, call you, and wait."

"And?"

"And what?" Jason said.

"What do you do when they enter the study?"

"Activate the gas."

"Well done," Patrick clapped his hands a couple of times. "Test the panic room's emergency shut-and-seal as well as the house alarm system. Double check that all the hidden tear gas canisters are not obstructed by any books in the shelves and that they are pointing outwards."

"Why are you telling me this? What's going on?"

"There's unrest in the country again and tensions are running high in the black townships. The possibility of problems in our neighbourhood is very low, but we have to be ready just in case. Things can happen without notice and escalate very quickly. Especially now that Mandela has been released. Which brings me to my next point. Emma's son will take over the gardening from now on. He'll be here by one o'clock this afternoon to get settled before he starts on Monday. Make sure you're back before he arrives."

"What happened to Jefrey and Johannes? They've been here for just a few months."

"I let them go for security reasons. Emma's been with us for many years now, and I think it's better for someone she personally knows to work here, which gives me better control over things and reduces the risk of a break-in. And he was desperate for work, so things worked out well. Show him around the garden, where the tools are stored, and the swimming pool equipment. And make sure he knows how to operate the swimming pool pump. Not like that other imbecile who fucked up the machine in one week. Make sure he knows what the rules are when entering the property and which entrance he can use to get to the rear garden and the servants' quarters. *Hey*, are you listening? Did you hear what I just said?"

Patrick slammed his fist on the table right at the moment Jason took a large bite from his beloved egg on toast. Yellow yolk shot from the folded bread.

"Umm—not deaf," Jason mumbled with a stuffed mouth.

"How many times have I told you not to speak with food in your fucking mouth? You're not one of these goddamn monkeys. And sit up in your fucking chair like a normal human being. You better pull yourself together, young man. My god, my patience with you is running critically low."

Jason opened his mouth and dropped the half-chewed food on his plate and said, "You asked me a question."

Patrick kept silent and gave Jason *the look*, pulled his dark grey undercoat in place and slipped on a matching custom-cut suit jacket and petted his neatly trimmed beard. "My PA booked your driving test on the morning of your birthday." Patrick took his briefcase and walked out of the kitchen saying, "Fail it and you can walk for all I care. And make sure you're back before Thabo arrives, otherwise there will be hell in this house when I get back."

Jason kept silent as his father disappeared towards the front of the house.

"I can't hear you. Is that a yes?"

"Yes, *dad*," an irritated Jason said. "Fucking asshole," he whispered, "wish you fall down a mine pit."

"And don't forget to test the alarm system," Patrick's voice echoed from outside.

Jason lifted his middle finger and took another bite of his folded egg sandwich.

Several minutes passed while Jason gazed at his own reflection in the silver coffee pot and stirred the partially stiffening egg yolk on his plate with his middle finger, imagining what it would be like to pick rice in the fields of Vietnam. He could see himself wearing a nón lá, the distinctive Vietnamese palm-leaf conical hat, while being watched by a shirtless member of the Vietcong and shouted at with a weapon pointed at him. A scene he saw in a war movie not so long ago.

Like something controlled his hand, Jason slapped himself in the face. "You stupid," he said followed by another slap. "Fuck you." And another landing on the side of his head. "You did this to yourself."

"Good morning, master Jason," Emma the maid said as she quietly strolled into the dining room and caught Jason by surprise.

Jason froze in place as he watched the short, black-as-coal woman began to clear up the side of the table where Jason's father sat.

"Emma," Jason greeted and sat back up in the chair and took a sip of the lukewarm coffee. "I hear your son is going to work here."

"That's right, master Jason," the shy looking woman said while she stacked all the cutlery and glassware onto a wide silver tray. "You remember him?"

"No." Jason tried to remember but could only recall scant images from before his mother left them.

"You met him many years ago when you and him was still pikininis, *small boys.*"

"Really? I don't think so."

"Yes, madam Sarah-Jane was still here. I took Thabo with me to work that day." Emma chuckled and said, "Eish, you made me laugh that day when the master came looking for you, yoh."

Emma's distinctive laughter triggered a memory when he was about seven years old. "Oh my goodness, I remember."

Jason stood beside the swimming pool while playing with a remote controlled boat on the water when he heard some laughter coming from the servants' quarters, hidden away on the rear side of the mansion.

Jason walked in the direction of the laughter, which came from behind trimmed green hedges.

Jason peeked around the greenery and saw Emma playing with a small black boy.

The boy laughed as he ran circles around Emma while she tried to catch him.

The boy suddenly stopped and looked directly at Jason before he quickly hid behind his mother's dress with only his head peeking out.

"Hello, master Jason," Emma said.

"Hello," Jason said and walked up to Emma. "Is that your son?"

"Yes, master," Emma said proudly, "he's my little Thabo."

"How old is he?"

"He turned eight in April."

Jason looked at the big-eyed boy, almost half a head shorter than him. His clothes looked ragged and he had no shoes on and some mucus dripped from his nose.

"Hello," Jason greeted the boy and held out his hand to greet him.

"Say hello to master Jason," Emma said and pushed her son towards Jason.

Thabo held out his little hand and hesitantly shook Jason's hand and smiled from ear to ear, with a few missing milk teeth, before he quickly pulled back his hand.

"Come eat with us," Emma said.

"Eat with you?" Jason said, unsure if he should as he never eaten anything with a black person before. Thabo was the first black person he had ever touched.

"Yes, try some of my traditional cooking."

"I'm not sure if I should," Jason said. "I think I should ask mom first."

"Come," Emma said and waved at Jason and walked towards the door of the servants' quarters. "The madam won't have a problem. Come."

Thabo's clammy warm hand grabbed Jason's to pull him forward. He said, full of excitement, "Come, white boy, you eat with us. My mama cooks the best sheba in Soweto."

Jason walked up to the step leading into the servants room, feeling slightly hesitant to go any further and peeked inside the sparingly furnished room. There was one single bed covered with a thin sheet, a separate toilet, and a tiny little kitchen where a few pots stood on a stove, with a table and a chair to the side.

"You can come in," Emma said while she spooned some *stuff* onto a plate.

Jason smelled a peculiar and unrecognisable aroma hanging in the room, like nothing he had ever smelled before. Hard to describe, almost a whiff of burned toast mixed with sour milk and a hint of tomato.

"It's okay, I'll just stay here," Jason said and tried to be as polite as possible.

Thabo ran up to his mother and made a couple of licking sounds as she filled a bowl with more *stuff.*

Emma sat down on the step next to Jason. "Sit," she said and placed the two bowls on a little wooden crate acting as a table on the concrete floor.

Jason sat down cross-legged on the dirty floor and looked at the metal bowl and plate standing side by side right in front of him.

The bowl was filled with a reddish chunky tomato and onion sauce and the plate stacked with heaps of thick white paste like cooked ground maize.

"Please have some," Emma said to Jason.

Thabo hovered over the food like a vulture and looked eagerly at Jason and smiled.

Jason touched the stiff maize with his finger and swallowed hard. "What is this?"

"Yoh," Thabo said and began to laugh. "Eish, why the white boy doesn't know the food?"

"Hush," Emma said to Thabo then smiled at Jason. "It's called pap. You will like it. Look, I will show you how we eat it."

She scooped up a dollop of maize into her bare hand, rolled it between her palm and fingers, dipped the compressed maize into the reddish sauce and said, "And this is sheba," then took a bite.

Like a greedy vulture, Thabo grabbed a handful of maize and within a blink of an eye Emma slapped him on his hand, "Yoh, manners, boy."

She looked at Jason and said, "Please eat some, master Jason. Just try a little."

Jason dug his fingers into the warm, roughly textured maize that felt like heated mud, and took out half a handful.

"Now roll it between your palm and fingers and dip it in the sheba," Emma said and showed with her own hand.

Jason dipped the maize into the sauce and brought the unfamiliar foodstuff to his mouth. It smelled like heated corn and onion.

Thabo's big eyes followed Jason's every move as he brought the rolled maize all the way to his lips.

Jason took a tiny bite and said, "Tastes good," before he gobbled the rest in one bite.

Thabo smiled excitedly and stuffed his mouth too, and Emma happily motioned for Jason to eat more while she rolled another handful of maize for herself.

Jason rolled a second heap of maize and dipped it in the sauce and went in for another big bite, when suddenly the dreaded sound of Patrick's deep voice made Jason's blood run cold. His hand froze in place with a piece of rolled maize inside his mouth and his teeth partly sunk into it.

"Jason?" Patrick called out once again before he appeared from behind the hedges like Satan in a suit.

Jason slowly pulled his hand from his mouth and stood up and looked down, not knowing whether he should spit it out or swallow the piece he accidentally bit off when he heard the hated voice.

"What are you doing?" Patrick yelled. "Come here."

Jason slowly walked towards his father before Patrick grabbed him by the arm and pulled him towards the house. Just around the hedges, he slapped the sticky maize from Jason's hand. Sauce splattered against Patrick's expensive white shirt and onto his spectacles.

"Jesus," he snapped and wiped his face with a hanky. "I told you to stay away from the servants' quarters, didn't I?"

"I was just having a snack with auntie Emma."

"A snack? And she's not your bloody aunt. She is a worker like everyone else. How much did you eat?"

"Just a little bit," Jason said hesitantly and wiped his dirty hand on his shirt.

"For God's sake, you can't just go and eat everything people give you."

"But dad, it tasted so good, you should try some."

"Sarah-Jane!" Patrick called out as he rushed with Jason into the house. "Sarah-Jane, we need to get Jason to hospital, get the car keys."

Jason's mother came rushing into the kitchen. "Oh my god, what happened?"

"He ate some of *their* food."

"He did what? Who's food?"

"The maid's fucking cooked maize. Go get the car key."

"Oh my god, Patrick," Sarah-Jane laughed, "you're totally overreacting." Sarah-Jane kneeled beside Jason.

"Escherichia coli, noroviruses, rotavirus, the list goes on. God knows what was in that food. Go rinse your mouth with milk and drink a few glasses, then we need to get you to A&E."

"Seriously, Patrick, you're exaggerating. You're starting to scare him."

"I'm not scared, mama," Jason chipped in. "It tasted really good."

"See, he liked it," Sarah-Jane said and gave Jason a hug.

"Now you listen to me, Jason. Never eat anything they give you. Do you understand? You never ever do that again. You might get poisoned deliberately. Do you understand?"

Jason laughed and said, "But Emma cooks for us every day."

"Yes, but that's different."

"He's making a fair point," Sarah-Jane added. "We would be all dead by now if they wanted to poison us."

"You're grounded for a week," Patrick hissed.

"He's a very good boy and a good worker," Emma continued while she wiped the dining table with a white cloth. "He will make the garden beautiful again."

Jason stood up and walked away while Emma continued to speak, and headed directly to his father's study, closed the exotic wooden double doors and locked them behind him.

He walked up to the glass box housing the two French Boutet silver-mounted flintlock pistols dating back to 1803. The pistols Patrick described as 'more valuable than a human life.'

He deactivated the alarm and took out one of the heavy antique weapons and inspected the engraving on a silver plaque on the side of the handle that read, 'Jérôme Bonaparte.'

He pulled the cock handle back, causally lifted the pistol and pointed it towards the enormous oil painting of his father hanging on the wall and said, "Your money or your life." Jason smiled and pulled the trigger.

CHAPTER 9

12:14 p.m.

The scorching African sun burned down on Jason and Pedro as they struggled to cycle up the steep hill in the upmarket suburb of Northcliffe heading towards the Rothshen mansion located at the very top of the hill.

"Come, pussy, cycle faster." Jason could feel the sweat dripping down his face and back. In the distance, Jason could see a black man standing by the ten foot gates of their home.

Jason cycled faster and sped right up to the gate and braked sharply, which caused the bicycle's rear wheel to swing sideways and stop inches away from the tall, young man.

The man stood with his back pressed against the enormous wooden gates and turned his head as the bike almost hit him, with a light dust cloud swooping past him.

"Thabo?" Jason gasped as he caught his breath.

"Yes, sir," he said shyly.

Jason placed his bicycle flat on the ground. His heart beat extra fast as he looked at Thabo's tall, dark and slim physique.

So different, Jason thought to himself. Only the eyes were recognisable. Those distinctive big hazel brown eyes that looked like they were slightly glowing.

In a mere split second, Jason's gaze flashed down towards the bulge in Thabo's trousers, which distinctively outlined a section of his cock, and further down towards Thabo's worn out trainers with a part of his left big toe peeking through a small hole.

"You look so different, so much *taller.*"

Thabo smiled and shyly looked down while he rubbed his foot on the cobbled pathway. "Yes, of course. I grew up, sir."

Jason held out his hand and said, "You remember me, right?" and firmly shook Thabo's large clammy hand.

"Yes, of course, sir," Thabo said and smiled broadly. "You ate with me and my mama many years ago and the boss got very upset."

"Hello?" Pedro chipped in from behind Jason. "Are we having a Zulu reunion here or what?"

"It's Emma's son, asshole," Jason said without looking back at Pedro, keeping his eyes fixed on Thabo's large, dewy brown eyes. "The last time I saw Thabo was when I was about seven or eight."

"I'm going home," Pedro said. "I'll come back later when you finished your little *black* reunion."

"Ja, see you." Jason searched his bag for the gate's remote control.

"Can we do some shooting again?" Pedro said.

"Yeah," Jason said and pressed the remote button a couple of times, but the gate wouldn't open.

"Oh no, not again." Jason kicked the solid wooden gate before he kneeled down on his knees and stuck his hand into a small gap located between the gate and the wall and pulled the emergency release lever located on the inside of the gate.

"I'm going now," Pedro said.

"Yeah."

"I'll see you at three?"

"Yes, Pedro, see you at three. And remember to bring my tennis racket back. You've had it for way too long."

The gate made a loud clunk sound as the main chain released and the wooden gate moved slightly sideways.

"Give me a hand, will you?" Jason said to Thabo.

Both pushed the heavy gate just enough for a person to slip through the gap.

CHAPTER 10

One step behind, Thabo followed Jason up the winding cobblestone driveway. His eyes fixated on the fair skinned, milky blond teenager walking in front of him wearing a white t-shirt, white shorts and grey sneakers without socks. His curly blond hair gently lifted from a light breeze that carried a refreshing sweet smell from Jason. Thabo sniffed the air like a hyena as he deliberately walked just an arm's length behind Jason to get a better look at the watch on his right hand resting on the bicycle handle.

"You remember the house?" Jason said without looking at Thabo.

"Just a little, sir. The garden does look smaller than I remember."

Jason kept silent, and the wind blowing through the tall trees made an eerie howling sound.

The further up the steep pathway they walked, the more alive the garden became, with all sorts of creepy crawly insects and birds having fun in their own little paradise in the one hectare front garden filled with exotic ferns, bushes and sweet smelling wild flowers randomly peeking out from the rocks.

"Did your mother tell you about the job?"

"Yes, she did, sir."

"Did she tell you that you're the only one who will be working in the garden?"

"Yes, sir."

"You think you can do it? We used to have two people working in the garden, and they struggled."

"Yes, sir, I think I can do it. My mama told me they were lazy and didn't work hard."

Jason stopped and turned to Thabo and looked him straight in the eyes and said, "You know the boss is full of shit, don't you?"

Thabo smiled and kept quiet as he thought back to the day the master grabbed Jason when they were eating. He looked scary.

"I bet you right now that you'll get fired within a week from today." Jason held out his hand to shake Thabo's hand and smiled.

Thabo's smile suddenly disappeared and he thought *what?* He pondered for a second and said, "Fire me? For what?"

"For not doing the job good enough."

"How much?"

"You want to bet for money?"

"That's how a bet works, isn't it?" Thabo said arrogantly.

Jason gave Thabo a dirty look and said, "And how are you planning to pay me if you lose?"

"I won't lose."

"One thousand rand."

"Eish," Thabo sighed and swallowed nervously at the unexpectedly high number. "You pay me one thousand if I don't get fired in one week?"

"That's how much you will pay me because you will lose."

"I'm not going to lose." Thabo hesitantly shook Jason's hand.

"Well, then we have a bet." Jason continued walking.

You fucking arrogant spoiled white boy, Thabo thought and kept a few steps behind as they reached the summit of the front garden.

Thabo looked at the palatial house as they walked up to the front door. It looked slightly smaller than he could remember but still massive.

Jason unlocked the door and said, "Come in," and threw his backpack on the floor by the door.

As the huge wooden front door silently swung open, the first thing Thabo smelled was the distinctive aroma of pure leather and exotic woods that created a lavish sense of luxury that filled the entire entrance hall.

"Wait here. I'll go call your mother, and don't touch anything." Jason disappeared down the hallway.

So big, Thabo thought as he looked around the symmetrically balanced interior of the white opulent grand foyer with an array of artwork strategically placed on the walls to complement the elegantly styled interior. And in the centre of the grand foyer stood a stately white marble staircase curving toward the upper floor.

The interior was worlds apart from the tiny two bedroom tin shack Thabo shared with his mother and two brothers in the sewage filled slums of the Soweto township. *Ten of our houses would fit into the entrance alone.*

The house was completely silent, with only the faint sound of birds chirping in the garden.

Thabo stood frozen in one place but eager to explore the treasure chest. His stomach made an unsettling growl of hunger that lasted for about five seconds.

He looked up at the glittering mass of glass pieces hanging down from the ceiling in the centre of the foyer.

Thabo noticed a very large glossy black box beside the wide staircase, with part of it standing up slightly.

Thabo took a few steps with his shoes squeaking over the polished stone floor, stopping after every step to hear if someone was coming, until he reached the unfamiliar large shiny object.

On closer inspection, Thabo realised it was in fact a massive grand piano.

He slid his hand over the side of the piano to feel the glossy exterior, and he couldn't resist the urge to press one of the keys.

The loud low tone echoed through the entire front of the house and sounded like it had been amplified.

Thabo quickly took a few steps back and pretended not to have done anything as he stood there with his hands behind his back, still looking around at all the expensive looking artefacts.

He walked up to a wall filled with African tribal masks when his eye caught sight of several small, shiny, golden ornaments on a side table beside a comfy looking purple velvet chair in a room next to the foyer.

Thabo ran his hands over the soft fabric then picked up the heavy figurine that looked like a man blowing a horn.

He inspected the piece of art a little closer and felt the urge to put it into his bag. "They won't miss it."

"Thabo?" Jason called out from behind him.

Thabo dropped the figurine back on the table. His heart pounded in his chest and he stood frozen in place.

"Thabo," Jason called out again.

Thabo took a few big steps out of the room.

"There you are," Jason said as he walked up to Thabo. "Didn't I tell you to stay by the door?"

"Sorry sir, I was just looking at all the beautiful things you have in your house. You must be very rich."

Jason frowned at Thabo and said, "I can't find your mother. She might be in the servants quarters. You can walk with me through the house, but next time you'll need to go around the side and use that entrance. Do you understand?"

"Yes, of course," Thabo said and glanced at Jason's beautiful watch. "Nice watch. What make is it?"

"You won't know it."

"Why won't I know the brand? Is it because I'm black? Or because I'm poor?"

"Did I say that?" Jason stood there waiting for an answer. "It's a brand that you don't get in South Africa, so I highly doubt you would have heard of it."

"Try me."

"Patek Philippe. You know?"

"No."

Jason rolled his eyes at Thabo. "See, what did I tell you? Follow me."

CHAPTER 11

19 October 1990.

Two weeks had passed since Thabo began working as the garden caretaker at the Rothshen mansion. Thabo scraped dead leaves together at the very far end of the back garden, near the border where the lawn ended and the exotic plants began.

A colourful little bird swept past Thabo and landed in the tree just above his head. The bird chirped then flew off into the bush.

Thabo continued his chore and seconds later the bird appeared once more, chirped a couple of times and flew back into the bush. Thabo wondered what type of bird it could be, then dropped the rake and walked into the shrubs to see if he could find it.

Perhaps it has a nest somewhere with babies.

Thorny branches and twigs grabbed at Thabo as he walked deeper and followed a barely visible overgrown path between the exotic plants. He could smell a peculiar whiff hanging in the air. For a moment it smelled the same as in the township. The smell of something decomposing.

The bird appeared once more above his head then flew away.

Thabo carefully stepped over some ferns while he searched for where the smell came from.

Something cracked under his shoe.

He slowly lifted his foot and saw the remains of a bird.

"Oh no," Thabo whispered and kneeled down to take a better look. "What happened to you, my furry friend?" He inspected the few colourful feathers with a stick. "You must be family of that other bird. Looks like you've been dead for a couple of days now."

Thabo spotted something shiny, took a stick and scraped the ground with it. He lifted a thin necklace with pieces of dried earth stuck to it.

"Wow," he said and inspected the treasure, thinking there must be more hidden somewhere near. "Maybe they hide their gold in here." He looked around him to see if he could spot anything else.

That familiar smell of a dead animal increased and he knew it had to be very near him.

He took a few more steps and noticed more remains of another bird, which looked like a dove that had been dead for at least a couple of weeks.

He looked around him and began to realise there were dozens of bird carcasses strewed around the area. "It's like a graveyard."

Thabo spotted a dirty orange soccer ball partly hidden behind a fern a couple of meters away. He walked towards the ball and the decomposing smell became overwhelming.

Thabo carefully took a step closer and kneeled beside the remains partly hidden underneath leaves.

He covered his mouth with his hand and prodded the stiff corpse with the stick then lifted the side of the body.

A colony of flesh-eating maggots crawled in all directions as he lifted it, with a few fat flies flying away.

"Looks like a cat."

Suddenly, loud dance music came from the direction of the house.

Thabo scrambled through the bushes back in the direction he came from.

As he stepped into the open and onto the lawn, he saw Jason walking onto the patio only in his underwear, singing and dancing along with the music.

CHAPTER 12

With a jug full of juice in one hand and clutching a glass under his arm, Jason walked onto the patio. He'd just gotten home from a squash game with Pedro and thrown his sweaty clothes in the direction of the laundry room. As he was about to place the drink on the patio table, his eye caught movement coming from the far end of the garden. A shirtless Thabo stood on the opposite side of the swimming pool holding a ball and looking straight at him.

The thought of quickly walking back into the house crossed his mind, but too late as Thabo enthusiastically waved at Jason and shouted, "Hello, sir Jason."

In a state of embarrassment, Jason waved back and said, "You alright?"

"I'm fine," Thabo said and walked in his direction.

"I see you found my ball."

"Yes, sir, all the way back between the plants."

"You know there are snakes in there, don't you?" Jason thought Thabo must be a real idiot for walking in there.

"Snakes?" Thabo laughed and shook his head. "There are no snakes here."

"Of course there are."

"No, there are not."

"How would you know?" Jason suddenly felt the urge to tell Thabo off as his attitude had become slightly cocky since he began work.

"I just know," Thabo said as he walked up the patio steps. "I know what it looks like when snakes are around. I haven't seen any signs yet."

"Signs like what?"

"Skin. They shed skin. And holes in the ground. But then again, I was wondering why there are so many dead birds laying around. Perhaps there must be a snake."

"Yeah, perhaps there is." *Fucking idiot.* Jason took a sip of juice while eyeing Thabo's well-toned upper body and suddenly caught a whiff of Thabo's manly musk.

"Today is two weeks already. I think you owe me one thousand Rand."

"Has it been two weeks?" Jason said with a hint of sarcasm. "How about we play a game for it? You win, I give you the money. I win, you don't receive a cent. Yes?"

Thabo frowned angrily. "I already won the bet. You owe me money. One thousand cash. A bet is a bet."

Jason could see he touched a sensitive spot and thought he'd push it even further to see how much the hot gardener would and could take.

"Best of ten. Let's see how good you are." Jason kicked the ball to the other side of the pool. "Go get it," Jason instructed.

Thabo looked at Jason with surprise and shook his head as he walked in the direction of the ball, muttering something in another language.

Jason walked onto the grass sipping on his juice when Thabo kicked the ball back towards Jason. It landed in a puddle of water near him created by the garden sprinklers about an hour earlier.

As the ball hit the water, Thabo gasped when the muddy water shot up against Jason and left a brown muddy stripe across his face and upper body. Some splashed into his juice.

"Jesus," Jason bellowed and spat. "Are you fucking mad?"

"I'm very sorry, sir," Thabo said. He clearly thought it was very amusing.

"You're a real wanker." Jason laughed and spat a few times and saw the funny side. "I see someone who's going home without a prize."

"But you're already home." Thabo laughed while he created two miniature goal posts from sticks on either side of the lawn.

Jason stood facing Thabo in the centre of the makeshift pitch. Their feet were beside the ball and Jason looked Thabo in his hazel brown eyes. He noticed small sweat droplets on the bridge of Thabo's nose.

"Ready?" Jason said.

"One thousand," Thabo said right before Jason pushed Thabo backwards and kicked the ball towards the goalpost.

"Bam! Fuck yeah." Jason jumped with joy. "One-zero."

"You cheat," Thabo shouted and walked after the ball and picked it up.

Ten minutes later and Thabo took the lead with the most goals; nine to seven, his favour.

Jason took control of the ball and ran to the side of the garden, in an attempt to circle around Thabo, but Thabo caught up and tackled Jason from the side, looking like a spider with his long legs.

Both tripped and skidded through one of the puddles while the ball carried on towards the makeshift goalpost, giving Thabo the point.

At the same time, Jason slid face down in the mud with Thabo's torso halfway underneath Jason's legs. Their tangled bodies stopped right at the edge of the lawn where the flowerbed began.

Jason turned onto his back, one leg still on Thabo's torso with muddy water dripping from his head. "What the fuck, Thabo," Jason growled. "This is now the second time."

"You okay, sir?" Thabo wiped the muddy grass from his face.

"I'm fine, not my undies, though." Jason pointed down to his crotch where his wet underwear was pulled down to below his buttocks. Just enough to reveal Jason's ginger pubic hair and part of his pale white cock, also covered in the dirt.

Jason noticed Thabo looking at his exposed manhood before he shyly looked away and moved his body from underneath Jason's legs.

"Last one in the pool is a girl," Jason said as he jumped up and took off his muddy underwear.

Thabo jumped up and took off his soaked knee-high trousers but tripped and fell on the grass as his right foot got caught in one of the legs.

Jason kicked the soggy underwear in Thabo's face and went into a laughing fit while Thabo spat profusely and chased Jason in the direction of the pool.

Jason dove into the pool like a professional swimmer and his body cut through the crystal clear water that washed away the brown gunk. He rose on the other side of the pool and looked back at Thabo crouching by the side of the water.

"Don't be a pussy," Jason shouted. "Jump."

Thabo looked anxious and stood up and shook his head. "No, I can't."

"Come on, Thabo, jump in."

"I can't swim."

"What? Seriously?"

"Yes."

Jason could see Thabo looked anxiously at the water. "It's not deep. Come on, pussy, jump."

"Of course it's deep. I cleaned the pool."

"Look, I'm standing. See? It's not deep." Meanwhile, Jason kicked hard underwater to keep himself afloat to make it look like he was standing.

"Jump, or you don't get your money."

"Yoh, why are you doing this to me? You're so mean."

Thabo took a few steps back then ran and jumped into the deep end of the pool and disappeared under the water.

Jason looked on for a few seconds with only bubbles popping up.

"Oh fuck." Jason swam towards Thabo who suddenly emerged with both hands slapping the water as he tried to keep his head above the surface.

Jason grabbed Thabo across his torso to keep him from sinking.

Thabo frantically waved his arms and hit Jason on the side of the head.

"Calm down," Jason said and wrestled with Thabo to keep him under control.

Thabo managed to turn around and grabbed onto Jason like an octopus, wrapping his arms and legs around Jason.

Jason wrestled from Thabo's grip. He then grabbed Thabo with one arm from the back and swam towards the side of the pool. "I got you. Keep still."

When they reached the side of the pool, Thabo pulled himself out, coughing and gasping for air, and rolled onto his side.

"Are you okay, Thabo?"

Thabo coughed violently and began to vomit water.

"I'm so sorry," Jason said. "I thought you were just messing about when you said you can't swim."

Thabo slapped Jason's hand away from his shoulder. "Don't touch me." A string of mucus dangled from Thabo's chin as he caught his breath. "I told you I can't swim, and you lied to me. Why would you do that? I want my money. No more games."

"Fine, I'll give you the cash before you go home. No more games. I promise."

Jason glanced at Thabo as he laid on his back beside the pool. His smooth wet chocolate skin glittered in the afternoon sun. The musky body odour had vanished.

Jason laid down beside Thabo. He realised how small Thabo's nipples were. His eyes followed the contours of Thabo's naked body down towards his thighs, but with Thabo's legs raised, he could only see the black curly pubes, nothing more.

Jason wondered if a black man's skin smelled any different from a white person's, so he moved slightly closer to Thabo and tried to smell the skin on his shoulder.

"What are you doing?" Thabo said with Jason's nose just inches away from his arm.

"Nothing," Jason said and elegantly moved away and made as if he was adjusting his position.

"Were you trying to smell me just now?"

"No, most definitely not. Why the hell would I do that?"

"Yes, you were. I just saw you."

"Fine. I tried to see what your skin smelled like."

"You're so weird," Thabo said and looked away. "It's quite funny that the boss's son is hanging out with the gardener, don't you think?"

"I can do whatever I want."

"I bet you can. Why do you do it?"

"Bored, I guess. Nothing much to do. And besides, I think you're cool."

"Am I cool?" Thabo gave an unconvincing laugh. "White boy think black boy is *cool*. Fucking apartheid turned upside down. I wish more people were like you. Then we'd be free."

Deep down, Jason felt an urge to touch Thabo's chocolate skin. The attraction grew stronger every minute he spent in Thabo's company.

"What happened on your hip?" Jason lightly touched a prominent scar just above Thabo's hip bone.

Thabo gently pushed Jason's hand away and sat up. "Long story."

Jason noticed more long, crisscrossing scars on Thabo's back,

"You have a lot of scars, Thabo." Jason reached out to touch the scars, but then stopped short of doing so as Thabo already pushed him away.

Thabo kept quiet with his head resting on his knees.

"Do you want to tell me how you got them?"

"I can. But please don't judge me once I've told you."

Chapter 13

March 1983.

Deep inside the slums of Soweto, Johannesburg, Thabo, a skinny ten-year-old, sat outside the tin shack home of the Molefe family.

His stomach made unholy growling sounds as he hadn't eaten for days. Life in the slums at its worst.

In the distance, Thabo spotted his friend Vussi, an athletically built black teenage boy five years older than Thabo.

As Vussi got closer, Thabo noticed he was eating something and ran up to Vussi. "Oi, brah, Vussi, what're you eating there, my brah?"

"Chicken," Vussi said and increased his pace.

"Where did you find it?"

"Who wants to know?" Vussi said.

"Me, idiot."

"Then no one wants to know. Go home."

"C'mon man, you got more?"

"No," Vussi said. "I said go home, Thabo."

"I thought we're friends," Thabo said and grabbed Vussi by the arm.

Thabo's mouth dribbled from hunger as he eyed the chicken bone with a few tiny pieces of meat still left on it.

"Fuck it, boy, don't you ever get fed?"

Thabo looked down and said, "We don't have food, my brah. I'm so very hungry."

"Eish, man, what's wrong with your mother? Why doesn't she get some food? She's supposed to look after you, brother. I thought she was working for a rich white man now."

Thabo shrugged his shoulders and firmly fixated on the chicken bone in Vussi's hand. He said, "I don't know, but what I do know is I want that bone."

"Take it."

Thabo grabbed the bone from Vussi and began chewing away on it.

"Yoh, you just grab it like that. No 'thank you'?"

"Thank you, brah. Can you get some more?"

"No." Vussi began to walk again.

"Are you going to tell me where you got it from or not?"

"From somewhere. I'm in a hurry. Go home."

"Come on, Vussi. Don't be so selfish. We're like brothers. Tell me where you got the chicken from."

Vussi stopped, turned around and said, "If you wanna find out, meet me at Mr. Naido's corner shop tomorrow morning at eleven. And don't be late."

The following morning, Thabo sat outside Mr. Naido's Tikka Masala corner shop. The local cash and carry and takeaway shop sold everything except for tikka masala, of course.

A frail looking elderly black woman walking like a question mark handed Thabo a piece of candy wrapped in paper while holding onto her back with one hand and said, "Don't eat it all at once. I know there is some good inside you, boy. You just need to find it and know how to use it. Don't be tempted to do bad things for a little gain because it will come back and haunt you sometime in the future."

Thabo nodded and shyly said, "Yebo, gogo." *Yes, grandma.* He stuck the sweet with wrapping paper and all into his mouth and began to chew.

The old woman just shook her head and shuffled down the dusty gravel road while talking to herself.

Every couple of minutes Thabo looked at the wall clock hanging inside the shop behind the counter where the cash register stood.

All of a sudden, Mr. Naido appeared in the doorway holding a stick in his hand and prodded Thabo with the stick in the ribs. In a north Indian accent, he said, "Move away from my shop door. You've been sitting here too long. Go sit somewhere else or I call the police."

"I just want to see the time."

"I said move, you little fuck. You're banned from my shop."

"Does it look like I'm inside your ugly shop?" Thabo shouted.

"These steps are part of my shop. Now fuck off from them before I cane you myself, you bastard boy." Mr. Naido bobbed his head like a car window doll and lifted the stick in the air and made as if he wanted to hit Thabo.

Thabo stood up and walked a few meters and gave Mr. Naido the middle finger.

"Fuck you too," Mr. Naido said and returned the middle finger. "Fucking rat bastard."

Thabo waited for Vussi around the corner from Mr. Naido's shop. Not knowing the time, Thabo waited what felt like ages with no sign of Vussi.

"Vussi, you cat-fucker," Thabo muttered and began walking home on the dusty gravel path.

"Thabo," a voice called from behind.

As Thabo turned around, Vussi casually strolled out from behind a shack while sucking on something yet again.

Thabo ran up to Vussi. "Why are you so late? You said eleven."

"Calm down, brah, I was here all along. I was just making sure you don't shoplift again."

"Eish, Vussi, fuck off. I thought you weren't coming anymore. I'm so hungry, man."

Vussi began to laugh. "I see Mr. Naido still hasn't forgiven you."

"Can we just go? I'm so fucking hungry, I'll bloody eat you, man."

"Watch it, skinny boy. You might be eaten yourself if you're not careful."

"So where are we going?" Thabo said impatiently.

"You'll see," Vussi said with a smirk on his face.

The two boys made their way to the other side of the slums and arrived at an old industrial building with rows upon rows of scrapped cars and mountains of used car tyres.

"What is this place?" Thabo said.

"It used to be a scrapyard. It's uncle Sam's place."

"Who is uncle Sam?"

"You're asking too many questions, skinny boy. Keep that big mouth of yours shut and let me do the talking. You hear me?"

They walked into the empty brick building with a few pigeons flying about, their flapping wings echoing inside the large empty space.

They walked up to three black men that stood by the door at the far end of the warehouse, dressed in funky-looking outfits and decorated in gold rings and chains, smoking marijuana.

"Yo, Vussi, my man," one of the men called out. "Who's this with you, brotha?"

"Yo, Snake-fucker," Vussi said and greeted him with some kind of ritual handshake. "This here's my good friend Thabo. He's like my brother and he wanna earn some food today."

"And what special talents does your little skinny *friend* have?" said Snake-fucker.

"That's for uncle Sam to find out."

They walked up the flight of metal stairs to the first floor with Thabo holding onto the back of Vussi's t-shirt.

"Why do you call him Snake-fucker?" Thabo said.

"Because one day a snake bit him while he jiga-jiga his squeeze, *girlfriend*. He grabbed the snake, bit its head off and began to fuck the snake. They say it's the snake's poison that made him a little crazy. He hasn't been the same ever since that day."

Thabo gasped from shock. "Yoh, that's wild, man."

They entered a dirty-looking room with one of its walls completely demolished which overlooked a courtyard to the side of the building. A few empty plastic bags swirled around in the slight draft.

Thabo followed Vussi into a second room where a man prepared what looked like raw chicken.

"Come, skinny boy," Vussi said and pulled Thabo by the arm into a third room. It was much darker than the first two, with burning candles all around the room and an odd smell lingering in the air. A large dirty mattress lay on the floor to the side of the room. Two funky-looking men stood in the corner, chatting away in an unrecognisable language.

One of the men had a distinctive super-size afro with a comb tucked into the side, while the other was completely bald and wore a rolled bandana wrapped around his head just above his eyebrows.

On the other side of the room, two young boys roughly the same age as Thabo, danced to distorted pop music blaring from a portable FM radio player. They were dressed only in shorts and were smoking.

"Vussi, my man," the man with the super-sized afro said as he walked over. He had on a black tank top and white trousers and a number of thick golden chains around his neck. "And who's this?"

"Uncle Sam, this is my friend. He wants to earn some food."

"Good, I like hungry boys." Uncle Sam took a lit candle from the floor and walked up to Thabo and Vussi. "There is more than enough food for hungry boys like him. More than enough, yes." He spat a gob of mucus on the floor.

Thabo smiled, eager for the eating to begin. His stomach growled extra loud with the mention of food.

"And what's your little friend's name?" uncle Sam said.

"I'm Thabo."

"Thabo, my man, welcome to little Nigeria where everyone is welcome and chicken is king, brotha."

Uncle Sam inspected Thabo under the candlelight, which illuminated uncle Sam's face. Thabo could see his teeth were covered in gold and glittered like a black treasure chest every time he opened his mouth.

He must be very rich, Thabo thought while eyeing uncle Sam's golden jewellery.

"Now tell me, boy, what did Vussi tell you about me and my establishment?"

"Thabo—," Vussi began to talk.

"Hush, Vussi," uncle Sam cut him off. "He's got a mouth, so let the boy speak for himself."

"Nothing," Thabo said and glanced at Vussi. "He didn't tell me anything. He just said there's some food, that's all."

"Why didn't you tell this young man what we do here?"

"Eish, uncle Sam, because the last time I did that, you got very angry with me."

"Okay, okay, fair enough. That is another matter I wish to forget about. Anyway, I like young boys and I'm always ready to help them out. Especially the ones who can help me out. You know, one hand washes the other, as they say. You help me, I help you. Get it?" Uncle Sam had a deep chesty laugh and inspected Thabo one more time under the candlelight.

Thabo smiled excitedly. His eyes fixed on uncle Sam's treasure chest mouth and he wished he could have golden teeth like that.

"Oi, you two, come here," uncle Sam called the other two dancing boys. "Take off your clothes. You too, Thabo, strip."

"Why he want me to strip?" Thabo said to Vussi and felt a knot in his stomach.

"Just take your clothes off, dammit," Vussi said and pushed Thabo over to uncle Sam. "Do you want to eat or not?"

Thabo took his shirt off, then his shorts and stood beside the other two naked boys in front of uncle Sam, feeling scared and wanting to go home.

"Shall we start with you, Thabo?" uncle Sam said. "And don't look so frightened, young man, chill. Now tell me, how much do you want to eat today?"

"I don't know," Thabo said.

"One mouth full, two mouths full, or three?"

"Three," Thabo said full of excitement. In his mind, he visualised stuffing his mouth with barbecued chicken so much that he could not close his tiny gob-hole while he licked the juices from his fingers.

"Come closer," uncle Sam instructed and took a silver pot standing on a table. He stuck his hand inside and scooped out a dollop of petroleum jelly.

"Now bend over and touch your toes," uncle Sam said to Thabo.

"What? No."

"Bend over or you go home without eating a nice juicy piece of chicken thigh. And you two as well, do the same," uncle Sam said to the other two boys.

Thabo slowly bent forward while keeping his eye firmly on the hand that held the petroleum jelly.

"Now, can you do the same backwards?" said uncle Sam.

Thabo stood up and looked at Vussi. "Eish, I don't know if I want to do this anymore."

"Just do what uncle Sam asks and stop being a pissy boy."

"Don't call me a pissy boy." Thabo pondered for a moment whether he should continue or go home hungry. His stomach gave an audible growl. Thabo bent backward and placed his palms firmly on the ground and made a complete three-sixty backflip and stood up.

The two other boys lost their balance and fell backwards.

"Thabo, now that, my boy, was fucking impressive. I have to say I didn't think you had it in you. You're like a skinny gymnast. You stay, and you two useless rats, get the fuck out of my building. Fucking useless. Fell over like bags of shit. Get out. I said get the fuck out!"

The other two boys grabbed their shorts and looked angrily at Thabo, as if he stole something from them.

"Thabo, come over here," uncle Sam said and held petroleum jelly in his hand.

Thabo cautiously walked closer, unsure whether he wanted to continue.

Uncle Sam began to smear Thabo's body.

"Why are you putting that stuff on me?"

"You need to be lubricated. It's not pleasant to get stuck inside a tiny hole."

Thabo pulled away and said, "Eish, what hole?"

"This hole." Uncle Sam pointed to a piece of black iron pipe laying to the side of the floor.

"That's where you need to slide through like a snake. If you can do that, then you can eat three mouths full today. If you can't, then you leave immediately without food like those other two useless rats."

Uncle Sam continued to smear Thabo's entire body with petroleum jelly, until Thabo gleamed like a brown diamond.

"Okay, now put on the shoes." Uncle Sam gave Thabo custom made rubber shoes that stretched and sucked to his feet. "Get into the pipe, head first and use your toes to push yourself through."

Thabo slipped into the pipe and slid through to the other side within two seconds.

"Fucking hell, Thabo, excellent job. Absolutely excellent. You definitely have some skills, boy. Now, can you do the same, but this time on your back?"

Thabo climbed into the pipe, turned onto his back and slipped through to the other side again within a couple of seconds.

"This boy is like a fucking snake sent from heaven."

Thabo got up and said, "Can I eat now?"

"Yes, of course," uncle Sam said and walked Thabo and Vussi outside to the rear of the warehouse where Snake-fucker stood busy barbecuing some chicken pieces.

"Three mouths full," uncle Sam said. "Don't eat too much. We don't want you to get fat and get stuck inside the pipe."

Without asking any more questions, Thabo stuffed his mouth with the oily chicken faster than he could swallow.

After a few bites, he stopped as the food began to push back up.

"Slow down, boy. The food is not going to run away."

The following afternoon, Thabo and Vussi arrived back at uncle Sam's warehouse.

"Well, Thabo," uncle Sam said, "it seems like you're truly *hungry* for success. How hungry are you today?"

"Very much hungry, uncle Sam, five mouths full." Thabo felt super enthusiastic and excited about the new-found food.

"Well, you'll have to work extra hard for those five mouths full. Today is peri-peri chicken and maize. You like?"

Thabo bobbed his head a couple of times. "Yes, I like very much, uncle Sam."

"Good boy. Now if you can do this tiny little job for me, then you can eat as much as you like. Would you like that?"

"Yes, uncle Sam," Thabo said and licked his lips. "Whatever you want."

"Perfect. Let's get you lubricated."

As uncle Sam covered Thabo's entire body in petroleum jelly and gave him the same custom made rubber shoes to wear, Thabo kept wondering what type of job he had to do.

"Down here," said uncle Sam and pushed away a square wood cover on the floor, which revealed a large hole in the concrete floor. He took out his flashlight and lowered himself into the hole.

"C'mon, boy, what you waiting for? Get that lubricated ass in here."

"Yoh, uncle Sam, I don't know if I can get in there." Being claustrophobic, Thabo eyed the dark hole in the ground and gave a nervous fart.

"Fuck, boy, you wanna gas us all down here with your fart?"

"Sorry, boss."

"Move your ass. I don't have all day."

"Come ,Thabo, it's not that bad," Vussi added.

"Yoh, why don't you get in there?" Thabo snapped.

"Because you're smaller than me, dumb-ass." Vussi pushed Thabo forward.

"Vussi, voetsek, *fuck off,* don't push me like that." Thabo lowered himself into the hole.

"See, not so bad, is it?" uncle Sam said. "Just think of the delicious chicken you will eat when you get back."

Thabo visualised stuffing his mouth with a fat chicken breast with juices dripping down the side of his lips. That distinctive smell of barbecued chicken urged him on.

Uncle Sam shone his torch light down the opening of the pipe, making a turn a couple of meters inward. "This pipe leads to a building down the road. Once you get to the end of the pipe, you will be in the basement of that building. When you get out of the pipe, you will see many wooden crates stacked on top of each other. To open the side of one of the crates you need to break the wood. You understand? There will be an iron bar inside to break it with. Once you manage to open it, fill this bag with as much of the red bullet casings as you can, then climb back into the pipe and come straight back. Do you understand?"

"Yes, uncle Sam."

Uncle Sam tied the purple handmade bag the size of a woman's handbag around Thabo's waist with a piece of white string.

"When you're back, you can eat all you want. We'll be waiting for you right here."

Thabo licked his lips and said, "What kind of bullets are they?"

"Bullets for a shotgun. Pump-action like the peri-urban use." He pointed at a shotgun standing against the wall in the corner.

With the torch tied around his head, Thabo slid headfirst into the dark pipe and into the unknown.

The temperature inside the pipe became unbearably hot within minutes. The pipe became narrower the further down Thabo slid. Many meters and half an hour later, Thabo reached a kink in the piping. Presumably the part he had auditioned for.

His body bent ninety degrees down at the first kink with his arms by his side.

He pushed through into the next kink, a ninety degree bend to the side. Thabo's body bent backward and his chin scraped against the bottom of the pipe, with his arms pressed flat against his body.

Uncle Sam's simple yet ingenious invention, the custom made rubber shoes, came in handy and Thabo managed to get a grip and pushed his sweaty body forward.

Suddenly, everything came to a halt and Thabo got stuck in the middle of the kink.

His chest pressed flat on the horizontal surface with his bum touching the top part of the previous kink.

Thabo tried to wiggle forwards, but with no luck as he lost traction under the shoes.

Thabo's bum and back muscles began to cramp and went into a painful spasm.

"Yoh, fuck you, Vussi," Thabo cried out. Unable to move as the muscles pulled stiff, he sobbed, "Why did I do this?"

Thabo's body tensed up and the stifling heat became overwhelming. He began to hyperventilate and seconds later Thabo lost consciousness.

A minute or so after losing consciousness, Thabo's limp, sweaty, petroleum smeared body slowly edged forward until it slipped through the kink in the pipe like a lubricated sausage and stopped.

Several minuets went by as Thabo laid unresponsive while dreaming of playing in mud on a cloud while eating chicken.

A rat came scurrying up towards him and sniffed a couple of times at his mouth before it bit into Thabo's bottom lip.

Thabo woke from the pain and jerked back and banged his head against the top of the pipe, looking straight at the rat illuminated under the torch light.

The rat sat in one spot for a moment before it slowly moved towards him, presumably to take another nibble.

"*Voetsek,*" Thabo shouted.

The rodent moved slightly back and assessed the situation, then came forward again.

Starting to panic and afraid the dirty animal might bite him again, Thabo forced his one arm past his body and managed to grab the torch from his head and swing it at the rat, which eventually scared it, and it scuttled down the pipe.

Thabo took a while to get back to his senses. Suddenly he could feel a slight draft gently flowing over his face.

He wormed himself through the last couple of meters until he reached a mesh cover and listened for a couple of seconds, with only the cooling system humming away.

He banged the cover with his head a couple of times until it came loose and fell to the floor.

Cool, fresh air blew into his face the moment he stuck his head out of the pipe. He shone the torch into the dark room and looked down at a drop of a couple of meters to the floor.

He slipped from the pipe and landed on his back on a concrete floor.

Thabo curled with pain from the fall and held onto his elbow, which hit the cold concrete floor the hardest.

He sat there for a minute before he pulled himself up. His lubricated body dripped with sweat and left a large human body splat print on the concrete where he fell.

He took in the scenery around him. And just like uncle Sam said, stacks of small wooden crates.

Thabo broke one of the wooden panels open with an iron bar he found standing in the corner, just like uncle Sam said. It seemed like he knew every detail.

A bunch of red bullet casings dropped from the crate onto the cement floor as he pulled the wooden plank away. Thabo grabbed the bullets as quickly as he could until the bag was half full.

Thabo tried to lift the bag. It had become too heavy to even lift above his head.

He walked back to where he fell from. The opening was too high to climb back into the pipe.

He searched for something to stand on. The only option was the crates, but they were too large to be moved by a small boy.

Left with no other option, Thabo walked to the only door and slowly opened it and listened for any sign of people. He tiptoed up the stairs that led into a big factory full of machinery with some lights switched on, but there was no sign of anyone, except for some whistling from the far end of the factory floor.

Thabo quietly walked to one of the windows located on the left side of the factory floor.

He opened the window slightly and the bag slipped from his hand and landed with a loud bang on the factory floor.

The whistling stopped. "Hello?" a male voice called out. "Robert, is that you?"

Thabo stood frozen in place for a moment and listened. He could hear footsteps but couldn't see anyone.

"Shit." Thabo grabbed the bag and wiggled himself through the narrow gap in the window, then suddenly heard someone running towards him yelling something. A hand grabbed Thabo's leg but it couldn't get a grip because of the petroleum jelly on Thabo's skin.

Thabo jumped and landed in some bushes and began to run for his life in an unknown direction along a path between the factory and a high brick wall.

"Stop!" someone called out. Thabo ran as fast as his little skinny legs could carry him until he reached the brick wall standing between him and freedom.

He glanced back and saw a fat white man running in his direction.

"You're not going anywhere, *kaffir*,"[1] the man said and slowed down as he ran out of breath and then stopped.

"Now," Thabo said to himself and began to scale the wall. His tiny fingers barely gripped the small gaps between each brick, with the bag hanging down behind him.

---

[1] A racist slur used to refer to a black African. A term now banned in South Africa.

He could hear the large man stomping towards him yet again, shouting, "Get back down, you fucking swine."

Thabo reached the top of the wall, lined with broken glass bottles cemented to the brick.

Something large hit Thabo on the back, making him lose his balance and fall over the wall. A piece of the security glass ripped into Thabo's skin just above his hip bone, and he tumbled down onto a pile of rubbish bags.

Thabo pressed his hand on a gaping wound with the flesh lifted up with a large amount of blood flowing from the cut. He stumbled over the bags of rubbish, looking for a way out. He recognised part of the building visible over another wall and realised he fell into the car scrapyard behind uncle Sam's warehouse. Thabo had to try and get over a mountain of bumped-up cars and tyres to get over uncle Sam's wall.

Thabo felt dizzy, and the almost unbearable noise ringing inside his ears just didn't want to go away.

Moments later, two men in blue overalls ran towards Thabo with a barking German shepherd on a lead, foaming from the mouth and looked like it wanted to rip Thabo into pieces.

Thabo dropped the bag of bullets and held one hand in the air while covering the ripped skin on his hip with the other. His naked, petroleum jellied body glittered in the sunlight.

One of the men wearing thick black glasses picked up the bag and smacked Thabo in the face. "Thought you'd get away with this?"

Right about the same time, a police van sped into the scrapyard with flashing blue lights and siren blaring.

Two police officers jumped out of the vehicle.

Thabo began to sob the moment he recognised the white police officer with the scary blue eyes. Officer Van Rooyen with his neatly combed blond hair.

"That's him," the man with black framed glasses said to Van Rooyen. "The glass did a good job on him."

"I recognise you," Van Rooyen said. "You're that boy who stole chocolates a few months ago from that corner shop."

Van Rooyen crouched in front of Thabo. "So, from chocolates to ammunition? That's a pretty big jump. A true criminal in the making. Tell me, who did you steal this for?"

Thabo sobbed as he tried to say sorry, but no words came out of his mouth as the salty flow of tears dripped from his lips and down his chin.

"Fine, we'll get it out of you at the station," Van Rooyen said and pushed Thabo into the back of the police van.

"They lashed me six times."

"Why didn't you tell them the truth?"

"Ratting someone out in the township is never a good idea. They always say snitches get stitches but in Soweto you get the Mama Winnie necklace."

"What is a Mama Winnie necklace?"

"They place a car tyre around your neck, fill it with petrol and then set it on fire."

"Winnie Mandela," Jason said.

"Yebo, Mama Winnie. She's very famous in Soweto, and so is her necklacing."

Jason reached out and touched the scars on his back, at which moment Thabo stood up.

"I need to finish my work, sir." Thabo picked up his muddy clothes from the grass.

"You haven't finished?"

"No, sir. There is too much to do. I have to finish the back garden today and tomorrow the front."

"Told you. It's a lot of work. I'm surprised you lasted two weeks."

"Yes," Thabo said and walked off.

"Do you have dry clothes?"

"No, sir."

"I'll give you some of mine."

Something dropped from Thabo's dirty clothes and landed on the floor.

Jason picked up a dirty looking chain and said, "Is this yours?"

"I found it over there behind the ferns in the mud."

Jason inspected the chain. "It looks like gold." He walked over to the pool and gave it a quick rinse.

"Why do you have so many dead animals laying in the bushes?"

"Where exactly did you find this?" Jason said.

"All the way to the back, near the wall."

"It looks like my mother's," Jason said, but he couldn't be sure as there were no markings. "There, take it. Finders keepers."

"No, I can't take it. It's your mother's."

"It's not. Take it."

"Thank you, sir." Thabo disappeared around the corner to the servants' quarters.

CHAPTER 14

9:20 p.m.

Thabo left the Rothshen's home and made his way in the direction of the bus stop, a forty-five minute walk that would take Thabo through the quiet, winding roads of upmarket suburban Northcliffe.

How will I finish the front garden? Thabo thought to himself. *I can't even finish the back garden. I don't think I want to do this work anymore. Too much. Just too much.*

A dark storm brewed over the city and quickly morphed into a dark grey beast from the soaring heat. The roaring thunder became louder as the storm floated closer to the city. The electricity in the air illuminated the drifting dark grey mass that tumbled and grew into bigger, darker balls of floating water.

A warm gust of wind that carried the distinctive sweet smell of summer rain began to get stronger and awoke the tall oak trees that hung lazily over the empty suburban streets and looked like they hugged the streetlights.

Thabo placed the one thousand Rand cash Jason gave him into the old plastic shopping bag with his dirty clothes, afraid it might get wet, and increased his pace to a light jog.

The blanket of heavy rain began to chase after him like a big grey ghost.

Thabo pulled the t-shirt over his head and made an attempt to outrun the natural shower, but he got completely soaked within seconds.

Steam rose from the warm tar road and created a layer of otherworldly fog, illuminated by the yellow-orange glow of the street lights.

Very quickly, large puddles of water began to form as the rain fell faster than it could drain.

A bolt of thunder clapped and rumbled through the air like African tribal drums and echoed against the surrounding hills.

A car approached Thabo from behind, and its headlights cast two thick yellow-white beams through the steamy fog.

"Hey," a man shouted from the car.

At first, Thabo thought it could be Jason and glanced back, then realised it wasn't. "Please go away," he whispered and wanted to run.

The car pulled up alongside Thabo. "What you doing here?" the man yelled in a broken South African English accent. "You know you shouldn't be here."

Thabo kept walking with his shirt pulled over his head.

The car pulled up behind him and Thabo could hear someone get out.

"Stop, *kaffir*, or I'll shoot!"

Thabo stopped. Streams of warm rainwater flooded over his smooth face and blurred his vision.

The car's headlights created a dark, stocky shadow in front of him as the man approached.

"What are you doing here?" the man said. His voice was barely audible through the heavy rain. "You know you shouldn't be in our neighbourhood at night. Where's your passbook?"

"I finished work late, sir," Thabo said with a quivering voice, busy searching for his passbook. "I have a passbook and permit to work here. I'm going home now, sir."

Thabo searched through his muddy clothes inside the plastic bag for his passbook then realised he left it on the steps near the pool in the rear garden.

"Don't talk shit with me, *kaffir* boy. Do I look fucking stupid? You're here to steal from us, isn't it? Caught in the fucking act, you black bastard. You fucking monkeys think you can just walk around in our neighbourhood and rob us."

The man grabbed the plastic bag from Thabo.

"No." Thabo tried to take it back from the man who wore a baseball cap that obstructing his face. The cap had a bright neon orange Nike logo on the front.

The man shoved Thabo to the side. "Who did you steal this from?" He pulled out the money Jason gave him.

An unexpected slap landed on the side of Thabo's face, partially over his ear. His vision filled with flashing dots, and he stumbled sideways.

As Thabo looked back, he could see the man stuffing the rolls of money with the golden chain into his own pocket.

A second slap landed on the back of Thabo's head, which caused Thabo to lose his balance and fall forward. He landed on his hands and knees on the rough, wet road. The loose stones on the road cut deep into the soft skin on his palms and knees.

"Please stop!"

A kick landed on Thabo's ribs. Thabo gasped for air and yelled, "Please please, *yoh-na-we*, I beg you, sir, please don't do this."

The man grabbed Thabo by the shirt and jerked him backward into a sitting position in front of the car. Thabo faced the car's powerful headlights and blocked the light with his hand, seeing diluted blood streaming from the cuts in his palm.

"Help!" Thabo called out.

"Shut your monkey mouth," the faceless man yelled and punched Thabo in the face.

The punch tore through the skin on Thabo's left eyebrow and knocked him semi-unconscious. He fell over like a sack of potatoes and bumped his head on the road where he lay on his side and stared at the car's headlights.

Blood gushed from the cut above his eye while the ringing sound in his ears drowned out the sound of the pouring rain.

The man's foot was inches away from Thabo's face. The neon Nike logo on the front of the cap stuck in Thabo's mind.

The man walked back to the car and sped away, leaving Thabo in the centre of the suburban street with a line of blood flowing into a puddle of water beside the road.

CHAPTER 15

Back at the Rothshen residence, Jason stood in his underwear by the bedroom window and gazed at the lightning display over the city.

The intercom buzzer broke the silence and echoed through the ground floor. Jason casually strolled down to the front door and lifted the handset and inspected the camera screen.

"Yeah?" Jason said.

"Please help me," a faint voice said over the scratchy speaker.

"Who's this?" Jason said impatiently, as the image on the CCTV camera was barely visible due to the pouring rain, and he could only make out the silhouette.

"Please, sir, it's me, Thabo."

"Thabo? What's going on?"

"I was attacked. Please help me."

"I can't see you. Move closer to the side of the gate." Jason immediately thought it could be one of the scenarios his father had constantly warned him about. The feared unrest due to the political situation in the country and someone trying to get onto the property.

Jason pondered for a moment, unsure if he should open the gate, then ran to his father's office and pulled the book to open the hidden door to the panic room so that he could escape in case it was a trap.

Jason pressed the button for the gate to open.

"Make sure it closes behind you before you come up."

Jason stood nervously by the front door and shone a powerful torch down the driveway, unsure of what to expect. Suddenly, in the distance, Thabo stumbled along the driveway towards him, and Jason could see the white t-shirt he gave to Thabo had large dark pink stains all over the front.

"What happened?" Jason said the moment Thabo reached the front door.

"Some bastard attacked and robbed me." Thabo began to cry. "And they took the money you gave me."

Jason could see the wounds looked real. "Stay where you are, I'll get some towels." Jason closed the door and locked it while Thabo stood outside. Jason didn't trust anything he said.

Moments later, Jason opened the front door. "Take off your clothes and cover yourself with this towel. Try not to drip any blood on the floor."

"No, I stay outside."

"My dad's not here. Hurry up."

Thabo did as instructed and followed Jason up the long marble staircase and into Jason's en-suite bathroom.

"Who would do such a stupid thing? Did you get a good look at him?"

"No, sir, I couldn't see his face. It happened so quickly and there was too much rain and he had a cap on."

"Sit on the toilet." Jason inspected the cut to Thabo's eye. The swollen wound on his eye gaped open and the exposed flesh looked pink against his dark skin.

"The cut looks really bad." Jason pressed some tissue over the wound. "Maybe you need to go to a hospital for stitches."

"No, I'm not going to hospital. I'm okay, I just need to rest a little, then I can go home."

"You're not leaving. It's already 10:30 p.m. What if the police sees you? Or what if that man finds you again? You shouldn't have left so late in the first place."

"I had to finish the work."

"You know the 10 p.m. curfew. Anyway, you can sleep in the servants' quarters where your mother usually sleeps when she stays over."

"Okay. Or maybe," Thabo hesitated for a moment, "I can stay in here with you." He smiled shyly.

Jason kept silent and wondered why Thabo would suddenly suggest that. Paranoia set in. *What if this is a setup? Maybe this has been his plan.*

A sudden fear overcame Jason that someone else might already be inside the house and he had to get downstairs to get a weapon and activate the alarm system.

"Go have a shower. I can patch the wounds afterwards."

Jason took out a small Thai engraved wooden box from underneath his bathroom sink and slid open a hidden compartment on the side of the box, which revealed a secret stash of prescription medication Jason had stolen from Patrick.

He took out a morphine pill, prescribed to Patrick after a skiing accident in France several years earlier.

"Take this, it should take the pain away for a while."

"Thank you, sir," Thabo said and swallowed the pill without any question. "You're very kind to me." Thabo stood up and walked to the door.

"Where are you going?" Jason said.

"To the servants' quarters to shower."

"Use my shower. I don't want you to walk outside."

Thabo nodded and smiled and dropped the towels on the floor, then walked straight into the massive shower.

Jason stood by the door and listened for the sound of falling water from the shower, then sprinted downstairs to the panic room. He got the keys for the safe and took out his father's semi-automatic pistol, loaded a magazine, locked it all up and enabled the home alarm system. Connected to the doors and windows, it would activate if it detected any forced entry.

Just as Jason walked back inside his bedroom, he noticed the shower had stopped. He quickly placed the loaded pistol inside his bedside table and closed the drawer at the same time Thabo appeared with a bath towel wrapped around his smooth, slim body.

"Eish, sir, that was the best shower I have ever had. It's like a waterfall. Oh, and I don't have any dry clothes."

Jason threw a pair of his silk boxer shorts at Thabo. "Use that."

"Yoh, this is such nice fabric. It feels like a king's underwear."

Jason smiled and his eyes fixated on Thabo as he took off the towel and put on the boxer shorts.

"Sir Jason?" Thabo said.

"Yeah?"

"I go out now?"

Jason took a deep breath and pondered for a moment whether he should take the chance and let Thabo, a person he hardly knew, stay inside the house. It wasn't just a security risk, but if his father found out, his reaction would be unthinkable.

"Sit down first so I can patch the wounds."

Jason sat down with Thabo on the carpet and blotted a piece of cotton with antiseptic ointment on the cut marks.

"Thank you for helping me, sir."

"Can you stop calling me sir? One more sir and you become *lady*, yeah?"

"Yes, sir," Thabo joked. "I mean Jason."

Thabo kept smiling with his eyes closed while Jason cleaned the cuts on his eye and hands.

"How are you feeling?" Jason said.

"I feel nice. My body doesn't hurt that much anymore." Thabo took a long, deep breath. "I feel good and nice."

They both sat on the carpet with their backs against the bed, Thabo's head tilted backward and his eyes shut.

Jason quietly measured the distance to the bedside table in case he had to grab the pistol if the situation turned out to be a trap.

Jason turned his head towards Thabo to smell his skin, which smelled like soap. Jason's tongue slowly and slightly touched the skin on Thabo's shoulder. He paused to see if Thabo reacted. But he kept still, eyes closed. Jason got excited as it had been his first mouth contact with a black man, and his skin tasted nothing like he had imagined it would taste like. It tasted like his own skin, the same as when he practice kissed himself on his arm. Jason moved a little lower and tried to smell Thabo's armpit. But the smell that turned him on before had gone, and he smelled the same as anyone else.

Jason went in for another lick on Thabo's arm, but the tiny lick turned into a bigger one with saliva oozing from the side of Jason's mouth. It suddenly turned into a full-on suck as his lips hungrily clamped around the soft, smooth skin on Thabo's muscular upper arm like a baby latching onto his mother's tit.

Jason could feel his own pre-cum seeping out of his erection, which left the top part of his boxers wet.

Thabo's breathing became more audible and he slightly moved his head and legs.

Jason looked down towards Thabo's blue boxer shorts and realised Thabo had an erection too. A big one, which slightly moved around underneath the fabric.

Wow, Jason thought and touched his own throbbing cock.

He moved his hand slowly towards Thabo's bulging boxer-shorts and reached a level of excitement he'd never experienced nor felt before.

He could feel his own erection become uncomfortably rock hard the moment his index finger lightly touched Thabo's bulging shorts, which caused the limb-like body part to move upwards and push against Jason's hand.

Suddenly Jason's cock contracted rapidly to the point of no return and an explosion of warm liquid shot uncontrollably inside his boxer shorts.

Jason grabbed hold of his own cock in an attempt to control the seemingly unstoppable bursts of ejaculation shooting against the inside of the fabric. Jason jumped up and ran straight to the bathroom.

"No," Jason said to himself as he pulled his cum-stained boxers down, filled with white sticky residue that smeared down his legs with more oozing from the tip if his cock.

"Jason?" Thabo called out.

"Yeah, I'm in the bathroom."

"I will sleep now. Is that okay?"

"Yeah sure, just get in the bed."

A minute earlier, Thabo felt like his body floated calm and free, with his thoughts drifting into short dreams.

All of a sudden, he felt a warm, wet tingling sensation on his arm.

Thabo slightly opened his one eye and watched as Jason's head touched his shoulder and could feel his warm tongue against his skin.

What is he doing? Thabo thought and kept still not to show that he could feel it. The sensation felt out of this world and he could hear Jason's breathing getting louder and the licking turned into a suck. He could feel Jason's teeth biting into his skin, but just a little, not too hard. Thabo could feel his erection bobbing in his shorts and wanted to turn towards Jason, but he stopped short of doing so.

Thabo watched as Jason's hand moved towards his boxers.

Touch it, white boy, Thabo thought and deliberately flexed his erection the moment Jason's finger grazed the head of his cock, causing it to move upwards against Jason's hand.

Thabo silently laughed when he saw Jason grab his own crotch before he jumped up and ran to the bathroom.

Fuck. Wow. That felt so good, Thabo thought and began to masturbate for a few seconds.

"Jason? I will sleep now."

Thabo climbed onto Jason's massive super kingsize bed. The mattress was the most comfortable thing he had ever laid on in his life. He rubbed his hand over the silky bed sheet then rubbed it over his chest.

CHAPTER 16

The balcony door off Jason's bedroom stood open. A cool breeze playfully lifted the side curtains like a dancing ballerina with streaks of moonlight landing over Jason's four-poster bed.

Jason opened his eyes. Above him, against the wall where it met the ceiling, hung the dark figure.

It made an unholy grunting sound as it moved from side to side.

Jason tried to scream but no sound came from his mouth, just muted puffs of air.

He tried to move his arm but his body was paralysed and it felt like his arms had been stuck to the bed.

The grunting of the dark figure became louder and it suddenly leaped from the ceiling onto Jason and bit him in the face, cracking his facial bones.

"No!" Jason screamed and sat up and held onto his face with one hand. His left arm hung to his side and felt like a dead person's hand as he touched it. It had gone completely numb.

His body trembled and was soaked in sweat, and he tried to catch his breath.

Thabo laid on the other side of the oversized bed, fast asleep with a slight snore. His head was turned towards Jason and his mouth was slightly open. A tiny amount of drool seeped from the side of his mouth and disappeared into the pillowcase.

Jason breathed a sigh of relief and slumped back onto his pillow. He lay quietly and listened to Thabo's breathing before he shifted closer and placed his ear near Thabo's chest to listen to his heartbeat. He could feel Thabo's warm skin that now smelled like a baby's skin.

I want you, Jason thought to himself and gently moved his hand underneath the silk sheet and ran his fingers over Thabo's smooth chest. *I can't believe he's actually in my bed. Patrick will shit himself.*

Jason's heart began to race as he gently moved his fingers over Thabo's tiny nipple and down over his smooth six-pack stomach.

Thabo mumbled a few unrecognisable words and turned his head to the other side, still fast asleep.

Jason slowly pushed his fingers underneath the waistband of Thabo's boxer shorts. He could feel Thabo's rough, curly pubic hair and playfully pulled on them, then stopped.

A sense of guilt overcame Jason as deep inside he knew it was wrong. But the excitement overrode everything else. He just couldn't resist touching Thabo's warm body.

Jason shuffled his body closer, just enough not to touch Thabo, then slowly and carefully laid his arm over Thabo's chest, settling into a hug.

We are going to be good friends, he thought to himself before he drifted off to sleep again.

CHAPTER 17

Friday, 2 November 1990.

Just after 1 p.m. in the afternoon, Patrick stood on the patio overlooking the rear garden like an Egyptian god under a large white patio umbrella, protecting his pale English skin from the harsh sun. He sipped a martini and gawked at the white open-sided tent being erected on the lawn beside the swimming pool for Jason's eighteenth birthday party.

He was fashionably dressed in a style that resembled a horseback riding outfit, with dark brown leather boots, light brown tight trousers and a white silk shirt with its sleeves rolled up to his elbows. His beloved round Versace tortoise shell sunglasses hid his *large* drug-dilated pupils.

"Thabo," Patrick called out, "come here."

"Yes, my boss." Thabo hurriedly made his way towards Patrick and up the stairs. "Yes, sir, my boss?"

"Clear-up those leaves from the pool." Patrick pointed at three small leaves floating in the centre of the gigantic swimming pool. "And sweep the driveway when you're done with that. I saw some debris near the gates when I drove in. I want this place immaculate before the guests arrive. No messy-messy. You understand?"

"Yes, sir."

"And where's that mother of yours? She's supposed to be working today."

"I think she is ill, my boss," Thabo said.

"You *think* she is ill?" Patrick gargled. "Again? Is she gonna be off sick all fucking year? Lazy. Drop dead lazy. The whole lot of you. She's treading on thin ice. She's next to go. Had enough of lazies."

"I'm so very sorry, my boss, for her being ill. I will tell her when I get home."

Patrick sniffed loudly and said, "God, what's that ghastly smell? Is that you that reeks like old sweat?" Patrick's deep voice echoed though the rear garden and attracted all the workers' attention in his direction. The way Patrick liked it, when all eyes are on him. "Jesus. I can smell you from all the way over there. Don't you people wash? Fucksake. Jason, come here for God's sake. Hurry."

Jason strolled onto the patio and said, "Yes, dad, what now?"

"Bring Thabo an apron and give him some of your old clothes, preferably black. And make sure he takes a bloody shower before the guests arrive. He can't walk around white people smelling like a god-damn rubbish dump. And get rid of those fucking hideous shoes he's wearing." Patrick pointed at Thabo's worn-out shoes, with his big toes creeping out on each side.

"Thabo, are you awake? I said that'll be all. Get moving. Time is ticking. Chop-chop."

Thabo shuffled down the stairs with his head hanging and disappeared around the corner as Patrick watched his every step.

Where is that imbecile going? "Thabo," Patrick called out.

Thabo's head peeked around the corner of the house.

"I said clean the pool first. For God's sake, you need to clean your ears and listen."

"Why do you treat people like that?" Jason said. "He's not an animal."

"He's on my patrol, so keep your wiseass comments to yourself. You think because you turn eighteen today you're *cool?* I'll cancel this fucking party in a blink. Yeah? You understand? I told you before, you're walking on very thin ice, young man."

"What did I do?" Jason said with teary eyes. "Why are you being like this?"

"Get moving. I'm not asking you again."

Patrick gulped down the rest of his martini and took a puff of his fat cigar. *I've fucking had it with this continent,* he thought and plunked his martini glass down and shouted, "Oi, I'm not paying you to sit on your fucking asses, get that fucking tent up." Patrick tramped down the stairs in their direction. "My guests will arrive soon, and this place looks like a campsite!"

Twenty minutes later, Jason called Thabo to the servants' quarters.

"Wear this," Jason said and handed a pair of black trousers and a black t-shirt to Thabo. "It's still new."

"Thank you, sir," Thabo said. "I'm sorry if I'm smelly. I did wash at home this morning."

"It's okay, Thabo. I think it's just your shirt that needs a bit of a wash. Anyway, I brought you this." Jason handed Thabo a bag filled with soap, shampoo, a toothbrush, toothpaste and a bottle of Chanel Pour Monsieur eau de perfum, and most importantly, the much-needed underarm deodorant.

"After you've showered, spray some of this perfume on you and then smear this stuff under your arms. And don't tell anyone I gave you this stuff. You understand? It's our little secret."

"Thank you so much, sir."

"Madam," Jason said and walked out.

"I'm not a madam," Thabo said and shyly laughed. He picked up the clothes and smelled them. Fresh and clean, and a little like Jason's room.

Thabo's thoughts went back to the night he was assaulted. The moment Jason sucked on his arm. That feeling he had. The tingling sensation. And the undescribable urge to love and be loved.

CHAPTER 18

18:15 p.m.

The lavish birthday party came to life with the first guests arriving at the Rothshen Mansion in their luxury cars. The hypnotic and soothing tunes of traditional Thai music drifted throughout the garden, which was decorated with colourful lanterns strategically placed around the footpaths and hanging lazily from the trees, giving the garden a magical ambience.

Elegant women in colourful silk Thai dresses, decorated in glittering emeralds and brass Thai finger claws on each finger, performed magical dances, and a couple of flame blowers added some excitement to the party.

Thabo stood to the side of the house, partly hiding behind some plants as he watched the dancing women, and was amazed by all the glittering jewellery the dancers wore. All he knew was that they came from very far away just for the event.

Thabo watched Jason's every move while he greeted the guests, then decided to get a little closer. His palms became sweaty and his heart beat in his throat with the feeling of being a nobody among the rich white people who didn't even look at him. To them he didn't exist. Just another peasant serving the rich white masters.

The meaty flavours of the spit roast filled the air and began to play havoc with his empty stomach.

He picked up a few glasses and glanced over at Jason, who spoke to the man whom he met with Jason on his first day of work. Pedro, Jason's olive-skinned friend. A handsome, fit teenager with amazing sea blue eyes and a beautiful face. Almost too beautiful to be a man.

Jason made eye contact with Thabo and smiled. Just as Thabo was about to smile and wave, Jason turned his head away.

Then Pedro turned around and looked directly at Thabo.

Thabo quickly looked away and searched for more glasses to pick up.

Why are you looking at me? Both Pedro and Jason looked at Thabo.

Pedro's smile disappeared and turned into a frown. It looked like he tried to say something in slow motion with his lips moving.

Thabo realised Pedro wasn't talking to Jason, as Jason looked the other way and spoke to someone else.

The lip movement looked like he tried to say *Monday,* and kept repeating the same word.

What about Monday? Thabo thought.

Then suddenly it dawned on Thabo. Pedro mimed the word *monkey.*

"Fuck you," Thabo whispered and wanted to throw a glass at him. Pedro got the last word by almost unnoticeably giving Thabo the middle finger as he pretended to touch his face.

CHAPTER 19

Patrick tapped a fork against his martini glass and said, "Ladies and gentlemen, if I may have a quick word before you all get too tipsy. Where is Jason? Jason? Where are you? Come here."

Jason walked up to his red-faced father, who had clearly taken some type of mood altering substance, again.

"A personal thanks to each and every one of you for making the effort to join us on this very special occasion, with every one of you looking as splendid as always. I'm sure Jason is absolutely thrilled that you made it tonight, aren't you, Jason? And I'm sure he's super excited to open all the generous gifts he has received. He is a very fortunate and lucky eighteen-year-old. Now, Jason, my dear son, I hope you've had a fantastic day, and I hope and pray you're going to be more responsible from now on, and for the rest of your life, and stop giving me all these fucking grey hairs." The crowd broke out in laughter with Patrick clearly enjoying the punch line for a couple of seconds. He continued, "And I'd like to take this opportunity to say congratulations to Jason for passing his driving test today. And I promise I had absolutely nothing to do with the outcome." Patrick laughed and held his glass in the air and said, "Happy birthday, my boy. And one last thing, your gift is in the driveway."

Without waiting a second longer, Jason ran to the front of the house, followed by a couple of his friends.

In the driveway stood his father's red Mercedes Benz 300SL roadster with its top down and a tiny blue ribbon tied around the steering wheel.

"Oh my god," Jason said and covered his mouth and jumped in the driver's seat. He eventually got what he wanted, yet again.

The excitement soon faded, and the party continued in the rear garden where Jason began to open some of his gifts.

One particular gift wrapped in brown paper stood out from the rest.

He got excited when he saw the package had been sent from England. *I hope it's from mom,* he thought to himself as he pulled out the package from the box. Inside was a Polaroid Colour-Pack instant camera.

A card fell from the box. He opened it and read:

Happy birthday, young man. Thought you might like one of these. They are great for taking some 'action' photos on the go (wink-wink).

Sorry I couldn't be there.

Uncle Jimmy.

Jason threw the card back into the box, took another look at the camera and dropped it back into the box. He was disappointed it hadn't been from his mother, whom he'd had no contact with for nine years.

Jason felt alone, sad, and pissed off. He took another look at the camera. "Why not," he said and put the device together.

Jason walked up to Thabo, who stood by himself to the side of the patio, holding a silver tray.

"Hey, Thabo, I was looking for you earlier. What're you doing here hiding from all those drunks?"

"Just resting." Thabo seemed tired.

"You okay?" Jason placed his hand on Thabo's shoulder. "You look sad."

"I'm okay. I just want to go home. I've had a long day."

"Yeah, I know the feeling. I'm tired too. Can't wait for this to be over. Can I take a photo of you?"

"Me?" Thabo laughed.

"Yes, come, let me take a photo of us."

"Eish, I don't know."

The camera made a clicking sound and an almighty flash, then a few more sounds before a white square emerged from the front of the camera.

Jason removed the photo and waved it a couple of times and handed Thabo the photo.

"You're really photogenic, Mr. Thabo."

Thabo glanced at the photo and laughed. "Eish, I look funny."

"Don't be silly, you look good."

"Oh, I almost forgot. I have something for you, too," Thabo said.

"What, like a gift?"

"Yes, I hope you like. It's in my bag in the servants' room."

I wonder what it is, Jason thought as he walked with Thabo to the servants' quarters.

Thabo took out a small package wrapped in newspaper from his bag and said proudly, "Happy birthday, sir Jason. This is my gift to you."

"Thank you, madam Thabo."

"Yoh, does it look like I have a pussy?" Thabo laughed and gave Jason a playful nudge.

Jason shook the package a couple of times. "What is it?"

"Open it."

Jason noticed Thabo's face light up with excitement the moment he tore the paper open. A handmade wristband slipped out of the package and landed on Jason's lap. Jason inspected the tribal-style wristband, made of pieces of wood, oxidised copper, stone and bone.

"Wow, this is nice. Where did you get it from?"

"I made it. I have one, too." Thabo held up his wrist to show off a similar bracelet.

"This is absolutely amazing. It really is. It's so simple, but so creative and beautiful. Very thoughtful, I have to say. Thank you so much, Thabo."

"You're welcome." Thabo shyly looked away.

"Help me put it on." Jason held his hand up and Thabo tied the bracelet. "This really is the best gift. Not even the car can beat this. You really made my day. Come, let's take a photo together."

Both teenagers posed idiotically as Jason held the camera in one hand with the lens pointed back at them.

"Say titties."

In the photo, Jason stood with his arm around Thabo's neck and showed a peace sign while Thabo was looking at Jason.

An overwhelming urge came over Jason to kiss Thabo, but he wasn't sure what Thabo's reaction would be. *Now*, Jason said to himself and kissed Thabo on the lips.

Thabo pulled away and looked at Jason with shock. "Yoh, why did you do that?"

"What?" Jason laughed and took a step back.

"You kissed me." Thabo's eyes grew to the size of golf balls.

Jason's smile faded, followed by an awkward silence. "I'm sorry," Jason stuttered. "I thought—," Jason paused and wanted to say he liked him. "Never mind. I need to go."

"You just kiss me like that?" Thabo clutched both hands into fists and frowned angrily with his nostrils flaring like an angry bull about to charge. He walked up to him, so close Jason looked into Thabo's hazelnut eyes and could smell the perfume he gave him.

Thabo's head slowly moved towards Jason and his soft, plump lips touched Jason's.

A feeling of euphoria shot through Jason's body as his lips lined-up against Thabo's warm mouth and Thabo's tongue slipped inside Jason's willing mouth.

The kiss became more intense as they explored each other's mouths with their tongues while they kept their eyes closed.

Suddenly, a loud bang came from outside the window, which ruined the magical moment.

Jason pushed Thabo away and glanced at the window and saw the shadow of a person disappearing. He ran outside to see who it could be.

Thabo plunked himself down on the bed and his heart raced from adrenaline and excitement. He wiped the saliva from his mouth. *That was so amazing,* he thought. He was about to pick up the wrapping paper from the floor when Jason charged into the room.

"You can go home. I'll take you to the bus."

"I can't go yet. The boss will be angry if I leave early."

"It's finished, everyone is leaving. You can go. Get your stuff and meet me at the front of the house."

"I have to clean up."

"You can do it tomorrow. Let's go."

"What's going on?"

"Someone saw what just happened."

"I'm sorry. I've never done that before."

"What you talkin' about?"

"I've never kissed anyone before."

"Just get your stuff and meet me at the front."

Moments later, Thabo made his way towards the front of the house, not knowing what to expect and starting to worry about not cleaning up. He tiptoed past a few drunk guests and sneaked through the plants. He could see the dimly lit driveway and could hear voices coming from somewhere between the rows of humming cars, most of them about to drive away.

Thabo walked closer and could see Jason talking to a man wearing a black baseball cap.

"Pedro, you should leave," Jason said to his swaying friend holding a bottle of beer.

"Don't tell me what to do, you're not my mother," Pedro said and downed the bottle of beer.

Thabo took a step closer to hear better, but his foot caught in a shrub and he fell over a bunch of plants.

"Thabo, let's go," Jason called out.

Thabo kept his head down and walked as fast as he could to the car with his dirty bag clutched under his arm. He got into Jason's new sports car, somewhere he never imagined he would be.

Jason started the engine and reversed down the driveway while the roof of the car folded open. The headlights illuminated Pedro's figure as he stood in the driveway with his hands in his pockets and the black baseball cap sitting sideways on his head. "I'm not fucking stupid!" Pedro yelled and gave Jason the middle finger.

As Pedro turned his head, Thabo saw the neon Nike logo on the baseball cap. The tone of voice was the same. Even the same words, 'I'm not stupid.' The person who assaulted him stood right there in front of him.

Jason pulled away and they raced towards the opening gate and narrowly missed hitting it.

The car tires screeched and the engine roared as they sped down the suburban road.

Thabo felt scared and held on for dear life as they navigated the narrow winding hillside roads. His stomach felt like it wanted to come out of his mouth as he had never in his life gone so fast in a car. It felt like he could fall out of the car at any second, or worse, crash into a tree. A constant beeped sound came from somewhere in the car.

"You really don't have to take me," Thabo shouted over the roaring engine and the wind.

"Nonsense," Jason said calmly and drove faster. "Put on your safety belt." Jason pointed to the extended black piece beside Thabo's shoulder.

Five minutes later, their journey came to a dramatic stop on the gravel beside the road next to the bus stop, and a cloud of dust swept over the car from behind, illuminated by the only street light in the area.

A handful of black people stood in a slant queue by the bus stop and covered their faces from the dust while they waited patiently for the last bus to Soweto.

Thabo breathed heavily and shook his head. "You drive like a crazy person."

"Yeah, okay, get out. I have to get back."

"Is everything okay?" Thabo said. "You look very upset."

"I'm fine."

"Good night, Jason," Thabo said before Jason sped off into the darkness.

Thabo tried to process what had happened in the last twenty minutes, going from an unexpected kiss to fearing for his life. His stomach cramped from hunger, so he squatted down hoping that the cramps would stop.

A dusty orange bus pulled up to the line of tired black men and women waiting to go back to their shacks.

Thabo plunked himself on the dirty seat one row behind the driver and leaned his head against the rattling window. He played the kiss over, wishing it had lasted longer. Jason's soft, moist lips and breath that smelled like honey. Thabo smelled the hand he used to wipe his mouth after the kiss and could still smell Jason's saliva.

His thoughts then jumped to Pedro.

He stole my money. You will pay for it, you white scum. I like Jason. Maybe I can let him do what he wants with me and get something in return. Maybe he can get me out of this place. They are so rich. Why can't we be rich? I don't know. I've never even kissed anyone. How do I know if I like boys or girls? He smelled so good. So fresh. I wish I could stay there. I think he's my best friend. Fuck Vussi. Vussi never helped me. He always just wants to get me in trouble. That Pedro is going to pay.

CHAPTER 20

The bus criss-crossed through Soweto and pulled up at its final stop at the slummiest area of the township.

Thabo, the only person left inside, stepped out onto the gravel road and walked through the maze of dark, smelly alleyways riddled with rats the size of cats that ate anything they could sink their rodent teeth into, even human flesh if given the chance.

Thabo approached the tiny shack he called home. A faint light seeped from a small front window and he could hear voices coming from inside. His heart began to race, hoping it might be his father who had finally come home. It had been seven years since he'd left and never returned.

Thabo walked up to the window and tried to peer inside, but the ragged piece of fabric used as a curtain blocked the view.

He opened the squeaking front door and stepped inside.

In the flickering candlelight, he saw two black men dressed in blue workers overalls, sitting to the left of a small square table, and his mother to the right. The centre of the table was riddled with bottles of locally brewed beer.

"Where have you been all day?" his mother slurred angrily.

"Helping at the boss's birthday party, mama. You know I had to work today. And you—."

Emma cut him off mid-sentence, "Until this time of the night? You are asking for trouble again, boy. You know those peri-urban bastards are looking to arrest people in that neighbourhood."

"Mama, the boss wanted me to stay and help, so I did. And who are these men?"

Emma frowned and said, "They are from the resistance movement. They are here to help us."

"Help us with what?" Thabo was unconvinced that any of these 'guests' had the intention to help them.

"Help us fight these white supremacists for a better life," she slurred. "Go to bed. I have guests."

Tired and not in the mood for an argument, Thabo stepped into the tiny room he shared with his two younger brothers and closed the worn-out piece of fabric that substituted for a door. The candlelight from where his mother sat cast just enough light into the room for Thabo to make out the shape of the bed, where his two brothers lay fast asleep on the double mattress propped six bricks high.

Thabo undressed and neatly folded the clothes Jason gave him and placed them on a wooden crate used as a bedside table, then laid down beside his brothers. He was barely able to lie on his back without falling off the side.

Thabo listened as his mother blurted out racist words and insults.

Just shut up. I hate you, he thought to himself and pressed his fingers into his ears in an attempt to drown out the drunken blabber.

Everyday I have to come back to this shit. I don't want this anymore. I want to have a life like Jason. My own room with a bathroom. I want to eat anything I want. I want money. I want to be rich. I want a better life. No more.

Thabo closed his eyes with warm teardrops sliding down the side of his face. *I don't want this anymore.*

CHAPTER 21

All the guests had left, and Jason indulged himself in a piece of chocolate cake while his father sat in his study listening to a violin concerto at full volume. His favourite music when on his *happy* pills.

"Jason," Patrick called.

"What?"

"Don't you 'what' me. Come here."

"I'm busy."

"Jason, I said come here now!"

"Fuck you," Jason whispered and threw the piece of cake against the inside of the kitchen window. "Asshole."

Jason took a knife and pressed the tip into his upper leg. "I wish you'd fucking die." He pierced the top layer of his skin.

"Jason, I'm not calling you again."

Jason charged angrily into Patrick's study where his father sat behind his wooden desk with his feet resting on top while puffing away on a Cuban cigar.

"Yes?"

"How many times do I have to call you?"

Jason kept silent and eyeballed his father, wishing he would swallow the cigar and choke.

"What happened on your leg?"

"Nothing."

"Don't lie to me. Did you start again?"

"No."

"Look at me. Did you start cutting again?"

"I said no, dad. Why did you call me?"

"Then what's that blood on your leg? For God's sake, do you want me to call Dr. Swanepoel?"

"I scraped my leg against the corner of one of the tables in the garden. Okay? You always try and make something from nothing."

"Start cutting again and you go back to hospital. Sit down."

Jason took a seat on a red leather armchair opposite his father's desk.

The only time Patrick ever called Jason to the study was when he had done something wrong. And when Patrick took his happy pills, he would rant on about the same subject for hours. Going in circles, repeating what he had said minutes earlier.

"I'm flying to New York tomorrow morning. You'll have to stay alone for a week."

"Can I go with you?"

"Sit in the hotel and work on my nerves all day? Absolutely not."

"Please, dad? I can do other things while you work. I'll keep myself busy. Please? You promised me last time I could go with you if you went back to New York."

"That's out of the question. I'll be in meetings all day and you're definitely not walking alone in the streets of that dirty city. It's a security risk and it's dangerous."

"More dangerous than here?"

"It's a different type of danger in this place. New York has had an increase in kidnappings and I refuse to pay ransom to anyone."

"So if I get kidnapped you won't pay for me?"

"Absolutely not."

"Well, that's reassuring then. So you'll just leave me so that they can do whatever they want to me?"

"Why? Are you planning a kidnapping?"

"Of course not. Why don't you get a bodyguard like you did when we went to Paris?"

"Jason, you're not going with me."

"Fine. Then I'll go to Cape Town and stay at the beach house."

Patrick took a puff of his cigar and closed his eyes and moved his hand in rhythm to the violin music.

"Dad?"

Patrick opened one eye and pressed his finger to his lips and said, "Shhhh." He continued to sway his hand in the air until the violin reached its climactic moment and stopped.

"Yes, go. And don't fuck up the house like you did last time. Do I make myself clear?"

"Yes."

"Close the door on your way out."

CHAPTER 22

The next morning, Jason woke from the roaring sound of the petrol lawnmower in the back garden. He rolled over and squinted at the electronic alarm clock that stood on the bedside table and said, "Not again."

The clock flashed 12:00 a.m., which meant it had stopped sometime during the night, probably due to a power outage.

He looked at his wristwatch. The time had gone just past 9:00 a.m.

Jason rolled out of bed and walked out on his bedroom balcony.

The sweet scent of cut grass floated through the crisp, fresh morning air. Jason watched from the top floor as Thabo pushed the lawnmower effortlessly from side to side with his black sweaty body glimmering in the sun.

"Thabo! Thabo!"

Thabo changed direction without looking at him.

In only his blue silk boxer shorts, Jason made his way down the cold marble staircase to the kitchen that had been left in a complete chaotic state from the previous night's party, with confetti scattered over the floor and dirty plates and cutlery sitting on any available space. The piece of chocolate cake still stuck to the kitchen window.

Jason picked up a note his father left on the breakfast table.

Jason, make sure Thabo cleans up the garden and cuts the grass. The money in the envelope is his wages for the week. If Emma is in today, make sure she cleans the house properly, including the cake on the window. She will have to sleep in for the week while you're away. I left the keys for the beach house in the drawer next to the fridge. Ensure you close all the windows when you leave the beach house. And no parties. I'll be back next Sunday.

Jason took the money from the envelope and walked to the patio door. "Thabo!"

Thabo kept going, unaware of Jason's calling, while he sang at the top of his voice and made funny hopping moves. The six long lash marks were clearly visible over his flexing back muscles.

Jason ran up behind Thabo and grabbed him on his sweaty shoulder.

Thabo jumped sideways like a wild cat and yelled, "Yoh-yoh mama wê yoh!" His eyes widened like he had seen a ghost.

"Wow," Jason laughed.

"Eish, you gave me such a fright." Thabo wiped the sweat from his face. "I thought it's the peri-urban."

"You looked funny when you jumped." Jason could smell the Chanel perfume he gave Thabo. It smelled fresh with a hint of cut grass.

While Thabo talked, Jason could hear Thabo's stomach growling with hunger. Jason's eyes drifted down to the broken zipper on Thabo's trousers. The fly hung slightly open, with

Thabo's curly pubic hair and part of the top of his cock slightly visible through the gaping fly.

Jason could feel an erection growing, and in an attempt to keep it under control, forced his hand over his crotch. But the escalation took just a few seconds and the hand motion over his boxer shorts only aggravated his now throbbing cock.

"Your pay for the week." Jason shoved the money into Thabo's hand and briskly walked back to the house while keeping his hand over the bulging boxers.

"Thank you, Jason."

"Why does this always happen?" Jason whispered to himself and slapped his cock and watched on as Thabo continued mowing the law.

Is it my imagination or is he starting to look really skinny? Jason thought. *His stomach always makes these weird sounds. Wonder if they have food. Poor guy.*

Twenty minutes later, a knock sounded on the rear door.

"Jason?" Thabo called out.

Jason walked to the rear wearing a white apron without a shirt. "Come in, it's only me. You hungry?"

"Yes."

"Take a shower first. There's a bathroom down the hallway to the right."

"Eish, my mother will not be happy if she knows I showered in your house."

"Oh, come on. You did before. Did she find out about that?"

"No, of course not."

"Hurry. I'm hungry."

CHAPTER 23

While Thabo cleansed himself in the shower, he realised the soap smelled just like the soap his mother always brought home. He stepped out of the shower and looked at himself in the mirror. *I want this every day. This feels so good.*

He got dressed in a pair of shorts and a shirt that Jason had left for him, yet again. He would soon have a whole wardrobe full of clothes at this rate.

Thabo opened the bathroom cupboard out of curiosity and saw a few small blue jars with sparkling golden lids that looked expensive. He took one out and unscrewed the top to smell it, then checked the label and read, "Invigorating body moisturiser. Made in New York."

Thabo picked up his dirty trousers and stuck one of the blue jars in his pocket before he walked out.

"Sit," Jason said as Thabo walked into the kitchen.

"Bacon and eggs with toast, just the way your mom taught me."

"Wow, thank you so much, Jason. I have never had such a nice breakfast. You make me feel so happy today."

Thabo's stomach growled in anticipation for Jason to start to eat.

"Sounds like our tummies are speaking to each other." Jason laughed and poured Thabo a glass of orange juice.

Thabo smiled and copied Jason as he picked up the fork and knife.

The utensils kept slipping from Thabo's hands as he tried to cut the bacon. He wasn't used to using basic utensils, as at the Molefe home they ate with their hands.

Jason put his utensils down and took a few pieces of bacon and folded it with the eggs inside a slice of toast and took a whopping bite.

Thabo smiled with a sense of relief and stuffed his mouth with bread.

"I'm going to Cape Town tomorrow," Jason muttered as he chewed. "You need to tell your mother to come over before tomorrow evening. She needs to stay here while I'm away."

Thabo nodded and took a moment to swallow. "Really? Just you?"

"Yeah. I'm leaving tomorrow morning."

"I will tell her when I get back home."

"Where is she, anyway? She hasn't been here for a couple of days now."

"I think she's not feeling well. How long will you stay there?"

"Five days."

Thabo pondered for a moment, scared of what Jason's reaction would be to his next question.

"Can—can I go with you?"

Jason paused for a moment. "You mean go with me to Cape Town?"

"Sorry, I shouldn't have asked." Thabo placed the sandwich down, feeling embarrassed for asking.

"You can, but you're aware that you're black and I'm white and the stupid rules in this country."

"It was stupid of me to have asked, sorry."

"It's okay, Thabo. If you don't ask, you'll never know."

"I think I'll go finish work now." Thabo stood up.

"What? Come on, what's the matter? You haven't finished your food."

Thabo looked back at Jason and felt an overwhelming urge to cry but fought back the tears and took the sandwich from the plate.

"Why are you acting so weird?"

"Sorry, I will go finish work now. Thank you for the food."

Jason watched as Thabo shuffled off with his dirty clothes in his one hand while munching on the bread.

"What a weirdo." Jason pondered for a moment. "Maybe taking him with me isn't such a bad idea. He can come in handy."

Jason jumped up and ran after Thabo.

"Hey," Jason said and took Thabo by the arm. "Why are you acting so weird?"

"Nothing, sir. I have a lot of work. I just want to finish."

"C'mon, stop calling me that. My name is Jason, not *sir*. And I invite you inside my house and give you food and you just walk out. What's that all about?"

"I just thought I can maybe go with you. I've never been to the sea. But it's okay, I understand if you don't want me to go with you. I'm just a *kaffir* after all."

Tears started to build up in Thabo's eyes before he turned his head away.

"Don't say that about yourself. I was just surprised that you want to take the risk to go with me. You'll be the one who'll get into shit, not me. I just don't know how we'll get you past the authorities if you travel with me. I was planning to fly."

"I've never flown before."

"I think it's better we drive down."

Thabo wiped his eyes and looked back at Jason and smiled, then unexpectedly hugged Jason. "Thank you, you make me so very happy now. I will tell my mother I'm going with you."

"Hang on." Jason frowned. "I haven't said you can come with me."

"Okay."

"But on this occasion, you can come with me, which means you owe me."

"What do you mean *I owe you?*"

"It means you owe me something in return."

"Oh, like a favour, you mean?"

"Something along those lines, but at a higher level."

"I will do anything for you. But I need to tell my mother I'm going with you."

"I don't think that's a good idea."

"I have to, otherwise she will wonder where I am. I can tell her when I get home."

"Why don't you tell her you're going to stay at your friend's house."

"She knows me, I never stay away, and I don't have many friends."

"Fine. Up to you."

"Can you take me?" Thabo said with a smile.

"Where? To your house?"

"Yes, but you don't have to go inside. Just drop me off near the gates and then I don't have to take the bus."

"Sure," Jason said with some hesitation. *Why is he asking me all these things all of a sudden? That's not like him. Something's not right.*

"Thank you so much. You make me very happy today."

"That's okay. You owe me now."

"Yes, of course, anything for you."

"Are you going to show me your house?"

"You don't want to see where I live. It's not nice."

"It can't be that bad, can it?"

"Maybe I'll show you one day. Right now, it's not safe for a white man like you who drives a fancy car into Soweto. They will rob you, stab you and then give you a Mama Winnie necklace." Thabo laughed. "But one day, I will show you. Promise."

CHAPTER 24

Later that afternoon, Jason and Thabo arrived at one of the main entrances leading into the Soweto township.

"Stop here," Thabo said. He looked around anxiously as they pulled over at a petrol station about four hundred meters away from the entrance. "Something doesn't look right." Thabo pointed at a roadblock with armed police halfway between them and the entrance of the township, and a police helicopter hovering over the centre of Soweto searching for something underneath a layer of smog that covered its quarter-million residents.

"I think there is trouble again. Since Madiba was released in February, there has been many police searches every day."

"Madiba?"

"Yoh, you don't know Madiba? Mama Winnie's husband, Mr. Nelson Mandela."

"Oh, so he's the Madiba they refer to," Jason said unenthusiastically. "I saw he was released from prison. My dad says he's a terrorist."

"I think one day he will become our president." Thabo pointed at a large white sign next to the road. "If he becomes president, then he can get rid of that."

The sign read: Warning: This road passes through proclaimed Bantu locations. Any person who enters the locations without a permit renders himself liable to prosecution for contravening the

Bantu (Urban Areas) Consolidation Act of 1945, and the Location Regulations of the City Council of Johannesburg.

"Is it that dangerous to go inside?" Jason said, and thought, *I should not have come here. Bad mistake.*

"*They* don't want the white people to see how the rest of us live."

"Who are they?"

"Your white regime."

"Hey, don't label me with that. I'm not like them."

"I know you are not." Thabo smiled at Jason and gave him a quick rub on his hand. "You are a good person. I'll walk from here."

"Be careful," Jason joked. "Don't get locked up."

Thabo tapped Jason's forearm, "You're the one who needs to be careful, white boy."

Thabo took the plastic shopping bag with his clothes and began to jog down the dusty gravel road, past the roadblock where a mixture of black and white armed police officers in combat gear checked each vehicle as they entered and exited the town.

Thabo slipped down one of the many sewage-filled alleyways. It was a smelly shortcut Thabo took on a regular basis, which took him through the worst part of the slums beside a stream filled with all sorts of shit. Literally. The part no one wanted to live in, but the desperate had no choice, including Thabo's family.

Neighbourhood dogs barked wildly as Thabo jumped over flimsy wired fences and stepped through the backyard of the residents' long narrow plots.

The clattering of the police helicopter became louder and slowly drifted sideways overhead like a yellow spaceship, and he could feel the powerful force of the rotor that made the shack roofs rattle. For a moment it felt like the helicopter followed Thabo before it slowly moved away.

Thabo reached the flimsy shack with the light blue front door. Number B43. Only two shacks away from the shit stream.

Thabo took a deep breath and opened the screeching front door, ready to tell his mother the news. But as he stepped inside, he saw no sign of Emma. Just loads of empty beer bottles from the night before that stood beside the door, ready to be sold back to the bottle store like Thabo had to do every week.

"Mama?" Thabo called.

"I'm in the back."

Thabo walked through the tiny shack and saw his mother standing in the small courtyard to the rear of the house. It was filled with nothing but dry gravel and a few loose bricks and stones scattered randomly. Emma was hanging laundry over the wire clothesline fixed to two slanting poles.

"Mama, why didn't you come to work today?"

Emma looked back at Thabo with bloodshot eyes. "Where's your manners, boy? You greet your mother with respect. 'Good afternoon, mama. How are you, mama? Can I help you with the laundry, mama?' Have you swallowed up your manners, boy?"

"Sorry, mama."

"Why are you back so early from work?"

"I finished my work early, mama."

"Good, then you can help me with some chores today. You can start by sweeping the floor inside and then start to cook some pap for dinner. We have guests from the resistance movement coming tonight."

Thabo sat down on the lopsided step by the back door. "The resistance movement again? Those two drunks from last night?"

"Don't be too big for your shoes, boy." Emma wagged her crooked finger at him. "You are not too old for a good hiding. Do you understand? You don't speak to me like that. Seems you've already been influenced by that spoiled trash of a white boy."

"Sorry, mama." Thabo sat for a moment and pondered while he waited for the right time to tell his mother. "Mama?"

"Yes, Lethabo?"

"Jason asked me if I can go with him to the sea in Cape Town tomorrow."

Emma stopped in mid-air, about to hang a shirt. "What did you say?"

"Jason asked me if I can go with him to Cape Town tomorrow. Just for a few days, mama. They have a house there. Please, mama, I've never been to the sea. Please-please-please."

Emma threw the shirt back into the tin bucket and gave a few huffs and puffs as she stomped towards Thabo. She looked him up and down a couple of times. "Where did you get those clothes?"

"Jason gave them to me."

"Oh, now you're even wearing his clothes. What's that spoiled white boy trying to do? Get you into trouble, I would say. Take off those clothes. I will take them back tomorrow. And why would a white man ask a black man to go with him on a holiday? What's going on?"

"He's my friend, mama."

"Lethabo, you listen to me very carefully today. White people are not your friends. Don't trick yourself to think such foolish things. That spoilt white bastard wants to get you into trouble. Nothing else."

"Mama, Jason is a good person. He is not like other white people. He is different. He's very kind to me. He's—," Thabo smiled and thought back to the kiss. "He's my best friend, mama. My best friend ever. And he's rich and can help us with a better life."

Emma looked at Thabo and shook her head in disappointment. "Did you smoke dagga?"[2]

----

[2] A regional term used in South Africa for the Cannabis plant.

"No, mama. You know I don't do those things."

"Then you are just a fool. You are going to learn your lesson the hard way. That day will be when that white spoilt brat gets you into big trouble. I know him. He is an evil child. As evil as you can get. I think it's better you don't go back to work there anymore. You understand? I will tell master Patrick you quit. You can find another job. Maybe you can ask that Indian man at the corner Tikka Masala shop if he can give you some work."

A vision of Mr. Naido grabbing him when he stole the chocolates flashed in his mind. "Eish mama, why are you such a bitter person? You always see the bad and never the good. And I don't want to work for that Naido man." Thabo stood up and was about to walk inside when Emma grabbed him by his shirt and pulled him close to her face.

She said with her alcohol reeking breath, "You are not talking to one of your friends now. If you want to become a coconut,[3] then you can leave this house immediately. You can go and pack your clothes and go live with your white best friend."

Thabo slapped his mother's hand away and his eyes filled with tears.

"Mama, you know what? The day I was beaten and robbed by the white man in Northcliffe, Jason was the person who helped me. He helped clean my cuts and gave me medicine and a place to sleep that night. He let me sleep in his bed, mama. Yes, the white man let the black man sleep in his bed. He is a good person, mama. You are so blinded by your bitterness. And you're just a drunk!"

---

[3] Slang for a black person who thinks he's white.

Emma smacked Thabo across the face. "You don't talk to me like that. How dare you!"

"I hate you." Thabo stormed into the small damp room he shared with his two younger brothers.

"You bloody black fool," Emma shouted from outside. "You will learn your lesson the hard way. You think you are a man now and know everything. If you don't want to listen to me, then you need to learn the hard way. You're becoming just as useless as that father of yours."

Thabo grabbed the few pieces of clothing he possessed and threw them into a plastic bag and ran out of the house shouting, "At least I'm not a drunk witch!"

The two women who lived in the shack next door stood in the road and gazed at Thabo.

The all too familiar scene coming from the Molefe household at shack B43. Soon gossip would follow, including that of the *activities* from the previous night between Emma and the two men from the resistance movement.

"What are you looking at, you old hags?" Thabo yelled and began to jog.

Several minutes later Thabo reached the car.

"Fuck, man, what took you so long? I thought you were never coming back. What did she say?"

"She said it's fine."

"Really?"

"Yes, let's go."

While they drove back to the Rothshen mansion, his mother's words kept repeating in Thabo's head. 'That boy's evil; as evil as you can get; he's a spoilt brat; he's going to get you into trouble.'

Why would she say that? Maybe it's the resistance people who are poisoning her thoughts. He's been nice to me. I think he likes me, too. No, he definitely likes me. Thabo smiled. *He can help me get out of this place for good. Whatever it takes from now on.*

Thabo turned his head towards Jason and watched him for a moment as he steered the car with his curly blond hair flapping in the wind from the open window.

Jason glanced back at Thabo and gave him a smile. The small gesture gave Thabo a warm, content feeling. A notion that someone actually cared about him.

CHAPTER 25

Later that evening, Thabo stood on Jason's bedroom balcony and could see the amazing bright city lights he had never seen before and thought, *no gunshots, no barking dogs, no noisy cockerels, no police helicopters. Just peace and quiet.*

Jason walked up to Thabo and said, "What're you doing out here?"

"Just looking at the view. It's so beautiful and peaceful here. It makes me want to stay out here all night."

The half moon hung weightlessly in the sky over the city, surrounded by the countless stars of the Milky Way.

A bright start shot past in the sky.

"Did you see that?" Jason said excitedly.

"Yes."

"Make a wish but don't say it out loud."

Thabo closed his eyes. *I wish I can be rich like him and have enough money to buy myself a house and buy mama one too and give her some money so she doesn't have to work anymore.*

Jason tapped Thabo on the shoulder and said, "Hope your dreams come true. I'm going to take a bath and go to bed. Wanna join?"

"Sure." Thabo followed Jason to his en-suite bathroom and was met with the invigorating, luxurious smell of bubble bath drifting in the air. Flickering candles gave a dreamlike atmosphere against foam from the bubble bath that slowly crept over the side of the tub.

"So many candles," Thabo said. "It looks amazing. Do you always bathe like this with so many candles and bubble bath?"

"Just sometimes. We can both get in, there's plenty of space in the bath."

"Yes, it's a massive bath."

The candles cast a vibrating shadow against the white tiled walls. Thabo undressed and gracefully immersed himself in the lukewarm skin-kissing water, which pushed over the sides and splashed onto the white marble floor. "Sorry," Thabo said and watched the water flow onto the tiles.

"The bathroom was designed for that," Jason said as he slipped down his shorts.

Thabo shyly ogled Jason's smooth, athletic body. It was the first time Thabo had ever seen a white person completely naked. Jason had an unmissable perfect six pack surrounding his beautiful round belly button, tiny pinkish-brownish nipples and many freckles. The most unusual and beautiful freckles he had ever seen. A sea of light brown dots sparsely spread over Jason's entire body, all the way down, including his cock, which Thabo saw the moment Jason took off his underwear and approached the bath.

It looked bigger than Thabo could remember as his thoughts jumped back to the day he tackled Jason on the grass and they slid through the mud and his underwear pulled down.

Thabo wanted to look away but forced himself not to. He kept his eyes firmly yet shyly on Jason, who lifted his leg over the side of the bath and immersed it into the foamy water. There were even some freckles on his white-pinkish balls, topped with a bush of curly ginger pubes.

Jason had short repeating scars on his upper left arm and upper right leg. A few of the cuts looked fresh.

Goosebumps covered Jason's skin as he sunk into the bath opposite Thabo.

Part of Jason's body gently slid against Thabo's leg.

"I told you about my scars," Thabo said. "You want to tell me about yours?"

"Not really." Jason submerged his arm under the foam.

"Fine." Thabo smiled and laid his head backward. "This feels so good. I have to tell you something."

"Sure, what is it?"

"I've never taken a bath before."

"No way."

"True. We don't have a bath or shower at home."

"How do you clean yourself?"

"With a bucket of water. You just splash the water over your body after you wash with soap."

He could feel Jason's leg slightly rub against his.

"When I showered in your house, it was the first time in my life I had a real shower."

Jason smiled and looked seductively at Thabo.

Thabo felt a weird knot in his stomach from excitement.

He's doing it again, Thabo thought, and his heart began to race, and he rubbed his leg back against Jason's leg. Thabo could feel Jason's hand sliding up his calf and over his knee, then up his inner thigh. Jason's hand touched Thabo's testicles before his fingers wrapped around Thabo's cock and began to lightly stroke it.

Thabo swallowed nervously and didn't know what to do next, but he felt aroused and excited.

Should I touch him back? Thabo thought and moved forward, reaching towards Jason's body under the water. He touched Jason's chest and could feel his nipple and played with it.

Jason leaned towards Thabo and he felt the same weird euphoric feeling as the night before. Then Jason kissed him.

His warm, soft mouth gaped open over Thabo's lips and sucked on them. As if nature took over, Thabo slid his tongue into Jason's slippery, moist mouth and met his tongue while he gently touched Jason's face with his foamy hand and looked him in the eyes. Jason looked passive, his eyes dreamlike.

The kiss quickly became more sensual and intimate before it turned into pure raw lust and passion as nature intended humans to kiss. The most amazing moment Thabo had ever experienced in his entire life.

Jason stood up in the bath with his erect cock right in front of Thabo's face.

Yoh, what do I do? Lick it?

Jason breathed heavily and took hold of Thabo's head and pulled him towards his cock.

Thabo held back as he looked at the pinkish looking pieces of meaty muscle and could feel Jason's hand pulling his head forward. With his other hand, Jason pulled his foreskin back to reveal his purple-pinkish mushroom head.

Jason's cock smelled like bubblebath.

"Do you want to suck it?" Jason muttered.

Thabo looked up at his tall, gleaming, slender body covered in patches of white foam, then looked back at the thick, veiny, throbbing cock pointing north with a slight curve.

A droplet of pre-cum pushed out from the exposed swollen head.

Thabo stuck his tongue out and touched the top part of the pre-cum just to test it. It had a sweet taste, almost the way it smelled. It tasted different from his own, which was slightly saltier.

Thabo wrapped his lips around Jason's head, pushing it into his mouth as deep as he could and suckled on the throbbing cock for about a minute, trying his best not to gag as Jason moved back and forth.

Jason suddenly let out a loud moan and pulled back, then pulled his cock from Thabo's mouth.

A flood of warm cum shot across Thabo's face, into his nostril and into his left eye.

Thabo fell back into the bath. "My eye." He tried to wipe it with his soapy hands.

Jason went into a laughing fit and sat down on the rim of the tub, trying to control his laughter.

"Your jizz went in my eye. Stop laughing, it burns." Thabo hung over the side of the tub. "I can't see."

"Are you okay?" Jason struggled to get the words out.

"It burns very much. Stop laughing and help me."

"I didn't mean it," Jason said and helped Thabo out of the bath with a string of cum dripping from his now half-flaccid cock.

Thabo rinsed his eye in the sink and looked into the mirror. It was bloodshot, and he had cum dripping from his chin and nostril. His body shaking from a moment that went from excitement to shock and disappointment at something he always wanted to try.

"Look at my eye. What if I go blind?"

"You won't go blind silly, it's just semen."

Thabo rinsed the remaining cum from his face and rinsed his mouth.

Despite the burning and humiliation, he couldn't be mad at Jason. He was more ashamed at himself for letting it happen, for giving in to his friend. Maybe mama was right, the white man just wanted to control us.

"Let's go to bed," he suggested to Jason and took one more look at his eye in the mirror. In the reflection he could see Jason had a smirk on his face.

CHAPTER 26

"Come here," uncle Jimmy from London said and took a puff from his cigar. "Don't you greet me anymore? I haven't seen you in ages."

"You saw me last year," Jason said. He reluctantly strolled towards the man he called uncle J. He had scruffy, almost white-blond hair that hung just above his shoulders in a mullet, always dressed up in a tracksuit, and had a prominent mole on his nose.

"Come on, on my lap, young man," he said and pulled Jason closer.

"I have to go," Jason said. He pulled away.

But uncle J didn't let go and pulled him onto his lap.

"There you go. Have you been a good lad? You studying hard?"

"Yes, uncle J," Jason said. The overwhelming cigar breath smelled like burnt timber and ash.

"How old are you now?"

"Twelve."

"You're getting big. What's wrong? Are you not happy to see me?"

"I am." Jason tried his best to be polite to the man with an ugly mole on his face and a short temper. He feared him as much as Patrick.

"Are you still working in the television industry?" Jason said.

"Yes, still doing my duties to the nation. You want to join the limelight and become famous like me?"

"I didn't know you're famous, uncle J."

"Well, maybe not over here, but in England I am. I think you'll do well in the industry, especially with those good looks of yours and that curly blond mop of hair." Uncle J's hand swept over Jason's hair and he could feel his hand go down his back over his shirt before his arm curved around Jason. His other hand rested on Jason's knee while he kept talking about acting and being a famous television talk show host.

Jason didn't hear a word uncle J said and feared the clammy hand that slowly moved from his knee and crept further up his leg.

Jason looked the other way and held his breath and closed his eyes, hoping it would stop.

He opened his eyes again.

Above him stood uncle J with a cigar in his mouth, laughing like a witch, pushing his hand down Jason's throat.

Jason choked and couldn't breathe or move his body. Behind uncle J stood the dark figure, staring back at Jason with its red eyes and making the skin-crawling grunting noise.

Jason sat up in bed and gasped for air, his body soaked in night sweat.

He sighed of relief and slumped back onto his pillow.

He looked towards his right and realised Thabo had disappeared.

Thabo had woken and walked to the toilet to pee. The deafening, eerie silence was overwhelmingly strange to him. Thabo looked back at the four-poster bed where Jason lay fast asleep.

He suddenly felt hungry and sneaked along the hallway and down the marble staircase, everywhere dimly lit with nightlights. He went straight to the kitchen and opened the fridge where Jason earlier stored the leftover chicken. The fridge was stacked with enough food for ten people to last a month, mostly food Thabo had never heard of.

He took out the chicken and took a few bites from a drumstick, then a mouthful of strawberry yogurt, and another mouthful of chocolate sauce as a dessert. A delicious combination he had just discovered.

Thabo strolled back into the grand foyer and looked up at the huge, sparkly chandelier in the centre, then walked along the ground floor to a double door that stood slightly ajar. It seemed like only one light was on behind it.

Thabo peeked inside.

A humungous painting of the boss hung against the wall. Thabo began to backtrack when his eye caught something glittering on the desk.

He looked nervously around and tiptoed nearer to the object to take a closer look. *Wow wow wow,* Thabo thought and picked up a sparkling golden pen with many tiny diamonds encrusting its length.

After inspecting the pen, he placed it back on the desk, then picked it up again. He looked at it for a second time and glanced at the boss's painting, then stuck it into the waistband of his boxer shorts before he quickly made his way back to the bedroom.

Thabo looked at Jason on the other side of the bed and quietly crawled back in.

"Where were you?"

Thabo's body went numb from shock. "You gave me such a big fright," Thabo whispered. He gave a nervous giggle. "I went to the toilet."

Jason moved closer to Thabo and placed his arm over his chest.

"You feel warm and sticky," Thabo said.

"I had a bad dream."

Thabo turned towards Jason and slowly leaned forward and kissed Jason on the lips.

Jason sniffed. "Did you eat chicken?"

"I did, sorry. I got hungry again."

"That's okay." Jason hugged him. "You can eat as much as you want."

Thabo placed his hand on the side of Jason's face. "Why are you so kind to me?"

Jason kept silent for a moment. "I like you. I think we can be good friends."

Thabo could feel the tears building. "Thank you."

"Do you have a passport?"

"No, why?"

"Just asking."

"Come on, tell me. Are we going to travel to another country?"

"Do you like me?"

Thabo kept silent. *Should I say yes? Maybe? Don't know?* "Yes?" Thabo answered with a slight hesitation.

Jason's hand moved from Thabo's chest down to his hip.

Shit, Thabo flipped onto his back before Jason could feel the pen stuck in his waistband.

"I'll tell you later," Jason said. "I have an idea."

Thabo kept his hand over the pen. Jason came within inches as his hand rested just above Thabo's pubic hair.

"Sure." Thabo lay in the same position for several minutes, waiting for Jason to move his hand. But he never did. Eventually Thabo fell asleep.

CHAPTER 27

Thabo woke up from the sound of an alarm clock. Confused and half asleep, it took him a couple of seconds to recognise his surroundings.

The alarm clock kept ringing.

The sheet pulled to the side and Jason fell on the carpet with a loud thump.

"Fuck," Jason groaned and hit the alarm clock with his hand before he emerged from the side of the bed and gazed at Thabo with only his head peeking above the bed.

"Wakey-wakey, Thabo."

"Morning." Thabo watched as Jason walked to the curtains stark naked and jerked the heavy drapes open.

Thabo squinted and blocked the bright morning rays with his hand.

"You ready?" Jason said excitedly.

"Yes." Thabo laughed and pointed at Jason. "Your hair. It's standing like a porcupine."

Jason jumped onto the bed and playfully hit Thabo a couple of times with a pillow, then stopped and gaped at him for a brief moment. "Shit, keep still."

"What's wrong?"

"Don't move." Jason reached over the side of the bed and brought out the camera.

"Turn your head slightly to the right. Perfect."

Jason took a photo of Thabo laying sideways in the bed. His chocolate skin was accentuated by the white bedsheets and orange rays of sun falling over his smooth brown skin. And a red and partly swollen eye.

"Can I see?"

"Later. We need to be quick. There's only one train going down and if we miss it, we'll have to wait till tomorrow."

"I thought we're going in your car?"

"We take the car on the train."

"Yoh, we can do that?"

"We can do anything."

CHAPTER 28

Thabo looked at his reflection in the mirror. "Look at my eye. Why didn't you tell me it's swollen like this?"

"I was afraid of that reaction."

"That's why you don't want to show me the photo."

"Exactly," Jason smiled.

While both began to lather themselves with shampoo, Thabo just couldn't resist any longer. "You're not really a man."

"What?" Jason said.

"You didn't go to initiation school."

"What do you mean?" Jason said and wiped foam from his face.

"In our culture, boys go to initiation school for two weeks where we're taught the facts of life and how to become a man."

"I know what you mean. We have it too. It's called survival school."

Thabo pondered for a moment, unsure if they were talking about the same thing. "I guess so."

"Yeah, I did survival school. We went camping in the bush for a couple of weeks. Boys and girls stay in separate camps. They taught us how to read a map and shit like that, how to make a fire, and what insects you can eat to survive. It was quite useless really. I hated it. Did you do the same in your survival school?"

Thabo giggled. "You are funny. I'm not sure if we're talking about the same thing, but what you just said sounds more like a normal day where I live. No. We spent two weeks living deep in the mountains feeding off the land."

Jason frowned, "What's the point of living rough for two weeks in the mountains?" He knew Thabo tried to mock him.

Thabo sighed with disappointment. "To become a man. That's what I'm trying to tell you. That's why I asked you."

"I still don't get it. It's the same."

"Yes, no, but it's different."

"It's different? Bullshit. Just because you sleep in a bush like a homeless person, it suddenly makes you a man?"

"No, sir, that's not what I'm saying."

Jason noticed Thabo began to get agitated. He decided to see how far he could push him, in the hope that Thabo would decide not to go with him to Cape Town. "Of course that's what you're saying. If that's the case, then I've been a man much earlier than you. I've camped many times with my dad when we went hunting. When I was thirteen, we camped in the Moroccan desert for a week and slept under the stars and ate camel meat. Of course I didn't slaughter it myself like you did, but it's the same. And when I was fifteen, we went skiing in France. My dad had a skiing accident and we were caught up in a snow storm and trapped in our cabin for three days. I had to look after my dad and had to eat tinned soup every day. So *bam*, I win. I was a man before you." Jason laughed and tried his best to provoke Thabo and jokingly flexed his bicep and mimicked the roaring sound of a lion.

"This is not some game. What you just told me sounds more like a holiday. Just look at yourself." Thabo pointed at Jason's cock. "That's what I was trying to tell you before you began to show off with your skiing and hunting adventures and trying to show how rich you are. I am a real man, and you are not. You are still a boy in my culture. You even behave like a boy."

"Really funny." Jason filled his mouth with water from the shower and spat it into Thabo's face.

Thabo shoved Jason against the wall, which caused Jason to slip and fall.

"You fuck." Jason jumped up and pushed Thabo out of the shower and he too fell to the floor.

Thabo got up and they began to wrestle each other on the wet tiles and slipped and slid all over until Thabo wrapped his arm around Jason's neck in a choking manoeuvre.

"Can't breath," Jason gargled as his face turned red. He slapped a couple of times against Thabo's body as panic set in.

Thabo loosened his grip and stood up.

"What the fuck," Jason coughed and caught his breath. "You tried to strangle me." Jason got up and wiped blood from a cut on his lip.

"I'm sorry, Jason. I didn't mean to hurt you."

"I was making a stupid fucking joke. What's wrong with you? Get out."

"Sorry."

"I said get out. You're fired. Get the fuck out. Now!" Jason grabbed a towel and walked to his room. "Fucking asshole trying to choke me in my own house." He was surprised by Thabo's strength and his short temper.

Thabo appeared with his head hanging and walking very slowly towards him. "Jason?"

"I said get out of my house."

Fuck off, Jason thought and continued packing a bag with clothes and ignored Thabo. "Can't believe I'm so fucking stupid to let you inside."

"Jason, please, I want to go with you. I will do anything for you. Please. I beg you so much. Please, Jason. I'm sorry."

Jason kept his attention on packing and watched from the corner of his eye as Thabo shuffled on his knees closer to Jason before he lightly touched Jason's arm with his hand. Jason found it slightly amusing to see Thabo shuffle on his knees and wanted to smile, but he kept a straight face.

"Please, sir, I am so very sorry I hurt you. You are my best friend. Please forgive me. I will never hurt you again."

Jason looked into Thabo's sad brown eyes filled with tears and could see Thabo meant what he said. But Jason wanted to take it to the extreme and make Thabo suffer with guilt. He liked the fact that Thabo kept apologising. But instead, he let it go.

"Fine. Use that bag over there and put your clothes in that."

"Thank you so much." Thabo kissed Jason's hand like a peasant to his master and began to cry.

"Why are you crying?"

"Nothing." Thabo stood and wiped his tears and said, "I was so scared that you would really fire me and I'd have to go back home and never see you again."

Jason suddenly felt overpowered with emotion as no one had ever showed so much affection towards him. He pulled Thabo closer and hugged him.

"I love you, Jason."

"I've asked one of my friends if we can borrow one of her mom's niqab and some makeup. She'll be here in about thirty minutes. You'll have to wear that, otherwise you won't be able to travel with me. You owe me for this."

"Yes," Thabo said and shoved his few pieces of clothing into the bag. "Jason, can I ask you something?

"What?"

"What's a niqab?"

"A type of dress and face veil some Muslim women wear."

CHAPTER 29

"Hold still," Jason said as he puffed the last section of powder on Thabo's face.

"Can I see?" Thabo said anxiously.

"Wait." Jason took out a pair of women's sunglasses. "You need to wear this at all times."

"Why? The sun is not shining in here."

"It's to hide your eyes."

"But I thought the mascara will make me look like a woman."

"Have a look."

Thabo stood up and walked to a mirror and inspected himself for a few seconds from all angles and then put the sunglasses on.

"Wow, Jason, where did you learn to do this?"

The thick layer of makeup gave Thabo a Mediterranean appearance and much lighter than his own skin tone.

"Drama class. The girls liked to do transformation makeup. I picked up a few tricks."

"It's very good. But why only my face? What about my neck and arms? What about my hair?"

"You're going to wear this." Jason carefully placed the niqab over Thabo's head, which left only his eyes visible.

"This is such a good plan. They can't see the rest of me. You're so clever Jason."

"Well, I hope it works, otherwise we're not going anywhere."

An hour later, Jason and Thabo sped down the winding driveway with the car's top down. Part of the black niqab flapped in the wind.

In the distance, by the border wall to the property next to the Rothshen estate, stood a person wearing a black baseball cap and a white t-shirt, with his back turned towards them.

Jason slowly drove past the person who kept his back turned to them as they passed.

Jason suddenly stopped.

"What's wrong?" Thabo said.

"I think I know who that is." Jason reversed and pulled up beside the person.

Thabo's body went numb the moment Pedro turned around and walked up to the car.

"Jason, buddy," Pedro said. "Who's the freaking ninja?" Pedro looked right at Thabo with his dewy sapphire eyes.

"What's going?" Jason said.

"Nothing much, just having a walk."

"What are you doing here?"

"I know you're hiding underneath that Muslim outfit, black boy, I can smell you."

"What are you doing here?" Jason repeated.

"Told you, having a walk."

"You're spying on me, aren't you?" Jason said.

"What? Don't be fucking silly, man." Pedro laughed and adjusted his cap with the Nike logo on it.

"C'mon, Pedro. What are you doing in front of my house? You live two blocks away."

"Jesus, mister paranoid, like I just told you, I was taking a walk. Am I allowed to walk freely or did papa Patrick buy this whole fucking block too?"

Jason smiled and said, "It's unusual for you to walk all the way up here to a dead end road. You've never done that before unless you visit me. So why are you here?"

"Oh, come on, don't accuse me of shit. And what is that fucking *thing* doing in your car? I'm sure the police would be very interested to know that you befriended a black man and let him stay in your house and do *things*."

"You mean Thabo," Jason said calmly. "Do whatever you want, Pedro. We've done absolutely nothing wrong. Thabo has a permit to work for us, and that's exactly what he does. So go ahead, do whatever makes you happy. Oh, and while you're at it, why don't you tell the police about your preferred out-of-school activities, too. I bet your mommy and daddy would be ecstatic to hear about their little beloved innocent boy's secret hobby, wouldn't you say?"

"What are you getting at?" Pedro said innocently and tapped his fingers on the side of the door as he held onto it.

"Sethole and the Jesus juice. Remember?"

Jason was referring to an incident a year ago in which he and Pedro had gotten drunk and high and plied the Rothshens' gardener at the time, a black man named Sethole, with his father's expensive champagne. They had convinced him to take off his clothes and dance naked for them. Jason then paid both and watched on as Pedro performed oral sex on Sethole.

"You remember now?" Jason said. "It's rather shameless for someone who's so anti-black to have done what you did that day. I never told you, but I saw what you did afterwards."

Pedro kept quiet and gawked at Jason, and his surprised facial expression said it all.

"I watched you through the bathroom window that day. I saw you kiss Sethole. I watched him fuck you like a lion in heat. And you disappeared to your house and never said a thing about that day."

"Fuck you," Pedro barked. "You're fucking sick in your head."

Jason smiled and pulled away, then suddenly stopped again and looked back at Pedro. "And yes, we own every house on this block. We don't need to *pretend* to be wealthy, Pedro, we are." Jason sped off and covered Pedro in a plume of dust.

CHAPTER 30

Jason and Thabo arrived at the train station with enough time to catch the morning train to Cape Town.

"I'll leave the car running with the air-con on," Jason said. "And keep that thing on your head. I'll be quick." He ran into the station.

"I'm so hot and itchy," Thabo said to himself and scratched his head and tried to cool down by flapping the side of the niqab and leaning against the air vent blowing at full blast.

An elderly White man and woman approached the car. It looked like they headed directly towards Thabo, and the man pointed at the window, presumably at Thabo.

"Go-away-go-away-go-away."

The old man tapped on the window with his ring.

Fuck, Thabo slowly turned his head and looked straight into the old man's face.

Thabo didn't know what to do and looked the other way.

"Open," the old man said and knocked on the window a second time.

Thabo hoped Jason would come to the rescue, but there was no sign of him.

The man knocked on the window once again. "Excuse me, can you open the window?"

Thabo pressed the button and the window slid down.

"Whose car is this?" said the partially bald man with a funny grey piss-pot haircut.

"It's my boss's car," Thabo said, trying to pitch his voice higher like a woman's, but then realised what he had just said. "I mean my friend, it's my friend's car."

"Really?" the old man said suspiciously. "And who's that? Where's your *friend*?"

"Inside buying a ticket." Thabo's heart pounded inside his throat and he could hear it thumping in his ears.

"Where are you from?" the man said.

Thabo didn't know what to answer. "I'm from—," Thabo hesitated, "I'm from South."

"South what? Durban? Cape Town?"

"Yes, Cape Town, my boss, I mean sir." *Fuck, what am I doing?*

"You're a Muslim?"

Thabo hesitated, not sure what to answer, then said, "A little."

The old man eyed Thabo for a brief moment then took the woman by the arm and walked off. At the same moment, Jason came running out of the station waving tickets in his hand.

"Cape Town, here we come," Jason said, feeling super excited.

Just as Jason opened the car door, a familiar voice called from behind him, "Jason?"

Jason looked around and recognised the old man with a grey piss-pot haircut. "Father Michael," Jason said.

"I haven't seen you at the parish for quite some time, young man. What's going on?"

"I've been busy," Jason said and tried to get into the car.

Father Michael pushed the car door closed. "Too busy for God?"

"Busy with life, father. Can you let go of the door, please? I'm in a hurry."

"Why is there a man dressed in a Muslim woman's outfit inside your father's car?"

"It's my car, father Michael. Now, if you don't mind, I need to go."

"Oh, I get it," father Michael said and pushed the door closed again. "Now all of a sudden it's your car. How does that saying go, 'when the cat's gone, the mouse is boss,' hey?"

"Whatever, *father*. Excuse me, please." Jason opened the door again.

"What's going on here?" father Michael pressed. "What evil are you up to now?"

"What the hell do you want?" Jason said and felt like punching the annoying prick.

"God is going to punish you for your sins, Jason," father Michael's wife chipped in. "You're bringing shame to this community with your despicable behaviour."

"Let him be, wife," father Michael said. "God is watching and will strike down with force upon he who sins before God all mighty as Satan seeks out the weak and lodges his poisonous way deep within them."

"What the fuck are you two fossils going on about?" Jason laughed. "It doesn't even make sense what you just said."

"That poisonous tongue of yours is the devil's work himself," the wife added. "It should be dealt with accordingly."

"What do you want from me?" Jason screamed. "Tell me."

"Like the great Cecil John Rhodes once said, 'we were the first in the world and should not be poisoned by the unpure,'" father Michael said and made the cross sign on his chest.

Jason pushed father Michael out of the way and stepped into the car. "I think you're the one possessed."

"I'm going to tell your father about your doings, mister," father Michael shouted and tapped his finger against the car window.

"Fuck off, whore." Jason pointed his middle finger at them both and sped off.

"What an asshole," Jason said.

"Yoh, I thought they could see I'm not white. That man asked if I'm Muslim."

"What did you say?"

"A little?"

Jason burst into laughter. "Thabo, you're supposed to be a Muslim woman."

"Yoh, I forgot," Thabo said and felt utter embarrassment. "I got so nervous, I forgot what to do. Maybe I should not go."

"There's no turning back now. I already bought the tickets."

"I don't want to get you in trouble."

"Act like a woman and you'll be fine. That old prick could only make out you're a man, but not a black man. Just keep quiet and let me do the talking. That's the only way."

CHAPTER 31

They drove through large black gates to the loading bay at the side of the station.

A caucasian man dressed in a brown railway uniform waved Jason down to stop. "Drive up to carriage three and leave the key in the ignition. There's no access to the car for the duration of the journey, so you'll have to remove your belongings from the car, then make your way over to the Whites Only entrance booth to the right."

"Just act normal and keep your gloves on," Jason whispered to Thabo before they got out.

"How do I act normal if I don't know how to act like a woman?"

"Improvise." Jason took out their bags and pulled Thabo by the arm in the direction of the Whites Only entrance booth.

Inside the tiny hut-like structure sat a woman the size of a baby elephant, cramped in behind a small wooden desk. Her face was plastered with a thick layer of makeup two shades lighter than her real skin tone, giving it a slight ghostly illusion. Her thin lips were smeared with bright red lipstick to make them look bigger. The rosy-cheeked woman indulged herself on a chunk of milk chocolate while she glowered at Jason then at Thabo's disguise as they approached her.

Without uttering a word, the fat woman pointed at the sign to the side of the booth, which read: Whites Only Entrance/Slegs Blankes Ingang.

The fat woman held out her red puffy hand with a smudge of chocolate on her finger.

Jason handed the two tickets to the woman. He smiled as much as he could.

"You're in first class, compartment eight. It's to your left as you enter the third carriage. Who's travelling with you?"

"My wife's travelling with me."

The woman looked at Thabo for a couple of seconds with a raised eyebrow. "I need to see her face." The fat woman stamped their tickets.

"It is against our religion for a woman to show her face in public."

"Madam, I need to ask you a few questions then."

"For goodness sake," Jason chipped in and kicked Thabo against his leg to make sure he kept quiet. "We're travelling within the country, not on an international flight. Why the interrogation?"

"I need to make sure who she is. Madam, can you take off that head cover thing and your sunglasses?"

"My wife is from Jordan and she can't speak English."

"What language does she speak?"

"Arabic."

"Then tell your wife in Arabic to lift that face thing and show me her face."

Jason looked at Thabo and began to speak in a made-up language, indicating to Thabo to show his face.

Thabo took off his sunglasses and made a few body movements and a few hand gestures and mumbled in a high-pitched voice something that made him look slightly agitated. He then looked away like he got upset.

"See, my wife said there's no way on this earth that she will show her face in public."

Thabo muttered a couple more unrecognisable words and blinked his eyes a couple of times at the woman.

The fat woman's breasts wobbled as she burst into a chuckle and pushed her large square glasses up her nose to try and see better. "You're not going anywhere until I see your entire face, madam."

"I want to speak to the manager," Jason said calmly.

The woman pursed her thin red lips. "You can speak to me. I am the manager. Do you have some identification on you?"

Jason pushed his identification book over.

"And how about your *wife's?* "

"She's travelling with me, and like I said before, this is not an airport, so I don't see the need to check for identification on a domestic train."

"So you're British, mister Jason Rothshen?"

"Yes, I'm indeed British, madam, from London."

"Doesn't sound like you are."

"I grew up here, hence the accent."

"I can hear that clearly. Any relation to Sir Patrick Rothshen from the diamond mines?" The fat woman took a sneaky bite from a piece of melting chocolate that left a thin brown string hanging from the side of her mouth.

Patrick funded the construction of a new section of the train station a couple of years earlier and personally opened the new section himself just a few weeks ago.

"I've heard of him," Jason said, "but unfortunately I don't have any affiliation to Patrick Rothshen." He was unwilling to let anyone know his relationship to Patrick since this type of situation would attract attention.

Thabo looked at Jason with surprise and said, "But—."

Jason kicked Thabo on the leg and gave him a *look*.

"Oh, did your wife want to say something?"

"She wants to use the ladies' room."

"For goodness sake, is this going to take much longer?" a person in the queue behind them said.

"Fine, Mr. Rothshen. Enjoy your trip." The fat woman gave Thabo a final dirty look and stuffed the last piece of tempting chocolate in her mouth.

CHAPTER 32

Two hours into the one-thousand-four-hundred kilometre train journey that would take twenty-seven hours to complete, the rocking motion of the train proved to be an effective sleeping aid for both Jason and Thabo. Each stretched out semi-naked on separate single beds with a tiny table between them. The niqab hung on a hook on the back of the door.

The dull brown curtains flapped erratically outside the open compartment window and the noise from the window and the clucking of the wheels on the track drained out everything else.

The makeup on Thabo's face began to melt from the excessive heat and sweat.

Jason woke up from knocking.

He looked at the flapping curtain through one eye. It danced like a raver on a super trip.

He closed his eye again.

"Ticket inspector!" a male voice called from outside the compartment, followed by three abrupt knocks on the door. "Please open."

"Fuck," Jason whispered. "Thabo, Thabo, wake up."

"What?" Thabo said with a long trail of drool hanging from the side of his mouth.

"Shhhh," Jason hissed and covered Thabo's mouth with his hand. "Fuck, man, you need to brush your teeth. You need to hide, quickly."

"But—," Thabo said. Jason covered Thabo's mouth again.

"Shut up and lie still."

Jason grabbed both their hold-all bags and scattered their clothes over Thabo's body.

"Ticket inspector! Please open," the man called followed by more knocks, much louder than the last.

"Just a second." Jason frantically spread the clothes over Thabo's face and body.

"Don't move," Jason said to Thabo.

He took off his trousers and underwear and slid open the compartment door.

In front of him stood a short, overweight, caucasian man in a faded khaki railway uniform, wearing a sweat-stained brown railway cap and thick, dirty spectacles.

"Hello, mister ticket inspector," Jason said. "Sorry, I was taking a nap."

The red-faced ticket inspector glared at him for a moment. "Ticket please?"

"Sure thing, I just need to find it." Jason turned around and bent over and reached for his trousers on the floor, while deliberately pointing his smooth, athletic bum towards the sweaty inspector.

As Jason reached into his trouser pocket, his eye picked up movement coming from the pile of clothes Thabo hid under.

"Found it." Jason quickly handed the ticket over to the inspector and fanned himself with a magazine.

"Are you travelling alone?" the ticket inspector said.

"Yes—I mean no, my *wife* is travelling with me."

"Where's your wife?"

"Toilet."

The ticket inspector glanced at the open door to the tiny shower and toilet room in the compartment. "There's no one in there."

"I mean the toilet down the hallway. She's not feeling well and wanted some privacy. Think she might have eaten something bad."

Thabo's distinctive musky armpit smell swirled around the compartment and Jason could smell it.

The ticket inspector could clearly smell it too. He touched his nose a couple of times. "What's that smell?"

"Oh, it's probably me. I need a shower." Jason lifted his arm and smelled his pit. "Haven't had a shower for a while. And this hot weather doesn't help."

Jason watched the inspector's eyes and could see him looking towards the clothes behind Jason, and then glanced down towards Jason's manhood.

Jason smiled wickedly and leaned against the doorframe. "Do you like, mister inspector?" Jason seductively pulled on his cock in full view of the ticket inspector.

The ticket inspector swallowed nervously and swiftly pushed the ticket back at Jason, turned around and walked down the corridor to the next compartment.

"Fuck," Jason said as he shut the door, followed by a couple of thrusting moves. "That was fucking close."

Thabo's head popped out from underneath the pile of clothes. "You are crazy. What if that man calls the police?"

"Relax your tits. People feel uncomfortable if a naked person stands in front of them. It was the quickest way to get rid of him. I have to say I enjoyed that. I think I want to do it again." Jason pulled the compartment door open.

"No, please, Jason," Thabo pleaded and jumped from the bed. "Please don't. You're going to get us into trouble."

"Be a little more adventurous, Thabo. You're so scared to do things."

"No, I'm not," Thabo said and looked agitated.

Jason stepped into the aisle.

The ticket inspector stood at the very end of the carriage and handed a ticket back to another passenger.

Jason made a couple of thrusting moves with his cock slapping up and down between his legs. The inspector gawked back at Jason, shook his head and then casually made his way through the carriage door to the adjacent carriage.

Jason ran back into the compartment and shut the door.

"You're going to make big trouble now," Thabo said angrily.

CHAPTER 33

The sun crept lower and the landscape became dry and flat as the train snaked through the farmlands in central South Africa.

Jason and Thabo discovered a bunch of magazines hidden under one of the mattresses and laid lazily on a bed as they flicked through the dated books.

"I'm getting something to drink. I'm dying of thirst." Jason took out a roll of bank notes from his bag. "What do you want?"

"Coke, please. Can you get something to eat, too?"

"Yes. Lock the door behind me."

Jason strolled through the swaying aisle to the next carriage towards the restaurant located between the first and second class cars.

He stepped through the door and was met by piano music and laughter from other passengers. The carriage consisted of a bar to the left with a dozen fixed barstools, and to the right, restaurant style tables and chairs strategically placed beside the windows.

Jason found a gap near the centre of the bar next to a young man with a darker skin complexion, similar to that of Pedro, and long black curly hair neatly tied into a ponytail. He was having a conversation in Spanish with a tall, young woman.

"Hola," Jason interrupted the man in mid-sentence.

"Joder, qué casualidad, ¡otro español en el mismo tren," the man said in a deep voice. *Fuck, what a coincidence, another Spaniard in the same train.*

"Yo solo hablo un poco de castellano," Jason said. *I only speak a little Spanish.*

"¡Qué va. ¡Está perfecto. Incluso tienes buen acento. ¿Vives en España?" the man said and looked at Jason with his seductive hazelnut eyes and long eyelashes. *No way. It's perfect. You even have a good accent. You live in Spain?*

"No, mi profe era de Madrid. Supongo que me pasó su forma de hablar." *No, my Spanish teacher was from Madrid. I guess he passed his accent onto me.*

"That's impressive, man," the Spaniard said.

"What are you doing in Africa?" Jason said and glanced at the woman, who smiled back at him.

"We travel round the world. Cape Town is our final destination before we go back to Spain. We came to see Montaña de la Mesa."

"Table Mountain?"

" Sí sí, Table Mountain, of course. Sorry, my English not so good, man."

"That sounds great," Jason said.

"Yes, we love to travel. How about you? You go same place?"

"Yup, heading to Cape Town. We have a house there."

"¡Genial!" *Magnificent!* The Spanish man laughed and patted Jason on his shoulder. "Igual nos puedes recomendar un lugar para quedarnos unos días." *Maybe you can recommend a place to stay for a few days.*

"Tal vez," Jason said. *Perhaps.*

The man's unexpected touch surged through Jason's body, and he could feel the Spanish man's warm, firm fingers caressing his shoulder while he continued to smile at Jason. An awkward moment of smiles and extended laughter followed as each one waited for the other to say something else.

"I am José, this is Carla. How do you say—mi novia?"

"Your girlfriend?" Jason said.

"Sí sí, my garl-friend," José laughed. "Soon wife."

José's girlfriend Carla smiled seductively at Jason with her red plump lips, flicked her hair back and said, "Es muy guapo." *He's very handsome.*

"Sí, ¿lo quieres?" *Yes, you want him?*

"No seas tonto," Carla said and playfully slapped José on the arm. *Don't be silly.*

"Wanna come for a drink in our compartment?" Jason said.

"Sí sí, of course," José said. "We are always up for a good party."

"Perfecto," Jason said. "We're in compartment eight in the next carriage."

"¿Viajas en primera clase?" José said big-eyed. *You travel in first class?*

"Yeah."

"That must be very nice, yes?"

"Nah, basic, small and smelly. The only difference is we have a shower and toilet."

"¡Tienen ducha!" Carla shouted out with excitement. *They have a shower!* "Mi nuevo mejor amigo." *My new best friend.* Carla grabbed Jason's arm and pulled him closer.

Jason hesitantly held back and just smiled at the unexpected attention from Carla. *Let go, come on let go of my hand.* It smelled like Carla hadn't washed her hair for a while.

"We visit you very soon, yes?" Carla said. "We bring drink and come for a shower too, yes?"

"Sure thing," Jason said. "You can have a shower with me, I mean with us, I mean at ours."

Jason felt like he wanted to jump to the other side of the carriage as Carla kept pulling his body against her breast.

"I go now," Jason said and pulled free from Carla's grip. "See you when I see you." He took the two bottles of water he'd ordered and retreated backwards.

"You travel with your girlfriend?" Carla said.

"Shit, yes, I mean no. Well, I'm travelling with a *friend*. But it's slightly complicated for very obvious reasons once you actually understand the situation."

Jason leaned slightly forward and covered his mouth with one hand. "You need to promise you won't say anything to anyone when you come for a drink."

"Why? You're hiding a killer?" Carla laughed.

"Now you making us very curious, my friend," José added.

"Can I trust you?"

"Okay, we promise," Carla said. "Come, José, I need that shower. Promise the man."

"We promise." José smiled.

CHAPTER 34

Thirty minutes later, a couple of knocks landed on the compartment door.

"Yes?" Jason said.

"Hola, it's José."

Jason slid the door open and quickly glanced outside to make sure they didn't have anyone else with them. "Come in. This is my friend Thabo. Thabo, this is Carla and José from Spain."

Carla and José both looked slightly shocked as they stepped into the compartment, clearly not expecting to see a black person inside a *whites only* section of the train.

Thabo got up and shook both the Spaniards' hands and sat back down.

"I thought all black people are travelling in the last few carriages," José said.

"Do you have a problem with Thabo being here?"

"No, no, not a problem," Carla said. "En Madrid protestamos contra tu gobierno y el Apartheid. Tienes lo que hay que tener para desobedecer a tu gobierno. Me mola." *In Madrid we protested against your government and Apartheid. You have what it takes to disobey your government. It's cool.*

"Anyway, we brought Sambuca, so let's celebrate to new friendship," José said and pulled out a bottle of Molinari.

Carla pulled out some glasses they nabbed from the bar and poured the drinks.

"¡Salud!" José shouted and held his glass in the air.

"¡Salud!" everyone cheered.

Jason pulled out his cassette player from his bag and said, "Let's party."

Pop hits pumped from the tiny cassette deck speakers and drowned out the clucking sounds of the train tracks.

About an hour later, a tipsy Thabo stood up and began to dance and took his shirt off.

"Go, Thabo, go!" they all cheered as Thabo stripped down to his underwear.

José and Jason quickly followed, and Carla joined them in only her matching purple bra and panties.

Jason pulled out his Polaroid camera and began to take random photos of everyone.

"Can I take some photos?" Thabo slurred.

"Take one of me," Jason said and stood against the compartment door and flexed his muscles, then pulled down the front part of his underwear and revealed his ginger pubic hair.

"Hola, guapo," Carla said and danced provocatively beside Jason and slid her hand over his six pack stomach and pulled one bra cup down to expose her perfectly formed, round, firm breast right at the moment Thabo took a photo.

"Let's take a group photo," Jason said. "Say titties."

In the photo, Jason stood to the left with his arm around Thabo's neck. Thabo stood between Jason and Carla with his eyes fixed on Carla's exposed breast. Carla looked like a woman possessed as she rolled her eyes back, with only the whites visible, and her lipstick smeared over the side of her face. José stood to the right with one arm around Carla's neck showing a peace sign and about to lick Carla on the side of her face.

"Okay, I shower now," Carla said and unclipped her bra in front of them, followed by the panties that dropped to the floor.

"Voy a ducharme con mi chica," José said and took off his underwear. *I'm going to shower with my girl.*

Neither of them showed any sign of embarrassment.

I want you, Jason thought to himself as he eyed José's Mediterranean body with a light layer of hair on his chest and a narrow line of hair running down from his belly button into his pubes.

José's dark, uncut cock looked like it had slightly woken up as José pushed against Carla and squeezed into the tiny shower just big enough for the two of them.

"Estoy cachondo," José said. *I'm feeling horny.* "You want to join?" José flashed a smile and began to kiss Carla.

"I'm good," Jason said and glanced at Thabo, who just sat there with his mouth open, gawking at the foreigners, clearly shocked at what he had just witnessed.

"You sure? We can make room for two more," José said and cupped Carla's breast.

"We're alright," Jason said.

A minute later, moaning came from inside the closed shower, followed by a rhythmic bumping sound, which got louder and faster, with the moaning becoming more intense.

"Fóllame más fuerte así, sí, más profundo, joder, sí." *Fuck me harder, like this, yeah deeper, fuck yeah.*

Jason looked at Thabo, who looked back at him. Jason couldn't hold it anymore and kissed Thabo.

"¡Me voy a correr!," José shouted. *I'm going to cum!*

Jason went down and sucked on Thabo's cock.

A minute later, the shower door swung open. Jason pulled away from Thabo, who covered his third arm with a t-shirt.

"I feel so fresh now," Carla said. She smiled as she stepped out of the shower with some noticeable cum dripping down the inside of her leg.

Jason wiped his mouth and could not believe that a woman could be so vile. He felt slightly embarrassed on her behalf.

"I need more drink," Carla said, and with absolutely no care in the world, plunked her wet, naked body on the bed opposite Jason and Thabo.

Jason threw her panties at her. "Maybe you need those."

"Oh, I was looking for them," she said, stood up and put them on right in front of them as if she knew them.

"Okay," José said and glanced at Jason from the corner of his e. "I think you come from rich family."

Jason just smiled, reluctant to say anything.

The rocking motion of the train rubbed their arms against h other and Jason looked at José once more and smiled.

José smiled back at Jason and flicked his cigarette out into the d and looked away, then looked back at Jason. He took Jason the head and kissed him on the lips, then pulled away to look Jason for a second before kissing him more violently. He led his tongue deep inside Jason's gaping mouth. José pulled y and looked out of the window as if nothing happened.

Jason wiped the spit from his mouth. "What just happened?"

osé laughed and kept his gaze on the landscape.

ason knew he couldn't let this opportunity pass and grabbed by the shirt, pulling him backwards, and forced him against wall and kissed him.

They began to passionately wrestle each other and kissed with lust. A release of sexual tension that had been building up they'd met in the bar.

Jason stumbled sideways against the wall when his shirt ht on something sharp. It ripped the side of the shirt open, as he slid down against the wall, the object cut him in the of his head.

Fuck, wait-wait-wait," Jason said and held onto the back of ead.

Sometime early the next morning, Jason woke from a knock on the compartment door, with the morning sun burning down on his face. A stream of warm air gushed through the open compartment window.

Jason pulled himself up.

Beside him on the floor lay Thabo in his underwear with a blanket pulled over his head. He was snoring.

"Thabo-Thabo," Jason whispered and pushed against Thabo's bum with his foot.

Thabo just snored louder.

"Jason?" a woman's voice called from outside the door.

"Carla?" he said.

"Yes, can you open please?"

"Just a second." *What happened here?* Jason thought and looked around at the food and drink scattered all over the compartment. One of the brown curtains was missing, and the other flapped halfway outside the window.

His dry mouth was accompanied by a pounding headache.

Thabo woke up and rose from the dirty floor. "What happened to your head?" he said to Jason.

"Jason, open," Carla yelled and banged the door.

Jason touched the back of his head and slid the door open. Carla looked as rough as a homeless person who just woke up. Her makeup was smeared and her hair looked like a perm had gone wrong.

"Is José here? He did not come back to our compartment."

"No. He left about ten minutes after you. Have you checked the bar?"

"I just looked there," she said and walked off.

Jason closed the door and suddenly felt numb and wanted to faint.

"You have blood on the back of your head," Thabo said.

Jason touched his head again and could feel the clotted, hardened blood in the centre back of his skull.

CHAPTER 36

Jason slowly began to remember what happen[ed] before. About twenty minutes after Carla left, Thab[o passed] out on the floor, so Jason and José chatted and dran[k]

"We had a great time," José slurred and stumbl[ed] He hugged Jason and kissed him on both cheeks th[en] in Europe and walked out the door.

Jason watched José stagger along the aisle [to the next] carriage. He followed José a couple of carriages t[o] where José stopped by an open window and lit a ci[garette]

Jason walked up to José and said, "Can I have [one]

"Ah, Jason my friend, you come to join me? [...] me you smoke." José lit a cigarette, put his arm shoulders and placed the cigarette between Jason'[s]

"We had very much fun last night, yes?" José s[aid] time in unexpected place."

"Yeah, we did indeed."

A couple minutes of silence followed as Jaso[n] in the dimly lit carriage aisle and puffed on th[e] gazed out at the moonlit landscape with the w[ind on] their faces.

"Your parents, they rich, yes?" José said.

Jason thought to himself what an odd quest[ion] shook his head to indicate *no*.

"You okay?" José said.

"I'm fine." Jason pulled his shirt off and then José's and began to suck José's nipple while he pulled José's shorts down to unveil his semi-hard uncut manhood. As Jason took hold of the Spanish meat, a roll of banknotes dropped from José's shorts.

Jason reached out and picked up the money while José drunkenly leaned his head back against the wall and said, "Come, you suck me now."

Jason saw the green elastic band holding the roll of notes together, which had his father's company logo on it.

Jason stood up and said, "Where did you get this?"

"You give to me. Now suck. I can see you look at me all night." José's tone of voice suddenly became more belligerent and he pulled Jason's head closer. "Suck it."

"He's lying," the familiar, deep voice said.

Jason slapped José's hand away. "I didn't give this to you."

"No no no, you make story now. You gave me the money. You very drunk. You forget. Come suck. I want to sleep."

"Bullshit," Jason said and stuck the money into his pocket. "You took this from my bag." Jason walked away, and José grabbed him by the back of his trousers.

"Give me the money," José said and tried to reach for the cash.

"Get the fuck off me." Jason pushed José and opened the carriage door.

"Le diré al revisor que un hombre negro está escondido en tu compartimento y que ambos sois homosexuales." *I'll tell the ticket inspector that a black man is hiding in your compartment and you're both homosexuals.*

Jason stopped and slowly turned around and walked up to José. "Will you really do that?"

"Give me money," José slurred and held on to a handle beside one of the emergency exit doors, "or I tell everyone on this train there is a black faggot hiding in first class. You give me back the money, then my lips are sealed."

"Fine, you can have it, but I want something in return."

"What?" José said impatiently and lit another cigarette.

"Te la quiero chupar." *I want to suck you.*

"What are you waiting for, faggot?" José held out this hand for the money and pulled his underwear all the way down. "Money now."

Jason handed him the money and went down on his knees and looked at José's limp cock that smelled like a dead fish.

"Quiero que me vacíes." *I want you to empty it out.* José leaned back against the door.

"Fuck you," Jason said and pulled the emergency exit lever beside him, which caused the emergency exit door to swing outward, then pushed José.

The Spaniard disappeared into the dark passing landscape without making a sound.

Jason fell to the floor while the cold wind blew into the carriage, and he smelled his hand that had held José's cock.

"Good boy," the voice said.

"Leave me alone," Jason said and closed the emergency door, then picked up the roll of money and walked back to his compartment.

He immediately popped a morphine pill from his secret stash and gawked at the ceiling until he fell asleep.

CHAPTER 37

Six hours after Carla came looking for José, the train reached the station in Cape Town.

"Why are you so quiet?" Thabo said.

"Just tired."

"You didn't tell me what happened to your head."

"Can you keep quiet? I'm trying to finish the makeup."

"Okay, sorry."

"There, put on the niqab. And remember to be a woman this time. And if someone asks you something, pretend not to speak English. Let me do the talking."

"Yes, sir," Thabo said and mimicked a woman's voice and flapped his writs. "My name is Madam Rothshen and I am a lady."

Jason frowned at Thabo.

"Do you think Carla found José?" Thabo said.

"Yes, most probably."

"Will they come with us?"

"No."

"You don't look happy like always. What's wrong?"

"Like I said, I'm tired."

CHAPTER 35

Sometime early the next morning, Jason woke from a knock on the compartment door, with the morning sun burning down on his face. A stream of warm air gushed through the open compartment window.

Jason pulled himself up.

Beside him on the floor lay Thabo in his underwear with a blanket pulled over his head. He was snoring.

"Thabo-Thabo," Jason whispered and pushed against Thabo's bum with his foot.

Thabo just snored louder.

"Jason?" a woman's voice called from outside the door.

"Carla?" he said.

"Yes, can you open please?"

"Just a second." *What happened here?* Jason thought and looked around at the food and drink scattered all over the compartment. One of the brown curtains was missing, and the other flapped halfway outside the window.

His dry mouth was accompanied by a pounding headache.

Thabo woke up and rose from the dirty floor. "What happened to your head?" he said to Jason.

"Jason, open," Carla yelled and banged the door.

Jason touched the back of his head and slid the door open. Carla looked as rough as a homeless person who just woke up. Her makeup was smeared and her hair looked like a perm had gone wrong.

"Is José here? He did not come back to our compartment."

"No. He left about ten minutes after you. Have you checked the bar?"

"I just looked there," she said and walked off.

Jason closed the door and suddenly felt numb and wanted to faint.

"You have blood on the back of your head," Thabo said.

Jason touched his head again and could feel the clotted, hardened blood in the centre back of his skull.

CHAPTER 36

Jason slowly began to remember what happened the night before. About twenty minutes after Carla left, Thabo was passed out on the floor, so Jason and José chatted and drank more beer.

"We had a great time," José slurred and stumbled to his feet. He hugged Jason and kissed him on both cheeks the way they do in Europe and walked out the door.

Jason watched José stagger along the aisle into the next carriage. He followed José a couple of carriages towards the rear where José stopped by an open window and lit a cigarette.

Jason walked up to José and said, "Can I have one?"

"Ah, Jason my friend, you come to join me? You never told me you smoke." José lit a cigarette, put his arm around Jason's shoulders and placed the cigarette between Jason's lips.

"We had very much fun last night, yes?" José said. "Such good time in unexpected place."

"Yeah, we did indeed."

A couple minutes of silence followed as Jason and José stood in the dimly lit carriage aisle and puffed on their cigarettes and gazed out at the moonlit landscape with the wind blowing over their faces.

"Your parents, they rich, yes?" José said.

Jason thought to himself what an odd question to ask and just shook his head to indicate *no.*

"Okay," José said and glanced at Jason from the corner of his eye. "I think you come from rich family."

Jason just smiled, reluctant to say anything.

The rocking motion of the train rubbed their arms against each other and Jason looked at José once more and smiled.

José smiled back at Jason and flicked his cigarette out into the wind and looked away, then looked back at Jason. He took Jason by the head and kissed him on the lips, then pulled away to look at Jason for a second before kissing him more violently. He drilled his tongue deep inside Jason's gaping mouth. José pulled away and looked out of the window as if nothing happened.

Jason wiped the spit from his mouth. "What just happened?"

José laughed and kept his gaze on the landscape.

Jason knew he couldn't let this opportunity pass and grabbed José by the shirt, pulling him backwards, and forced him against the wall and kissed him.

They began to passionately wrestle each other and kissed with pure lust. A release of sexual tension that had been building up since they'd met in the bar.

Jason stumbled sideways against the wall when his shirt caught on something sharp. It ripped the side of the shirt open, and as he slid down against the wall, the object cut him in the back of his head.

"Fuck, wait-wait-wait," Jason said and held onto the back of his head.

"You okay?" José said.

"I'm fine." Jason pulled his shirt off and then José's and began to suck José's nipple while he pulled José's shorts down to unveil his semi-hard uncut manhood. As Jason took hold of the Spanish meat, a roll of banknotes dropped from José's shorts.

Jason reached out and picked up the money while José drunkenly leaned his head back against the wall and said, "Come, you suck me now."

Jason saw the green elastic band holding the roll of notes together, which had his father's company logo on it.

Jason stood up and said, "Where did you get this?"

"You give to me. Now suck. I can see you look at me all night." José's tone of voice suddenly became more belligerent and he pulled Jason's head closer. "Suck it."

"He's lying," the familiar, deep voice said.

Jason slapped José's hand away. "I didn't give this to you."

"No no no, you make story now. You gave me the money. You very drunk. You forget. Come suck. I want to sleep."

"Bullshit," Jason said and stuck the money into his pocket. "You took this from my bag." Jason walked away, and José grabbed him by the back of his trousers.

"Give me the money," José said and tried to reach for the cash.

"Get the fuck off me." Jason pushed José and opened the carriage door.

"Le diré al revisor que un hombre negro está escondido en tu compartimento y que ambos sois homosexuales." *I'll tell the ticket inspector that a black man is hiding in your compartment and you're both homosexuals.*

Jason stopped and slowly turned around and walked up to José. "Will you really do that?"

"Give me money," José slurred and held on to a handle beside one of the emergency exit doors, "or I tell everyone on this train there is a black faggot hiding in first class. You give me back the money, then my lips are sealed."

"Fine, you can have it, but I want something in return."

"What?" José said impatiently and lit another cigarette.

"Te la quiero chupar." *I want to suck you.*

"What are you waiting for, faggot?" José held out this hand for the money and pulled his underwear all the way down. "Money now."

Jason handed him the money and went down on his knees and looked at José's limp cock that smelled like a dead fish.

"Quiero que me vacíes." *I want you to empty it out.* José leaned back against the door.

"Fuck you," Jason said and pulled the emergency exit lever beside him, which caused the emergency exit door to swing outward, then pushed José.

The Spaniard disappeared into the dark passing landscape without making a sound.

Jason fell to the floor while the cold wind blew into the carriage, and he smelled his hand that had held José's cock.

"Good boy," the voice said.

"Leave me alone," Jason said and closed the emergency door, then picked up the roll of money and walked back to his compartment.

He immediately popped a morphine pill from his secret stash and gawked at the ceiling until he fell asleep.

CHAPTER 37

Six hours after Carla came looking for José, the train reached the station in Cape Town.

"Why are you so quiet?" Thabo said.

"Just tired."

"You didn't tell me what happened to your head."

"Can you keep quiet? I'm trying to finish the makeup."

"Okay, sorry."

"There, put on the niqab. And remember to be a woman this time. And if someone asks you something, pretend not to speak English. Let me do the talking."

"Yes, sir," Thabo said and mimicked a woman's voice and flapped his writs. "My name is Madam Rothshen and I am a lady."

Jason frowned at Thabo.

"Do you think Carla found José?" Thabo said.

"Yes, most probably."

"Will they come with us?"

"No."

"You don't look happy like always. What's wrong?"

"Like I said, I'm tired."

They sat in silence until the train came to a full stop.

"We're gonna get off on the other side of the train. It should be easier to get past all the people."

They climbed out on the opposite side by the emergency exits.

Jason looked around nervously and walked towards the station entrance.

"No sign of her," Jason whispered to himself and pulled Thabo by the arm. "In here."

They briskly walked towards the car collection point.

On the other side of the tracks, through the gap of the train, Jason noticed a couple of police officers walking towards the train, closely followed by a few members of the train staff.

"Excuse me," Jason said to one of the staff members. "My car is in that carriage and we're in a slight hurry."

"Which one?" the man said.

"The Mercedes."

"That one's next. It's a very nice car."

"Thanks," Jason said and anxiously waited for the car to appear.

As soon as it pulled up, Jason threw the bags in the trunk.

A little white girl with her parents shouted at her mother, "Look, mommy, it's a ninja woman," and pointed at Thabo, who in return made a karate kick.

"Get in the car," Jason said.

In the distance, Jason saw two police officers with a German Shepard walking in his direction, speaking on their radios, clearly looking for something.

Thabo stood beside the car, fooling around with the little girl by making a few more karate moves in his disguise.

"Get in the fucking car!"

Jason drove slowly towards the exit.

"Why you so angry with me?" Thabo said.

Jason kept quiet and saw Carla speaking to three police officers, crying and gesturing with her hands.

Don't look at me, Jason thought and slowly drove in the opposite direction. He kept looking in the rearview mirror to see if they might have seen him, until they left the station.

Thirty minutes later, Jason and Thabo arrived at the Rothshens' beach house.

"Come in, Thabo," Jason said with excitement. His attitude was completely different from half an hour earlier.

He pulled Thabo by the arm and led him into the stunning open plan kitchen and living room area with large floor to ceiling windows overlooking the blue Atlantic Ocean.

Thabo stared slack-jawed at the view while Jason slid the balcony doors open. "Come check outside."

Thabo walked onto the balcony. Below him, the gigantic roaring waves of the ocean crashed against the rocks and spewed fine mist into the air.

"Can we go to the beach?" Thabo said, full of excitement.

"In a minute, I just need to do something."

Dressed in white t-shirts and white swimming trunks, Jason and Thabo made their way to the beach, barefoot on a narrow white sandy path through dense bush.

"This way." Jason pulled Thabo by the arm into the lush bushes.

Thabo could hear the roaring ocean somewhere on the other side of the bush as they followed the barely visible footpath snaking through the dense shrubs until it opened up to enormous, smooth boulders with the untamed sea on the other side.

Jason and Thabo climbed over one of the rocks and slid down and followed another narrow path flanked by two large, smooth, round rocks with tiny sea creatures going about their business in the small puddles of seawater.

The path opened up to a secluded pure-white sandy beach.

"The only way to get here is the way we came," Jason said. "We have it all to ourselves."

Waves crashed against the large rocks then pulled back in.

Thabo took a step into the water and immediately jumped back out. "It's freezing."

Jason sat down on the powdery white sand and Thabo joined him.

"This is more amazing than I thought it would be. It's so beautiful," Thabo said.

"It sure is. There's something powerful and magical about the sea."

"Thank you for bringing me with you." Thabo gave Jason a hug. "I was really scared you would leave me behind after I pushed you in the shower."

"Would you like to live here?" Jason said.

"How? With you?"

"You and me, in the house."

"Yoh, you're joking."

"No. I'm serious."

"Wow, sounds like a dream. Can I come to the beach every day?"

"You can do whatever you want."

"Eish, I can walk in the nice white sand every day, and maybe catch some fish, and we can have a braai."

"And maybe you can go to London with me and meet my mother. She'll like you."

"London? No. Serious?" Thabo shyly looked at Jason. "Where is London again?"

"Far away from here, where people like you are free."

"Then I want to go with you." Thabo hugged Jason once more and rested his head on Jason's shoulder.

"We just need to get you a passport."

"Yes."

Jason looked at Thabo and said, "Hey."

Thabo looked back at him.

"I like you, Thabo." Jason peered deep into Thabo's eyes. "I like you a lot."

Thabo smiled and shyly pushed his face against Jason's shoulder. "I love you."

"Do you mean that?" Jason said.

While keeping his face hidden, Thabo nodded his head, indicating *yes*.

"Hey, look at me."

"Everything feels like a dream to me. Why are you so kind to me?"

"Because you are real. Because you make me laugh. Because you are an amazing kisser, and because you make me feel happy. And I love your chocolate skin. You want me to go on?"

"Do you love me, too?" Thabo said.

"Yes, I love you, Thabo. I want to take you away from this bad place and give you freedom, a better life."

"You make me happy, too," Thabo said.

Jason could see tears building up in Thabo's eyes right before he hid his face again.

"I will inherit everything if something happens to my dad."

"What do you mean?"

"I mean, if he dies in an accident or has a heart attack or something, I will get everything."

"You don't love your father?"

Jason kept silent for a moment, thinking what the best answer would be to pull more empathy out of Thabo. *Tell him.*

"He's not a good person. Look how he treated you the other day at my birthday party."

"Yes, I remember. But I'm used to it. I'm black. Most white people treat me like that, except for you."

"He treats everyone like that. Even me. I don't think he loves me. I don't think he loves anyone but himself."

"What about your mother?"

"She left many years ago. They had an argument about some photo I found when I was still a boy. It was my fault she left."

"What was the photo of?"

"I don't want to talk about it. All I'm saying is he's a bad person. I wish he died so that I can be free, too."

"Don't say that. He's your father and he has worked hard to give you a good life."

"I would rather have a simple life and be happy than to have all of this and no happiness or freedom."

"You have everything, Jason. Why are you so unhappy?"

"See these scars?" Jason pulled his sleeve all the way up to his shoulder. "You asked me about these cut marks. I did this to drain out the pain he caused me and what he has allowed to happen to me."

Thabo looked at Jason with a sombre face. "What did he do to you?"

"It's what he allowed to be done to me."

"I'm sorry," Thabo said and kissed the scars. "Do you want to talk about it?"

"Are you happy?"

"With you, yes, very happy. I'm always happy when I'm with you. I still can't believe I'm sitting here with you on a beach. Since the first day I met you, I was walking behind you and I could smell you. It made me want to be close to you."

"So you planned all of this?"

"No," Thabo said and laughed. "I never plan anything."

"Life is strange. Sometimes things happen when you least expect it."

"How can I help to make you feel happy?"

Jason pondered for a moment. "If you can kill him, that would be a start. Let's go back to the house and make something to eat. I'm starving."

Thabo walked behind Jason, holding onto his shirt from behind as they navigated the lush bush heading back to the house.

Why did he say that? He wants me to do something bad to the boss and then I can be free?

CHAPTER 38

Jason prepared steaks for the two of them to barbecue when a couple of loud knocks landed on the front door. Jason peered through the keyhole but couldn't see anyone.

Dressed only in his swimming trunks, Jason opened the door and cautiously walked in the direction of the garages situated at the front of the house where a cream coloured Italian-style scooter parked in the driveway. A yellow, open-faced helmet dangled from the handlebar.

Pedro, Jason thought as he recognised a green alien sticker stuck on the side the helmet, and immediately retraced his steps backwards.

"Boo!" a voice shouted from behind him.

Jason turned around and looked straight into Pedro's face. "What are you doing, Pedro?" Jason shrieked and pushed Pedro.

"Don't be like that," Pedro said, looking slightly tipsy. His eyes were red. "You not happy to see me?"

"How did you know I was here?"

"Oh yes, well," Pedro shook his head with a half-smile, "yesterday I went over to your house to play some tennis, and your lovely maid Emma told me you went to Cape Town. So I thought, fuck that, I might just as well go to Cape Town myself. And where else would you be?"

"You mean after you spied on me and saw me leave?"

"You're exaggerating now."

"How did you manage to get here so fast?"

"That large metal thing that flies in the sky." Pedro laughed and held out his arms to mimic a aeroplane.

"You said your *hello*. Now go."

"Come on, Jason, why are you so rude to me? I just want to hang out with you."

"You're an asshole."

"Fine. By the way, aunt Coco sends her regards. You remember her?"

"How can I forget the hair and the fake boobs?"

"Yeah, well, I'm staying with her."

Jason kept quiet and gawked at Pedro for a moment.

"What're we waiting for?" Pedro said. "Let's fucking party, man."

"Not today,"

"Oh, come on, don't be like that. What are you up to now? I didn't mean to upset you. I just want to spend some time with you."

"Don't you ever shut up? Fuck-sake, we're having a braai. Okay? Go home." Jason walked into the house and was about to shut the door.

"Did you say *we?*" Pedro said and pushed his way past Jason. "Who's with you?"

"You're an imbecile, Pedro."

Pedro walked straight to the open plan kitchen with views of the ocean and plunked himself on the kitchen counter. "So where's the mysterious guest?" He began to stuff his mouth with crisps.

"It's just myself and Thabo."

"Oh God, what?" Pedro barked with pieces of crisps falling from his mouth. "Don't tell me you brought that monkey into your house."

"Stop your shit or leave right now, yeah?"

"Okay okay, calm down, mister sensitive. I'm just horsing around. I won't say another word. But I can just imagine what papa Patrick will do if he found out there was a black man inside his house. Oh my god. Daddy Rothshen will totally shit himself." Pedro laughed out loud and continued to stuff his gob with crisps.

"He won't," Jason said and walked right up to Pedro, close enough to smell the crisps in his mouth. "Do you understand?"

"Do you understand?" Pedro mocked and planted a quick kiss on Jason's lips. "Yes, sir, lips sealed and ready to p-a-r-t-y, baby."

CHAPTER 39

Thabo sat on the wall of the patio in the late afternoon sun, overlooking the waves crashing into the sharp rocks, while pondering what Jason had said earlier. *Will he really take me with him? Why me? He can do whatever he wants. Mama was so wrong about him. She just don't want me to have a better life than her. One day I will live here. I will sit on this wall every day and just look at the ocean for hours. It's so beautiful. I feel so happy.*

"Thabo," Jason called out from behind him.

As Thabo turned around, Pedro stepped around Jason. Thabo's body went numb as Pedro approached him and eyeballed Thabo with his deep, dark blue eyes.

"You remember Pedro?" Jason said.

"Yes, of course," Thabo said with a fake smile and firmly shook Pedro's hand.

Pedro returned a half-smile with his perfect set of pearly white teeth. He quickly wiped his hands on his trousers right after he shook Thabo's hand.

"God, this is going to be a long night," Jason said. "I'm gonna get us some drinks."

As Jason disappeared into the house, Pedro took a seat beside Thabo on the wall. "So, Thabo, where are you from and what do you do for a living?"

Thabo could smell the alcohol on Pedro's breath and knew he should just stay calm as this guy was a loose cannon. "The same city as you," Thabo said and kept his gaze on the breaking waves below.

"Okay, fair enough. And what work is it that you do again? Oh yes, how could I forget, you are a garden boy. The one who dressed up in a Muslim woman's outfit."

Jason walked up to them with beer. "What are you chatting about?"

Pedro stood up and said, "I'm going for a piss," before he disappeared into the house.

Jason took a seat on the wall next to Thabo. "Don't mind him, okay? He can be a prick sometimes, but he's okay."

"You don't know him that well, do you?" Thabo said.

"Why are you saying that? I've known him since I was nine."

"I'm just saying."

"Did he say something to you?"

"No."

Jason placed his arm around Thabo and said, "Don't worry, I know how to handle him," and planted a kiss on Thabo's cheek.

CHAPTER 40

Pedro strolled into the master bedroom where Jason and Thabo's luggage sat on the floor, and piled in the corner was the black dress Thabo wore. Pedro began to snoop around in one of the open duffle bags and pulled out some clothes and the Polaroid camera Jason got for his birthday.

"Here we go," Pedro whispered and pulled out a stiff and stained pair of white underwear.

Pedro sniffed the part of the fabric that had dried and gave it a lick. "That's definitely cum." He threw the underwear to the side.

He dug further and pulled out a handful of developed Polaroid photographs. "And what do we have here?"

"Pedro?" Jason called from outside. "Did you flush down the toilet?"

Pedro quickly flicked thought the photos. "Who are you?" he said as he looked at the photos taken on the train with Thabo and another man and woman.

He flicked further until he came upon a naked photo of Thabo. "Fuck." He flicked further. "I knew it, I fucking knew it. Disgusting."

"Pedro?" Jason called again.

Pedro shoved the photos back into the bag and began to search through the other bag and pulled out a t-shirt and smelled it. "Oh my fuck. It could only be his." He threw the shirt to the side while he carefully continued to search for something unknown.

Pedro pulled out a few folded shirts when an object dropped on the floor. A golden, diamond-encrusted pen had the initials 'PR' engraved on the side.

"Pedro?" Jason called once more.

Pedro pushed the clothes back into the bag and walked back to the patio.

"What took you so long?" Jason said as Pedro approached them. "Did you have a wank?"

Pedro laughed and said, "Had a shit."

"Eww," Jason shrieked. "Too much info, man."

Pedro pulled out a thick hand-rolled cigarette from his pocket. "Let's lighten up the mood a little, shall we?" He placed the oversized cigarette between his lips and searched for his matches.

"Thought you quit smoking," Jason said.

"This, my friend, is a *special* cigarette for *special* occasions," Pedro said as he lit it and took a deep drag and held his breath for a couple of seconds before he coughed violently. "G—god! Fuckin' mother of Moses, it's strong."

Pedro handed the dagga[4] to Jason, who in turn took a deep draw and began to cough violently as well and spat, "Jesus fuck, what is this?"

---

[4] A regional term used in South Africa for the Cannabis plant.

"Durban Poison dude," Pedro said.

Jason handed the hybrid cigarette to Thabo.

"I don't smoke," Thabo said.

"Bullshit," Pedro said. "You all smoke, so don't pretend." Pedro gawked at Thabo. *You fucking lying kaffir thief.*

"Come, Thabo," Jason said. "After our twenty-seven-hour trip we deserve a chill-out session."

Jason and Pedro began to chant, "Thabo-Thabo-Thabo-Thabo," until Thabo took a long drag and blew it out like an old smoker.

"Thought you don't smoke, Thabo," Pedro said.

"Not with whites," Thabo said halfway through a light cough and spat.

CHAPTER 41

Jason, Thabo and Pedro sat on the wall with their feet hanging over the twenty-meter drop and smoked a second dagga cigarette while they took in the amazing sunset over the ocean. Red-orange rays of a half sun stretched out over the ocean towards them while the waves crashed against the rocks below, and fine droplets of sea spray blew up into their faces.

Random topics and half-finished sentences were followed by uncontrollable giggles about nothing logical.

Jason could feel Thabo's warm skin touching against his arm, the sweat feeling cool as the wind blew past them.

"It's so bu-pi-pul," Thabo muttered. "I mean, beau-ti-ful. This is the most beau-ti-ful sunset I have ever seen. And-and this is the best time of my life. Thank you, Jason." Thabo leaned his head on Jason's shoulder and whispered, "I love you."

"Did he just say, 'I love you'?" Pedro said.

"I think you're hearing things," Jason said. "It's probably the Durban Poison talking."

Pedro shuffled against Jason and looked Thabo right in the eyes and said, "I love you, Jason," and burst into a laughing fit.

Jason elbowed Pedro in the ribs.

Pedro moved his face so close to Jason's that their noses almost touched. "You love me back?" Pedro said. His lips edged closer to Jason's lips.

Jason gave Pedro a quick lick on the lips and stood. *Maybe we should have a threesome,* he thought and imagined what it would look like if Thabo fucked Pedro.

Jason walked towards the kitchen then stopped and looked back and saw Pedro's head leaning towards Thabo.

Should I ask? I'm so fucking high right now. Fucking awkward. What time is it? Did I finish my wine? I want more wine. Pedro, do you want to try a threesome? Yes? Fuck yeah. I want to see Thabo fuck you with that massive cock. I think it's bigger than José's. Oh fuck. José.

Jason crouched, holding onto the wall, seeing José's expression the moment he fell from the moving carriage door.

CHAPTER 42

Pedro sighed deeply and shifted closer to Thabo and sniffed his neck and said, "Are you wearing Jason's perfume?"

Thabo looked at Pedro from the corner of his eye and kept quiet.

"You know Jason is *my* friend," Pedro said. "So whatever's going on here, if his dad, *your boss*, finds out, you're fucked, man. You're as good as gone. He'll probably shoot you. Bam, right in the head."

Thabo kept his gaze towards the horizon.

"Why do you have such small ears and such thick lips? Like a monkey. What's that mark above your eye?" Pedro touched the scar Thabo got from the night of the assault.

Thabo grabbed Pedro's hand and smiled, then stood up and gently dug his fingers onto Pedro's thick mop of dark brown hair and began to massage his scalp.

"What're you doing?"

"Just a massage," Thabo said. He noticed Pedro's smart silver watch and gold necklace, then looked down at the sharp rocks below. *You're not getting in my way of freedom,* Thabo thought and gently moved Pedro's head from side to side in a subtle, controlled manner.

Pedro closed his eyes and said, "Ja man, that feels really good."

Thabo took a second look at the sharp rocks below and slowly began to push Pedro's head forward.

"Hey, stop, I'm going to fall off," Pedro said and pushed back.

Thabo stepped away.

"Let's go to the beach," Jason suggested as he walked up behind them.

Pedro looked big-eyed at Thabo and said, "What the fuck, man?"

"What's going on?" Jason said.

"I think he wanted to push me off."

Jason looked at Thabo, who in turn shrugged his shoulders and frowned, and said, "Maybe you're a little paranoid."

"Ja, that's what dagga does," Jason said. "Told you, you should quit that shit. Come on, grab your drinks and let's go for a swim."

"Come, Thabo!" Jason yelled over the roaring ocean as he and Pedro ran naked over the beach and into the rolling waves. The orange-red sun had completely disappeared in the horizon, but it was still light enough for Thabo to see the shapes of their bodies.

Thabo dug his feet into the soft white sand and sat down. He was reluctant to step into the ice-cold seawater, even less so with that blue-eyed bastard in the vicinity.

Jason and Pedro jumped over the waves and screamed like children, their voices barely audible over the roaring waves.

"Come on, Thabo," Jason shouted and waved.

Still high from the dagga, Thabo lay down and looked up at the dark blue sky slowly turning a deeper blue-grey with a few early stars appearing.

A few minutes later, Pedro walked up to Thabo, naked. "You scared of water or what?"

Thabo looked past Pedro and didn't say a word and felt like punching him in the face so that he would shut up.

"And now you lost your tongue, too?" Pedro said. He deliberately stood in front of Thabo. He took a step closer with his cock inches away from Thabo's face. "How about you give me some head, black boy?" Pedro pushed his semi-erect cock towards Thabo's face.

Thabo looked at the tiny thing inches away from him. He almost began to laugh, then slapped Pedro on his testicles.

Pedro squealed like a pig and fell to the sand in a bundle and gasped for air.

Thabo grabbed Pedro by the throat and forced Pedro onto his back, then sat on his chest with his knees pinning both Pedro's arms to the ground. He held Pedro's neck with one hand and grabbed Pedro's testicles with the other.

"You like this?" Thabo said in a calm and composed tone, and squeezed Pedro's testicles harder. Pedro's skin felt cold and smooth in his palms.

"G-get off m-me, you f-fucking *kaffir*," Pedro gargled. It looked like he couldn't breathe.

Thabo moved closer to Pedro's face. "You asked me about this cut on my eye. You don't remember this black monkey *kaffir* face?"

Pedro began to cry and tried to get out of Thabo's grip, but couldn't.

"You punched and kicked me and called me a *kaffir*, then stole my money like a thief."

Pedro spat in Thabo's face.

Thabo spat back. "Next time I'll cut your fucking throat like a goat if you get in my way, you white bastard." Thabo loosened his grip and stood up. "Good thing Jason took care of me that night."

Pedro coughed and crawled away over the white sand like a wounded animal before he gathered momentum and stumbled naked in the direction of the footpath that led back to the house and disappeared into the bushy shrubs.

Not long after, Jason emerged from the rolling waves and strolled up the beach towards Thabo.

"Where did Pedro go?"

"He left," Thabo said and handed Jason a towel.

"Without his clothes?"

"He said he felt sick and went back to the house."

"The way I know him, he probably went back to smoke more of that shit."

CHAPTER 43

Thirty minutes later, back at the beach house, Jason and Thabo lay slumped over a sofa listening to pop music.

"It's really odd of Pedro to just leave like that," Jason said.

"Yes, very strange," Thabo said and gently stroked Jason's arm.

"I just realised he had to ride his scooter naked. Imagine that. Crazy. I think I know where he might have gone."

"Where?"

"His aunt's club. Come on, let's go." Jason pulled Thabo by the leg. "Come, Thabo."

"I don't want to go."

"Why not?"

"I'm tired."

"Bullshit. You won't be tired once you get there, believe me. Come on."

Jason walked to the bedroom and threw all his bags' contents on the bed. "What will I wear?"

One of the photos of their train trip lay on the carpet to the side of the bag. The photo with Carla and José. "Fuck, I need to get rid of this," Jason said to himself and tore the photo into small pieces and searched through the clothes for the other photos.

"Thabo, have you seen the photos we took on the train?"

"No," Thabo said as he walked into the shower.

Jason opened Thabo's bag and began to search through Thabo's stuff. He picked up the golden pen with PR engraved on the side. *No—no—no.*

Jason just stood there, shocked to see the pen in Thabo's bag.

He looked at the pen once more to make sure. "This can't be."

Moments later the shower stopped.

"Now I feel fresh again," Thabo said as he walked into the room butt naked patting the towel at the back of his head.

Jason eyeballed Thabo.

"What's wrong? Why're you looking at me like that?"

"For a moment, you sounded like Carla when she stepped out of the shower in the train."

"Oh yes, I remember. She was a wild woman." Thabo giggled and sat down on the corner of the bed.

Jason noticed Thabo glancing towards his own bag.

"Did you find the photos?"

"No, I've looked everywhere." Jason tipped Thabo's bag upside down on a mission to see if something else might surface.

"The photos are not in my bag." *Hope he didn't find it,* Thabo thought as he quickly gathered his clothes again and shoved them back into the bag. But the shirt he used to hide the glittering pen lay to the side, open. *No-no-no-no-no, my life is over. Fuck. He found it.*

"I'll take a quick shower, then we'll go," Jason said.

"Do I need to wear the Muslim dress again?"

"Nah, they're fairly relaxed over here, and it's nighttime so no need for that." Jason stood there for a couple of seconds, not saying anything.

"Are you okay?"

"Yeah," Jason said and disappeared into the opulent bathroom.

As soon as he could hear the shower water, Thabo threw all his clothes out and searched for the pen in the hope it hadn't been discovered. He turned his attention to Jason's bag and, just as he opened it, he noticed the diamond and gold pen on the floor beside the bag.

Thabo's body went cold and it felt like being sucked into the ground. *You just fucked it all up for yourself. Fuck. What will I say? Jason, I found it in the garden. Or, Jason I saw it laying on the floor and wasn't sure whose it was.*

Thabo sat down on the bed. "I don't know what you're talking about," Thabo practiced. "I found it in the garden." He kept practicing different replies he could use until he heard the shower go silent.

Thabo looked down at his feet, trying to avoid eye contact from embarrassment.

"You ready?" Jason said as he walked naked into the bedroom.

"Yes, no, almost, I'm just waiting for you."

Jason walked up to Thabo and stood in front of him with that strange look in his eyes again. Thabo could see the disappointment on his face as Jason half-smiled at him.

Thabo felt so embarrassed that he wanted to run away. He held out his hand to touch Jason's hand.

Jason leaned forward and kissed Thabo on the lips, then looked him in the eyes and said, "Do you love me?"

"Yes." Thabo's entire body suddenly flushed with cold sweat out of fear of what Jason would say next.

"Good," Jason said and touched Thabo's face with his soft hand. "Let's go. We're going to have some fun tonight."

CHAPTER 44

Jason and Thabo arrived in the city centre and drove down a dimly lit street behind an old grey concrete building that looked deserted. They parked the car and walked in silence down an alleyway, sparsely illuminated by a few scattered streetlights. A couple of men stood smoking to the side of the alley, just out of reach of the streetlight. Their faces were hidden in the darkness of the night and only their deep voices gave away their gender. The glowing coals of their cigarettes floated in the air like red fireflies.

Laughter could be heard coming from somewhere near the other side of the concrete building.

"This way," Jason said and walked up to a flight of stairs that led to a door with a large red flashing neon sign above it that read 'Madam Coco.'

To the side of the steps stood another group of men, smoking and laughing. They eyeballed Jason and Thabo as they began to climb the stairs. The muffled sound of music escaped when the metal door flung open and two men emerged from the smoky doorway like two models. One was a dark-skinned Indian man with a curly mop of black hair and a little moustache. He wore a denim jacket that was unbuttoned, and no shirt underneath, his chest hair puffed out like a carpet with a golden chain around his neck, and tight dark blue denim jeans. His manhood bulged against the front of the fly. The other man was a white guy, young-looking, with milky blond hair slicked back to the side with an undercut. He wore a white shirt, unbuttoned at the bottom and tied in a knot just above his perfect six-pack, and skinny white trousers like a couture model.

The blond man eyed Thabo as they passed and said, "Hello."

Thabo shyly waved back at the friendly man and watched the two of them disappear into the darkness of the alleyway, just before the man looked back one more time.

"You nervous?" Jason said.

"I'm scared. What is this place?"

"You'll see. Don't worry, it's nothing like Jo'burg. People are nice over here. Black, White, Coloured, Indian, everyone's welcome at Madam Coco."

They walked through the metal door into a thick, musky wave of warm air, with a hint of body odour that tickled the back of the nose.

The disco music got louder the deeper they walked towards a table lamp at the end of the corridor. Thabo looked up at the low ceiling. It had been covered with hundreds of Barbie dolls stuck to the ceiling.

Thabo held onto Jason's arm as they ventured towards an elegantly dressed woman in a sparkly evening dress who sat cross-legged on a bar stool beside the table lamp. Her skin looking sun-kissed, almost like that of José.

Her elaborately large blonde hairdo was done up like a beehive and her face was plastered in a thick layer of foundation, but a hint of five o'clock shadow could be seen underneath. Her breasts were the size of balloons, hidden underneath the glittering dress. The look was topped off with red stiletto heels that would have made Elizabeth Taylor choke with envy.

"Welcome to Madam Coco," the woman said in a deep theatrical voice.

"Hello, aunt Coco," Jason said.

The woman quickly put on her reading glasses and said, "Oh my goodness, Jason darling." Coco jumped up from her chair and stood a head taller than Jason and Thabo. "My darling, I haven't seen you in ages. Come give me a hug, you handsome young man."

"Yeah, it's been just over a year since I last saw you."

"Feels like much longer," she said and turned her attention to Thabo.

"This is Pedro's aunt," Jason said to Thabo.

Thabo didn't know how to react.

"And who's this handsome man with you?" Coco said.

"This is Thabo," Jason said.

Thabo reached out his hand to shake hers when she grabbed him and gave him a hug, too.

Thabo could feel her massive breasts pressing against his face. They felt like balloons.

"Oh, at last someone who has the same taste as me," Coco said and laughed. "Like the saying goes, 'once you've tried black, you never go back.'" She laughed out loud and playfully nudged Thabo on the shoulder.

"God, he's almost as dark as I am," she said. "He could just as well have been Portuguese. You're in the Mother City now, my dear. Most probably the only place in this godforsaken country that's open to everyone. We're all family in here. Viva Mandela."

Thabo looked at the lady with big eyes, smiled and said, "Viva Mandela."

She lit a cigarette and said, "And if anyone in here gives you shit, tell them I'll fuck them up, and I mean literally with my dildo." She pointed at a fire extinguisher canister standing beside the stool. "By the way, where is that nephew of mine?"

"I thought he might be here," Jason said.

"No, darling. He said he was going to your place. Maybe he's back at mine getting ready. You know how long he takes to get dressed. Even longer than me. Little narcissistic shit." She laughed and took a long drag from her cigarette. "Now, Jason, you know the rule to enter. Come-come, lift those shirts so mama can see what's hiding under there."

They both lifted their t-shirts as instructed while Coco inspected Thabo from top to bottom and ran her perfectly manicured index finger over his stomach. "My-my, what a handsome young specimen you are. Say hallelujah for being such strapping young men. And remember, shirts off and bottoms out."

Coco winked at Thabo with her lavish, long, black lashes while she pouted her juicy lips.

"We've had a few raids by the police recently, so if there's some action again, run like it's the end of the world and don't look back."

Jason gave aunt Coco a final smile and ushered Thabo through a bunch of glittering fringed curtains along the narrow black-walled corridor where they passed two shadowy figures holding on to each other.

The music became louder and the heat increased as they approached a small dance floor lit by a few flashing disco lights and a large mirrored disco ball swirling in the centre. A thick layer of cigarette smoke hung over the dance floor with glittering figures of shirtless men trembling with the beat of the music.

Jason and Thabo walked up to a tiny bar beside the dance floor with a shirtless Chinese barman sporting a cowboy hat and tight jeans and a laundry peg on each nipple.

"What can I get you fellows?" the barman shouted as he petted his thick black moustache that almost looked like some Kung-Fu master's facial hair.

"Two beers, please," Jason said and took his shirt off.

"Are you twenty-one?" the barman said.

"Yes, of course we're twenty-one," Jason said and twitched his nipple at the barman and smiled.

"Coming up," the barman said and disappeared behind the counter.

"Are you okay, Thabo?"

"Yes."

"You sure? You look a little down."

"I am fine," Thabo said as he gazed at the crowd of faceless bodies moving to the rhythm of the music on the smoggy dance floor.

"It's just—I've never been to a place like this before."

"There's always a first time for everything," Jason said and handed Thabo a beer.

"Just relax and go with the flow. Just enjoy yourself."

Thabo's stomach began to cramp from nerves. "Where's the toilet?"

"The other side of the dance floor. You can see the blue light, just in there."

Jason pulled Thabo's shirt up. "Take it off."

Thabo melted into the sea of multicoloured sweaty bodies as he wrestled his way through the crowded dance floor. He eventually managed to get to the other side past the blue light and down a corridor where a slant queue of semi-naked men stood by the toilet door, waiting for a cubicle to open.

People's shoes made sticking sounds as they walked over the dirty floor partly covered in a mixture of spilled alcohol, urine and other bodily fluids.

Thabo joined the queue and peeked around the corner into the toilet hall, lit by a single flickering fluorescent tube light. To the right stood a long stainless steel urinal trough. The sound of urine shooting against the hollow metal urinal could be heard echoing through the restroom while the sweaty men eyed each other's cock's and moved their bodies to the beat of the music. At the very end of the urinal stood two sweaty shirtless men who kissed lustfully yet passionately with their hands deep inside each other's trousers.

Thabo rubbed his eyes and looked again. *They just all do it in here?* he thought and felt slightly aroused by this new experience. He had the urge to look at the unusual sight, but was scared someone might see that he was looking.

An arm suddenly grabbed Thabo around his neck and said, "Mind if I join you?" Jason pressed his head against Thabo's while doing silly twisting moves with his eyes fixated in the direction of the urinal trough.

"I need to use the toilet," Thabo whispered. "My tummy doesn't feel well."

"That's ok," Jason said. "We can go together. I'll piss first, then you can take a dump."

A toilet cubicle opened and as they entered, Thabo was hit by an overwhelming stench of old urine.

Jason unzipped his trousers and started to pee. "I got us something special," he said and reached into his pocket and pulled out two pills. "One for you and one for me. It's to give you energy." Jason began to sing, "Super-c, super-c, super-c for energy, so we can dance the night away. Ready?"

Thabo popped the mysterious bitter pill into his mouth and swallowed it with a mouthful of beer.

"See you on the other side," Jason said and gave Thabo a kiss before he disappeared back towards the music.

CHAPTER 45

Thabo sat on the stained toilet seat for about fifteen minutes and listened to the strange conversations happening around him while he did his business, including constant loud sniffing sounds coming from the cubicle next door.

Thabo flushed and unlocked the toilet door and slowly opened it. He felt anxious, more than ever before. A strange tingling sensation surged through the back of his neck, and for a moment he felt like he was about to float into the air.

He took a deep breath and walked past the queue of men who all gawked at him.

A short, bald, skinny man with countless earrings and an orange t-shirt stepped out of the queue and pushed his arm against the wall to block Thabo.

The man's eyes widened like a person who struggled to see, and he fidgeted and ground his teeth like a cow chewing on grass. "What do we have here?" the big-eyed man said and moved his sweaty face closer to Thabo.

"Please excuse me," Thabo said. His heart pounded in his chest as he sensed imminent danger. His thoughts jumped back to the night of the assault. Thabo clenched his fists, ready to fight. "I don't want trouble, sir."

"Relax," the man said and lowered his arm. "It's not every day we see a sexy chocolate brownie in here." The fidgeting man held out his hand to shake Thabo's. "Wish we had more like you visiting. It's hard to find anyone Black and hot like you in here."

Thabo felt relieved yet scared that it might be a trap as he hesitantly shook the man's soft, clammy hand.

"I'm Albert," the man said and stared right through Thabo with tarsier- sized eyes. "And you are?"

"I'm Thabo, sir."

"Are you here on your own tonight or with friends?" The man touched his crotch, unable to stand still, almost like he was doing little dancing moves like Michael Jackson.

"I came with a friend," Thabo said. "He's dancing, I think."

"Oh, a friend with a capital 'F,' I presume." The man gave an unexpected half-giggle. "Do you like this place?"

"I've never been to a place like this, sir."

"Really? Where you from, then?" The man breathed heavily, followed by a couple more half-giggles while he moved his body to the rhythm of the music.

Thabo paused as a sudden strange euphoric feeling crawled through his body and underneath his skin. "Johannesburg, sir."

"Oh God, no wonder," the man said. "The heart of the regime."

A small crowd of semi-naked men began to form around Thabo.

"Look at that body, all sweaty and smooth and not a single hair in sight," the fidgeting man said.

Thabo stood in one spot like a mannequin in a shop window with everyone gawking at him. He began to feel uncomfortable and sweaty as his body rapidly heated. He wanted to leave, but the man blocked his way.

"Now, I have a question for you," said the man whose name Thabo couldn't remember. "Is it true what they say about Black men?"

Thabo began to blink rapidly and could feel the unknown substance Jason gave him take effect on his brain. The slight vibration in his eyes lasted for a mere second, then turned into a mild mid-eye hallucination.

Thabo forgot what the man said. "What did you ask again?"

"Is it true about Black men?"

"About what?"

Thabo blinked continuously in an attempt to stop the unexpected vision, at which point his eyes began to move rapidly from side-to-side as if searching for something. He tried his best to keep his eyes open and straight to focus on the man in front of him.

"They say Black men tie a rope around their dicks and use a stone to make it longer."

Thabo laughed and suddenly felt a boost of confidence.

"Yes, we tie a string around it," Thabo said and smiled.

"So it's true," the man said to one of the other men beside him. "See, I told you."

The small crowd of sweaty men stood in a half circle while twitching and grinding as they looked at Thabo like hungry wolves with big eyes, ready to feast on their prey.

Thabo looked down towards his stomach and smeared the sweat droplets that formed as he stood under the blue light, giving his skin an almost alien look.

"Pop out that black snake so we can see for ourselves then," Albert said.

"Yoh," was the only word that came out of Thabo's mouth. His heart raced and felt like it wanted to jump from his chest while his breathing increased rapidly and his palms felt like wet sponges as they touched his stomach. Every muscle in his body felt like it tensed up. Thabo realised he had also begun to bite constantly. Then another mild mid-eye vibration.

Thabo's head tilted backward and stared straight into the blue light bulb above his head that bounced rapidly from side to side like a blue glowing rabbit hopping around in a dark blue forest of music.

A feeling of euphoria surged through Thabo's body and crawled underneath his skin, and a layer of goosebumps formed all over his body.

Thabo moved his hand down his smooth, sweaty chest and opened the top button of his trousers, then unzipped the fly.

The group of men looked on in anticipation.

Thabo's legs twitched and wiggled with the beat of the music as his hand disappeared into the front of his trousers.

"That's right," a random voice in the semi-circle said, "get that thing out."

Thabo could feel his testicles contract deep into his body, and without looking down, he pulled the much-anticipated object of desire into the dim blue light.

Thabo opened his hand and moved it away.

Humming sounds of surprise and lust came from the crowd of fidgeting men as they edged closer to take a better look.

It felt like one moment lasted an hour as Thabo stood against the wall and closed his eyes, then drifted off into a dream-like world of music and disco lights. He moved his body to the rhythm, then drifted back into reality as he opened his eyes.

Thabo suddenly felt a warm tingling sensation on the tip of his cock and looked down. He was unsure what he saw as his eyes couldn't look straight but constantly bobbed around in his skull. The sensation increased. Thabo opened his eyes as wide as he could hoping it would make him recognise what he was looking at. For a moment the rapid eye movement stopped. A faceless person crouched below him, indulging himself on Thabo's cock.

Thabo pushed the faceless figure away from him and stumbled down the dark corridor in the direction of the music and lights, while he struggled to close his trousers.

He stopped and tried to compose himself, but stumbled further towards the glittering figures moving in succession to the rhythm of the music. He pushed his way through a swarm of sweaty bodies as they danced provocatively to the beats while their hands slid all over Thabo's own sweaty body. He wrestled his way in an uncertain direction until he recognised the Chinese barman with the cowboy hat who smiled at him while making kung-fu moves like Bruce Lee.

Thabo looked back at the crowd of moving bodies under the colourful flashing disco lights. He couldn't stop grinding his teeth or stand still.

The hallucinations occurred as before, and the light danced with the beat of the music. Seconds felt like minutes and minutes felt like hours.

Thabo opened his eyes and recognised the blue light on the other side of the dance floor near the men's toilets. He stumbled back in the direction of the toilets, feeling the urge to pee.

Thabo's body began to overheat and he felt like he wanted to faint.

"Jason," Thabo called out, looking for him as he walked into the toilets.

He recognised Jason standing naked by the metal urinals masturbating in full view of a few other men doing the same.

Jason looked at Thabo, then looked away and continued with his public exhibitionism.

Thabo shuffled towards Jason and said, "No," and tried to pull Jason away from the wolves.

Jason just smiled and continued.

"Why you do that?" Thabo muttered before he shuffled off towards one of the stained sinks.

He looked at himself in the dirty cracked mirror and couldn't recognise the person who looked back at him in the reflection. Thabo splashed his face with water from the tap and looked in the mirror once more. Eyes big and pupils dilated to the size of tennis balls. Everything looked magnified.

The light began to flicker and his legs began to wobble.

Thabo held onto the sink as he began to sway. "Help," he whispered before it all went pitch black.

Thabo fell sideways against the wall and onto the floor.

Jason touched one of the men's nipples and was about to cum when someone shouted, "Help, someone fell on the floor."

Jason looked back towards where the shouting came from and saw a black figure lying on the floor. "Thabo?" he said and shuffled towards him. "Thabo," Jason called out and tried his best to fight the mind-altering substance while he lifted Thabo's head from the dirty concrete floor. "Thabo, wake up," he said and patted him in the face. "Give me some water." Jason took a cup from the floor and handed it to one of the men.

Jason felt something warm and wet in his fingers coming from somewhere underneath Thabo's head.

He pulled his hand out and looked at the blood.

"Call an ambulance!" Jason shouted. "Fuck, no-no-no Thabo, wake up!" Jason slapped Thabo a couple of times in the face. "Thabo, wake up!"

Thabo began to foam from the mouth and his body went into convulsion.

"Someone, help," Jason yelled.

Two men came running in and pushed Jason to the side. "What happened?" one of them said.

"He just collapsed," Jason said.

"He's having a seizure," the other man said. "Give him space."

"Help him, he's going to swallow his tongue," Jason cried and wanted to help.

"Don't touch him," the man said and held on to Jason. "Wait for the seizure to stop."

White foam bubbled from Thabo's mouth and his eyes were wide open looking sightlessly at Jason.

"Do you know him?" one of the men said.

"Yes," Jason said and could feel himself grinding his teeth.

"Has he taken any substances?"

"I think so," Jason said, afraid to admit he gave it to Thabo.

Thabo's body slowly calmed down and the fit suddenly came to an end. His eyes were still wide open and fixed on Jason.

"Oh my god, he's dead." Jason rushed to Thabo's side. "Thabo, hang on," Jason said and sobbed. "Please don't leave me."

"He's got a pulse and he's breathing," one of the men said and rolled him into recovery position.

"Has he had an episode like this before?"

"Not that I know of," Jason said.

Thabo slowly moved his body, looking like an old person trying to push himself up and said, "Help me."

"Thabo, stay still, we're waiting for an ambulance," one of the men said.

"No hospital," Thabo said and grabbed onto Jason's arm, then vomited.

Jason helped Thabo sit up. "You gave me such a fright."

Thabo looked pale and completely off his head. His pupils were super dilated and a mixture of vomit and spit was smeared on his cheek and down the side of his mouth and into his hair.

Moments later, two paramedics walked in with their equipment.

"Clear out the area," one of paramedics said, then crouched beside Thabo. "What happened?"

"He just fell down and had some kind of seizure," Jason said as he struggled to keep his eyes on the man who spoke to him.

"What's his name?"

"Thabo," Jason said.

"Thabo, can you hear me?" The paramedic shone a light into Thabo's eyes.

"Yes," Thabo whispered.

"Hyperthermia, you're overheating. Did you take any drugs?"

Thabo nodded his head.

"What did you take?"

"I don't know."

"You need to tell me so that I can help him," the paramedic addressed Jason.

"I think it was Ecstasy," Jason said with some hesitation.

The paramedic opened his bag and took out a kit. "This American shit is flooding our streets. Thabo, I'm going to inject you with some medicine to stabilise you. Someone get me a jug or tub of ice cold water."

The paramedic injected Thabo with the counteracting medicine. "It will take a few minutes to kick in, okay?"

Moments later, someone brought in a bucket of ice water.

"Put both your hands into the water and keep them inside for as long as you can. It should help to cool down your body."

The medic attended to the small cut to the side of Thabo's head.

"I don't want to go to hospital," Thabo said to Jason.

"You might not need to go," the paramedic said. "You have a small cut on your head, but you will live. How much Ecstasy did you take?"

"The what?" Thabo said.

"The drugs, how much did you take?"

"You gave it to me," Thabo said and looked at Jason.

"How much did he take?" the paramedic said to Jason and stood up.

"Just one pill," Jason said.

"I should call the police," the paramedic said.

"That will not be necessary," the familiar voice of Coco said as she elegantly kneeled down beside Thabo in her sparkly dress and high heels.

"How are you feeling, darling?" she said.

"I'm okay," Thabo said. "I feel better now."

"I'll take it from here," Coco said to the paramedic. "Thank you very much for your help."

"Fine," the paramedic said, stood up and looked at Jason. "I hope you learned a very good lesson today. Don't take drugs."

As the medics walked out, Coco stood up and looked down at Jason and said, "Take yourself and your friend and get the fuck out of my establishment. We don't need this type of attention drawn to us. Get up." She pulled Jason by the arm, then Thabo and manhandled both of them towards the emergency exit door of the club.

"You will never set foot inside here for as long as I live." She pushed them out and shut the door.

Jason and Thabo stumbled into the dark alleyway and sat down on a couple of crates outside Madam Coco's.

"Are you okay, Thabo?" Jason said.

"There's blood inside my mouth. But I'm fine."

"I really thought you're going to die," Jason said and hugged Thabo. "I'm so sorry, Thabo," Jason sniffed. "I should never have given you that stuff."

"Don't worry," Thabo said. "I kind of liked it. I've never felt so weird in my life."

CHAPTER 46

Thursday, 8 November 1990.

Patrick arrived home two days earlier than planned.

He parked his new Mercedes near the front door of the house, took his briefcase and walked up to the door and noticed the garden looking slightly unkempt as he glanced over his shoulder.

Patrick walked straight to his home office and poured himself a glass of single malt whiskey, kicked off his shoes and slumped back into a brown leather Le Corbusier chaise lounge before he lit a thick Cuban cigar. A potential deal kept repeating in his head and the amount of money he could make would be the biggest deal he had ever done. All of the excitement made him want to get some stimulation. A line of Charlie would make it all blend in together.

He looked back at the garden through the large windows while orange-red rays of dusk sunshine trickled through the trees and highlighted the cigar smoke swirling in the air.

He stood up, walked to the window and gazed over the front garden that was partly covered in afternoon shade.

The intercom buzzer by the front door broke the silence.

"Not now," he muttered as he marched towards the intercom.

Patrick lifted the handset and looked at the black and white CCTV footage of the car with a head stuck out from the window.

"Yes?" Patrick said rudely.

"It's Inspector Van Rooyen to see Patrick," the man said over the scratchy intercom speaker.

"About?"

"Patrick, is that you?"

"What do you want, inspector?"

"It's about your safety. Will you let me in please?"

Patrick watched as the gate opened and the car drove in.

Van Rooyen parked his cream-coloured sedan behind Patrick's car. The tall, well-built, clean-shaven Caucasian man stepped out of the car. He was dressed in a dark blue suit, no tie and immaculately polished shiny black shoes, and he clutched a brown folder under his arm.

"Patrick, good to see you," Van Rooyen said and held out his hand to shake Patrick's.

"Inspector," Patrick said and snubbed the inspector's handshake. "This way." Patrick led the way to his office.

"Have a seat," Patrick said when they arrived. Van Rooyen sat down on a red leather armchair opposite the large wooden office desk. "Whiskey?" Patrick offered.

"Still on duty," the inspector said.

"Since when did that stop you from drinking? I know you guys like your tipple."

"I guess one won't hurt."

"Ice?"

"Straight, thanks. I have to say, every time I come here I'm taken aback by the sheer size of this house. And you always seem to have new paintings."

"I'm an art collector."

"Business must be thriving."

"Business is doing great. Never been better." Patrick held out a wooden box of Cuban cigars to Van Rooyen. "Diamonds never go out of fashion. We just can't get them out of the ground fast enough."

"Seems I'm in the wrong industry," Van Rooyen said and lit the cigar.

"So, inspector, enlighten me on what's so important that you had to drive all the way out here to tell me."

"Two things. Firstly, we have evidence that suggests your domestic worker is plotting to assassinate you."

Patrick broke out into laughter. "You must be fucking joking me. Emma? The short black woman who can't read or even write her own name? Come on, is this some kind of a wind-up or what?"

"I'm dead serious, Patrick."

"She's been with me for many years. Never had any problems with her. It sounds a little bit far-fetched."

"She has meetings with an anti-apartheid activist group."

"Mandela has been released and the Apartheid era is nearly at its end. And what do I have to do with it in the first place? I'm a businessman, not a politician."

"Your connection with the South African Apartheid government, of course. You are well known and what better way to make a final statement."

"Oh, fucking come on, this is absolutely absurd. Look, I think you guys are great at your jobs, but on this occasion someone along the line has misinterpreted something. This sounds more like some Hollywood movie plot. Who's in charge of this so-called *intelligence* operation anyway?

"I am."

"And what are they planning?"

"At this point we're still not one hundred percent certain what, but only that something is being planned."

Patrick pushed back in his chair and took a puff of his cigar. "That sounds rather vague to me. So how long have you known about this so-called plot?"

"Two weeks. She's met with these activists at her home on several occasions. We think one of her sons might be involved too."

"Oh my fucking god, now one of her sons too? Let me guess, the one who works in my garden, right?"

"Indeed, the eldest one, Lethabo."

Patrick gulped down his drink and thought back to the moment he smelled the ghastly body odour of Thabo. "They have had direct access to this property. She has access to our bedrooms and makes us bloody breakfast each morning. She could have poisoned us already. It just doesn't stick. This whole plot smells like the work of Deventer. You sure he's not behind this so-called plot?"

"Patrick, I'm here to give you a heads up."

"Heads up about what? You sure Deventer is not in charge of this operation, because it really sounds a little off to me."

"Lethabo, your garden boy, has a history of running into the law. I had the pleasure of arresting him twice many years ago when I was stationed in Soweto. He's had contact with a person called Uncle Sam, a Nigerian drug and arms dealer who is now one the most wanted drug trafficking fugitives in the country. We suspect Lethabo still has contact with him."

"And?" Patrick said and served himself another drink.

"He's not all he seems, Patrick. None of them are."

"The only thing I can see is an uneducated, smelly black boy who doesn't care about anything other than stuffing his mouth with my food. I don't think either of them has the brains nor the capability to plan an *assassination* or anything else for that matter, except for stealing food from my bloody kitchen, of course."

"Where's Jason?"

"What does Jason have to do with this?"

Van Rooyen opened the brown folder and took out some photographs and pushed them over to Patrick. "This is the second point I wanted to bring to your attention. Have a look."

"And what is this?"

"Just have a look. Maybe this will change your mind. Do you know where your son is?"

"As far as I know, he's in Cape Town at the beach house." Patrick picked up the pack and looked at the first photograph and shoved back in his chair and went red in his face as he flicked through a few more before he dropped the photos on the desk. "Where did you get this?" Patrick suddenly got the urge to do a line of coke to help cope with what he just saw.

"Someone handed it in at the police station with a note giving your address. Luckily, I was with the officer on duty when he opened the envelope. I told him our department would deal with it after I recognised Jason and the black man in a couple of the photographs. Do you know the whereabouts of Lethabo?"

"Should be at home in Soweto."

"Do you have any idea when these photos were taken?"

"Must have been recently. Jason got one of those instant cameras for his birthday."

"It appears that some of the photos were taken on a train." Van Rooyen pointed at the background landscape in one of the photos.

"Who else saw these?"

"Just the officer on duty, myself, and of course my boss, Superintendent Deventer."

"Deventer? You just told me you're in charge of this operation."

"The intelligence gathering of the plot against you is my domain. However, Superintendent Deventer said he's personally taking charge of the operation after he saw these photos."

"I fucking knew that bastard had something to do with this. Did he send you?"

"I'm here on my own accord purely to give you the warning. Deventer wants me to arrest Lethabo as well as Jason."

"Arrest them for what?"

"The Immorality Amendment Act of 1969 on suspicion of performing homosexual acts, sodomy and interracial sex."

"That's absurd. This is clearly something for the *normal* police to pursue, not your branch. For fuck sake, you people need to deal with terrorists and other threats, not this petty shit. Why did you decide to let your department deal with it in the first place?"

"I'm just following orders from Superintendent Deventer."

"Tell that fat faced cunt to mind his own fucking business. He's been nabbing on me for years, and now that he got promoted he's trying a new tactic. I can see what he's doing. He's trying to get at me through my son. *You* need to take control of this situation before it gets out of hand."

Patrick poured himself another whiskey and downed it, then looked at the tiny metal bottle where his white psychotropic friend Charlie was hidden.

"This is fucking honey to the press. This cannot get out. That's what that motherfucker Deventer has been trying to do for years. Making up fake stories and feeding them to the press."

"I've heard a few rumours. Are they true?"

"All fake. Are you sure these were the only photos?"

"Yes."

"I'm keeping them," Patrick said and shoved them into his desk drawer.

"I have to take them back. I risked my career showing that to you. Deventer kept them in his desk and will know they're gone."

"It won't be in vain." Patrick stood up, went to the safe in the panic room and took out a couple packs of bank notes. He walked back to Van Rooyen and placed it on the table.

"You did the right thing to come to me. There's sixty-k, which should cover your next three years' salary in case you get fired. You'll get another sixty when the shitstorm is over. And I keep the photos."

Van Rooyen looked at the money then at Patrick and said, "I'll sort it out." He stood and walked out.

Patrick listened as Van Rooyen started his car and drove off. He couldn't get the top on the tiny bottle off quick enough and spread two long, thick lines of coke, rolled a note and double-sniffed the lines in one go.

"Motherfucker," he yelled and jolted back in his chair with a white powder circle around his left nostril.

He took the pack of photos and looked at them one more time.

A photo of Jason with Thabo and another man and woman who exposed part of her breast. Another photo of Jason's mouth over Thabo's erect cock, and another with Jason squatting down onto an erect black cock. It looked like it had been taken just a moment before it slid inside.

"This is the last shit," Patrick gargled and did another line.

CHAPTER 47

Later that evening, Thabo and Jason arrived back in the city.

Jason pulled up to the petrol station near the entrance to Soweto, in the same spot as before, with Thabo fast asleep in the passenger seat. He sat for a moment, pondering whether he should ask Thabo about the pen he found in Thabo's bag. He recited the correct words to use not to upset him.

"Hey, wake up," Jason said and gently rubbed his hand on Thabo's shoulder.

Thabo sat up. He had an indentation on the side of his face.

"We're here," Jason said and unclipped his safety belt.

Thabo gave a yawn and a stretch and smiled at Jason.

"Have you given any thought to what we talked about?"

"What?"

"The plan, you know, *the plan*."

"I will do it," Thabo said.

"You serious?"

"Yes."

"Okay." Jason suddenly didn't know whether to feel happy or sad.

"Shall we start to work on the plan tomorrow?" Thabo said.

"Yes, Patrick won't be home until the weekend. You sure you don't want to stay over at my place?"

"Maybe tomorrow I can stay there, but I have to go home now." Thabo stepped out of the car and took his bag from the trunk.

"I need to ask you something," Jason said and got out of the car.

"What is it?" Thabo said.

No, no, don't, Jason thought as he looked at Thabo's tired eyes. He didn't want to fuck up their friendship and, most importantly, the *plan.*

"What do you want to ask?"

"Nah, nothing important. We can talk about it tomorrow."

"You sure?" Thabo smiled and gave Jason a hug. "Thank you for taking me with you."

"That's okay. Sorry about what happened the other day."

"It's okay. I told you before, don't worry about me, I'm tough." Thabo tapped himself on the chest with his fist. "I'll see you tomorrow morning at eight?"

"See you at eight. I'll make us some nice breakfast with that Kenyan coffee you like so much."

Thabo smiled and looked super happy. "Sounds like a plan. I need to go now. Good night, Jason." Thabo held the bag to the side of their faces as a cover as he kissed Jason.

"I miss you already," Thabo winked before he walked off.

"See you later, alligator," Jason said and gave a partly hidden wave. He watched Thabo as he disappeared into the deep, depressing darkness of Soweto with its thick blanket of smog hanging over it.

CHAPTER 48

Thabo made his way through the maze of narrow, smelly alleys, past stray dogs barking relentlessly and scavenging for anything edible. He passed hundreds of tilted, patched tin shacks illuminated from inside by candle light. The air tasted bitter and thick from makeshift fires in old oil drums that polluted the oxygen with dangerous toxins.

Thabo hid behind a couple of empty oil drums and watched through the gap while an armoured patrol vehicle slowly passed with its loud engine, causing everything around it to vibrate. He could hear someone speaking over the two-way radio inside the van while they searched for someone.

Just as the vehicle disappeared behind the shacks, Thabo jumped up and ran as fast as he could down another narrow footpath, crisscrossing between rows of closely stacked shacks, with more dogs barking aggressively until he reached the small shack with the blue door. But there was no sign of life inside the tin abode, except for the sound of crickets.

Thabo unlocked the flimsy door that scratched on the concrete floor as he opened it and walked into the pitch black room.

"Mama?" he called, but heard no response.

Thabo felt his way around the table and lit a candle and saw a note one of his brother's had left him.

Thabo. Mother has gone to the blue overalls again. Petros and I is staying at uncle. Watch out for the peri-urban. They arrest many people yesterday. Letsepo.

He put down the piece of cardboard his brother wrote the note on and took a good look around him. For the first time he could smell the damp coming from the floor and cooked maize and burnt meat hanging thick in the air. A breeze filtered through the gaps in the metal walls and carried the distinctive smell of sewage from the nearby ravine.

"I don't want to live like this anymore," he said and tossed the cardboard note across the bed. He knew Jason was the key to a better life.

CHAPTER 49

Forty-five minutes after dropping Thabo off, Jason arrived at the Rothshen mansion, unaware of Patrick's early return. He drove up the long dimly-lit gravel driveway, and as he reached the top, he saw his father's car parked near the front door of the house.

"What the fuck," Jason whispered and slowly drove up to the garage and got out. He took his bag out and tiptoed towards the front of the house.

The door stood wide open with all the lights on and eerily quiet.

"Dad?" Jason called out and stood inside the foyer and listened for any sign of Patrick. "Dad?"

But the only sound came from the crickets in the garden.

Jason walked into the kitchen and poured himself a glass of water and gulped it down.

"Jason?" a calm, deep voice said from behind him.

Jason shrieked and jumped with water shooting from his mouth.

"Don't do that," Jason said and wiped his mouth with his forearm. "Why are you back so early?"

"Because I'm back early. And when did you get back from Cape Town?"

"Just now."

Patrick gazed at him for a moment. "Just now?" Patrick shook his head like he understood. "Did you have a good time?"

"It was okay. Can we talk tomorrow? I'm tired and want to sleep early."

"Of course, but before you go to bed, is there anything you'd like to share with me about your little *adventure* to Cape Town?"

"No, not particularly, why?" Jason sensed something odd about Patrick's sudden interest in his trip, and the way he looked at him just didn't feel right. Perhaps the priest with his wife said something.

An uncomfortable moment of silence followed as Patrick gazed at him yet again, then suddenly said, "We'll speak in the morning," before he disappeared around the corner.

Jason stood in the same spot for a moment, trying to figure out whether Patrick knew Thabo went with him or maybe because of the money he took from the safe. "Father Michael. It could only be him." Jason grabbed his bag, and briskly walked to his bedroom and locked the door.

He fell onto his bed, still in the same clothes, exhausted from travel, and drifted off into dreamland while thinking about how he and Thabo could get rid of Patrick for good.

CHAPTER 50

1:13 a.m. the following morning.

An armoured police personnel carrier drove down a narrow alleyway in the slums of Zone B, Soweto. The large bulletproof vehicle shook violently as it slowly navigated through the pothole-filled gravel road. A bright hand-operated spotlight on the front of the vehicle illuminated the closely stacked shacks in succession, searching.

Rats the size of cats crisscrossed the road and scattered for safety.

"B50, 49, 48," a deep voice counted as the vehicle crawled along the path. "Hard to make out some of these numbers."

Then suddenly, he said, "Stop," and switched off the spotlight. "That one over there, two shacks to the right of the one with the light on."

The heavy side door of the vehicle opened and three men stepped out, geared up in combat uniforms. Each carried a pump action single barrel shotgun with a flashlight mounted to the front.

"Close the door and keep your eyes peeled," one of the men said to the driver.

Barks from stray dogs came from all directions as the loose gravel cracked under their boots while they tactically walked towards shack B43, the house with the blue door which belonged to the Molefe family.

A flimsy fence cordoned off the front section of the shack and was held up by a wire connected to a pole, which hung over the entrance at the right height to hit a man on the Adam's apple, barely visible with a torch.

One of the men gestured to his two colleagues to watch out for the wire as they walked into the front yard and approached the blue door.

The man raised his fist in the air as they reached the door and stood there quietly for a couple of seconds, then counted down with his fingers, three—two—one, and kicked the door open. It split in half on impact and slid into the dark shack.

Thabo jumped at the loud bang and commotion and looked straight into a storm of dust and flashlights heading towards him.

"Don't fucking move," a man shouted. "Hands where I can see them. Stay down, don't you fucking move or I'll blow your fucking head off."

Thabo froze and didn't know what was happening.

A vice-like hand grabbed Thabo by the ankle and jerked him from the bed onto the damp concrete floor.

Thabo looked up at the man, who then forced Thabo to lay facedown on the dirty floor and pushed his head against the floor and twisted Thabo's arm backward.

"Hands behind your back," the man shouted and grabbed Thabo's other arm and jerked it backward, but Thabo got his arm out of his grip.

"I said hands behind your back."

The man punched Thabo on the back ribs, which left Thabo gasping for air. "I'm not telling you again," he said and clamped Thabo's arm between his legs and cuffed him.

"Clear," one of the other men said and began to throw things onto the floor.

The man with his shoe against Thabo's head shone the torch in Thabo's eyes and said, "What's your name?"

"Thabo," he said in a shivering voice.

"Surname?"

"Molefe, sir."

Thabo's head lay flat on the floor, facing the door, and he saw the figure of another man who stood silently in the doorway holding a weapon while smoking.

"Where's your passbook?" the man said and pinned Thabo's head to the ground with his foot.

Thabo gasped for air and said, "Bag," with a mixture of mucus and tears dripping onto the floor.

"Where's Emma?"

"Don't know," Thabo struggled to speak from shock.

"Your brothers?"

"I don't know."

"Don't talk shit with me, boy."

Thabo noticed one of the men dropped the contents of his bag on the floor.

"Where did you steal this Chanel perfume from?" he said as he picked up the bottle Jason had given Thabo.

Thabo kept quiet, afraid to say anything.

"What does a Black man like you do with this expensive perfume? Trying to be like the White man, or shall I say woman, hey? You can get them out of the bush, but you can never get the bush out of them. No matter how much you spray yourself, that stench never goes away."

"And what do we have here?" one of the other men said as he picked up a bunch of banknotes.

The man grabbed Thabo by the neck with his vice-like grip and said, "Who did you steal this from?"

Thabo shook his head, unable to breathe as the man's grip tightened.

"Looks like Emma is getting fucked by the blue overalls again," one of the men said and walked towards Thabo with a piece of cardboard in his hand. "And the brothers are at *uncle*. Is that uncle Sam?"

"No," Thabo said and trembled from fear as he laid in his underwear on the concrete floor.

"Don't try and bullshit us," he said and slapped Thabo a couple of times in the face with the cardboard. "We know everything."

"Got it," one of the men said as he flicked through Thabo's passbook.

The third man approached and his shoes cracked over the debris before he kneeled down beside Thabo. He took out a photograph from his shirt pocket and held it beside Thabo's face.

The driver called over the two-way radio, "We're starting to draw a crowd, I suggest you get out now."

"Copy that," the third man said over the radio and stood up. "Bag it and let's roll."

"Where are you taking me?" Thabo said angrily and tried to resist.

One of men stuffed a piece of fabric into Thabo's mouth, duct-taped it to his face, pulled a canvas bag over Thabo's head and ushered him into a vehicle and shut the door.

A crowd of people began to gather outside in the dark, holding torches and candles as they tried to see what the commotion had been about.

One of the people in the crowd shouted something and a stone landed on the front windscreen of the police truck.

"What're we waiting for? Let's go!" the third man shouted and pushed Thabo onto the floor and kept him down with his foot on top of him.

The personnel carrier began to move forward then suddenly braked sharply. "They're blocking the fucking road and there are dozens of them."

The headlights of the truck illuminated a small mountain of tyres, wood, rubbish and things the crowd had thrown onto the road to prevent them from exiting. About a dozen people holding sticks and stones started to shout and chant. The crowd grew by the second.

"Fucking drive through it, that's what the thing was built for," the third man yelled, "let's go!"

The driver put the vehicle in gear. "Strap in, men, we're gonna go off-road." The driver laughed and revved the engine and drove straight at the angry mob. He dodged the mountain of debris by cutting through part of a shack. Pieces of metal flew in all directions as the armoured vehicle ripped the tiny house apart.

Suddenly, objects hailed down on the bulletproof truck from all directions, popping and clapping as they bounced off the metal. A large stone hit the front right side of the windscreen and immediately followed by a petrol bomb, with flames spilling over the entire front of the vehicle, moments before the driver mowed down a few of the angry protestors and sped down a narrow alleyway.

The heavy four-wheel drive truck bounced up and down as they sped along the road riddled with potholes.

"Shit," the driver said and slammed on the brakes just before a ravine.

"What the fuck are you doing?" the third man said. "Go-go-go!"

"The truck is too long. We'll get stuck between the banks."

The third man looked towards the rear and could see the sea of lights bobbing in their direction. He ran over to the driver. "Move, I'll show you how to drive this thing."

Another petrol bomb landed on the rear of the truck, engulfing the back and side windows with bright blue and orange flames. The hail of stones and bottles began again soon after.

The smell of petrol filled the cabin along with the deafening claps against the steel and bulletproof windows.

The third man put the vehicle in reverse and mowed a couple more people down and dragged them for several feet underneath the truck before he stopped.

Then another hail of bullets sprayed over the front of the vehicle.

"Fucking AK's," one of the police men shouted at the same time a bullet pierced the ultra-thick window and ricocheted past the third man and inside the cabin a couple of times.

The third man shifted the truck into second gear and floored it, heading directly for the sewage-filled ravine.

The heavy vehicle shot through the air and hit the opposite bank with stones and sand bursting over the front of the vehicle.

The force of the impact flung everyone inside the van forward, each of the occupants hitting their heads against something, including Thabo, who flew against the bottom of the seating.

They sped across an open field through some barbed wire fences towards one of the main roads leading out of the township, with flames illuminating the side of the vehicle.

Twenty minutes later, the dramatic journey came to a screeching halt inside the basement parking lot of 1 Commissioner Street at John Vorster Square Police Station. The notorious powder blue thirteen-storey building nicknamed 'Timol Heights' by locals. The central police station was also home to the South African Police's National Security Branch.

Thabo lay curled up in a bundle, his body bruised from being flung around inside the cabin with the erratic driving.

The door opened and the familiar strong grip of one of the men grabbed Thabo's arm and pulled him up and took the canvas bag from his head, before he ripped the sticky duct-tape from Thabo's mouth.

"Why are you doing this to me? I have done nothing wrong."

The men ignored Thabo and forced him towards an elevator.

To the right of the elevator stood a tiny security office with a police officer sitting behind thick bulletproof glass.

The third man with his back towards Thabo showed his ID to the security guard and said, "Inspector Van Rooyen."

The elevator doors opened and an overwhelming smell of ammonia filled Thabo's nose as they walked inside.

Thabo looked at Van Rooyen with his blond hair and ghostly blue eyes and got a flashback from Mr. Naido's tikka masala shop. The man who whipped him, which left the six long marks over his back after the uncle Sam saga.

"You recognise me, don't you?" Van Rooyen said.

"What have I done?" Thabo said. "Why have you brought me to this place? I want a lawyer."

The three men looked at Thabo and kept quiet as the elevator rose to floor nine. They got out of the elevator and one of the officer's escorted Thabo down a long corridor with shiny grey floors and lime green walls, with rows of humming fluorescent tube lights down the centre of the ceiling. The stench of the same ammonia cleaning chemicals filled the entire corridor as far as they walked.

"I want a lawyer," Thabo yelled and stopped.

"Shut the fuck up. No one cares what you want. Move."

The police officer unlocked the metal door of cell three-one-one and pushed Thabo inside, with his arms still cuffed behind his back.

Thabo stumbled and fell shoulder first on the concrete floor.

The heavy metal door slammed shut behind him, the lock clanking, and the footsteps and dangling keys faded into an eerily silence.

Thabo slowly gathered his senses and managed to sit himself up against the green wall. He faced the cream coloured door with a square flap at eye level. Presumably where they shoved the food through. A metal toilet stood in one corner of the four square-meter cell next to a concrete slab painted the same lime green as the walls. No mattress or pillow, just a concrete block for a bed.

A cockroach scurried over the floor and disappeared into the gap underneath the door.

Thabo shuffled towards the toilet. His body ached and he had some blood on his shoulder and knees. He stood by the toilet and tried out a few manoeuvres to pull down his underwear to pee, with his hands cuffed to his back.

"Why is this always happening to me?" Thabo sobbed. His vision blurred with the tears.

He couldn't hold it anymore and urinated in his underwear.

He slid down against the wall and wept, "Why me?"

Suddenly, a few random screams came from somewhere down the hall, closely followed by the sound of slamming metal doors, and then more screams.

Thabo looked up towards the light fixed to the high ceiling, which had been covered with metal mesh. There was a window far up the wall, also covered with a layer of metal mesh and a thick layer of Perspex to prevent any tampering.

Thabo shuffled over to the makeshift bed and laid down sideways, then pulled his legs through his arms until he managed to get his arms in front of him. He held onto his legs and rested his head on his knees until he fell asleep.

CHAPTER 51

Patrick sat behind his desk puffing away on a cigar while he gazed at a new abstract painting he recently acquired that reminded him of a yellow canary taken down a mineshaft.

He could hear the back door to the kitchen unlock and open.

"Here we go," Patrick said and took the whip from his desk, pulled his undercoat in place and casually walked towards the kitchen with the cigar clutched between his teeth.

"Good morning, sir," Emma greeted as Patrick walked into the kitchen. She placed some coffee into the coffee maker.

Patrick looked at his Patek watch. The time was 6:04 a.m.

Without uttering a word, Patrick struck Emma over her back with the whip.

Emma dropped the glass coffee pot and stumbled to the side, clearly in shock and pain, then began to scream. Patrick hit her a second time, and she covered her head with her arms.

"I let you into my house," Patrick yelled and struck her again.

"No, please," she screamed and scrambled towards the back door, but Patrick struck her again across her head.

"Help!" Emma ran around the kitchen island towards the front of the house and slipped on one of the Persian rugs in the ground floor hallway.

"I will teach you a lesson," Patrick yelled and swiped again, but this time missed as Emma ducked and ran for the patio doors with Patrick right on her heels.

Jason woke up from a woman's blood-curdling screams coming from somewhere in the house. He sat up and thought he had been having a dream.

Then he heard another scream.

Jason ran towards his bedroom door and pulled the handle, but the door had been locked from the outside.

Jason ran out onto his balcony.

The ground floor patio door burst open and window glass scattered everywhere. Emma ran out onto the patio towards the lawn, screaming. Red stripes blossomed over the back of her maid's uniform. She looked up towards Jason, "Help me!"

For a moment, Jason thought they're being robbed and wanted to run back in, but watched as Emma stumbled onto the grass in the direction of the swimming pool before she slipped and slid, then began to crawl, all seemingly in slow motion.

Then Patrick appeared, walking calmly in Emma's direction, holding a long, black leather whip.

"Dad!" Jason screamed, "what're you doing?"

Patrick kept walking towards Emma without looking back.

"Dad, no," Jason yelled the moment his father lifted the whip and swung at Emma.

The whip cut through the air with a swoosh and landed across Emma's face and arm with an immediate clapping sound, and a mist of blood puffed from her body as the toughened leather tore through the top layer of her skin.

Emma's screams echoed through the rear garden as she crawled over the grass.

Jason wanted to jump off the balcony to stop Patrick, but had second thoughts as he might break his legs, and instead stood helpless as Patrick continued his lashing.

"No, please, boss. I'm sorry, my boss. Please!" Emma pleaded as the blows landed over her.

"You have one minute to get off my property," Patrick grumbled and pulled his grey waistcoat in place and walked back into the house.

Jason looked on as a badly injured Emma crawled over the wet grass and disappeared around the corner of the house.

Just as Jason rushed back into the bedroom and headed for his door, a sudden ear-popping boom came from the rear garden that shook the entire house. At the same time, Jason could hear police sirens approaching.

Jason ran back onto the balcony and saw his father standing with a shotgun in his hand by the corner of the house at the same spot where Emma disappeared earlier, with a plume of gunpowder smoke going up into the air.

CHAPTER 52

Ten minutes later, Jason's bedroom door unlocked.

"Jason," Patrick said.

Jason stood on his balcony and looked inward as his father approached. He was afraid Patrick might have another angry outburst.

"Why did you hit her like that?" Jason said.

"They were planning to hurt us," Patrick said as he wiped his forehead with a white handkerchief.

"Hurt us how?"

"The less you know, the better. You stay in the house and keep all the doors locked. You do not leave the property under any circumstances, and you keep the alarm system activated. If the alarm is triggered, you go to the panic room and call the me."

"You're scaring me now. What's happening?"

"Do you understand, Jason?"

"Yes, I heard you. But why is this happening? Who's trying to hurt us?"

"I need to get to the office for an important meeting."

"Why don't you want to tell?"

"That bitch was planning to kill us."

Jason shook his head in disbelief and a loss for words. "That can't be. There must be a mistake."

"There might be some media vultures hanging around. Don't speak to anyone. Do you understand? You do not open the gates for anyone under any circumstances."

"Yes."

"Give me your car keys."

"Why?"

"I said, give me your damn keys." Patrick had *that look* in his eyes again. The kind of look that would make any person shit themselves. "I said keys, now."

"Fine," Jason said and stomped towards his bedside table, grabbed the keys and realised the wristband Thabo gave him was still around his wrist.

Patrick took the keys from Jason and stormed out of the room and down the stairs.

Moments later, the telephone rang. Jason quietly lifted the handset in his bedroom. All the telephone lines in the house connected to each other, which meant Jason could hear everything over any of the phones in the house.

Jason listened to a conversation between his father and a man.

"… She's on her way to the police station as we speak. They found some articles of interest in her house and the accomplices houses."

"This is absolutely unbelievable."

"We were lucky. Fortunately, or shall I say unfortunately, those photos of your son with the gardener certainly woke Deventer up to push forward with the arrest of her and her mongrel son. I think if it wasn't for that, Deventer would probably still be *waiting* for the right moment."

"So you got my gardener too?" Patrick said.

"Yes, I was there when he was arrested during the night. Got a little heated when we left. We took a few stones and bullets but managed to get the job done. They're just waiting for his Emma to arrive before the interrogation begins."

"Well done, Van Rooyen."

"There's a but," Van Rooyen said.

"What do you mean?"

"Deventer wants to arrest Jason, too. He wants to charge both of them under the Immorality Amendment Act of 1969 for performing homosexual acts in a public space."

Jason slowly put the phone down and began to cry and shook from fear. "This is not happening."

In his study, Patrick continued the conversation with Van Rooyen. "I won't let that happen," Patrick said.

"But without those photos, we can't keep the Black boy in here," Van Rooyen said. "There's not enough evidence to suggest the gardener had any involvement in the plot."

"So the motherfucker can just walk away without any fucking charge?"

"Unfortunately, you have the only thing that can keep him inside—those photos. Without them, we can only keep him for maximum of fourteen days under current rules. It's your choice, Patrick. But if that's what you want, then we need those photos, which means Jason will join him."

"It's one of those things I will have to deal with myself then. All I'm concerned with right now is the media. They're like fucking infected stray dogs looking to attack."

"We've done things quietly and by the book. Kept it all under wraps with only a small team working on this. However, your trigger-happy moment from this morning didn't do you any good."

"I just couldn't control myself. I want to go back to what you said. Was Deventer actually waiting for something to happen before he would give the order to make the arrests?"

"Not so sure about that. Perhaps he just wanted to make sure he was going after the right people. Deventer is not a bad guy. Maybe a little anal about certain things, OCD some would say, but a decent guy and doing things by the book."

Patrick gave one of his fake dry laughs. "I've known Deventer for years and he's a cunt, so I'm not surprised."

"Well, not everyone likes him, that I would agree on. By the way, where's Jason?"

"He's in the house. Saw everything this morning."

"Is he aware the photos have been handed in to the police?"

"No, and I think it should stay that way for now. Well, it's a darn good thing you came to me first. You'll see the rest of the leaves once this wind has calmed down."

"I suggest you destroy those photos if you haven't already. Patrick, I need to go, looks like Deventer just walked in."

"Keep me posted," Patrick said and put the phone down.

Jason sat on his bed. "You fucking two-faced asshole." He swept everything from his bedside table and walked to his bathroom, splashed his face with water and stared into his own eyes in the mirror.

"Fuck you," Jason said and slapped himself in the face again and again until his right cheek turned rosy pink. He then grabbed a small pair of scissors from his bathroom cupboard and cut himself on the side of his bicep with the sharp blade until blood began to seep from the cut and trickled down his arm and dripped onto the white marble floor.

Jason slid down the wall crying.

He walked to his bag and dumped all his clothes on the bed. A folded piece of paper stuck out from between his clothes. Jason opened it and read.

Dear Jason,

Thank you for treating me as your friend. I did not know I will find a person like you in the world. You treat me like I am your brother and a friend. My heart is very happy. Thank you for taking me with you. I had the best time in my life. I think this is what they call 'being in love.' It feels weird and nice.

From your secret special friend T

"Jason," Patrick called.

Jason wiped the tears from his face, placed a bandage over the cut on his arm and hid it with a long-sleeved shirt, then strolled downstairs.

Patrick stood by the front door, dusting something from his jacket. "I'm heading to the office. I should be back before 5 p.m. You'll not set foot out of this house until I am back. Do you understand me?"

"Yes," Jason said and gaped at his father, who, for a second, looked like he wanted to say something else to Jason, with his hand raised and wagging his index finger.

Jason could see the anger in Patrick's face. But Patrick didn't say anything else and walked out the door and locked it.

Jason walked to the window and watched as Patrick drove away.

"I know what your plan is," Jason said to himself, "and I ain't going back to that place."

Jason walked back to his room and dialled a number on the phone.

"Hello?" a man answered.

"Pedro?" Jason said.

"Ja, who's this?"

"Jason."

The phone line went quiet for a moment.

"Ah, how are you?" Pedro said.

"Fine."

"You back already?"

"Yeah."

"What happened at your house this morning? We heard some gun shots and some police cars went to your house."

"Apparently, Emma was planning to bomb us or something."

"No fucking way. You serious? That sounds like crazy shit."

"It was bad. I thought my dad was going to shoot her dead. I keep hearing her screams over and over in my head."

"Now that you mention it, I heard some screaming, but it was kinda faint. Anyway, are you okay? Fuck, that sounds seriously fucked up, man. To think she was in the house all the time. Oh my god, she could have done something to me when I was there the other day. Imagine if she slit my throat."

Always about you, Jason thought. "What do you want, Pedro?"

"You called me, moron. You okay? Did you lose your memory?"

"I'm fine. Don't feel so good."

"Sounds like you're having a hard time remembering. Come over to my house."

"I've been told to stay inside the house."

"Why do you have to stay there? Thought everything is over now."

"Apparently, I am not allowed to leave the house, just in case."

"Do you have police guards?"

"Nope. Not even a bodyguard. Nada."

"Thought they would have given you some type of protection after something like that."

"Fuck knows. Anyway, you wanna come over?"

The phone went quiet for a moment. "Sure. By the way, how's your Black friend doing?"

Two-faced fucking asshole, Jason thought, and politely said, "I guess he's at home." He knew from the conversation he overheard that Thabo had been arrested too.

"Your new best friend?"

"Are you jealous of my friendship with Thabo?"

"Not at all. I'm just curious as to why you would befriend a Black person."

"I think you're jealous. I've noticed your attitude changed. And the other night on the beach you just vanished without saying anything."

"Hang on, don't you pin that one on me," Pedro said. "You are the one who has been ignoring me for the last month and then accused me of spying on you and your gardener."

"You know you're my best friend, Pedro. You will always be my best friend."

"I thought I was more than that."

"You know I have a very special place for you, and we had some fun a few times, and you're still my friend."

The telephone went silent again.

"Hello?" Jason said.

"Yeah, I'm still here," Pedro said. "So you're not angry with me?"

"Why would I be angry?"

"Just thought, never mind. I'm just glad we're still friends."

"So you coming over or what?"

"I don't know, my mom wants me to go buy some stuff for her in the city later."

"We can drink some of my dad's champagne like last time and play video games. I got a new zombie game a couple of weeks ago."

The phone line went quiet again for a few seconds.

"Don't know," Pedro said.

"Come on, Pedro, I'm feeling lonely."

"Okay, okay, I'll see you in about thirty minutes."

CHAPTER 53

Pedro strolled up to the large wooden gate of the Rothshen estate just after 11 a.m. and pressed the grey intercom button.

"Hello?" a voice answered over the scratchy connection.

"It's me," Pedro said.

"I'll open," Jason said, and the heavy gate opened with a grinding sound.

Pedro walked up the long winding cobbled driveway, whistling a tune until he reached the front door that stood wide open.

"Jason?" Pedro called out as he entered the house.

"I'm in the kitchen."

Pedro cautiously stepped into the reception hall and took a quick look at Patrick's extensive collection of tribal masks from his trips around Africa. The scary-looking masks were all strategically placed on the wall in the main entrance of the house.

"Hey," Pedro said as he walked into the kitchen.

Jason stood on the other side of the kitchen island with his back to Pedro, in only a pair of white underwear.

"You eventually decided to come over?" Jason said and handed Pedro a glass of Patrick's expensive champagne.

Pedro laughed and walked to the patio and saw a heap of shattered glass.

"What happened to your door?"

"It was this morning when my dad chased Emma out of the house."

"Fuck," Pedro said and inspected the damaged door for a moment. When he turned around, Jason stood right behind him.

"What happened to your arm?" Pedro said and wanted to touch the bandage.

"Nothing. Let's sit outside."

"You sure you're okay?"

"I'm perfectly fine. Just want to forget what happened this morning. I keep hearing her screams."

Pedro could see Jason's eyes become slightly watery.

Pedro plunked himself onto a deckchair beside the pool and watched as Jason took off his underwear and dove into the pool.

"Come," Jason said.

"I don't feel like swimming."

"Then what did I invite you for?" Jason said from the other side of the pool. "Come, the water is nice."

"I thought we were going to play video games."

"We have plenty of time. Come on, pussy."

Pedro gave Jason the middle finger, but eventually took off his clothes and dove in.

"Who're you calling pussy, boy bitch," Pedro said and playfully grabbed Jason by the head and pushed him under the water.

Afterwards, Jason hung onto the side of the pool with his head resting on his arms and his eyes closed. Pedro mirrored Jason and looked at Jason's pale, smooth skin and the light brown freckles on his nose.

Pedro moved closer and kissed Jason on the lips.

Jason opened his eyes and said, "I'm gonna get some music," and got out of the pool.

He's acting weird, Pedro thought as he watched Jason walk naked towards the house.

CHAPTER 54

On the other side of the city, Thabo sat on the concrete block of a bed with his legs pulled up against his chest and his arms wrapped around his legs. His hands were still cuffed and he was laying with his forehead on his knees, while he listened to the singing prayers coming from a nearby mosque's loudspeaker.

The squeaking sound of shoes stopped outside the cell door, followed by clunking keys and the sounds of the mechanism unlocking.

The door swung open and one of the men who arrested him walked in. "Get up."

Thabo stayed in one place and held out his hands in front of him. "Cuffs."

"I said, get up."

"Why are you keeping me here?" Thabo said and slowly stood up, afraid the man might hurt him again.

"You don't speak unless spoken to," the uniformed man barked and pulled Thabo by the arm.

"Why is no one telling me what is going on? You don't have the right to keep me here."

"Keep quiet."

Thabo refused to move and pulled his arms back.

"Move your fucking black ass." The man lifted his truncheon.

"Hit me," Thabo said and moved towards the man. "Come on, hit me."

"I'll fucking break your skull boy, don't try me."

"Then do it."

The man suddenly let loose and hit Thabo on his femur with the truncheon.

Thabo sunk to the ground and could feel the pain deep in the bone and regretted the taunt.

"Next time it will be your head. Get up and move before I lose my temper."

Thabo slowly got up and limped out of the cell in front of the man.

"Did you piss yourself?" the man said. "There's a fucking toilet right next to you, but you go and piss yourself. Don't you know how to use a toilet?"

Thabo stayed silent and kept walking down the lime green hallway until they reached a metal gate leading to stairs with mesh above it.

"Walk faster," the man said and pushed Thabo. "I don't want to smell your stinky ass all day. Move."

They walked up a flight of stairs then into a sixteen square-meter room with a small window on the opposite side and a single light bulb hanging in the centre above a wooden table. There were three chairs around the table.

"Sit," the man instructed and pushed Thabo down into the lone chair facing the window. The other two chairs were opposite him.

The man walked out and locked the door behind himself.

Thabo trembled with fear. The stories he heard in the township of people who had been detained in the police station began to play in his head. The humming light bulb above the desk went dim for a second, immediately followed by screams coming from somewhere down the hallway.

The door opened behind Thabo. He kept his head down, afraid to look, and could smell perfume which reminded him of lemons. Someone sat down on a seat opposite him. He could see a briefcase placed on the table but didn't dare to look up.

"Hello, Thabo," the person said.

Thabo slowly looked up to see a clean-shaven man with blond hair neatly combed to the side and dressed in a grey suit and purple tie. The dreaded inspector Van Rooyen.

The morning sun was just about to peek its head over the horizon, giving an angelic orange glow behind Van Rooyen as he took out a thick brown folder from his briefcase and placed it on the table. Then he took out a packet of cigarettes and a lighter and placed them next to the folder before he placed the briefcase on the floor.

"Please, sir," Thabo muttered, "why have you brought me to this place? What did I do wrong?"

Van Rooyen kept silent, took out a cigarette and lit it while he looked at Thabo. He opened the brown folder.

"Please, I didn't do anything wrong. Please. I want to go home. Please, sir."

Van Rooyen gazed at Thabo with his ice-cold blue eyes and took a long drag from his cigarette. He blew the smoke into Thabo's face with a smile.

"How many times have we met? Three, four times? I lost count."

"I don't know," Thabo said faintly and looked down at the table, feeling tired, scared and confused. His stomach cramped from hunger and his shoulder throbbed with pain.

"Right, let's start from the top. Name?"

"Thabo, sir."

Van Rooyen's smile disappeared. "I'm going to ask you again, what's your name?"

"It's Thabo, Thabo Molefe, my boss. You already know my name."

"Don't talk shit with me, boy. What's your real name?"

"Thabo Molefe." Thabo's stomach made an unholy growling sound from stress.

"Sounds like someone hasn't had their breakfast this morning." Van Rooyen took out a sandwich wrapped in plastic from his briefcase. "My breakfast. Toasted bacon and egg with avocado on whole grain." He took a bite and placed the sandwich beside his burning cigarette, then looked curiously at Thabo while he chewed with a fake smile.

"Fuck, I love my girlfriend's sandwiches. They make me feel all warm and fuzzy." Van Rooyen licked his lips and took another bite.

"Do you see this nice little brown folder in front of me?" Van Rooyen said. "This folder contains everything about you, your father, mother and brothers, the whole lot of you. And of course, I already know this, but it's written here on this piece of paper in front of me, your name is actually *Lethabo* Sephile Molefe. Your mother is Emma Wenize Molefe. Your brothers are Petros Molefe and Letsepo Molefe and Johannes Molefe, who died of tuberculosis two years ago. I asked you these same questions many years ago and now you tried the same trick again."

"I'm sorry, my boss," Thabo said graciously.

"Then why the fuck are you lying to me?"

"How do you know my brother died?" Thabo said and gave a little cough from the smoke.

Van Rooyen twirled a pencil between his fingers without answering while he flipped through a couple of pages. "Are you part of the African Freedom Fighters Alliance?"

"No, sir, I don't know what that is."

"Don't spin me bullshit, boy. Everyone knows the AFFA. And we know about your connections with a known terrorist who also coincidently belongs to the AFFA."

"I don't belong to any groups."

"And how about uncle Sam? You must remember him very well. The man you stole ammunition for."

Thabo shuffled uncomfortably when he heard the name. A shiver raced down his spine as his thoughts jumped back to the moment he fell over the wall.

"Who do you work for?"

"I work for Mr. Rothshen," Thabo stuttered.

"Mr. Rothshen," Van Rooyen repeated and pretended to write it down on the paper with an imaginary pen. "And what do you do there?"

"I work in the garden, sir. I am the garden boy. My mother also works for Mr. Patrick in the house. I have my permit to work, sir. It's in my passbook, sir."

"I ask one question and then you start blabbering things I didn't ask for. But now that we're on that subject, let's have a little peek inside." Van Rooyen turned his attention to Thabo's dirty passbook and opened it. "So you don't have any connection with the resistance movement?"

"No, sir, I don't. I don't want any troubles."

Van Rooyen skimmed through the pages. "I don't see any permit in this passbook." Van Rooyen dangled the passbook in front of Thabo's face. "Where's your permit to work?"

"It's there, sir, in the front of the book."

"I don't see any permit in this passbook, Lethabo."

"It's there, I can see it."

"Your passbook is not in order. You don't have a permit to work in the city. You have been breaking the law and have been working illegally. You know very well non-whites must have a work permit to work in this city, and every other city in our supreme white Christian society."

"No, sir, it's there. Look on the first page. My boss signed the pages."

Van Rooyen flicked back to the first page.

"There, I can see the permit, it's there." Thabo stood up and leaned over the table.

"Sit your dirty fucking black ass down in that chair. You don't move from that fucking chair unless I tell you to. Do I make myself clear? I said, do I make myself clear?" Spit shot from Van Rooyen's mouth like an angry dog about to bite.

Thabo sank back into the chair and the tears began to build up.

"Aw, did I make him cry?" Van Rooyen said with a hint of sarcasm before he ripped out the first page of the passbook and set it alight.

"What are you doing?" Thabo gasped as he watched the orange flame engulf the page.

Van Rooyen smiled evilly at Thabo and dropped the burning page on the floor, and ripped out another page and set it on fire, and then another, and continued until all the pages burned.

"Like I said, Lethabo, there's nothing in your passbook. Oh wait, hang on, you never had a passbook. That's right, you've been working without a work permit or passbook. You live in the city without a residence permit, and that's just the first set of crimes you have committed. You broke the law, Lethabo. You already know what we do to people like you who break the law in this country. We break those who break the law. Looks like you didn't learn your lesson the previous time, I should have broken your back when I had the chance, then we wouldn't be sitting here right now wasting my precious time."

"Why are you doing this to me?" Thabo slammed his fist on the table. "You make up all these stories and then destroy my passbook because you have nothing else. I want a lawyer."

"Well, now, look at that." Van Rooyen laughed out loud. "You want a lawyer? How the fuck are you going to pay for a lawyer to defend your dirty skinny ass? You can't even afford a decent pair of underwear."

"I know my rights," Thabo said. "I might be poor, but I'm not an idiot."

"In here, Mr. Molefe, you have no rights." Van Rooyen stood up and walked out of the room and shut the door.

"Why is this happening to me?" Thabo sobbed and looked at Van Rooyen's burning cigarette that hung on the small metal ashtray beside the sandwich.

His stomach growled with hunger. He wanted to grab the sandwich then escape through the window.

The small room began to fill with smoke from the smouldering passbook paper.

Thabo stood up and opened one window.

A gust of cool city air blew into his face, carrying the distinctive morning smell of car fumes and the sound of life.

Freedom was right there, right in front of Thabo. So close, yet so far.

He looked back at the door before he grabbed the chair and pulled it up to the window. In only his stained underwear, Thabo climbed out and stepped onto the concrete ledge below the windowsill. Just wide enough to walk on.

Thabo faced the wall and tried to cling onto the brickwork.

He looked to his right where the ledge ended against a wall, then looked to the left where the ledge disappeared around a corner. "Left," he said and took a small step. A gust of wind swept over him and almost pulled him backwards.

"Yoh, mama," Thabo said and froze in place. His fingers burned from gripping the small gaps between the coarse brickwork.

Out of nowhere, something grabbed his arm and pulled him back through the window.

"You're not going anywhere," Van Rooyen cautioned and punched Thabo in the ribs.

One of the other officers cuffed Thabo to the chair, as tightly as the handcuffs would allow, causing them to slice into the already raw cuts on Thabo's wrists from earlier.

Van Rooyen scraped the ash from the burnt passbook onto a sheet of paper and tossed it out of the window before he sat down.

"Now, where were we?" Van Rooyen said and took a bite from his sandwich while eyeballing Thabo, displaying intense pleasure with every bite, with a slurp of coffee in between.

"You want a bite? Maybe not. I don't want to catch AIDS now, do I?"

Moments later, a tall, smartly dressed man with a full set of thick black hair and eyebrows the size of two black fuzzy caterpillars, took a seat beside Van Rooyen and placed a file on the table.

The man's eyes looked puffy, like he hadn't slept for a long time.

"Superintendent Deventer will be joining us," Van Rooyen said.

A trail of mucus dripped from Thabo's nose as he recovered from the punch in the ribs and stomach.

"Get some tissues and clean that mess up," Deventer said in a deep voice. "And bring the man some water, he looks thirsty."

Deventer looked through a few pages in the file before he said in a calm tone, "So, Mr. Molefe, I have been told that you are living in the city without the correct paperwork and that you've been working without the required permit. Is that correct?"

"No, it's not true. That man burned my passbook just now. Please, sir," Thabo sobbed, "you have to believe me. I have done nothing wrong. I had a permit in my passbook which my boss signed, but that man burned it all."

"It's okay, Mr. Molefe," Deventer said. "Calm down, I'm here to listen. Let me get this right, what you're saying is that you had a passbook with a work permit, but inspector Van Rooyen here took the passbook and set it on fire for no apparent reason. Is that correct?"

Thabo nodded with an overwhelming sense of relief that someone believed him at last. "Yes, that's right, sir."

"Did you burn this man's passbook, inspector?" Deventer said to Van Rooyen.

"Me? I would do no such thing, superintendent. I have no idea what this Black man is talking about. You know what they say about these crooked glue sniffing *tsotsis* from the Soweto slums. Always trying to bullshit their way out of every situation. And Mr. Molefe has a history of that, don't you, Lethabo?"

"So where is the burnt passbook, Mr. Molefe?" Deventer said.

"He threw it out the window."

Van Rooyen laughed. "See, what did I tell you."

Deventer gave an unconvinced and uncomfortable laugh and took a long drag from his cigarette. "On a more serious note, Mr. Molefe, I would assume that you're going to categorically deny the fact that you and your mother, Emma Molefe, have been having secret meetings with the resistance movement at your house on several occasions during the past couple of weeks. I will also assume that you have no recollection of your mother's plan to assassinate her employer, the honourable Sir Patrick Rothshen, by planting an improvised explosive device in his car, with the aim to assassinate him and his only son, Jason Rothshen."

Thabo shook his head in disbelief. "No, that's not true, my boss. I don't know anything of that."

"I'm one better than you," Deventer said to Van Rooyen. "I can read minds." He opened the folder and read a few notes. "Okay, moving onto the next point. I'm going to ask you a simple straightforward question, and might I remind you, I have evidence of this, but for the record, I have to ask you this question. Have you had a homosexual relationship with your employer's son, Jason Rothshen?"

"No." Thabo's heart suddenly went haywire as he realised the police knew about the secret sexual encounters with Jason.

"We have photos and witnesses suggesting otherwise, Mr. Molefe," Deventer said. "We have photo evidence of you and Jason taken on a train not so long ago."

Thabo's mind wandered back to the moment Jason took a specific photo of them both, and he thought Deventer referred to that one. *But how would they know?*

"Take a photo while I suck you," Jason had said and wrapped his lips around the tip of Thabo's cock, then looked seductively into the camera. "Your pre-cum tastes so sweet."

Jason had stood up. "Okay, now let's take another one." Jason spat heavily on Thabo's cock and slowly slid the dark tool inside him and gave a slight moan as it went deeper. "Fuck, it hurts."

"You okay?" Thabo had said.

"I'm fine, just so thick." Jason held out the instant camera and took a photo of Thabo's cock halfway inside him.

Jason sunk down on it before he'd said, "I want you to fuck me hard," and forced Thabo's cock deeper into him, so much so that it began to hurt Thabo.

"Harder," Jason had said while he bounced up and down like a jockey riding a racehorse at Ascot.

"I'll tell you what it looks like to me, Mr. Molefe," Deventer continued, breaking into Thabo's memory. "You and your mother concocted a plan to kill Patrick Rothshen, and the best way to take out both in one go was for you to get closer to Jason. Your mother knew very well he's a faggot after working for them for many years, so she got him to use you for his own gratification, thereby gaining his trust. And may I remind you, performing unnatural *homosexual* acts in this country is still a crime, as is performing sexual acts between a White person and a non-white person. That's two crimes in one go. Your *faggot* partner in crime will be arrested as well."

Deventer searched through all the papers in his file and suddenly looked bewildered. "Where are the photos?"

"Should be in the folder," Van Rooyen said.

Deventer threw all the papers on the table. "No, they're not in here."

"Maybe in your desk?"

"I put the photos in here myself and kept the file in my drawer."

"Maybe they fell out on the way here."

Deventer grabbed the folder and said, "In my office, now," and stormed out of the room.

Van Rooyen closed his folder, placed it inside his briefcase and smiled at Thabo. "Take him back to the cell," he said to the guard before he walked out.

"Close the damn door behind you," Deventer instructed. "Where the fuck are those photos?"

"I haven't the faintest idea, superintendent," Van Rooyen said and took another sip of his coffee.

"They were in this file and you're the only one who knew about them."

"I honestly don't know, sir. Everyone has access to your office, not just me."

"The shit will hit the fan when I find out who's behind the disappearance of those photos. I want an internal investigation conducted immediately." Deventer picked up the phone and punched in a few numbers.

"What about the Lethabo boy? Do we book him?"

"With what evidence? You know as well as I do that the only credible evidence we had were those photos. And from the little evidence you have, there's nothing that connects Lethabo Molefe with the plot, nor his mother. Fucking two men who are members of an anti-apartheid group is not a crime."

Deventer slammed the phone down and pulled out each drawer in his desk, dumping the contents on the floor. "A TV crew is on standby, ready to record the arrest of Jason Rothshen the moment Patrick Rothshen arrives at his house. But instead, I'm left with jack shit. The only thing we can do is to detain that Lethabo fella under the Internal Security Act for a maximum of fourteen days without charge, then he's free to go. The same goes for his whore mother. I keep asking myself the question, how did we get to this point? This whole so-called *terrorist plot* your division uncovered is a complete shambles."

"Sorry for my ignorance, superintendent, but why then did you order us to bring Molefe in?"

"Are you fucking serious right now? Because if you are, then I suggest you clear your desk and find another job. Otherwise, get the fuck out of my office and find me some real evidence. And find those mother-fucking photos."

CHAPTER 55

The loud pulsing sound of cicadas drifted through the hot summer air while Jason and Pedro lazily baked in the sun beside the pool like two human lizards.

"Drink," Jason said and pushed a glass of champagne into Pedro's hand.

"Do you have suntan lotion?" Pedro said.

"Yeah. I'll put some on your back."

"Now we're talking," Pedro said and turned onto his stomach.

Jason began to rub Pedro's sunburned skin with baby oil.

"Ah, that feels really good," Pedro slurred. "You gonna make me horny if you keep doing that."

"Just drink and keep quiet." Jason moved his hands down toward Pedro's bum and into his inner thigh. He pushed his fingers slightly under the hem of Pedro's underwear and gently touched the skin of Pedro's testicles.

Pedro began to move uncomfortably and pushed his bottom into the air as he tried to reposition himself.

"Keep your ass down, you're interrupting the massage."

"Don't tease me like that, man," Pedro said.

"Finish your drink."

"My head is already spinning."

Jason slid his oiled fingers deeper inside Pedro's underwear.

"Fuck, Jason, what're you doing?" Pedro moved onto his side and opened his legs like a dog in heat.

Jason began to give him a hand job.

Pedro moaned and gulped down his drink with half of it spilling down the side of his face and chest.

"Can I kiss you?" Pedro slobbered and began so suck on Jason's arm.

"Let me get another drink, then we can kiss."

"No more drinks. My head's already spinning. If my mom finds out I've been drinking, she's gonna be super pissed off. Told her I'm going to the shop."

"You'll be fine. I'll take you home."

"No," Pedro said and helped Jason's hand along to wank him more.

Jason pulled his hand out of Pedro's underwear with a string of pre-cum hanging from his finger and licked the pre-cum before he walked off to the house.

After several minutes lying in the burning sun, Pedro heard the familiar tune of Liszt's Piano Sonata in B Minor being played on the grand piano inside the house. Jason's favourite piece.

Snippets of memory from the day Patrick hosted a big party at the house many years ago came to him.

The mansion had been packed with smartly dressed people and the same melody was being played on the piano in the reception hall.

"Wanna check out my dad's secret door in his office?" Jason had said. They snaked through the guests, pretending to be secret agents, and disappeared into his father's home office.

Jason had walked to a floor-to-ceiling bookshelf located behind his dad's office desk that spanned the whole wall. "Check this out," Jason had said and pulled on one of the books. The bookshelf had slid open.

"Wow," Pedro had said. "It's like in a movie. What is this?"

"The panic room."

As they'd walked inside the panic room, Pedro noticed something lying on the floor, partly sticking out from underneath a sofa.

Pedro remembered picking up a photograph with some writing on the back, but he couldn't remember what he saw in the photo before Jason had snatched it from his hand and stuck it into his trousers.

Beside the pool, Pedro sat up and began to feel sick. The piano music suddenly stopped.

"Why'm I feeling so weird?" he said to himself and stumbled onto the lawn beside the patio stairs with his head spinning. His body was numb and trembled as he stood holding onto the railing.

Pedro pushed his fingers into his throat. A stream of rose-brownish liquid shot from his mouth and splashed onto the grass.

Pedro fell down onto his knees like an altar boy about to pray for his sins, followed by a second wave of brown foamy vomit.

"Pedro, you okay?" Jason said as he walked up to Pedro.

"Don't touch me." Pedro slapped Jason's hand away and tried to keep his balance as everything around him spun. "What did you put in my drink?"

"What do you mean?" Jason said.

"You poisoned me."

"You're being paranoid, man." Jason tried to help him up.

"Leave me alone." Pedro struggled to pull himself up on the handrail and stumbled up the patio stairs with everything spinning around him.

"Pedro, come back, you're being silly now."

Pedro felt his way into the house, his vision spinning and arms stretched out like a blind person. He tripped over a clay pot and scraped a couple of tribal masks from the wall as he fell onto the floor and began to crawl towards the front door.

"Pedro," Jason called from somewhere behind him.

Pedro pulled himself up against the enormous wooden door. He managed to find the long handle and pulled it open with the last bit of strength he had left.

"You're not leaving," Jason said and stuck his foot against the bottom of the door to block it from opening further. "The party's only getting started." Jason closed the door and locked it.

"Why are you doing this?"

"You know why," Jason said and slapped Pedro across the face.

Pedro fell backwards. "Help me!" He began to crawl away.

"Help," Jason mocked and broke out into laughter. "No one can hear you, stupid." He punched Pedro in the face. "Now shut your fucking hole, you two faced pig."

Pedro slumped back against the wall and covered his face, crying.

Jason kneeled down in front of Pedro, with his face inches from him, holding him by his hair, and said, "You took those photos from my bag and gave them to the police, didn't you?"

"Fuck you," Pedro bawled and punched Jason on his nose and crawled for his life in the direction of the front door. He managed to grab onto the handle a second time and attempted to unlock the door.

A loud thump echoed through the reception hall. Pedro fell face down on the floor with blood gushing from a gaping wound to the back of his head.

Jason stood over Pedro with one of Patrick's African tribal masks in his hand.

He dropped the mask and then kneeled beside Pedro. He slapped him a couple of times, but Pedro was unresponsive and motionless, with blood seeping from the wound.

"Fuck," Jason said and sat down beside Pedro and held onto his own nose with blood coming out.

"What have I done? Think, Jason, think."

He rushed to the kitchen, pushed pieces of paper towel in his nose, washed his hands and threw the empty red Seconal capsules down the drain. Enough pills to tranquillise a horse.

He heard a noise come from the front door and walked cautiously in the direction of the reception hall and found only a pool of blood left where Pedro had been a few minutes earlier.

Jason ran out the front door, and in the distance, Pedro stumbled over the lawn in his red briefs, heading down the slope towards the gate.

Jason ran after Pedro and tackled him rugby-style.

They both slid on the grass for a couple of meters before Jason began to punch Pedro continuously on the back of the head until Pedro stopped moving.

He looked around nervously, afraid someone might have witnessed the fight, then lifted Pedro over his shoulder and carried him back to the house.

Warm urine flowed over the front of Jason's chest from Pedro's lifeless body.

He tried to think of a place to put Pedro's body but Jason couldn't think straight.

"Car," he muttered and stumbled towards his car parked in the garage. He opened the trunk and slowly lowered Pedro inside, then ran back into the house, cleaned the blood from the floor with bleach, showered, and got dressed in a white t-shirt and shorts and a pair of sneakers. He threw the blood-stained clothes, including Pedro's, and the towels into the built-in barbecue on the patio, dosed the lot with petrol from a jerrycan and set it ablaze. Some useless advice from a television programme he once watched about crime scene investigation that just came in handy.

Jason walked back to the car and dropped the jerrycan behind the passenger seat.

"The key. Where's the key? Fuck no-no-no. He took the key. Fuck!"

Jason ran back into the house, into Patrick's office, and glanced over the desk to see if Patrick might have left it there. "Where would it be?"

Jason stood in one spot and slowly spun around.

"Kitchen," Jason ran to the kitchen, opened one of the cupboards where all the spare keys hung on hooks, and found his car key.

The buzzer at the main gate rang by the front door.

"Oh my god." Jason began to panic. It couldn't be Patrick. Maybe the press, or the police. Jason walked to the intercom and looked at the CCTV image of a woman.

"Yes?"

"Oh, hello, it's Mrs. Padwick from next door," a woman said in a Texan accent. "Is that you, Jason?"

"Yes, Mrs. Padwick, it's me." His legs felt like jelly and he wanted to sit down.

"Young man, have you by any chance seen my little Moo-Moo? My pussy has gone missing and I'm starting to get really worried. He has never been away for so long."

"No, Mrs. Padwick, I haven't seen your pussy. Maybe he's in heat again?"

"No, my dear, he's been a good boy since he was snipped many years ago."

"I'll keep an eye out for him."

"Please be so kind as to bring him home for me if you do see him. I just hope nothing happened to my little tomcat. I'm so worried about him."

"Yes, Mrs. Padwick, I'll be sure to let you know if I spot your pussy somewhere in our garden chasing birds."

"Thank you, dear. God bless you and your family. Oh, by the way, how's your mother doing? Have you heard anything from her? It's been such a long time."

Jason looked at the frail old woman in black and white on the screen. "No, ma'am. I need to go."

"What happened this morning? I heard some police and a gun shot and some screaming."

"Nothing. I need to go."

"That must—," Mrs. Padwick continued before Jason pressed the mute button and watched her stand there for a while as she continued to speak, but she eventually walked off.

Jason slowly and cautiously drove out through the gate, making sure no police or security waited outside. He drove for fifty minutes out of the city into bushland.

He turned onto a dirt road and continued down the narrow, bumpy, partially overgrown track, which suddenly opened up to a dried-out salt pan surrounded by lush bush on all sides. A giant tree stood in the centre. Its branches draped over like greedy fingers.

Jason pulled up beside the tree.

The curled, dried earth cracked under his sneakers as he walked towards the rear of the car with the deafening mating calls of cicadas pulsating through the hot African air. A pack of hungry blow flies dove for his bloodied nostrils and he tried to wave them away.

As he opened the trunk, Pedro's hand swung out and hit Jason on the side of his ribcage with a wheel spanner.

Jason stumbled back a safe distance.

Pedro breathed heavily and looked dazed and confused as he hung halfway from the trunk with dried blood all over his face and part of his body. His hair looked like that of a calf who had just been born.

Pedro fell from the trunk onto the ground in his underwear. He slowly stood. Half of his body was now covered in whitish ash from the dried dam. Within seconds, a cloud of flies zoomed around Pedro's head like black vultures ready to feast on the exposed hole on his scalp.

"Get away from me," Pedro said and swung the spanner one more time.

"I'm sorry," Jason said. He took a step closer. "Put down the wheel spanner." Jason reached out to Pedro with his left hand. "It's okay, Pedro, I don't want to hurt you."

"You already hurt me," Pedro sobbed and swayed from side to side. Tears left snail tracks through the dust on the side of his bloodied cheek.

Jason took another step closer, then touched Pedro's face. "I didn't mean to hurt you." He touched the dried blood on Pedro's face, which felt soft and smelled metallic.

Pedro tilted his head slightly against Jason's palm and looked at him. His left eye was bloodshot, and a mixture of mucus and blood hung from his nose. "Please take me home."

"Okay, don't cry. I will take you back, but first you need to tell me why you did it."

"Did what?"

"Gave those photos to the police."

"I did it for you," Pedro sobbed and took Jason's hand and squeezed it. Pedro's hand felt cold and damp.

"They want to lock me up. Was that your plan?"

"I wanted to protect you from him."

"Protect me? That's not what you do when you want to protect someone, is it?"

"No, please, you have to believe me. I will never do anything to hurt you. I love you."

"You fucked up my plan to get rid of Patrick. Thabo agreed to help me. But no, Pedro the moron just had to do something stupid yet again."

"You wanted to kill your dad?"

"Yes, you fucking idiot. I'll inherit everything when he's gone and I'll be free. But thanks to you, that's not going to happen now because Thabo's been locked up and I'll be next."

"You're fucking sick, man." Pedro begun to laugh hysterically. "You've been using that *kaffir* boy all along." Pedro spat blood into Jason's face. "*You* need to be locked up. You fucking sick fuck."

Jason pulled out a hunting knife from the back of his trousers and casually swung the knife in an uppercut motion into Pedro's stomach. The razor sharp blade slipped into Pedro's abdomen like a warm knife into butter and completely disappeared to the hilt.

"What are—," Pedro gasped with utter disbelief and surprise in his eyes and clung onto Jason's arm.

Jason pulled the knife out and grabbed Pedro by his blood-clotted hair and said, "I love him." Then he began to stab Pedro like a man possessed. He stabbed wherever his hand guided the blade, in Pedro's neck, in the arm, his face through his cheek, in his hand, ribs, legs. A fountain of bright red blood pulsated from a neck wound and spurted down on the thirsty, dry ground.

Pedro stumbled sideways and held onto his intestines rolling out like thread from the gaping stomach wound with one hand, while he tried to staunch the severed artery in his neck with the other.

Jason took a step back and looked at his handiwork as Pedro stumbled and fell onto his knees. The moment felt surreal, like a dream. It felt good.

Within seconds, Pedro's gasps and moaning turned into wordless gurgles as his punctured lung filled with blood. His breaths became spurts while he held his stretched hand at Jason in a desperate final plea for help. But they both knew they had reached the point of no return the moment the knife slid into Pedro's abdomen.

Jason stood there and watched as the dreadful glint of death crept into Pedro's eyes and he slumped over onto his side gasping for air. His breaths became fewer and shorter as he drowned in his own blood.

The swarm of hungry blow flies droned around Pedro and began feasting for life from the dead.

Jason stood frozen, his eyes transfixed on Pedro's gasping mouth, which opened and closed like that of a fish out of water.

After a few minutes Jason took out the jerrycan from behind the passenger seat and walked back to the red-stained ground. Tears rolled down his cheeks while he doused Pedro's body with petrol.

Jason lit his father's gold Zippo lighter and threw it onto Pedro. An immediate loud whoosh of flames shot into the air and the hungry orange fire engulfed Pedro's entire body and began to eat away at his beautiful olive skin.

Pedro's limbs twitched violently as a last spurt of adrenaline surged through him and he suddenly sat up as his muscles contracted. Inhuman gargles were barely drowned out by the sound of cooking flesh.

The erratic movements grew fewer and fainter and eventually stopped, and Pedro's body fell over onto its side. His flesh hissed as the blood under his skin boiled from the intense heat. The skin became black and cracked open. The air filled with the sweet smell of burnt human flesh, similar to that of burned pig skin, mixed with fat and burning hair.

Jason squatted down and vomited violently, with Pedro's screams repeating in his head.

CHAPTER 56

Jason sped down the dirt track with the top down and the jerrycan bouncing on the passenger seat as he headed back to the main road. He looked down at his bloody hands clinging on to the steering wheel. The skin on his knuckles were split from the blows to Pedro's head.

He stopped the car, got out and wiped the blood from his face with his shirt and then rinsed his hands with petrol from the jerrycan.

"Fuck! Shit!" The fuel burned the exposed flesh on his knuckles and instantly dissolved the blood from his skin.

Pedro's gargle kept repeating in his head and the smell of burned body fat stuck deep inside his nose.

Jason stumbled to the centre of the dirt track and vomited once more, mostly foamy gunk.

He took off his clothes and doused them with the small amount of petrol left, then realised he threw Patrick's golden Zippo lighter onto Pedro.

For a moment it crossed Jason's mind to go back to get it.

But instead he threw the blood stained clothes into the bush, jumped back into his sports car only in his underwear, and sped onto the main road with the radio playing at full volume to try and drain out the screams, while he sang at the top of his voice to a Tracy Chapman song.

In the distance, the silhouette of a person stood in the centre of the road and looked like it made stretching moves, like someone doing yoga in the middle of the road.

"Move, fucker." Jason began honking at the pedestrian, but then suddenly realised a traffic officer in a brown uniform waved him down.

Jason slammed on the car brakes, with tires screeching and burning rubber trailing the car, and narrowly missed the man. The car swerved off the road and came to a dusty stop on the gravel.

A moment of dead silence followed while Jason's eyes gawked at the rearview mirror. "Oh my fuck," Jason said. His arms shook and felt numb. He watched as an overweight traffic officer stormed towards him with his pistol drawn.

Jason looked around to see if anything looked out of place inside the car, then at his hands for any blood left, then down at his legs, bare in his underwear.

Jason took a deep breath. "Stay calm. Inhale, exhale."

"Turn off the engine and get out of the car with your hands on your head."

Jason turned off the ignition, unclipped his safety belt, opened the door and slowly stepped out, placing his hands behind his head.

He could feel the cooling sweat rolling down from his armpits over the side of his ribs while the cicadas' deafening calls screeched through the warm air.

"Move towards the rear of the car and keep your hands on your head."

Jason did as instructed and slowly walked towards the rear. His legs shook and felt like jelly, and he suddenly felt the urge to vomit as he could still smell the burning hair inside his nose.

"Have you been drinking, sir?" the traffic cop said as he pulled the car key from the ignition.

"No, sir," Jason said and watched as the man briskly inspected the interior of the car before he walked to where Jason stood.

"Who're you running from?" The officer inspected the scrape marks on the side of the car caused by bushes.

"No, sir, I'm not." Jason tried his best to look as cool and calm as he could.

"Then what's the excuse for driving like a maniac on a public road?" The cop walked around the other side of the car.

"I didn't realise how fast I was driving."

The officer puffed an unconvinced humph and turned his attention towards Jason. "Driving without due care and attention is asking to cause an accident. And is there any reason for you to be driving only in your underwear?"

"I'm just feeling hot."

"Doesn't your expensive Mercedes sports car come with air-con?"

"It does, but I'm just enjoying the sun and the wind over my skin. Is there a law against driving in my underwear?"

"No, as long as you don't expose yourself or speed." The cop suddenly sniffed the air. "Is that petrol I smell?" He took a step away from Jason before he spat a ball of mucus onto the road.

Jason suddenly felt aroused as he looked at the traffic officer.

A few blow flies zoomed around the officer followed by an uncomfortable moment of silence as he gawked at Jason.

"I've asked you a question. Is that petrol I smell?"

"Yes," Jason said while concocting an excuse.

"I'm all ears," the cop said and kept his pistol still visible but slightly lowered.

"My car got stuck without petrol a few kilometres from here, and I had to fill the car with my jerrycan and I accidentally spilled some of the petrol on myself in the process."

The officer took off his sunglasses. "What happened to your face and hands? You got a bruise on your ribs too."

"Oh this? I box, sir." Jason made a few punching jabs in the air. "Bare knuckles."

"Do you now," the cop said unconvinced and walked to the rear of the car, clearly looking for something. "You broke the speed limit by twenty kilometres an hour."

"I didn't realise I did." Jason suddenly noticed the marks where Pedro's body slipped over the bumper, which left a bloody smear mark that had been covered by a layer of dust. *Fuck.*

It looked like the cop noticed the marks as he slightly bent forward and took a closer look.

Don't, Jason thought and glanced at a piece of rock beside his foot and back at the officer, who now had his back turned to Jason. He holstered his pistol and reached out towards the luggage compartment's handle.

Jason gracefully kneeled down. His hand reached for the rock beside his foot while he kept his eyes firmly on the man. *Please don't open it.*

The cicadas' pulsating sound got louder, like they cheered him on, or perhaps tried to warn the cop.

Jason's sweaty fingers stretched out and wrapped around the rock, then stood up.

The officer called on his radio, "Albert to dispatch."

"Dispatch. You may continue, Albert, over," a woman's voice said over the two-way radio.

"I need a check on a vehicle registration number, Lima-Zulu-Charlie-Seven-Nine-Nine-Tango, over."

"Copy that, give me a minute, over."

Jason took a step closer to the officer. Opening the luggage compartment would be the end of Mr. Traffic Officer.

Jason glanced to the side of the road for a place to ditch his body. He briskly walked up to the cop and hit him as hard as he could on the side of his head, just above the ear. He could feel the cop's scull crack before the cop dropped sideways into the long grass.

"Hey! I asked you a question," the cop said. "Where're you from?"

"Northcliffe, sir," Jason said.

"Rich boy driving daddy's car?"

Jason swallowed nervously and said, "It's my car."

"I see, so rich boy driving fancy car. Mommy and daddy must be pretty loaded then. Now tell me, what were you doing all the way out here in the first place?"

"Just wanted to test out the car. I got it last week."

"The dust and scrape marks—looks like you went off road."

"Yes, I drove down a dirt road."

"Going off road with a luxury car like this?"

"It's just a car."

"I need to see your drivers license."

"Albert, this is dispatch. It's a code green, over," the woman said over the radio.

"Copy that. Thank you, dispatch, over and out."

"What's code green?"

"I said, get your license."

As Jason turned around he made sure he hid the rock behind his body. He walked to the driver's side door and dropped the rock inside the car as he took out the paper license from the glove compartment. He walked back to the man, who stood behind the car, scribbling on a small notepad.

"Paper license? You recently passed your driving test and you're already driving like a maniac?" He opened the license and began to copy some of the information onto the notepad. "Jason Rothshen. You're Patrick's son, aren't you?"

"Yes," Jason said with slight hesitation.

The traffic officer stopped writing and closed his notepad and looked at Jason and shook his head with a fake smile. "I'm a little curious about something, Jason. Where exactly did you fill that jerrycan?"

"At a petrol station, of course." Jason smiled. "Why?"

"Which one was it?"

"BP."

"BP? There aren't any BP petrol stations in the area."

"The one near my home."

"The one near your home? You went all the way back home to get it?" The cop looked unconvinced.

"I didn't fill the jerrycan with petrol," Jason said. "It was already filled when I left home. At a BP petrol station in the city last week."

The traffic officer frowned. "Why would you have a can full of petrol with you in the car?"

"You never know when you might need it. Like today. I could have been stuck in the middle of nowhere if I didn't have it with me."

"You are a lucky man indeed, Jason," the officer said and handed back his license. "You can be bloody glad I know Patrick or you would be facing a big fine. Take your keys and get the fuck out of my sight. And if I catch you speeding again, you won't be so lucky, no matter who you are. Do you understand me?"

"Loud and clear, sir."

CHAPTER 57

Jason arrived back home and ran straight to his bedroom, took a shower, got dressed, grabbed a duffle bag and threw in a few pairs of clothes.

"Passport—safe," Jason ran to Patrick's office and pulled the Encyclopaedia Britannica book which opened the panic room. Jason moved the large painting to the side to reveal the five-foot tall safe, home to the most valuable artefacts in the house.

"Keys, where would he keep the keys? Desk, should be in his desk." Jason went straight for Patrick's desk and began to search through the drawers for the long key that opened the safe, with only the top centre drawer locked.

Jason use a large knife from the kitchen and pressed the knife into the side of the drawer and pulled it as hard as he could until it bent.

"Fuck!"

He ran outside to the garden shed on the side of the house next to the servants quarters' and found a large screwdriver, ran back and forced it into the side of the wooden drawer and pulled it with all his strength until the wood surrounding the lock broke.

Jason fell backward against the wooden wall panel which cracked on impact.

He got up and pulled out the drawer and found the twenty-centimetre long key for the safe.

Next to the key laid a small, thick, brown envelope. He opened it. He took a step back from shock. "Oh my fucking god, no, this can't be."

Jason sat on Patrick's chair and gaped at the photos of him and Thabo on the train, plus the one of him with José and Carla. "They were here all along."

The dreadful sound of Pedro drowning in his own blood started to repeat in his head once again.

Jason folded the photos and stuck them into his trousers and ran to the safe. He unlocked it, pulled the heavy reinforced door open, which revealed packs of hard currency in US Dollars and British Pounds, as well as a few small paintings standing at the bottom. One of the paintings was a Picasso which used to hang in Patrick's office. Next to the paintings, was a pistol and a shotgun with enough ammunition to start a small war, and three military-style gas masks.

Jason wiped the tears from his eyes and looked for his passport. He pulled everything from the top shelf, where he found three passports. He opened the first, which belonged to Patrick. The second was his, and he stuck it into his trousers.

He opened the third passport and took a step back.

"Why would her passport be here?" Jason threw Patrick's passport back inside. He grabbed several packs of British currency and walked back to the desk while trying to figure out why his mother's passport was in the safe.

His eye caught a glimpse of something shiny coming from behind the wall panel behind Patrick's desk that he broke minutes earlier.

It looked like another secret storage compartment. He pulled it open and found a cupboard with a silver metal box the size of three men's shoeboxes.

Jason pulled it out and placed it on the desk. It had a removable lock on the side. Jason remembered seeing a bunch of small keys in the locked drawer.

He took out the keys and worked through them until he unlocked the box, then opened the lid. A thin sheet of paper lay on top, similar to the kind in a shoebox covering the shoes.

Jason lifted the sheet of paper, which revealed dozens of photographs turned face down, and VHS video tapes neatly stacked underneath, each labelled with dates and locations.

Jason took out a handful of photos and flicked through them. Each photo contained a different image but of the same nature. Older men with a younger person, some boys and some girls. Most of them looked distressed and teary-eyed, others looked unconscious or semi-unconscious. The photos looked like they had been taken secretly.

Jason turned one of the photos around. A girl's name, age and nationality was written in blue pen. *Maria, 14, Italian, Roger Sheddard MP, London, July 1989.*

"MP? What's MP? Military police? Member of parliament?"

Jason suddenly remembered the photo he grabbed from Pedro many years ago. The photo of uncle Jimmy, which Jason showed to his mother the night before she left.

He pulled out one of the video cassettes dated *1988* and pushed it into the video machine in the office and switched on the TV. Jason glanced at the clock on the wall. Patrick should be back in about two hours.

The video, which had muffled sound, looked like it bad been recorded from the top of a table. It showed a naked older man, partly bald with glasses, overweight with a belly, walking towards a bed with a very young-looking girl, much younger than Jason, sitting on the side of the bed. She looked drunk.

"Lay down on your back," the man instructed the girl and lifted her dress before he pulled her underwear down.

He quickly glanced through the rest of the contents in the box and found a video with the name *Jimmy* written on it.

When he played the tape, he recognised his own bedroom from several years earlier. It was recorded from an angle which appeared to be somewhere near the wardrobe or the bookshelf.

Uncle Jimmy walked into the room and stood beside Jason's bed.

Jason suddenly had a flashback of the man standing in the corner. The smell of burnt timber.

Jason hit the eject button. He couldn't watch any more.

He picked up a small black book with a red string tied around it and removed the string with shaking hands. Inside were the names, dates and telephone numbers of men with titles such as Lord and Sir, written in black ink, in Patrick's distinctive handwriting. Next to them were numbers that looked like payments of some sort.

Father Michael's name appeared at the very bottom of one of the pages with a location and a date not so long ago.

Jason heard a car driving up towards the front of the house and quickly glanced through the window. "Oh, no-no-no." Jason threw the money into his bag with the black book and both passports and ran towards the rear of the house. He flew out of the back door by the kitchen and slipped around the house through the plants, and watched as Patrick got out of the car and took a large bag out of the car's trunk and walked towards the front door.

Jason tiptoed to his car, quietly opened the door, shifted it into neutral and let it roll down towards the gate. He didn't take his eyes off the rearview mirror.

Chapter 58

Patrick entered the house, threw his jacket onto the chair near the door and noticed a strong smell of bleach in the reception hall. He looked at his beloved collection of tribal masks but couldn't figure out what was out of place.

Then it occurred to him: it looked like someone had swapped two of the masks.

Patrick switched them back and called, "Jason," before he made his way to the kitchen.

"Jason, come down to the kitchen." Patrick poured himself a glass of orange juice and placed a black pouch on the counter. He opened it and took out a syringe doctor Swanepoel had given him.

He took a sip of his juice and listened. Not a single sound except from his watch ticking away the seconds.

"Jason." He walked towards the stairs, waited for a few seconds. "Jason, I'm calling you."

Patrick climbed the stairs to Jason's room. Clothes and things were strewn around everywhere, and the wardrobes stood open.

"Jason, I'm not calling you again!"

Patrick briskly marched to his office and, as he entered, he almost screamed from shock when he saw the silver box on his desk and the panic room door wide open.

"What the fuck." A robbery was the first thing that came to his mind.

Patrick grabbed the phone and began to dial the police. "Fuck, I can't," he said and looked at the silver box and placed the phone down.

He went through the contents of the box and couldn't find the black book. "Where the fuck is it?" He searched all around. "Fuck." Patrick ran into the panic room and saw the safe stood open.

The first things he checked were the small black velvet bags that contained diamonds, and the Picasso painting, both still there. The weapons were also accounted for.

He looked at the top shelf and realised some of the cash had been taken and two passports were gone.

Patrick opened the remaining passport, which belonged to him.

"No." Patrick burst into a cold sweat and ran to his desk, punched in a phone number. The phone rang a few times.

"Van Rooyen," the person answered.

"It's Patrick. You need to get your men and find Jason, now."

"Why, what happened?"

"He stole money from my safe and he's got his passport."

"What am I supposed to do about that? That's a domestic issue."

"He stole valuable documents and money from my safe. Do you understand? You need to find him."

"What type of documents are we talking about?"

"A small black notebook with a red string around it and an old passport of my ex-wife."

"Passport?"

"Find him, find the documents and I'll take care of the rest."

"Well, if you told me that earlier we could have brought him in with the gardener."

"You have to stop him before he gets on a plane."

"Where do we start?"

"The fucking airport, obviously."

"There are several airports around the city, Patrick."

Fucking imbecile. "The main airport with an international terminal, of which there's only one, yes? He has a passport, which means he's about to leave the country."

"Do you really think your son is that clever to grab documents and jump on an international flight?"

"Just do as I ask and find that little shit."

"Fine, but you know Deventer will find out about this as soon as we head out."

"Fuck no, it's out of the question. I need this done discreetly. Please, Van Rooyen, you need to get those two items without anyone else knowing."

"He's my boss, Patrick, he knows everything that happens in our unit, and he went ballistic when he realised the photos had disappeared."

"If this situation gets out of control, things will go south for many people, including you. I will not be pulled down by a weak link. Get your shit together and find him as soon as possible and let me know once you have him, then I'll take it from there. And keep that cunt Deventer out of the picture, otherwise *you* might disappear from the face of the earth."

Patrick placed the phone down and took out his little secret stash of powder. The ultimate remedy for a stressful situation.

He scraped two lines and snorted it.

CHAPTER 59

Jason parked the car in an industrial area very near to the airport, on a quiet street beside an abandoned building. Before he got out, he put on a baseball cap, then took his bag out. He poured the remaining petrol from the jerrycan over the interior of the car and the trunk and threw a match inside.

The car burst into flames.

He took out the pack of photos of him and Thabo and tossed it into the burning car.

Jason briskly walked down a narrow path in the direction of the airport.

Twenty minutes later, Jason walked into the concrete terminal building and looked back from where he just came and saw a plume of grey smoke drifting into the air.

He was neatly dressed up in a white shirt with the sleeves rolled up, light brown Chinos and blue boat shoes. He took off the cap and quickly finger-combed his curly milky blond hair before going directly to the flight reservations counter.

A young Caucasian woman stood behind the counter and smiled at him with perfect teeth and a flawless face, sea blue eyes and blood red lips, and dressed immaculately in a figure-hugging navy blue jacket with a white blouse conservatively buttoned to the top. "Good afternoon, sir," she said as Jason approached. "How may I help today?"

"I need a ticket to London. What time is your next flight?"

"We have one flight to London daily and it departs at 7:30 p.m."

Jason looked at his watch. It was just after 5 p.m. "It's too late. Just give me a second." He pondered for a moment. "How about Paris or Madrid?"

"There's a flight to Paris which departs twenty minutes earlier."

"I'll take the one to Paris then."

"Certainly, sir. Please give me a moment while I check if there are still available seats on tonight's flight."

Jason placed his leather bag on the counter and tapped his fingers impatiently. "What time does the flight depart again?"

"Boarding is at six-thirty, departure is at seven-ten."

"Anything?"

"I'm sorry, sir. Unfortunately, there are no available seats left in economy on tonight's flight. Would you perhaps like to reserve a seat on tomorrow evening's flight?"

"How about first class?"

She leaned forward. Her hand slightly covered her mouth as if about to reveal a big secret, and whispered, "The seats in first class are rather pricey going to Paris, sir, especially when booked last minute."

Jason pulled out a pack of banknotes from his bag and plonked it in front of her. "How much?"

The reservations clerk smiled and pushed over a form and said, "If you could sign this form, the amount for a first class seat is displayed at the bottom, then all I need from you is your passport."

Jason slid his passport across the counter.

"Oh wow," the reservations clerk said. "Now that's a surprise. I didn't realise you were British, sir. You don't have an accent."

"No, I don't," Jason said and pushed the signed form back with a pile of banknotes.

The reservations clerk took a step closer and ogled Jason with her sea blue eyes and pointed at her own nose.

"What?" Jason said.

"You have some *blood* coming from your nose." She handed him a tissue. "Were you in some kind of a physical altercation, sir?"

Jason noticed she was looking at his bruised knuckles.

His thoughts jumped back to Pedro's hysterical screams as he fell to the dried earth and gasped for air. The stench of burning human flesh returned to his nose.

Jason took a deep breath and gathered his thoughts. "No, just a little accident I had earlier. Could you please just give me the ticket? I'm in a hurry."

"Oh, yes, certainly," the reservations clerk said with a flirtatious giggle, her hand slightly over her plump red lips. She took the money and paperwork. "Let me quickly process this for you. If you don't mind taking a seat, you can wait beside the lady over there."

Jason took the indicated seat next to an old woman in a dull purple dress with a matching hat, busy indulging in a sandwich while reading a book.

Jason leaned forward and rested his elbows on his knees. The gargling sound of Pedro gasping for air repeated in his head.

An unpleasant and overwhelming plume of granny perfume with strong floral notes hung like a curtain around the old woman. The stench of the perfume invaded Jason's nostrils and he could feel a sneeze developing. He tried to contain the sneeze, but it erupted from Jason's swollen nose and broke the silence. A clot of blood shot out from his nostrils and splattered on the floor.

"Oh deary-dear," the old woman said and took out a white handkerchief from her brown crocodile leather handbag and held the embroidered fabric out at Jason. "Are you alright, young man?" she said in a toff British accent.

"Why?" Jason said rudely.

"There's blood coming from your nose, young man. Is everything alright?"

"How about you mind your own fucking business," Jason said and stuffed the tissue the reservations clerk gave him inside his nostril.

"You rude little twerp," the old woman muttered and shoved back into her seat. "Youth of today. No respect for anyone."

"Mr. Jason Rothshen?" the reservations clerk called out a few minutes later. "It's all done for you, sir."

Jason walked up to the counter where the reservations clerk stood holding the ticket against her chest.

Her jacket had miraculously disappeared, and her white formal work shirt was unbuttoned to the centre, just enough to reveal her curvy, youthful breasts. She leaned forward with the ticket in her hand and said, "Here you go, Jason," and pointed with her red nails. "This is the departure time and gate number. Just follow the signs to the international departures check-in area, which is located just to the right. You can see the big sign."

"Thank you so much," Jason said with a sense of relief, fully aware of the reservations clerk's flirtatious behaviour.

Jason winked at her with a cheeky smile, grabbed his bag and walked in the direction of the check-in counter.

CHAPTER 60

Jason sat in the VIP departure lounge beside a window that overlooked the runway. He opened his bag and took out the tiny wooden box, swallowed one of the morphine pills and stretched out on the comfy sofa. Soon his eyes began to feel heavy. The lounge became quieter as he drifted off.

A slight breeze blew over Jason's face and rustled his blond hair.

He opened his eyes from a grunting sound beside him.

He looked towards his left. The dark figure stood in the doorway of a tin shack and a cool breeze came from his direction. The figure wore some type of mask with a pipe mounted to the front, similar to that of a chemical warfare gas mask. He swayed from side to side and excreted a sweet cucumber smell.

"I haven't seen you for some time," Jason whispered and reached out to the figure.

"I will keep you safe. But only if you stop taking the pills."

"Or what?"

The figure took hold of Jason's head and began to crush it between his hands.

"No," Jason yelled.

Jason opened his eyes. He laid on the carpet, soaked in sweat. Bewildered passengers pointed and whispered amongst themselves.

Jason took his bag, and out of embarrassment, kept his head down as he briskly walked to the restroom. He splashed his face with water, then inspected his swollen bruised nose and dark circles under each eye.

Suddenly he saw Pedro's reflection in the mirror.

He turned around.

It had only been an illusion. His eyes began to play tricks on him.

He patted his face with paper towel and took another morphine tablet.

An announcement came over the P.A. system. "AF zero-three-zero to Paris is now boarding at gate B. All passengers on Air France flight zero-three-zero to Paris, please make your way to boarding gate B."

CHAPTER 61

Jason wiped tears from his eyes and returned to the departure gate, then joined the crowd of passengers crossing the tarmac to the humming Boeing aeroplane.

"Good evening, sir, welcome aboard," a flight attendant greeted and checked Jason's ticket. "First class is to your left. Have a pleasant flight, sir."

Jason walked through an open curtain and searched for his seat.

He could smell granny's floral perfume hanging in the air. The old woman in the purple dress sat in the seat next to his.

The old woman looked at Jason through her massive reading glasses and said, "Now look at that." She pulled out a pack of cigarettes from her handbag. "They just had to give you a seat next to me."

"Seems to be my lucky day," Jason said and plunked down next to her.

A half hour later, after everyone had been seated and the aeroplane door securely closed, a voice came through the speakers. "Good evening, ladies and gentlemen. On behalf of Captain Dupont and the entire crew, we would like to welcome you aboard Air France flight zero-three-zero, non-stop service to Paris. My name is Juliette and I am your cabin crew in charge. Our flight time to Paris will be approximately ten hours and forty minutes. Please ensure your seat is in its upright position, your tray table is stowed, and your seat belt is fastened. If you need any assistance, please ask a member of the crew, who will be happy to assist. Thank you."

The old woman in purple smoked away on a long colourful cigarette and blew her smoke in Jason's direction.

"Excuse me, can you blow your smoke the other way?" Jason said.

"Maybe you should find a different seat," the old woman said and blew another cloud of smoke in his face.

"Excuse me," Jason said to a passing flight attendant and pointed at the woman smoking beside him.

In a friendly but assertive tone, the flight attendant said, "Madam, please extinguish your cigarette immediately. We are about to take off, and you need to put your seat belt on."

The old woman huffed and puffed and extinguished her cigarette in the armrest ashtray and said, "Get your bloody hands off me. I can do the seat belt myself, thank you very much. I might be old but I'm not paralysed."

Jason stood and moved to an empty seat beside the window.

He took out his mother's passport and looked at it again as the aeroplane began to taxi towards the runway.

It suddenly stopped, and an announcement came over the P.A. system:

"Ladies and gentlemen, this is your captain. We're experiencing a slight technical issue and will be returning to the terminal. Please remain seated and keep your seat belt fastened at all times and wait for further instructions. Head crew, please report to the flight deck immediately."

"This is not fucking happening," Jason whispered to himself and nervously looked out the window and then at his watch. The time had passed 7:15 p.m.

The aeroplane crept in the direction of the terminal building. The old woman in the purple dress grabbed Juliette as she walked past, and in a distressed tone said, "What on earth is going on? What technical problem is there? Is there a bomb on the aeroplane?"

"Madam, like the captain said, everything is okay. Please remain seated and wait for further instructions. And please, madam, could you refrain from smoking?" She took the cigarette from the old woman's fingers and briskly marched into the flight deck and shut the door.

Seconds later, Juliette reappeared and walked briskly toward the rear of first class and disappeared behind the dark blue curtain cordoning off first class from the cabin crew area.

Whispers between members of the cabin crew grew louder from behind the closed curtains. Juliette peeked her head through the curtains and appeared to be searching for something or someone, then pulled her head back and swiftly closed the curtains.

Jason reclined his seat and looked towards the blue curtains. He could hear the aeroplane door being unlocked and opened soon after they stopped taxiing.

Juliette came over to him and said, "Excuse me, are you Jason Rothshen?"

Jason's body went cold the moment he heard his name.

"This is not happening," he whispered to himself.

He heard some commotion from behind, turned around and saw a police officer through the gap between the seats.

"Fuck," Jason said to himself and felt like he wanted to melt into the seat.

"Mr. Rothshen? Please come with us," Juliette said.

Jason looked away and pretended to be somewhere else.

The police officer grabbed Jason by his shirt and jerked him into the aisle. Buttons from his shirt flew in all directions.

Still wearing his seat belt, Jason hung halfway over the side of the seat into the aisle and looked up at the police office and said, "I don't know anything."

"You are under arrest," the police officer said and cuffed Jason. He marched him out of the humming aeroplane towards the terminal building, where a police car waited for them.

CHAPTER 62

Patrick waited in anticipation in his office for *the* call.

"Where the fuck are they?" he said and tapped impatiently on his desk.

The phone finally rang.

"Yes?" Patrick answered before he even brought the phone to his ear.

"We got him," Van Rooyen said.

"Where are you now?"

"I'm at the station."

"The police station? Then where's Jason?"

"We had to book him in. Deventer's instructions."

Patrick felt like he wanted to break the telephone over Van Rooyen's head. "Jesus, Van Rooyen, what the fuck. I clearly said to you I will deal with it, for fuck's sake. Which station is he held at?"

"Central."

"Did you find *it*?"

"We'll do a search of his bag now. Will keep you posted."

Patrick slammed the phone down. "What a fucking moron." He punched a number on the phone and it rang.

"Put me through to Dr. Swanepoel, tell him it's Patrick Rothshen. It's an emergency."

"Patrick, what can I do for you?" Swanepoel answered.

"We have a little situation. You need to get Jason out of the central police station ASAP."

"Why is he in a police station?"

"He stole from me and was about to leave the country when the police intercepted him. They stupidly took him to the central police station where he's being held."

"I can do that, but you need to arrange a court order to release him into my care under the mental health act."

"One of the judges owes me a favour. I'll get my lawyer to accompany you to the police station. Give me a minute and I'll call you back."

Patrick hung up and made another call.

"Richard Edwards," a man answered.

"Richard, it's Patrick, how are you my friend?"

"What do you want, Patrick?" the judge said, sounding slightly agitated.

"Jason has been locked up."

"What does that have to do with me?"

"I need you to sign a court order for Jason to be released into the custody of Dr. Swanepoel. You see, he's suffering from a mental illness and he got himself into a little bit of a mess."

"And why should I help you?"

"Let's just say that he laid his hands on *something* that will incriminate you and will point back to me eventually."

"You're not talking about what I think you're talking about."

"I wouldn't call you if it wasn't serious."

"Jesus, Patrick, I thought we were over this after the previous favour I did for you."

"After this everything will disappear. You have my word. But it's important that he gets released as soon as the doctor gets there."

"Fine, I'll do it, but on one condition. I get everything you have on me. I will destroy it myself."

"You can collect it tonight if you want, in person at my house."

"Send your lawyer to my office. I'll get an order set up."

"Thank you, Richard."

"Fuck you, Patrick." The judge slammed the phone down.

"Someone's slightly pissed off," Patrick said and sniffed a line of coke and pushed back in his chair. "This has turned into a complete shit show."

CHAPTER 63

Van Rooyen walked into the interrogation room where Jason was being detained. Jason sat in a chair opposite one of the booking officers with his hands cuffed in front of him. "Where's the bag?" Van Rooyen said.

"On the floor behind me," the booking officer said while he scribbled something in a book.

"Has the bag been searched?"

"Not yet. I'm just finishing this then I'll do it."

"Go get us a coffee, then I'll get things started," Van Rooyen said and stood to the side and waited for the booking officer to walk out.

One of Van Rooyen's cronies entered as the booking office walked out and stood in front of Jason and said, "Take off your clothes."

"For what?" Jason said.

"Routine search to make sure you don't have any weapons on you. Now get them off. I don't have all day."

"You're gonna regret treating me like this," Jason said and pulled down his trousers and underwear and looked straight into Van Rooyen's eyes, who in turn looked at him with a smirk.

"Are you just going to stand there and look at me?" Jason said.

"Arrogant little shit," Van Rooyen said and took Jason's brown leather duffel bag and opened it. "Can see it runs in the family."

"Bend over," the other officer instructed.

Jason kept his eyes on Van Rooyen who had his hands deep inside the bag.

"All the way," the man said and pushed Jason's head down before he grabbed Jason's bum cheeks and pulled them apart to check for any forbidden objects.

Van Rooyen began to take out Jason's clothes, piece by piece as he looked for the objects as instructed.

"Get dressed and sit down," the officer said. "He's clean."

"Are you going to tell me why I've been arrested?"

Van Rooyen placed a pack of banknotes that he found in the bag on the table. "Care to tell me where you got all this money?"

"Do you know who my dad is?" Jason said with a haughty expression on his face. "I demand a phone call." Jason stood up.

"Please sit down, Jason," Van Rooyen said calmly and bit on his lip to keep himself from smacking the spoilt brat.

"I want my fucking phone call now."

Van Rooyen turned the bag upside down and dropped the rest of the contents on the table. He knew he had to find the items before the booking officer returned. A small wooden box engraved in a foreign script fell out with a few other items, including a golden pen and another passport.

Just as Van Rooyen picked up the other passport, the door opened and his boss, superintendent Deventer, walked in. "I told you to wait for me before you begin the search," Deventer said and looked slightly bewildered as he walked up to the desk.

"Only started," Van Rooyen said and put the passport down partly hidden behind some shirts.

"You should've called me before you opened that bag."

"Like I said, I just opened it. I wanted to get this done as soon as possible so we can get him processed."

"You need to follow protocol, Van Rooyen. I'm not telling you again."

Fuck off, you anal fuck. "Yes, superintendent."

Deventer picked up Jason's passport and inspected it for a moment. Van Rooyen knew Deventer saw the other passport partly hidden behind some clothes. "So who's passport is that one then?" Deventer said.

Van Rooyen kept quiet and watched as Deventer picked up the other passport.

"Sarah-Jane Rothshen," Deventer said and looked at Jason. "Why are you carrying your mother's passport?"

"Who the fuck are you?" Jason said. "Lawyer. Now."

"Like father, like son," Deventer said, "rude to the core. Everyone seems to want a lawyer these days, even your garden boy, what's his name?" Deventer snapped his fingers as he pretend to think. "Lethabo, that's right, Lethabo Molefe. Stinky little fucker, he is. Tell me, did you teach him that while he was fucking you?"

"Where is Thabo?" Jason kicked against the table. "Where is he?"

"Bag it, book it and make copies of Sarah-Janes's passport and leave it on my desk," Deventer said to Van Rooyen.

"Get up," Deventer instructed Jason and took him by the arm.

"I want my fucking call," Jason demanded.

"You've been watching too many American movies, boy. In here you don't have any rights, no matter how much money you have."

Deventer pushed Jason out the door to the holding cells.

Thabo pulled himself up and walked towards the door and listened. He recognised the familiar voice of Jason swearing and arguing with Deventer. It got louder as they got closer.

The cell door beside him closed and locked.

"I want my fucking call," Jason yelled.

Thabo began to laugh, but he wasn't sure why. Perhaps out of happiness that he was reunited with Jason in a way, or maybe because the behaviour was so typical of Jason.

Thabo waited for the clicking keys and squeaking shoes to disappear. "Jason?" Thabo whispered through the food slot in the door.

"Thabo, is that you?"

"Yes." Thabo felt like he had regained some energy. "I'm so glad to hear your voice."

"Are you okay?" Jason said.

"I'm okay, are you okay?"

"I'm fine, just need to get out of this place."

"Why are you here?" Thabo said. "What happened?"

"I think it's about the photos we took on the train. No one wants to tell me what the fuck is going on. They don't even want to give me my phone call."

"Me too. We should never have taken those photos in the first place," Thabo said with a raised voice.

"Keep your voice down," Jason hissed.

"How did they find the photos?"

"Pedro."

"I knew it." Thabo kicked the door.

"Shh," Jason hissed. "I don't think that's why we were arrested because those photos were given to my dad the same night we arrived back."

"Who gave it to your dad?"

"Someone in the police is secretly working for my dad."

Thabo stopped for a moment and tried to process what Jason said. "So the police don't have them anymore?"

"No."

"I think I know who it is," Thabo said.

"What do you mean?"

"The pig working for your dad. I think I know who it is."

"Who?"

"Van Rooyen."

"He was the guy in the room when they searched me."

"Tall guy with short blond hair and very blue eyes?"

"That's him."

"He's the one who lashed me many years ago."

"The marks on your back?"

"Yes."

"Asshole. He does look like a real cunt. I have to ask you something. You need to be honest with me now."

Thabo waited for the question. "Yes?"

"Were you planning to kill us?"

"Don't be crazy," Thabo said. "You know every part of me. I'm not like that. Why would you even think that?"

"The police told my dad your mother was planning something to harm us and you were involved too."

"My mother was drinking with those two guys from some resistance movement, nothing else. She's not like that. And I have done nothing wrong, except for loving you."

"You mean that?"

"Yes, of course."

"Fuck." Jason sighed. "We have to get out of this place."

"We need to make a plan. Whoever comes out first waits for the other one at a secret place."

"I agree," Jason said.

"Where?"

"Let me think," Jason said and went silent.

"How about the bus stop?" Thabo said. "The one where you dropped me off the one night."

"Okay, but how?"

"There is a large rock near the roadside," Thabo whispered, then paused as he listened for any footsteps. He continued, "We can leave some type of mark on the rock. Whoever gets there first makes the mark and has to go back every day to check if the other person made a second mark. If there's a second mark made by me, then you must wait there the following day. If it's you, I know you will be at your house."

"Sounds a bit silly."

"Do you have a better suggestion?"

"Fine. We can use a simple sign. How about you're the plus sign and I'm the equal sign."

And you said my idea is silly, Thabo thought. "Okay, I'll be the plus. I'm so hungry now. I haven't eaten for a long time. My stomach hurts so much."

"When we get out of this place, we will go to the best restaurant in London, just the two of us, and we will eat the biggest and best steaks you have ever tasted."

"I've never tasted a steak."

"You're kidding me."

"Don't you remember? I don't eat beef."

"No, you never mentioned that. Anyway, imagine the biggest, fattest, juiciest succulent chicken breast you have ever had."

"Fried?"

"Fried to perfection by the best chef in Mayfair."

"Whoo," Thabo said with his back against the door and slowly slid down to the ground while he visualised taking a big bite out of a juicy fried chicken breast.

Thabo began to cry and couldn't imagine what it would be like to live without the daily discrimination he's gotten so used to.

"Are you crying?" Jason whispered.

"No," Thabo said and wiped the tears from his face with his cold, shrivelled hands. "I'm just so happy you are here with me."

"Happy I got fucking locked up?"

Suddenly, a stampede of footsteps headed their way, accompanied by the voices of several men, perhaps four or five speaking at the same time.

Thabo stood up and moved away from the door and waited for his door to open. But the shoes went past.

Jason moved away from the door the moment it was unlocked and watched as the door swung open. In walked a tall man with large, black, square glasses and bushy sideburns, flanked by two men in white uniform. Van Rooyen, Deventer and some other person, presumably Patrick's lawyer, followed.

Jason backed up against the wall as he recognised the man with the sideburns. Dr. Swanepoel, who he hadn't seen for several years. Not since the last time he got treated.

The doctor placed his briefcase on the concrete bed. "Hello, Jason, remember me?"

"Of course I remember you," Jason said and slowly moved along the wall to get away from him. "My dad sent you, didn't he?"

"I'm here on behalf of the Rothshen trust to take you to a better facility."

"Why have I been locked up in this fucking shithole in the first place?"

"From my understanding, you've already been informed by the police about the details of your arrest. Any uncertainties should be raised with them, as this falls outside my scope of work. Right now, my job is to assess you in order for us to move forward from here without any hiccups."

"I haven't been informed of anything by these uneducated pigs. Not even a phone call."

Dr. Swanepoel approached Jason and took out a penlight from his jacket pocket. "I just need to check your eyes."

"Don't touch me." Jason slapped the penlight out of the doctor's hand.

"Calm down, Jason, there's no need to panic. I'm on your side."

The doctor bent over and whispered, "Let me do my job so that I can get you out of this dirty place."

"Yeah fucking right, like you did the last time?"

"The quicker you cooperate, the quicker we can all get out of this cell and the faster you can get back to normal life."

"Get your fucking hands off me!" Jason shoved against the wall in the corner of the bed and curled into a ball like a frightened little boy.

"Jason, I'm not going to hurt you," the doctor said and leaned closer.

Jason kicked Swanepoel on his arm. "Get off me, you motherfucker." Jason began to scream hysterically.

"That's it," Swanepoel said and pinned Jason down on the concrete bed, and said to the two men in white uniform, "grab his arms."

Van Rooyen stood there and laughed and said something to Deventer.

"Get off me!" Jason cried out and spat one of the men in the face.

Swanepoel pulled out a syringe with a long needle and a tiny bottle from his jacket pocket and said to one of the uniforms, "Pull his pants down." The doctor extracted some light yellow liquid from the bottle.

Jason twisted violently and kept screaming and crying. "Please, why are you doing this? Help! Please stop, no please, not again."

"Hold him still, for God's sake." Swanepoel jabbed the syringe into Jason's inner thigh and emptied the yellowish content in two seconds flat.

"Fuck," Jason cried out with saliva shooting from his mouth like a dog infected with rabies.

"He's definitely displaying symptoms of drug withdrawal," Swanepoel said as he casually placed the syringe into the briefcase.

"You quack," Jason yelled. He felt the drug crawl into his muscles and fell back onto the ground and looked upwards at distant people standing over him. His muscles began to tense and the sound of white noise got louder in his ears until the ground sucked him in and everything blurred. He couldn't move.

Swanepoel took out a cigarette and lit it. He stood back and watched with the others while Jason's body pulled and shuffled as the anti-psychotic medication took control of his entire body.

Within five minutes, Jason lay on his back in a dream-like state with his body tensed and his head turned sideways. His eyes gazed sightlessly forward. His teeth were clenched. He breathed heavily. Swanepoel pulled down Jason's bottom eyelid and shone the penlight into his eye. "Bring the jacket."

The two assistants dressed Jason with a white straitjacket and tied the brown leather straps to the rear of the jacket, then lifted him by the shoulders and the feet and carried him out into a waiting vehicle.

CHAPTER 64

Tuesday, 13 November 1990.

Random coughs and the occasional scream broke the cold silence in the row of tiny cells in the central police station.

Thabo laid naked and curled up in a bundle on the concrete bed in the corner, weak from hunger. His stomach cramped and made the most unholy sounds. The unbearable throbbing pain in his abdomen increased and crept deeper into his intestines.

The haunting sound of squeaking shoes and dangling keys came closer. Thabo's cell door unlocked, and two men walked in. One of them held a pair of handcuffs.

"Get up."

"Please, sir," Thabo pleaded, "no more."

"Get up," the man repeated. "You better get up or I will pull you like a sack of potatoes down this corridor."

"Please, no," Thabo sobbed.

"Fine, have it your way." The man put Thabo in a headlock while the second one cuffed him.

Both the men pulled Thabo up the stairs to the tenth floor and into room 1026, a sparse room with only a desk and a few chairs and some paperwork lying around.

Inspector Van Rooyen sat behind the desk and smoked a cigarette. A cloud of smoke hung above his head. To the right of Van Rooyen hung an analog wall clock reading 6:40 a.m.

"Is he refusing to cooperate?" Van Rooyen said and took a long drag from his cigarette.

"He's been acting up again," one of the officers said. "Pretending he can't walk."

Van Rooyen rose from the squeaking green office chair and walked up to Thabo. "Look at me."

Thabo looked at Van Rooyen as he hung limp between the two police officers. A plume of smoke left Van Rooyen's mouth like an angry dragon. Van Rooyen took another long drag from his cigarette with its coal turning red and long.

Without any warning, Van Rooyen brought the burning cigarette down with a swift movement and extinguished it on Thabo's forehead. Red pieces of smouldering ash scattered in all directions.

Thabo screamed with pain and stood upright and tried to break free from the two officers.

"Oh, now the thing can stand," Van Rooyen said and began to laugh and held his arms in the air like a priest. "Say hallelujah, it's a miracle. The black man can walk again."

Van Rooyen walked to the other side of the table. "Bring him over here so I can do those fingerprints and get his smelly ass out of my office.

"Open your hand," Van Rooyen ordered and pressed Thabo's fingers on a black ink pad and forcefully rolled them one by one on a piece of paper.

"Other hand," Van Rooyen said and slapped Thabo over the head. "I said other fucking hand."

Van Rooyen slapped Thabo a second time, hitting him in the same place.

Thabo broke free from Van Rooyen's grip and punched him in the mouth.

The unexpected blow threw Van Rooyen backward. He stumbled against the corner of the desk and touched his mouth with his left hand, and with the other gestured to the two police officers to stay back as he spat out a broken piece of tooth.

"You motherfucking black bastard," Van Rooyen said and walked up to Thabo and punched him in the face, then grabbed Thabo's arms and pulled them behind his back.

He pushed Thabo in the direction of the window. "Assaulting a police officer. Someone needs to teach this fucker a lesson."

Van Rooyen cuffed Thabo's hands and pushed the window open. A gust of city air grabbed the window and swung it wide. The echoes of morning prayers from the nearby mosque floated along the morning breeze.

"Do you know Humpty Dumpty?" Van Rooyen said and began to sing, "Humpty Dumpty sat on the wall," and pushed Thabo's head through the open window and lifted Thabo by his torso and pushed his upper body through the opening.

Thabo's body twisted around. He tried to grab hold of the bottom of the window frame as he looked back at Van Rooyen, who had a glint of evil in his eyes.

"Please," Thabo said and could feel himself falling backwards and the air blowing over his naked skin. His life flashed before his eyes. His mother giving him a hug, his brothers laughing with him, and Jason holding his hand.

Thabo could feel Van Rooyen loosen his grip. Thabo knew this moment would come. His mother warned him about it the day she got so angry when he left with Jason.

"What the fuck are you doing?" superintendent Deventer grabbed Thabo's arm and pulled him in and at the same time pushed Van Rooyen out of the way.

Thabo fell to the floor. Everything felt like a dream to him.

"What the fuck did you just try to do Van Rooyen?" Deventer yelled.

"This black bastard assaulted me. Look at my mouth."

"I gave you clear instructions to process his fingerprints and let him go, didn't I?"

"He fucking assaulted me." Van Rooyen spat a gob of blood.

"Did I give you an instruction, Van Rooyen?"

"Yes, superintendent."

"Then why the fuck is he hanging from an open window like a scene from Batman? I have had it with your shit, up to fucking here."

Deventer took a key from his pocket and unlocked the cuffs and threw an old shirt and trousers at Thabo. "Put that on and get the fuck out of here. You are free to go."

Thabo looked up at Deventer and said, "Why?"

"Because we're not going to charge you."

"Why have I been arrested? You locked me up for no reason and then let me go without any explanation."

"Mr. Molefe, you are free to go, so I'm telling you now to take this opportunity and get dressed in the clean clothes I gave you and walk out of this police station before I change my mind."

Thabo gathered the strength and put on the brown t-shirt and olive trousers and followed Deventer to an elevator. He took them to the basement car park, the same way they came in, and escorted him past the security booth to a large iron gate that led to freedom. Deventer opened the gate.

Thabo stepped outside and looked back at Deventer, who glanced at Thabo for a brief moment before he disappeared back into the dark car park.

Thabo stumbled along the sidewalk towards the hustle and bustle of people and shops and street vendors. Hungry and tired, he desperately needed something to eat in the hope it would stop the burning and cramping inside his stomach.

Thabo looked like a malnourished homeless person with a fresh burn mark on his forehead and dirt stuck in his nappy hair. He wore only the oversized clothes Deventer gave him—not even shoes.

People stepped around him and looked at him with disgust.

Thabo followed the distinctive aroma of freshly baked bread to the entrance of a small bakery with an orange sign above the door proclaiming Bettie's Bakery. He stopped and peered inside.

A white woman behind the counter was busy packing pasties into a glass display. She stopped and glanced back at Thabo. "What do you want?" she said in a tone that could only be described as hostile.

"Something to eat please, madam," Thabo said and held his hands together like a beggar.

"I don't have anything," she said and shunned him with a wave. "Move away from the door, you're blocking the entrance." She continued to stack the pasties on display.

"Please, madam, all I ask is for something small to eat. Please help me."

The woman gave him another look and ushered him away.

Thabo began to feel lightheaded from the morning sun burning down on his head. He shuffled further along the sidewalk, lost.

"Hey," a voice called from behind.

Thabo unhurriedly turned toward the voice.

The woman from the bakery stood in the door and held out a small blue plastic bag. "Take this."

Thabo shuffled towards her with his eyes fixated on the bag.

It felt like he couldn't get to her quick enough, afraid that she might pull the gift away the moment he reached her.

"Thank you very much, madam," he said and clapped his hands in appreciation before he slowly reached out. His hands shook like a person with Parkinson's as he took hold of the bag.

"Are you sick or something?" the woman said and took a step backwards.

"No, madam," Thabo said and looked into the bag and saw a few delicious looking pasties inside. "I was locked up by the police for many days for nothing. Now they let me go. No food for many days, madam. I just want to eat something and go home."

The woman looked at Thabo with slight disbelief for a couple of seconds, followed by an angry frown and shook her head. "Wait here."

She came back with another bag filled with food and a bottle of cold milk. "Take this. Drink plenty of milk to get your strength back."

"I am very grateful for your help, madam." Tears rolled down his sunken cheeks as he clutched both bags against his body.

"Take care of yourself, young man," she said.

Thabo nodded and gave a half-smile before he shuffled off and immediately stuck his hand inside the bag and felt the warm crusty dough of a sausage roll. He brought the piece of food to his mouth and gobbled three quarters of the pasty in one bite and washed it down with a mouthful of cold milk from the bottle. He stuffed the remaining piece into his mouth and immediately dug in the bag for another pasty. He devoured three in under two minutes.

Thabo's stomach began to cramp. He stopped and held onto his stomach and felt a lump that slowly moved.

He suddenly felt sick and vomited.

Out of desperation, Thabo wanted to pick it back up, but stopped short of doing so as a few passersby made sounds of disgust before they crossed the street.

The sick drained the last bit of energy from his already frail body.

Thabo sunk down to the ground and sat with his back against the wall like a drunk in a dreamlike state and watched blurry-eyed as people and cars passed by. His eyes slowly closed, and he drifted off while he lay on the pavement with the bags of pasties beside him. The bottle tipped on its side and the milk seeped from the unscrewed top and formed a white stream that flowed over the pavement towards the road.

"Thabo?" a voice said next to him and lightly moved his shoulder.

Thabo slowly opened his eyes and looked into the face of someone he knew, but he couldn't remember the person's name.

It felt like a dream and he closed his eyes again.

"Thabo, wake up," the male voice said.

Thabo opened his eyes once more.

The man crouched beside him. "Brother, what happened to you? Are you high on glue?"

"Who are you?" Thabo couldn't make out the familiar face.

"Vussi, you silly shit," he said. "Come, let me help you up before the police see you laying on the sidewalk and take you away."

Vussi pulled Thabo into an upright position. "Thabo, open your eyes. Look at me."

"I'm awake, baba," he said. "I'm just so very tired."

"Let's get you home. Come, let me help you up. Fuck, boy, you need to wash. You smell fucking bad, man. Have you been hanging around that glue sniffing gang?"

Thabo just shook his head.

Vussi helped Thabo get a bus and made it all the way back to his house in Soweto. The front door was missing and there was no sign of life inside.

The nosy woman in the shack next door walked over to Thabo and Vussi and said, "We watched the house for you. We saw what happened to you when the police came and took you away. We tried to stop them, but we all failed. Mama Nkozi from two shacks down died that night. She was run over by that police truck when we tried to block it. Anyway, have you heard anything from your mother?"

"No," Thabo said and walked inside.

The inside of the house lay in ruins. The few possessions they had were broken and strewn around the interior. And the front door was propped against the wall, in pieces.

Thabo walked to the bed he got pulled from and sat down.

"You didn't tell me you were taken away by the police. I thought you were fucking glued-up, boy. You're like a hero now, brotha." Vussi sat down beside Thabo and gave him a hug.

Thabo slumped back onto his bed and curled up into a fetal position.

"Are you okay, Thabo?"

"Thank you for helping me."

"That's alright, skinny boy. You owe me now." Vussi playfully poked Thabo in the ribs.

Thabo felt sad, tired and sick and just wanted to sleep.

"Please go," Thabo said. "I just want to rest."

PART 3

CHAPTER 65

Jason opened his eyes and felt a warm sensation on the side of his face. He looked around with blurry vision that quickly came into focus. His body ached and his muscles felt stiff. The inside of his mouth was raw, like he bit himself. He could smell burnt cookies.

Jason lifted his hand to touch his pounding head but couldn't. His hands and legs had been strapped to a bed.

Jason scanned the small room with cream walls. Only a brown arm chair stood in the corner in front of a large window with mesh wiring on the inside.

For a moment, it felt like being trapped inside a bad dream. Jason began to jerk his hands in the leather straps around his wrists, but they were fixed to the bed.

"Oh good, you're awake," a man said in a calm voice as he approached the bed accompanied by another person in white.

"How are you feeling?" the man said and placed his hand on Jason's forehead.

"Where am I?" Jason whispered and struggled to speak.

"You're in a hospital," the man said and shone a light into Jason's eyes. "Do you recognise me?"

Jason thought deeply for a moment, but even his thoughts felt fuzzy and he couldn't think properly. "I've seen you before."

"I'm Doctor Swanepoel. Can you tell me your name?"

"Jason," he whispered.

"Very good."

"What happened? Why am I strapped to the bed?"

Swanepoel scribbled a couple of lines on a notepad and said, "It's just a precaution while you're being treated. It's for your own safety."

"Precaution for what?"

"Addiction is a serious illness, young man," Swanepoel said and held up a small plastic bag in the air. "The police found these prescription painkillers in your bag, which you stole from your father, along with a large amount of money. And as you may recall, you are no stranger to our facility. To put it in simple terms, Jason, your abuse of prescription drugs coupled with your known schizophrenic episodes, led to those very vivid and quite disturbing psychotic hallucinations you've been experiencing. They dramatically increased your risk for self-harm or maybe even worse."

Swanepoel pointed to the scars on Jason's upper arm. "The restraints are there just for now to make sure that doesn't happen while you are being treated."

Jason looked at the rays of sun that trickled through a large tree near the window.

"Liar, liar," a familiar voice said.

Jason looked at the doctor, who wrote on his notepad.

"The quack is talking bullshit," the deep voice said from somewhere in the room.

"Did you hear that?"

"Hear what, Jason?" the doctor said as he began to take Jason's pulse.

"Nothing," Jason said and looked back at the mesh-covered window.

"Is someone talking to you?"

"Don't tell him," the deep voice said. "Keep that big trap of yours shut."

"No," Jason said.

"You can tell me, Jason. No need to be afraid. We're here to help you get well."

"I'm sure. I just thought you said something, that's all."

"Do you recognise Nurse Ester?"

"She looks familiar."

"She's been taking care of you since you arrived. Now, we just need to run through a couple routine questions to test your cognitive responses after each treatment."

Jason kept silent and watched Swanepoel from the corner of his eye.

"Let's start with the last memory you have, excluding today. Anything you can remember before the last five minutes?"

Jason pondered for a second and suddenly remembered the moment Swanepoel jabbed the syringe into his leg. "You injecting me with something in that place."

"That's correct, in the police cell. Mind you, that was after you assaulted me. It was for your own good, otherwise you would still be in there."

Nurse Ester stood behind Swanepoel, biting her nails and then glanced at her watch.

"Now, going back before that moment, can you remember anything else?"

"They arrested me on the aeroplane."

"Anything else from that day before you were arrested? For instance, why were you on the aeroplane in the first place and how you got to be there? Can you run me through the sequence of events as you remember them?"

Jason had a flashback of the moment he plunged the knife into Pedro's stomach and the unholy gargling sounds Pedro made, and the nauseating sweet smell of burnt flesh and human hair, with hungry flames covering Pedro's naked, twitching body. Suddenly, Jason felt unsure if that actually happened.

"Whenever you're ready, Jason," the doctor said.

"Is Pedro okay?"

Swanepoel scribbled something on his notepad and said, "Pedro?"

"Pedro. You know—Pedro, my friend from school."

"Oh yes, Pedro. Of course. He's hunky-dory. He came to visit you a couple of times."

"Really?" Jason said.

"Yes, of course. He said he's looking forward to kicking your ass on the tennis court very soon."

Nurse Ester looked at Swanepoel with raised eyebrows.

"That's impossible," Jason said with another flashback to blood spurting from the gaping wound in Pedro's neck.

"Why would you say that?"

Jason suddenly felt sick and wanted to vomit.

"Jason are you alright?"

Jason spewed brown liquid all over the side of the bed.

"Bring the tray," Swanepoel instructed the nurse.

"I want to stop," Jason said.

"Just a few more questions, then you can have some rest. Can you tell me why you were in such a hurry to leave?"

"He's in on it as well," the voice interrupted again.

"Go away," Jason whispered.

"You're hearing the voice again, aren't you, Jason?" Swanepoel said.

"Hush, don't say a word, or we'll get *it* again," the voice said to Jason. "Don't be stupid."

"No," Jason said and searched the room.

"You were definitely speaking to someone just now."

"I was talking to you."

Swanepoel scribbled some more. "Is the dark figure talking to you right now?"

"No more. I don't feel well."

"Is he here inside the room with us?"

"I'm not hearing anything, you have to believe me."

"Can you see the figure, Jason?"

"No," Jason insisted and glanced towards the corner of the room behind the doctor.

"Who is Thabo?" Swanepoel said.

"I told you, don't say his fucking name," the dark figure shouted.

"How do you know Thabo?"

Swanepoel looked at Jason with surprise. "You just said his name."

"No, I didn't," Jason said and tried to pull his arms out of the restraints.

"Yes, you did," the voice chipped in. "The quack heard it this time."

"Nurse Ester, did you hear Jason say the name *Thabo* just now?"

"Yes, doctor," she said and looked at Jason like something was wrong with him.

"See? You said the name *Thabo*. So who is Thabo?"

"Fine. He's my friend."

"Okay, was he the reason why you were in such a rush to leave the country?"

"No."

"Then why were you in such a rush to get away from your family home?"

"I wanted to go to my mother."

"She lives in London, correct?"

"Yes."

"You haven't seen her since she left, correct?"

"Yes."

Swanepoel scribbled some more on his notepad.

"Can you stop writing every time I say something?"

Swanepoel gave Jason an angry frown and took a deep breath. "In one of our previous sessions, you mentioned that you opened your father's safe and found your mother's passport."

"What previous sessions?" Jason said.

"Jason, you've been here for seventeen days now and we've had these sessions on a daily basis, the same routine questions since day one. I'll ask again, did you find your mother's passport in the safe?"

"Yes, but why can't I remember those sessions?"

Swanepoel ignored him and continued, "Why would her passport be in the safe if she left the country?"

"I don't know. Maybe she never left."

"Or perhaps she had another passport," the doctor said.

Jason shook his head. "No, she didn't."

"You said to me in a previous session, and I quote, 'I think my dad killed my mother.' Can you remember that?"

"I can't remember saying that," Jason said.

"Would you agree with that statement?"

"Why else would it be there?"

"You mean, the passport?" Swanepoel said.

"Yes, that's what we were talking about."

"The brain is very clever and can play tricks on us, and make things look and feel real and convince us that things are real, even though they're not. Do you perhaps think you mistakenly thought you saw two passports instead of one?"

"I know what I saw. I had it in my hand. It was my mother's passport. Her face. Her name. Her date of birth."

"Calm down, Jason," Swanepoel said.

"I am calm."

"No, you're shouting and looking very agitated."

"I am fucking calm, motherfucker!"

"Nurse Ester, could you please prepare the other room for us?"

"But doctor—," she said.

"Nurse, do as I say," the doctor instructed.

Swanepoel moved closer to Jason. "I believe you, Jason, and it's my job to ask these questions, so bear with me. But I have to ask, why would you think your father killed your mother?"

"Because I showed her a photo many years ago."

"A photo," Swanepoel said. "Okay, how old were you when you showed her this photo?"

"Nine, I think."

"And what was the photo of?"

"A girl." Jason stopped and looked down at his hands. "Can you take these restraints off? They're hurting me."

"They can't hurt you. They're lined with wool on the inside."

"They are hurting me."

"How old was the girl?"

"She was young, probably twelve or thirteen."

"And what was it about this photo that was so bad that you had to show it to your mother?"

"She was standing naked beside a man who sat on a bed, with is hands on her."

"Did you recognise the man in the photo?"

Jason kept quiet.

The doctor wrote more notes.

"And you think your father killed your mother because you showed her a photo of a naked girl standing beside a man who sat on a bed?"

"Why do you keep asking me these questions?"

"Yes or no, Jason?"

"What if I say yes? You gonna punish me?"

"It's a straightforward question," Swanepoel said with a raised voice. "Do you think your father killed your mother?"

"Yes, yes, yes, fucking yes."

"You think she's dead because you found her passport in the safe?"

"Oh my god. Are you going to keep asking me the same stupid questions?"

"I'm well aware of the trauma caused to a young person when a parent suddenly leaves the home, especially if you had a very close bond with that parent, which in this case is your mother. Trauma causes the brain to react in unpredictable and fascinating ways, which we still try to understand ourselves."

"So you're trying to say I'm crazy?"

"You are a person with special needs, Jason. Now tell me about the black notebook you found in the silver metal box."

"Don't say anything else, you stupid retard," the dark figure said.

"It had the names and numbers of people my dad knows," Jason said as he tried to ignore the voice.

"You're doing it again," the voice said.

"In a previous session, you mentioned that the names in the notebook had dates and locations that corresponded to photos and videos of men performing lewd acts on boys and girls."

Jason looked at the doctor. Behind him, the shadowy figure stood in the corner and glared at him with its red eyes and shook its head to indicate *no*.

"Jason?" Swanepoel said then turned his head in the direction Jason looked, as if trying to see what Jason saw.

"You didn't tell him that," the dark figure said. "I was beside you all the time, and you never mentioned anything about the black book or the passport. He's trying to trick you, but you've just played right into his trap. Just play along and pretend you don't know anything about it so that we can get out of here."

"What are you looking at, Jason?" Swanepoel said. "Is the dark figure standing behind me?"

Jason looked back at Swanepoel. "I never told you about the black notebook."

"You stupid fuck," the dark figure said. "I just told you to keep your fucking trap shut."

Swanepoel scribbled on his notepad and stood up and smiled.

"How do you know about the metal box?" Jason said.

"Each session has been the same since the first day you arrived two weeks ago. And you're still hearing that voice, which means the treatment is not working properly."

"No, I'm not hearing anything," Jason said.

"Nurse Ester," Swanepoel called.

The nurse briskly walked into the room while chewing gum. "Yes, doctor?"

"Get him ready for treatment," the doctor said.

"But doctor, it's too soon," Nurse Ester said.

"For God's sake, do as you're told and stop backchatting me."

"Idiot," the dark figure said. "Now look what you've done."

"How do you know about the metal box?" Jason said. "You work for Patrick, don't you? He made you do this so that I can forget what I saw. That's why you came to the house the day after she left. You just made up all these things about me because he made you do it. Your name is probably in that black note book, too."

For a moment Swanepoel looked lost for words, then said, "Jason, you suffer from a very real mental illness which I diagnosed you with eight years ago. Your illness manifested into something much bigger because of improper treatment, and because of drug abuse. You are still showing symptoms of disordered thoughts, which is a typical manifestation of psychosis in patients suffering from schizophrenia. You are a delusional young man. Tomorrow you'll think that today wasn't real, and that you were, in fact, somewhere else while having arguments with the *dark figure*."

Jason looked down at the self-inflicted cut marks on his arm. "I'm not, you just want me to forget about what I saw," he whispered to himself. "I know what I saw."

CHAPTER 66

With his arms and legs strapped to the bed, Nurse Ester wheeled Jason down a long white corridor. They passed a person who stood facing the wall and twiddled his fingers while mumbling and rocking back and forth. He looked back at Jason and giggled with his hand over his mouth.

They passed a woman dressed in a nightgown, holding a doll and repeating the words, "Mama, mama's little girl, good girl." She suddenly turned to Jason and said in a deep voice, "I know what you did," and pulled the doll's head off and laughed.

Nurse Ester pushed Jason through two swinging doors into an operating suite.

"Right, Jason," Swanepoel said, "you'll stay in the bed as you are to reduce any discomfort while we perform the treatment."

"Why are you doing this to me?" Jason said and tried to get out of the leather cuffs. "There is nothing wrong with me."

"As mention before, we use a modern technique called electro-convulsive therapy which will help you to get better. It stimulates the medial temporal lobe of the brain. Kind of like massaging your brain to get your thoughts back together. Nothing to worry about. The name sounds a tad worse than what it actually is, or maybe not. Anyway, Nurse Ester will insert a nice little mouthpiece to protect you from biting yourself while the treatment is in progress. We don't want you to bite off your own tongue now, do we? Everything will be over in a jiffy. Okay?"

Nurse Ester brought a large black mouthpiece towards Jason and said, "Open wide." She dangled the black grog-like rubber that smelled like shit in front of his mouth.

Jason turned his head away, "No."

"Jason, you need to cooperate," Swanepoel said impatiently. "You're just making things hard for yourself. Do we have to go through this every single time? Really, this is starting to get a little boring, don't you think?"

"Fuck you!" Jason spat and jerked his arms and legs as he tried to get out of the leather cuffs.

Nurse Ester took hold of Jason's chin with one hand and said, "Come on, open wide," and began to force his jaw open by pulling it downward, while the other hand forced the black rubber mouthpiece against his lips.

Jason clenched his teeth together and jerked his head from side to side like a person possessed by some evil spirit. Without warning, he dug his teeth into the side of Nurse Ester's hand and bit as hard as he could.

"Ouch, you little fucking swine," she screamed and slapped Jason in the face. "Let go of my hand," she yelled and slapped Jason again before he let go.

"Thirty-three CCs of succinylcholine," Swanepoel said. "Jab him in his fucking jaw this time."

"I can't, my hand," the nurse cried out and held her bloodied hand in the air.

"I'll do it," Swanepoel said and grabbed the syringe from her and stabbed it into the side of Jason's jaw and emptied it, then refilled and jabbed another dose into Jason's arm while Jason screamed with pain.

Jason slowly got weaker and his mouth gaped open.

Swanepoel stuck the mouthpiece into his mouth and picked up his instrument. He moved closer with two handlebar-like prods, each fitted with a round circular pad at the end, and pressed the flat side of each prod against Jason's temples.

"Set to one sixty," Swanepoel said.

"Affirmative, one sixty set, doctor," the nurse said.

"See you on the other side," the dark figure said, looking down from the ceiling.

"Ready," Swanepoel said. "Initiate."

"Initiating," the nurse said.

An electrical current of hundred and sixty volts charged through Jason's brain continuously for two seconds.

The black figure screamed at an ear popping high pitch while Jason's body went into a violent convulsion.

CHAPTER 67

"Jason, guess what?" a nurse said as they walked into the hospital room. "You have a visitor."

Patrick covered his mouth and nose with a white handkerchief as he walked up to Jason, who sat in the brownish chair by the window with his head slightly tilted. A thin trail of drool seeped from the side of his son's mouth and disappeared into the fabric of his hospital gown.

"Dear God," Patrick sighed.

"He loves sitting by the window, sir," the nurse said. "He's always staring into the distance. Such a lovely young man."

"What are his current cognitive responses like?" Patrick said.

"All I know is he hasn't spoken a word since the last procedure. I can ask Dr. Swanepoel to give you a detailed run-through of the entire process and the possible mid to long-term aftercare he'll need."

"That won't be necessary," Patrick said. "He's your responsibility now."

The nurse looked at Patrick with amazement and surprise. "As you wish, sir," the nurse said and walked to the door, then stopped and turned around. "My apologies, sir, but he did mutter a few words a while back. I think it was the day before he received his last ECT. It's probably nothing, but it's one of those rare moments that just stuck with me for some reason."

A moment of silence followed as Patrick stood beside Jason before he looked back at the nurse and said, "Yes, I'm waiting, what was it?"

"Well, it sounded like *back buck* or *lack hook*. I couldn't really make out what he was trying to say. He was heavily medicated at that point and had already completed several procedures. He kept repeating it a couple of times until he fell asleep, and then he hasn't spoken since. But like I said, it's probably nothing."

"Was there anyone else with you in the room when he said that?"

"No, it was just me preparing him for theatre."

"Doesn't make any sense to me either," Patrick said. "Was that all he said?"

"Yes, that was all, sir."

"Very good, now may I have a few moments alone with my son, please?"

"Certainly, sir," the nurse said, turned around and was about to walk out of the room when she stopped again. "You know what, sir, it's really strange that after the multiple ECT sessions, he never asked for you."

Patrick sighed loudly and gave the nurse an annoyed look. "What's your point, nurse?"

"It's just that in my twenty-five years of doing this work, I've never seen any patient at his level who doesn't ask for a close family member or someone they trust, which I just found very odd."

"Nurse Veronica, correct?"

"Yes, sir," she smiled.

"Are you a psychologist?"

"Oh, no, sir," she said shyly.

"Are you a psychiatrist?"

"Of course not, sir."

"Do you know his full medical history?"

"Yes, from what I've read on his notes, sir."

"His full medical history since he was born?"

"No, sir."

"How long have you been working here?"

"I've only been at this hospital for five months now."

"I see," Patrick said and glanced at his watch. "He was not in his right frame of mind when he was taken into this institution, and hasn't been for many years, and as you said, he was heavily medicated. Combine that with the treatment he received, which could cause temporary memory loss, it's very obvious to me why he might have stopped asking for me. So why don't you keep whatever theory you have in the back of your head to yourself and stick to your qualifications, which is to look after ill people, and stop psychoanalysing them, and leave that to the real professionals."

"My apologies, sir. I've seen many patients over the years—."

"Nurse Veronica," Patrick cut her off mid-sentence with a raised hand. "That will be all. If you don't mind, I'd like to have the room now. Close the door on your way out."

Nurse Veronica quickly said, "The point I'm trying to make is, he *never* asked for you in the first place," then shut the door.

"Arrogant bitch," Patrick muttered and took a deep breath to calm himself down. He took out a tinny metal tube he kept his stash in, scooped a little onto the side of his hand and sniffed into each nostril.

Patrick looked out the window at a large pond with some ducks and swans drifting on it. "What a beautiful view," Patrick said and turned around and took Jason's soft, warm hand and held it for a while. He looked at his pale son, who just sat in the chair with his head still tilted, breathing slowly.

Patrick felt absolutely no sense of guilt or remorse. In fact, he felt quite the opposite. He felt relieved. Like a heavy weight had been lifted off his shoulders.

He gave Jason a kiss on the top of his head, then moved down to the side of Jason's ear and whispered, "Where's that black book?" He looked straight into Jason's glazed eyes to see if he could detect any response in his dilated pupils.

Jason's gaze remained fixed in the middle distance and he didn't blink. Patrick snapped his fingers in front of Jason's eyes, but there wasn't even a flinch. Only the drool slowly seeping from the side of his mouth was proof of life.

Patrick then briefly moved his hand over Jason's shaved hair. "This could all have been avoided if you just listened like a good child and stayed out of my fucking office from the beginning.

He gave Jason another kiss on his head. "Goodbye, son. Godspeed."

As Patrick walked out, he dropped his white handkerchief in the bin by the door before he disappeared around the corner.

CHAPTER 68

Monday, 3 December 1990.

Nurse Ester entered the room and said, "It's meds time. Sit up and open your mouth. Come on, chop-chop, I don't have all day."

Jason lay in his bed, eyes half open and directed at the ceiling.

The nurse stood by the foot of the bed and placed her hand on his ankle, and slowly moved it over his knee and over his cock before she squeezed one of Jason's testicles.

Jason's eyes shot to her before he slapped her hand away and slowly opened his mouth.

"There you go," she said. "Just a little nudge and the hole opens like magic. And if you bite me again, you know what's going to happen."

She dropped two pills from a small cup into his mouth and pressed a cup of water against his lips.

"Drink and swallow. Now open wide and let me see."

She pulled his mouth open and inspected it briefly before she ran her hand over his crotch and kept it there for a moment. "I'll see you a little later, big boy," she said and walked out of the room.

A few seconds later, Jason spat out the tablets into his hand and pushed them into a hole in the side of the mattress.

CHAPTER 69

Patrick sat in his office behind his desk, puffing away on a fat Cuban cigar while listening to his favourite violin melody by Wagner.

The telephone rang, jarring him out of his daze.

"Rothshen," Patrick answered.

"It's Swanepoel. He's gone."

"Who?" Patrick said.

"Jason, he's gone."

After a moment of silent comprehension, Patrick said, "How did it happen?"

"Don't know, still investigating the exact details."

"Fuck." Patrick sighed loudly.

"What do we do?"

"What kind of a question is that? A bloody funeral, of course."

"What? No, it's not like that. I mean he escaped sometime during the night."

"Wait, what? I thought he died, you silly cunt. Why didn't you say he escaped in the first place? Jesus."

"That's what I've been trying to tell you."

"You motherfucking imbecile. It's a high security psychiatric unit. How the fuck could a person just walk out? Jesus motherfucking shit." Patrick went into a rage and continuously hit the phone receiver against the corner of the desk.

"Patrick, Patrick, are you there?"

Patrick lifted the handset to his ear. "Clean up your fuck-up. You understand? That psychotic boy is dangerous and should be locked up forever. The *black book* is still missing and he's the only person who knows where he hid it. If your treatment didn't work, then that's exactly what he will be going for. And if that happens, you can kiss your fucking career and your life goodbye because your name is in there, too."

"Jesus, Patrick, I thought we're quits on that subject."

"We are, but your name is still in there."

"He won't get far. The antipsychotic medication takes at least seven hours to wear off."

Patrick laughed. "If he was on meds, then how the hell did he manage to get out of that place? Find him."

Jason climbed up the patio railing onto his bedroom balcony. He pulled the window open and climbed inside and heard a faint voice coming from somewhere in the house, then walked straight to his wardrobe and opened it.

It had been emptied. All his clothes and other belongings had been removed.

He looked back towards his bed. The bedding had been removed and the walls had a fresh coat of paint.

Jason crept down the staircase and heard his father's familiar angry voice shouting, followed by a number of loud bangs and more talking.

He tiptoed to the double doors of Patrick's office and listened as Patrick said, "Find him."

Jason peered around the corner into Patrick's office and watched as Patrick took a big gulp of his morning coffee before he took the long key from his desk drawer and made his way to the bookshelf. He pulled the book to open the panic room and stepped inside.

Jason sneaked into the office and crawled behind one of the sofas and waited for the sound of the safe opening. He heard the clunk and quietly swiped a letter opener from the desk on his way to the panic room. As Patrick took out a shotgun, Jason walked up to him with the letter opener in hand, but he bumped against a side table.

Patrick turned around and went completely pale. He staggered to the side in surprise. "My fucking god, what are you doing here? Stay where you are, Jason."

Jason kept quiet and approached his father, pointing the letter opener at him.

"Look at me," Jason said. "You did this to me." His hair was shaved short like a prisoner and he looked like a drug addict.

"Stay where you are, do not come any closer," Patrick positioned his back against the safe.

Jason noticed Patrick's hand behind his back, blindly searching inside the safe, presumably for bullets.

"Where's my mother?"

Patrick's posture and facial expression suddenly changed from being afraid to angry and defensive. "You need to get back to hospital. I'm going to call Dr. Swanepoel."

"Where is she?" Jason stuttered. Jason suddenly felt sick and violently vomited over the floor.

"Jesus Jason, look at the state of you." He pointed the shotgun at Jason. "Do not come closer, or I swear to God I will have to defend myself."

Jason walked closer and pointed the knife at Patrick. "Then shoot me. Where is my mother?"

"Where she belongs," Patrick said.

"What did you do with her?" Jason sobbed and tried to keep his eyes on Patrick as the tears blurred his vision. He saw Patrick try to sneak a bullet into the shotgun, which meant it had been empty all along.

Jason ran up to Patrick and jabbed the pointed letter opener into Patrick's upper arm.

Patrick dropped the gun.

"You fuck!" Patrick ran a circle around Jason towards the entrance of the panic room. He tripped over the corner of a rug and fell.

Jason picked up the shotgun, ran to the safe and grabbed a couple of bullets from a green box.

"What do you want?" Patrick staggered up and pulled his designer waistcoat in place. "Tell me, what the fuck do you want?"

Jason cocked the weapon. "I want you to make everything out to me."

"What do you mean?"

"I want it all, everything. The house, the car and everything you own." Jason took out the file containing Patrick's will from the safe and threw it at Patrick. "I knew you kept it in here."

"Don't get greedy, Jason. You would already get a percentage of it if something ever happened to me. And it's not that easy to just suddenly give it all to you." Patrick laughed.

"Then make it easy, *Patrick,*" Jason pointed the shotgun at Patrick's head.

"I need lawyers present to make these changes."

"No, you don't. You just write it down like a note. *This is my final will* and so on. Do it or I tell the police what you've been hiding in here. I saw everything, including the secret videos that were taken."

"Who's going to believe a schizophrenic pill popper who hears voices? You're a fucking psychopath."

"I am not a psychopath. You made me like this."

"Look at you. What are you doing right now? You're pointing a loaded weapon at me and making ridiculous demands."

"Why did you allow uncle Jimmy to touch me?"

"There you go, another confabulation."

"I saw the video of him coming into my bedroom. You knew all along."

Patrick shook his head and gave a dry laugh. "What video?"

"Of other children being abused. Start writing."

"Okay, calm down," Patrick said and picked up the file and walked towards his desk, then took one of his golden pens and began to write.

"To whom it may concern," Patrick said as he wrote. "This is my final will, amended and dated with today's date. I leave everything to my dearest son, Jason. I hereby request and order for the executors of my trust to fulfil my wishes and to execute my will on the day of my passing. Yours sincerely, Sir Patrick Rothshen. There goes my signature at the bottom, and done."

Patrick dropped the pen on the table. "Happy now?"

"Now give it to me," Jason instructed and approached him.

"You were the biggest mistake I ever made. You should have been aborted the day that whore of a mother of yours got pregnant with you. You both bring shame to this family."

Jason walked up to Patrick. "Get up and move to the other side."

Jason kicked the hidden door behind the desk and opened it.

"Where is it?" Jason said as he searched inside for the metal box with the videos and photos.

"What are you talking about? There's nothing in there, just a storage space."

"It was here. The box with the photos. Where are—are—," Jason stuttered, "where are the photos and the videos?"

Patrick held his hands in the air. "There you go again, another one. You need to get back to hospital Jason. Your medication clearly wore out."

"Stop saying that. You keep acting as if I'm crazy. I know what I saw."

"Jason, my boy, you need to calm down, you're becoming hysterical again."

"I'm not hysterical!" Jason swept his father's belongings from the desk onto the floor. "I'm not going back to that place. You made me like this. Look at me. Look at my face."

"Tell me what's on your mind."

"Stop trying to change the subject. Where is it?"

"Where's what?"

"The fucking photos."

"Watch your mouth, boy. You don't speak to me like that, you hear me."

"Fuck you, Patrick. Fuck—you." Jason threw some books at Patrick.

"Kill him," the voice of the dark figure said as it stood behind Patrick. "Kill the snake and cut him into pieces, and feed him to the pigs."

Jason sat down on Patrick's chair behind the desk and began to scratch ferociously at the scab on the back of his head. "You're a liar."

"Put down the gun, Jason. You can have anything you want, just put the gun down and do this like civil people. If it's money you want, then you can have it all. You already have my signed will. There's enough cash in the safe to last you a long time. I'll even give you more, just hand me my chequebook and I'll sign a blank cheque."

"Don't listen to him," the dark figure said. "Don't let him get away with it. Shoot him now, before they come."

"Shut up, leave me alone," Jason muttered and stood up.

"Who are you talking to?" Patrick said.

"No one," Jason said and looked at the dark figure moving towards the other side of the room away from Patrick.

"You're imaginary friend is back, isn't he? I'm highly disappointed in the treatment they've been giving you. Highly disappointed."

"Get on your knees," Jason yelled with spit shooting from his mouth.

"Jason?" his father said passively. "You don't want to do this. Think of what I said. You can take anything you want and walk away right now."

"Really?" Jason said and aimed the weapon at Patrick's head.

"That's it, now we're talking," the dark figure said and hid behind Patrick. "He let that old fuck abuse you. Remember? Uncle Jimmy with his cigar breath, while you were drugged. Daddy knew about it all along and let it be done and witnessed the same being done to many others. He sold you like a cheap whore for his own gain. Blow his fucking brains all over the wall and send his Catholic ass to hell where he will burn for eternity."

"Jason, you don't want to do this," his father pleaded.

"I said get down on your knees. Please." Jason sobbed.

"You need help, Jason," Patrick said as he lowered himself onto his knees on the rug.

"There's nothing wrong with me." Jason pressed the barrel of the shotgun against the side of Patrick's head.

"Put the fucking gun down," Jason's father yelled. "You're out of your mind, boy."

"Do it," the dark figure said. "Free him from his sins."

"Whatever the voice is telling you, don't listen to it."

"Shut up!" Jason pulled the trigger.

The powerful weapon made a dull *click*.

CHAPTER 70

Forty minutes earlier.

Thabo stepped off the bus at the bus stop near the Rothshen mansion and walked to the large rock near the road like he had been for many weeks since being released from the police station.

As he neared the rock, he saw the long awaited equal sign lightly scratched on the rock.

"Yoh, Jason, you are here," Thabo said full of excitement and touched the marking, then quickly looked around him in the hope that Jason would be lurking somewhere behind a bush and jump out and jokingly try and give him a fright.

Thabo looked back at the marking and stood in the same spot for a few minutes. He remembered what he said to Jason in the police cell, 'If I see your mark, I will know you are at your house.'

Thabo smiled with excitement and briskly hiked up the hill towards the Rothshen house with an extra spring in his step. He couldn't wait to see Jason again, energised with the notion of touching his skin once more.

Thabo reached the humungous gate and stood there for a while listening and looking around for any sign of Jason, but there were only the sounds of birds in the trees and an aeroplane crossing over.

He wanted to press the intercom button, but stopped just as his hand nearly touched it. He remembered how Jason opened the gate manually on the day they met after the mechanism malfunctioned, and pushed his hand through a hole in the wall feeling for a lever.

He pulled it, which was closely followed by a clunking sound, presumably from the mechanism.

The gate cracked open about ten centimetres.

Thabo pushed the gate further, just enough to slip inside, and cautiously walked to the house, cutting through the bushes and plants with a pack of blue butterflies dancing around him.

As he neared the side of the house, he could hear shouting coming from inside.

He cautiously peered inside one of the windows by Patrick's office but couldn't see anything, then sneaked around the rear of the house and saw Jason's bedroom window on his balcony stood open. He climbed up the wall and into Jason's bedroom and crept along the corridor towards the grand staircase, where he looked down at the ground floor.

Out of nowhere, the boss pulled Jason along the floor by one leg, leaving a thin trail of blood while Jason looked like a drunk waving his hands.

"Jason," Thabo whispered. "I have to do something. What do I do? Think, Thabo, think."

CHAPTER 71

"Wrong bullets." Patrick snatched the weapon from Jason. He hit Jason against the head with the butt of the shotgun.

Jason staggered to the side and held onto his head and saw blood dripping onto his shirt. He felt slightly dizzy and his ears pinged.

"The green box are duds," Patrick said and threw Jason against the wall, then stood there as he caught his breath and wiped sweat from his face with his white handkerchief.

"Fucking ungrateful brat," Patrick said and took Jason by one leg and pulled him towards the guest bathroom near the staircase.

Jason had no strength to fight back. His body squeaked over the polished stone tiles as Patrick pulled him along.

Water began to run into the bath.

Jason rolled over and tried to push himself up before a kick landed on his face, smashing his head against the side of the bath.

Patrick lifted Jason by the legs and lowered him head first into the cold water.

Jason tried to grab the side of the bath but was too weak. Submerged to the shoulders, with his body in need of oxygen, Jason reflexively opened his mouth and swallowed and breathed in at the same time.

His lungs filled with water.

He looked up at a blurry image of Patrick hovering above the moving water.

I don't want to die, Jason thought.

Suddenly, the dark figure came closer to the water and said in its gruff voice, "See you on the other side, my friend." The light became fainter and everything around him turned silent and faded to black.

"No," Thabo bawled and ran up to Patrick and stabbed a massive kitchen knife into his back.

Patrick gasped and dropped Jason into the bathtub. "Fucking bastard," Patrick said and turned blood red in the face and began to growl while he spun around like a drunk ballerina and grabbed the air as he attempted to reach for the blade.

Thabo stood in one spot, not knowing what to do next, and kept looking in all directions like a rabbit in a spotlight, unsure in which direction to run.

Patrick grabbed Thabo by his shirt collar just as he tried to run out, and placed Thabo into a chokehold and increased the deadly grip while they stumbled towards the wall.

Just like Bruce Lee in a movie he watched with Jason, Thabo pulled his legs up and kicked against the wall, which threw them both backward.

Patrick slipped on the wet floor and fell on his back. Thabo landed on top of him.

The knife disappeared into Patrick's back and he let out a loud groan before he loosened his grip around Thabo's neck.

Thabo rolled to the side and gasped for air and looked at Patrick, who gargled blood. His face turned purple-red and made his grey beard look almost pure white. Thabo looked back at the bath. Only Jason's legs hung over the side of the tub, displaced water spilling over the rim.

"Jason." Thabo crawled over the wet floor and pulled himself up against the side of the bath. For a split second, he looked at Jason's lifeless face under the water with his eyes closed and some blood coming from his face. "No," he cried and tried to pull Jason's heavy, limp body to the surface.

"Freeze," a voice shouted from behind.

Thabo looked back at two armed men in the doorway. One of them was superintendent Deventer with his caterpillar eyebrows, the same man who saved him from falling from the police window.

"Step back with your hands in the air or I will shoot!"

"He's drowning," Thabo said and desperately tried to pull Jason out when the other man jerked Thabo away.

"Help him," Thabo cried out as he got trampled to the floor and cuffed. "Please."

Deventer lifted Jason's lifeless body from the bathtub and laid him on the white marble floor and felt for a pulse in Jason's neck and arm.

"We need an ambulance at One City View Crescent at the Rothshen Mansion," Deventer said over his radio, "multiple casualties."

Deventer threw the police radio down and began to perform CPR on Jason. "Come on, breathe, boy." Deventer looked at his colleague while performing the compressions. "Check on Patrick."

The other police officer inspected Patrick and felt for a pulse on Patrick's neck, then shook his head. "He's gone."

"Fuck, dispatch, where is that ambulance?" Deventer said over his radio. "Drown victim with multiple injuries in need of urgent medical care. Performing CPR now."

"Medics are on their way," a man said over the radio. "ETA five minutes."

"We don't have five minutes," Deventer almost screamed in desperation as he continued to perform the kiss of life on Jason. His own heart raced and his arms felt like jelly as he pressed Jason's ribcage as hard as he could. He looked down at Jason's face, which turned purple.

The other officer kneeled beside Jason and took his pulse while Deventer gave more chest compressions. "He's gone, superintendent," the other officer said.

"Come on, Jason, breathe," Deventer said and slapped Jason in the face a couple of times and gave him two breaths.

Deventer performed the routine for several minutes with no luck.

"Breath," he repeated and slammed Jason on the chest.

Then, like a scene from a movie, Jason spat out a stream of water and coughed and wrenched a couple of times, gasping for air.

"That's it, cough it up, boy." Deventer pulled Jason into a recovery position. "That was fucking close." He fell onto his butt and looked at the other officer.

"You're a fucking hero, man. You saved his life," Deventer's colleague said and looked at Deventer with disbelief.

"I'm no hero." Deventer stood and walked over to Thabo, who lay on his stomach near the door with his hands cuffed, crying. "Get up," he said and pulled Thabo up.

"Thabo Molefe, you are under arrest for the murder of Patrick Rothshen and the attempted murder of Jason Rothshen."

"I tried to save him. Patrick tried to drown him, not me."

"That's not what it looks like to me."

"You have to believe me, I tried to save him," Thabo sobbed. "You can see that."

"Take him away," Deventer said to his colleague and walked over to Patrick. His face had turned pale grey-white as blood pooled below his designer suit. His eyes were open and glazed, with blood flowing from the side of his mouth and into his grey beard.

Deventer slowly moved Patrick's lifeless body onto its side and saw the wooden handle of a knife underneath.

"Superintendent," the officer called out as he jogged into the bathroom, "you need to come look at this."

"Tell me it's what I think it is," Deventer muttered to himself as he followed the officer into the panic room.

A safe stood wide open with money, paintings and other expensive items. Deventer glanced through the artefacts and found Sarah-Jane Rothshen's passport at the bottom of the safe, underneath and behind one of the small paintings.

He looked at his watch, it turned 9 a.m.

"Dispatch, we have one DOA at the Rothshen Mansion. We need forensics. I will also need a team of officers to assist."

"Copy that. They're on their way and should be with you in a few minutes."

At the same time, the paramedics ran into the house with equipment.

"Contact Inspector Van Rooyen and ask him to make his way over here ASAP," Deventer said. "We need all available resources to search the premises."

"Copy that, superintendent," the dispatch officer said.

Deventer met additional forces in the driveway. "Listen up, people. While forensics is busy inside the house, we will start to search the premises from corner to corner. We will begin outside and move the search inside as soon as we get the all-clear. This is no ordinary premises, so if anything looks out of place or you have doubts, you need to let me know immediately, no matter how small. And may I remind you to wear your gloves at all times, you have them for a reason. Come on, people, let's move, time is ticking."

Several hours after Jason had been taken away by the ambulance crew, a heave of activity took over the mansion with news reporters and camera crews outside the gates, trying their best to get any hint of video footage. A news helicopter hovered above the palatial house and gave the television viewers live footage of the drama unfolding at the Rothshen mansion.

As Deventer searched through the safe, one of the officers briskly said, "Superintendent, we found something in the back."

Deventer lit a cigarette and followed the officer to the rear garden. He looked up at the helicopter and smiled. "This is going to be a good day," he said to himself and gave the metal bird a thumbs up.

Deventer passed the gigantic swimming pool and went into the thick layer of exotic plants and scrubs at the back of the garden. He double puffed his cigarette as he got nearer to a part of the garden with overgrown plants.

A dog barked, and some flashes illuminated the plants as one of the police photographers took photos.

"In here, watch out for these thorns," the officer said.

Deventer walked past several remains of dead birds. "What's with the dead birds?"

"Fuck knows," the officer said and pointed at something sticking out of the soil where two other police officers scraped with sticks.

"What am I looking at?" Deventer said and crouched beside the spot and patted the sniffer dog on its head.

"Can you see it?" The officer pointed with his pen towards a piece of black plastic.

"All I can see is plastic."

"Look closer. There is a tiny piece of bone sticking out."

"Can't see anything," Deventer muttered and squinted his eyes.

"Maybe you should put on your glasses, superintendent," the officer joked.

"Very funny, wise-ass," Deventer said and put on his glasses and took the officer's flashlight. "Give me some gloves, too." He began to scrape away the soil around the tiny bone poking out.

"Looks like an animal, perhaps a dog?" the sniffer dog handler said.

"Why would someone bury a dog inside a black plastic bag?" another officer said.

"Perhaps it was a pet dog and they used a plastic bag to mask the smell when it decomposes," Deventer said and began to dig deeper. He wiped away some gravel and saw something much bigger, kind of grey-whitish. He blew some of the dirt off. "It looks like a bigger bone," Deventer said and continued to dig deeper.

He suddenly stopped and said, "Jesus," and stood up. "Go get someone from the forensics team. Hurry."

"Is that what I think it is?" one of the other officers said.

Deventer crouched back down and took a closer look with the torchlight. It looked like a forearm with the radius connecting to a hand.

"It looks human," Deventer said and sighed deeply and patted the dog once more. "Well done, boy."

CHAPTER 72

Jason opened his one eye. A faint peeping sound came from somewhere to his side. He touched his shirtless chest and could feel several wires stuck to it. He lifted his hand to see a heart rate monitor clipped to his index finger.

He could tell he was in hospital, but everything else left him confused.

Jason tried to open his other eye and lightly touched it, but it had been patched up with a bandage around his head. He tried to move sideways and had to stop from excruciating pain that left him breathless. A nurse on her rounds walked into the private hospital room as Jason tried to get out of the bed.

"Young man, that's not a good idea," she said and took him by his shoulder and slowly laid him back down.

"You're wearing a catheter and you don't want that thing to pull out, otherwise we'll all be swimming." She smiled.

"What?" Jason slurred like a drunk who just woke up.

"You can do your business in bed, so no need to go to a toilet, and I'm talking about number one."

"What happened?"

"You've suffered several broken bones, so moving is not a good idea. I'll go call the doctor and tell her you're awake."

Jason touched his tender ribcage and could feel the broken ribs underneath the inflamed skin, then moved his hand down his stomach underneath the bedsheet. He could feel his pubic hair had been shaven and the catheter tube going into his penis. His hand followed it down his side to where the bag with warm urine hung beside him.

"Hello, Jason, you're finally awake. Welcome back," a female doctor in blue scrubs said as she walked in and buttoned her white lab coat on. "You had us all a little worried there for a few days." She lightly moved her hand over his head.

"What happened to me?" Jason said and it felt like a *déjà vu* moment. He lifted his hands again just to double check if he could freely move them.

"You don't remember anything?"

"I can't."

"Young man, you suffered a severe blow to the left side of your head. That is most probably why you can't remember anything. You and your father were attacked inside your home."

"Is he okay?" Jason said.

The doctor took Jason's hand in her small, cold hand and said, "I'm very sorry to have to tell you like this, but your father passed away a couple of days ago."

"Really?" Jason said, unsure whether he felt shocked or not. "How?"

"He suffered a fatal stab wound to his back which punctured his heart and lung."

"Who stabbed him?"

"We should discuss those things at some other time. It's important that you recover first. You've clearly been through a lot in the past few weeks."

Jason moved his hand away from her and touched the intravenous line stuck into his hand, kept in place with see-through tape.

"We couldn't get a proper vein in your arm to put the IV in, so we had to go for the hand and neck." The doctor smiled and gave Jason a friendly rub on his shoulder.

"What happened to me? Why is my leg in plaster?"

"Your knee was broken, and you had two broken ribs and a collapsed left lung. You also had fluid in both your lungs from being submerged in water."

"I drowned?" he said and began to sob.

"You need to rest. We can talk about it later."

"No, tell me now."

"You were drowned by the attacker. Luckily for you, one of the first police officers on the scene saved your life."

Jason lay there and tried to process what the doctor just told him and touched the scar on his bicep, the self-harm marks that confirmed he was in fact awake.

"Was I stabbed too?"

"No, but you were beaten up pretty badly and suffered head and facial injuries."

"My eye, why is it patched?" Jason lightly touched the bandage.

The doctor looked at Jason and paused for a moment. "You suffered a heavy blow to the left side of your face, which shattered the eye socket and some of the bone fragments severed the cornea beyond repair. We've tried everything we could but were unable to save the eye. I'm very sorry."

"You took out my eye?"

"I'm very sorry. You really need to rest so that you can regain your strength, which will speed up the recovery."

"Who did this to me? Tell me what happened."

"I think it's best that someone from the police speak to you about it."

"No, tell me," Jason insisted and grabbed the doctor's arm.

"I can only tell what I know from the news, which was that you were attacked by a terrorist inside your home."

"Did they catch the people who did this?"

"I'm sorry, that's all I know. But there's a police officer sitting outside waiting to interview you. He's been here every day since you arrived. I told him he'll have to wait until you've recovered and feel comfortable to talk to him, so just let me know when you're ready, then I'll let him in."

"I want to see my face," Jason said and touched the patch once more.

"We don't keep mirrors in the ward for a reason, Jason. You should wait a while until the swelling and bruising subside before you inspect your handsome face again, okay? Focus on recovering. That is the most important thing in your life right now."

Jason searched for some kind of reflection so that he could see his face.

He made another attempt to turn to this side, but the excruciating bone-grinding pain left him crying.

"Are you okay?" the doctor said.

Jason gasped. "The side of my chest feels like the bones are moving."

"You need to take it slow. Your ribs need time to heal. In the meantime I'll get a nurse to give you something for the pain and then you need to rest."

A minute later, a nurse came in and injected something into the IV line going into Jason's hand. Within seconds of the drug being administered, a satisfying, warm sensation filled Jason's arm and he could feel the powerful sedative flowing into his chest and entering his heart. He could almost taste its sweetness.

Jason's body became numb and the pain melted away within thirty-seconds and everything faded to black.

Jason slowly opened his eyes and looked directly at a man beside him whispering on a dictaphone.

"Oh, hello there," the man said and smiled. "You're finally awake."

Jason didn't reply and just gazed at him while regaining his senses.

"I'm Inspector Otto and I'm in charge of the investigation into the attack at your home a week ago. Do you mind if I ask you a few questions?"

"I can't remember anything," Jason said. "Where's the doctor?"

"She's on her way. I'll ask anyway, maybe it will rustle a few brain cells and make you remember."

"No," Jason said.

"Can you remember anything about your time at the psychiatric hospital?"

"Can you leave?"

"Can you remember how long you were held there?"

"No, I just told you, I can't remember anything."

"Nothing at all?"

"Go away," Jason said and searched for the emergency call button.

Otto took out a photograph and held it in front of Jason. "Do you recognise him?"

In the photo, a mug shot of doctor Swanepoel. He held a board with his name and date of birth and prison number, and he was dressed in a green prison uniform.

"Yes, I recognise him."

Otto showed Jason another photo. "How about him?" It was Thabo, also dressed in a prison uniform.

"Yes," Jason said and took hold of the photo and brought it closer to get a better look.

"And how about him?" Otto showed a photo of Captain Van Rooyen in the same position as the other two, dressed in the same uniform.

"Yes."

"Good. We'll talk about it in more detail at a later date, but if you need to speak to me urgently, you can reach me day and night on this number."

Inspector Otto handed Jason a piece of paper. "As you are probably aware by now, you were attacked in your home, and after a thorough search of your property, we found human remains buried in the rear garden. DNA tests were carried out on the bones and hair and came back with a one hundred percent match to your mother, Sarah-Jane."

"That's impossible, she's in London." Jason had a faint memory of his mother sitting on his bed, smiling at him, and could smell her perfume the last time he saw her.

"I'm very sorry, Jason, but your mother is dead."

"I don't believe you."

"Believe me, she's dead."

Jason pressed the emergency call button.

Within a few seconds the same woman doctor rushed into the room. "Excuse me, I'll have to ask you to leave, inspector. I told you to wait outside until I gave you permission to speak to my patient."

"Oh, I'm so sorry nurse," inspector Otto said and looked at Jason.

"I'm not a nurse," the doctor said. "Now get out."

"We'll continue this conversation when I see you again. And if you remember anything, give me a buzz, okay?"

Chapter 73

Wednesday, 10 April 1991

Jason stood in the driveway by the front door and wore his large black sunglasses and watched as the driver loaded luggage into the car.

Another car drove up the driveway and a well-dressed man in his thirties stepped out in a grey suit with his brown hair slicked back. He wore tiny reading glasses and had a gleaming smile. He approached Jason and said, "Good afternoon, I'm looking for Mr. Jason Rothshen."

"And you are?" Jason said and quickly glanced down at the man's crotch as he approached.

"I'm Frank from Frank Realtors," the man said with an extended hand.

"You're the guy selling the house?" Jason said and shook his hand.

"Yes, I am indeed. Are you Mr. Rothshen's son?"

"Nope," Jason smiled.

"Okay, would you be able to call Mr. Rothshen and tell him I'm here?"

"You can speak to me," Jason said.

"And may I ask who you are, sir?"

"Jason," he said with a slight pause. "Jason Rothshen. You can speak to me." He gave a fake smile.

Frank looked slightly confused. "Have we spoken on the phone?"

"You probably spoke to one of the trustees of our estate, but certainly not me," Jason said.

"Oh, now that makes sense. The man I spoke to sounded much, much older than you."

"I bet he did," Jason said. He recognised the man's cologne, Tommy Hilfiger. Cheap, Jason thought and tried to see what make of watch he wore.

"Well, it's a pleasure to actually meet you, sir."

"Do you have good news?" Jason said.

"The place is officially on the market and we should have our first viewers tomorrow morning."

"Excellent," Jason said and noticed another car drove towards the house.

"I'm leaving in the next thirty minutes, so the house will be officially vacant," Jason glanced past Frank at the car now parked beside his, while Frank continued to speak.

Jason recognised the man who got out of the car and approached him, inspector Rick Otto. The same asshole who came by the hospital months earlier.

"How long do you think it will take to sell the house?" Jason said.

"I personally think it shouldn't be that long before this beautiful home is snapped up. Rest assured that we will do our very best to get it sold."

"That would be good," Jason said with a half-smile while he watched inspector Otto get closer from the corner of his eye.

"Jason Rothshen, just the man I was looking for," Inspector Otto interrupted.

"Would you please excuse me for a moment?" Jason said to Frank. "I just need to deal with this."

"Certainly," Frank said and walked through the front door.

"Leaving for London?" Otto said.

"I am indeed," Jason said and adjusted the eyepatch that began to feel slightly sweaty.

"Oh, so you're going to become a Pommy now, hey?"

Jason looked at Otto without showing any emotion, then suddenly burst into hysterical laughter for a couple of seconds. "You're so hilarious, Mr Otto. What do you want?"

"I just wanted to clarify a few things that puzzled me for the last couple of months since our last interview."

"Really? I think I've told you everything I could remember, didn't I?"

"I would certainly hope so," Otto chuckled. "But this is about your friend Pedro."

"Urg, again?" Jason sighed. "I have already been interviewed by one of your colleagues. All I've been doing the last few months was answering questions. If it's not the police then its reporters that just show up without any notice and expect me to welcome them with open arms and give them some kind of story. And everyone asks me the same shitty fucking questions. But not one of them asks me how *I* am doing. Oh no, it's all about everything else but Jason."

"Maybe you're over-exaggerating a little. We humble policemen are just doing our jobs. As for the media, they're just milking it as much as they can, that's their job. And my job is to follow up on leads. So I want to ask a few more questions, just to clarify some blurry details after we received a few more leads in the investigation. Then I will let you get on with your life."

"Fine. Can you keep it brief, I really need to finish up and get to the airport."

"I'm sure your private jet can wait for you until you get there."

A blond-haired muscle guy carried luggage towards the car. He stopped and said in an Eastern European accent, "Is everything okay?"

"Yes, it's all good, Sergei," Jason said. "You finish loading the car."

The beefy man gave Otto a dirty look and said, "We will be leaving in fifteen minutes, sir."

"Bodyguard?" Otto said as Sergei walked back in the house.

"A precaution forced upon me by the trustees of the estate. I guess they don't want anything bad to happen to me. Now, what was it you wanted to ask me?"

"Is he Russian?" Otto said.

"Polish."

"They all sound the same to me," Otto said. "Any reason for a Polish bodyguard?"

"Like I said, it was forced upon me. What do you want to ask?"

"Right, back to that. On the day of that vicious assault on you and your father, the forensics team found blood residue around the house. However, no DNA could be extracted due to bleach being used to clean it up. As you probably know by now, they only recently found Pedro's burnt corpse in a dried out dam about forty kilometres outside the city when a dog walker was so unfortunate to come across him."

"Thank you for reminding me of how my best friend died."

"My apologies, Jason," Otto said. "The reason why your father was the initial suspect was because a gold Zippo lighter with his initials on it was found at the scene. However, I believe it wasn't your father who murdered him, even though he was the main suspect of your mother's murder and he had connections with some shady business people. There was no reason for him to have killed Pedro."

"And?" Jason said and tried to look as cool as possible while his heart raced and sweat rolled down the centre of his back and armpits. Even the inside of his eyepatch began to sweat.

"I think Pedro was taken from here to that dried out dam, dumped and set alight to destroy any possible way of identifying him or how he was murdered. If it wasn't for his dental records, then perhaps the body would never have been identified. I'll jump straight to the point, Jason. I think the blood matter found in your reception hall belonged to Pedro, which means he was assaulted in the house as he tried to escape through the front door."

"Based on what?" Jason said.

"New evidence came to light his morning."

Jason yawned audibly. "Is this going to take long? Your muffling makes me feel so sleepy." He looked at his watch then towards the upper floor of the house. Jason's mouth felt dry and he tried his best to look and stay as calm as possible.

"Where were you on the day of Pedro's disappearance?"

"I told you before, I don't know when he disappeared."

"He was reported missing Saturday, 10 November after he didn't return home from supposedly buying some goods for his mother in the city."

"I can't remember much of what happened during that period, and I think that's what I told your colleague as well. Why do I have to keep repeating myself?"

"I know, it was the electroshock therapy forced upon you that made you forget. You already said that, fair enough. But according to the timeline, you were *not* in hospital yet when Pedro disappeared, which means you would have been at home at that time and should be able to remember something."

"You clearly don't understand how shock therapy work and what it does to your memory, do you?" Jason said.

"Maybe I don't, but what I do know is Pedro disappeared on the same day your gardener and his mother were arrested. The same gardener who attacked you in your house. And the same gardener who—," Otto swallowed hard and struggled to get the word out, "—fucked you, Jesus Christ." Otto took a deep breath.

"Fucked me?" Jason said. "You're insinuating that I had some kind of sexual relationship with the garden boy? Are you out of your fucking mind?"

"Watch your language, Jason."

"You don't tell me what to do," Jason said and crutch to the front door.

"It's true, isn't it? Rumours might be rumours, but they started for a reason. That same evening you were arrested at the airport and taken to the police station for reasons still unknown to this day, and then shipped off to a psychiatric hospital apparently against your will by a rogue psychiatrist and his team, where you were kept for weeks until you escaped. This whole thing sounds like a coverup to me. Care to explain why your car was found burnt out near the airport?"

"I just didn't like the car."

"You didn't like a very expensive sports car and casually burnt it?"

"It's just a car. I can afford it."

"You mean your deceased father could afford it, not you."

"Are we done here?"

"You know what's funny, Jason? You can remember that you burnt your car because you didn't like it, but you can't remember anything else." Otto pulled out a piece of paper from his pocket. "On the day of Pedro's disappearance, you were pulled over by a traffic officer whilst driving that very same expensive Mercedes at high speed on the same stretch of road that passes the field where Pedro's burnt remains were discovered."

Jason's thoughts jumped back to the moment he picked up the piece of rock while the traffic officer inspected the rear of the car. "You sure it was me?"

"The traffic officer is the eyewitness," Otto said.

I should have taken him out, Jason thought and said, "Is that it?"

"It gets even more interesting. On that specific day, your father was in meetings most of the day, with many witnesses confirming it, which removes him as the main suspect, and which brings me back to you. You were the only person in this house on that day at that time."

"What makes you think I was at home?"

"Your lovely neighbour, Mrs. Padwick. She said she spoke to you that morning on the intercom by the front gate regarding her missing cat." Otto looked at his notebook. "Moo-Moo, if I got it right. Apparently, the cat's fur looked like a dairy cow, correct?"

Jason began to laugh.

"You find it amusing, Jason?"

"She suffers from Alzheimer's," Jason said. "For the last twelve months she's been calling us at least once a week about her missing pussy. Both on the phone and the front gate."

Otto looked slightly taken aback and glanced at his notes once more. "I'm not sure if we're talking about the same person here, but the Mrs. Padwick I spoke to from next door, with her distinctive American accent, looked perfectly healthy to me. She was in fact busy writing her fifteenth novel when I visited her."

"Looks can be deceiving."

"Indeed, they can, but in my line of work I can quickly spot those who try and deceive, like you're doing right now."

Jason sighed and rolled his eyes and said, "Is that it? Are you done accusing me?"

"The remains of a cat was found in the rear garden which matched the description of her cat."

"Oh my god, so now you think I have something to do with Pedro's death because of a dead cat you found in our rear garden? Your theories are becoming more absurd, Mr Otto. This neighbourhood has dozens of cats roaming around every day. It could be anyone's cat who decided to end its own life in our rear garden."

"Since when do cats perform self-immolation?"

Jason rolled his eyes. "When cats are ill, they find a place away from their home to die."

"Interesting theory, is that your own?"

"Discovery Channel, unlike yours."

Jason could see Otto trying to process what he just said.

"Next thing you're going to tell me is that his cat friends held a kitty funeral for him, which reminds me—why were you not at your father's funeral?"

"What a stupid question," Jason said. "Have a good day."

Jason crutched towards the door and said to himself, "Just fuck off, please."

"Where did you come from when you were pulled over, Jason?"

Jason could feel the sweat under his armpits leaking out like a tap had been turned on, and his whole body became glowing hot from nerves. He stopped without looking back. "I can't remember anything from that day, sorry," he said and continued into the house.

"Let me tell you what I think—."

Jason held up his hand and said, "I really don't care. If you want to arrest me on your ridiculous theories, then do so right now. I'll be out before you get me to the police station. Otherwise, leave."

"Stop trying so hard to deflect the truth, Jason. Do yourself a favour and admit you killed Pedro."

"You have yourself a fantastic day, Mr. Otto," Jason said and quickly crutched into the reception hall and went directly to one of the downstairs bathrooms. He splashed his face with cold water and knew he had to leave immediately before Otto prevented him from leaving the country—if he really had any evidence.

CHAPTER 74

The black luxury car pulled up to the gates outside a maximum security prison on the outskirts of the city of Johannesburg. The bodyguard who is also the driver, got out of the car and opened the rear passenger door. "Can I give you hand, sir?"

"I can do it myself, but you can take this." He handed his two gold-plated crutches with black handles to the driver and pulled himself out of the car.

Jason smelled the air. "It smells like it looks," he said and took the crutches from the driver. "We'll go straight to the airport from here. I won't be long."

Dressed in black fashionable designer clothes and large black sunglasses with a matching black baseball cap to hide his face, he hobbled towards the only visible door to the side of the mammoth concrete wall with barbed wire at the top and flanked by watchtowers.

He walked inside the heavily guarded reception area.

"Who are you here to see?" a rough looking guard sitting behind a bulletproof window said.

"The governor," Jason said.

"Your name and some identification?"

"Jason Rothshen," he said and pushed his passport through the gap below the window.

"The governor is expecting you Mr. Rothshen. Please remove your sunglasses, hat, jewellery, and any firearms and place it inside this box."

Jason took off his large sunglasses, which revealed a custom-made burgundy leather eyepatch designed by his distant aunt, Vivienne Westwood, in London, encrusted with dozens of small sparkling diamonds.

"Cool eyepatch, sir," the prison officer said.

Jason gave the guard a half-smile and crutched towards the search area before another man escorted him to the waiting room.

The clanking keys and slamming doors suddenly brought back a faint memory, and he suddenly had a flashback of sitting on a concrete floor, but then it went away as quickly as a dream.

After waiting for fifteen minutes in the cold reception room with its plastic chairs, a prison officer brought Jason to a small, white cubicle with a basic wooden chair. A very thick window separated the sides, and a black telephone receiver was stuck to the wall.

A man in a brown suit walked into the room and said, "Mr. Rothshen, I'm Johan Brits, the governor of this prison. Please, have a seat. Mr. Molefe is on his way."

Jason slowly lowered himself onto the hard chair and watched his own reflection in the glass. He adjusted the eyepatch. He made a few smiles and frowned at himself, and inspected his nose that had been reconstructed by a plastic surgeon a few weeks earlier, still covered with a nose cast and flanked by a purple-black bruise underneath his one visible eye.

Jason heard a gate open and the shuffling of shoes and clinking of metal chains, then suddenly a person appeared right in front of him. Jason sat back for a moment and looked at Thabo on the other side of the glass. His hands were cuffed in front of him and he was dressed in an olive green prison uniform with his prison number written in white on the left side of his chest.

Thabo sat down and began to cry the moment he pressed his hand against the window. "Jason, is that really you?"

Jason kept quiet and tried to focus on Thabo with his one eye. Thabo picked up the black phone receiver and said, "Lift it." Thabo's hand shook as he held the hand piece against his ear.

Jason slowly took the telephone receiver with a white handkerchief and brought it closer to his ear.

"Jason, I'm so glad to see you. This place is so bad. You have to get me out. Please tell them I didn't try to kill you. You have to tell them the truth about what happened. Please, I beg you."

Jason leaned forward to get a better look at Thabo, who still had his hand pressed against the window glass. He lifted his glittery eyepatch and could see in the reflection of the glass his artificial eye that looked in a different direction.

Thabo gaped back at him, clearly shocked.

Jason slowly raised himself with the crutches and said to the governor, "I can confirm it's him. I'll wait outside."

"Please don't go, Jason. Don't leave me here. Jason!" Thabo cried and began to bang his fist against the thick glass window.

Jason glanced back at Thabo and smiled.

"Please don't leave me Jason." Thabo felt like he wanted to fall down and die as he watched Jason limp out the door.

"Jason come back! Please."

Thabo burst into a hysterical crying fit as the guards pulled him away from the window, his voice echoing around the cold prison walls.

"Molefe, you better calm down," one of the guards said as they escorted him down the hallway. They went through several security gates and into an empty grey room with another door on the opposite side of the room.

"Where are you taking me?" Thabo feared they were going to kill him.

The guard kept quiet and unlocked his cuffs on his wrists and feet. At the same time the other door opened.

"Get dressed," Jason said and threw a bag at Thabo. "You can't get on an aeroplane looking like that."

"Am I dreaming?" Thabo said and slapped himself on the cheek a couple of time to make sure he was awake. "This is not real, this is not real," Thabo repeated and fell down to his knees.

"Come Mr. Molefe, get your shit together and get the fuck out of my prison," the governor said. "You have one minute before that door is locked for good."

Thabo sat in the back on the car and leaned against Jason's shoulder and said, "You kept your promise and came back for me."

"Of course," Jason said. "This is your passport."

"Oh my gosh," Thabo said as he opened the document and saw the his mugshot. "So that's why they wanted to take a photo. You knew all along."

"Of course."

"How did you manage to do all of this?"

"The trustees of the estate," Jason said and looked the other way.

They arrived at the airport and drove straight to a waiting private jet humming on the tarmac, and greeted by an air stewardess with champagne. "Welcome Mr. Rothshen, welcome Mr. Molefe."

Chapter 75

Six months later.

London, England.

Jason stood by the window in his eighteenth floor penthouse apartment that overlooked Tower Bridge.

"It's time," the familiar voice said.

In the reflection of the window behind Jason stood the dark figure with its red glowing eyes.

Jason opened Patrick's little black book and whispered, "Jimmy S., Hampstead Heath—uncle Jimmy."

He opened his backpack which contained some rope, a scalpel, and two pairs of surgical gloves.

"Thabo, are you ready?"

"Yes," Thabo said and gave Jason a kiss. "Let's go make some history."

Don't miss Andrey's new novel
coming in 2020…

Connect with Andrey

 AndreyLondra

andreylondra.com